SCRATCHES

S F Lindsay

Whiteley Publishing

Published by Whiteley Publishing Ltd
www.whiteleypublishing.com
First paperback edition 2018
ISBN 978-1-908586-46-9
Cover images used under license from Shutterstock.com

Chapter 1

Eddie

I was home.

I was home with a different body, a different face. My brother still recognised me, but when he looked at me, did he see his little brother, or did he see a killer?

My name is Eddie Bodansky. When I was twenty-one, I did something terrible. Then, with the help of drugs, sex and painting, I forgot about it and had a wonderful time living and loving as I pleased until I was thirty-seven.

I was twenty-one when Jason died. After the accident, I spent some time in hospital then I was brought home, to Lake Martin Manor House Hotel, on Christmas Eve My older brother Ilya and his friend David Manpyre took me upstairs in the lift, got me out of the wheelchair and into bed. They were both treating me like a bomb that was about to detonate. I was on a mood stabiliser and a mild sedative which kept me on a level, but even so, my mind kept flashing maniacally from one thing to the next.

I fixated on Manpyre's hair, which was held back in a glossy, black ponytail. It caught the light and looked unnaturally pretty; shiny and soft like melting butter. I fantasised about ripping it from his scalp. I could feel him staring at my face when I was not looking but each time I turned my fierce glare on him, he looked away, mildly tucking in my sheets and arranging my pillows. I felt that he was fighting an urge to laugh at me. He ripped off my hospital ID band, tearing out half of my wrist hairs in the process.

'Christ, Dave,' I spat.

'Sorry,' he said insincerely.

A bit of drool dribbled from the corner of my mouth. Wiping it, I turned to Ilya. 'The funeral; Eel's funeral. When is it?'

My brother pursed his lips slightly as he organised the bedclothes around my bulky plaster casts. His eyes flicked, ever so briefly, towards Manpyre.

'It's already been and gone mate,' he said. He gave me a bland smile of fake sympathy, 'while you were in the nuthouse. We just went ahead and sorted it out.'

I took a deep, calming breath. I did not care about the funeral but I needed something to focus on. 'Will you take me to his grave?'

'Sure. When you're a little better.'

At that moment, Ilya's Russian nanny appeared in the bedroom doorway, holding one of the twins in her arms. I didn't know, or care, which one. I glanced at it; it was the girl, dressed in a pink sleepsuit, and when she saw Ilya she stretched her arms towards him. The sound of her fussing made me clench my hands into fists.

'Get her away from me,' I murmured warningly.

They all ignored me. The nanny came further into the room and passed the child to Ilya while both of them delighted over her. Why my brother even bothered to hire childcare, when he seemed to prefer doing everything himself, was beyond me. I stared up at the ceiling, fighting to stay calm as Ilya cooed to the child, 'What is it, my darling? My love, you can't fall

6

asleep without Papa?'

He continued in that same ridiculous, lilting tone, talking nonsense about Father Christmas and snow as he carried her out of the room.

I was left alone with Manpyre. His face broke into a strange grin and he said, 'Does it hurt?' Through the medication I felt a mercifully brief moment of lucidity, and I turned to him with what must have been hell in my eyes.

'More than anything,' I said.

It had now been sixteen years since the accident, and I still hated Martin, my home town, as much as the day I left it. I owned half of the town. I wanted both halves to burn. This was the town that Jason died in.

Jason James Prescott; Everyone called him 'Eel' because of his ability to get behind the scenes of any gallery, museum or private house, using only his looks and his charm. Before he agreed to work for my brother, Jason was being used by a gang of art-thieves. He was the fixer, the one who smoothed the way for the thieves and made it possible for them to carry out huge robberies that fed into our business, the one that Ilya and I inherited from our creatively entrepreneurial father. Jason was many things; he was a thief, a punk, a pansexual aspiring model and a heart-breaker. I knew him for four years (could it really only have been four years?) and during that time I called him many names; Baby, angel… Bastard. But, in general, to everyone else he was simply Eel.

For the past half hour I had been standing at the gates of the hotel that belonged to my brother Ilya and me. It was raining hard so my eyeliner was destroyed… I wiped under my eyes delicately and swore when the fingertip on my lace glove came away black. Not only that, but I was also wearing a wet fur coat. Fur is one of my great pleasures but the sodden heaviness of wet fur is so tiresome and should be avoided, at all costs.

I flipped out a small mirror and sorted my face out. I was about to reunite with a lot of my old acquaintances, so I had to look my best, especially as every last one of them was probably going to kick the shit out of me. I might as well take the punishment with a bit of dignity and, hell, a bit of style.

Any minute now, I would gather up my courage and head through the gates, and into the hotel. I leant my head back against the wall beside the gates, grinding my skull against the brick, to kill the whining sound within. Being back in this damned place meant that the memories, of my relationship with Eel, came flooding in. Every beautiful, fucking detail of it. No. No. Spare me, I begged my brain. With an effort, I smothered the memories and turned to face the hotel. It rose out of the ground, a broad white building over four floors. A modern addition had been placed in the driveway sometime during my sixteen-year absence; a red and gold sign with looped writing spelling 'Lake Martin Manor House Hotel'.

I took a breath, shook my hair out of my eyes and strode up to the main doors of the hotel. The doorman looked up. I smiled. It was Manpyre, that lousy prick.

His face greyed with disbelief as he recognised me. 'You,' he said softly. I opened my mouth to say something, but I could not be bothered wasting my breath on him. I chose to spit in his face instead.

I pushed open the big double doors and found myself in the entrance hall. The great staircase swept up in front of me, the twenty-foot mirror stretched above it. A sense of fascination at the familiarity of it all, gave way to my breathless rage as Ilya turned to me. Oh, Ilya, you have barely changed either. He was standing at the bottom of the wide, sweeping staircase, wearing a black tuxedo, greeting guests with a saccharine smile as they descended for dinner. His face paled when he saw me standing there.

'Hey big brother! Welcome me home, baby!' I yelled, my voice ringing all around the great hall. Although I had not planned it, I noticed that I was, automatically, using my 'Russian' accent. My parents came from Siberia and, although I was born, raised and educated in England, I had a strange habit of speaking in an exaggerated Russian accent from time-to-time, especially when I felt under pressure. The accent started out as an affectation, a joke, between myself and my older brother- it was a cruel impersonation of our Russian-language teacher (we were made to sit through Russian lessons every Sunday as children). As I grew older I honed the accent and based it more on my father's voice. I used it to entertain Ilya, to endear myself to my father, to distance myself from talking about emotions... sometime in my teens, I lost control of the accent and it seemed to happen spontaneously if I ever felt 'too' emotional. Later, I used my accent to make myself sound more 'exotic' when I was trying to seduce. The most beautiful creature I had ever seen, for the first two weeks of our relationship, believed the pretence that I, myself, had emigrated from Siberia. The conceit of it!

Manpyre came storming into the hall behind me, screaming, 'You fucking bastard. You fucking prick.' He punched me in the back of the head; puny, pathetic. It rattled my brain a little, but I just laughed and ignored him. I was staring at my brother, wondering what he was feeling. The pianist faltered, and then started up again in earnest. Ilya's face turned to ash. He abandoned the two well-heeled ladies he had been fawning over, and hurried in my direction.

'Oh my... Christ,' he murmured. 'Edvard, but for Christ's sake.' He pursed his lips and his eyes roved all over my mutilated face. For one moment, I actually thought that he... was about to embrace me. Ha... of course, he did not... not even after sixteen years. It was not Ilya's style. Instead he glanced at Manpyre who was ranting beside me with my spittle still streaked across his face.

'Leave it, Dave,' murmured Ilya, never taking his eyes off of me.

I became aware, as no doubt Ilya was, that a small crowd had assembled. Several guests, dressed in smart dinner clothing were gathered in the archway of the dining room, peering out to see what the commotion was. Additionally, various members of hotel staff were standing gaping at us. One caught my attention straight away; the bell-boy, a pretty little thing in his red jacket, no hat on his curly black hair. He hovered beside the receptionist, and I caught his eye and grinned. The bell-boy looked away.

Ilya had two high points of colour on his cheeks. He loosened his tie and cleared his throat. 'Edik,' he murmured, his voice very low. 'Please, please do not make a scene in here. Go and wait for me in the card room. I shall be two minutes.'

I looked at him and laughed. 'Don't make a scene?' I crowed loudly. 'Sixteen years and I get 'don't make a scene.'' I looked around, at all of the guests and treated myself to another look at that bell-boy giving him a wink. 'A scene, brother, is what all these fine people are waiting for!' I was amused to note that I had made the bell-boy blush.

'Edik- please,' Ilya said, teeth gritted. I blinked again, heavily. My head still did not feel quite right, and I was beginning to feel nauseous. Maybe that punch from Manpyre had been harder than it felt. I noticed slight movement in the corner of my eye, on the sweeping staircase. I looked up and there he was. I gasped. All of the air rushed out of my lungs. I staggered towards him, to where he stood in the middle of the stairs looking like a blond angel, elegantly holding the banister. He looked frightened.

'Jason,' I gasped, running at him. 'Eel, baby.' I fell on the steps at his feet, my hand clawing at the angel's shoe.

'Urgh! Dad!' He yelled, twisting away from me in aversion. He pelted past me, down the stairs and ran to Ilya. I lay on the carpet of the stairs, heaving. I vomited.

'It's not Jason, he's my son,' Ilya was saying. 'Christ, he's been sick. Alright, get everyone out of here. Get all the guests into the dining room, right now.'

Someone was touching me, holding my head. I opened my eyes slightly but the light was very bright. Someone peeled my eyelid open, gently. The pretty bell-boy. Wonderful. I was covered in vomit.

'Mr Bodansky- sir?' He spoke in a quiet, precise Scottish accent. His voice was the sound that came the clearest to my ears, through the humming fog of everything else going on. He kept on cradling my head against his warm thighs. 'Sir, I think he's got a wee touch of concussion. He's going to need-'

Ilya's voice snapped back at the boy, 'Colt- just clean up this vomit. Bidden, take him upstairs and give him some water. Get him out of here.' The boy paused. His hands were very gentle as he steadied my buzzing head.

'With all due respect- sir, could I go with him? Only, it would be best if he was monitored by someone who is medically-' I opened my eyes. The light was powerfully bright, so I squinted. I could see the boy's face, upside-down, gazing concernedly into my eyes. Ilya was kneeling in front of him, his face, contorted with rage directed at the young man.

'With 'all due respect' to you, doctor,' he snarled, 'I never asked for your opinion, now go and get your bloody mop and your bucket, and clean up this fucking puke.' I gave in and let my eyes flutter closed.

A maid and receptionist took me into the card room and laid me out on the couch. I felt extremely weak. I lay there blearily waiting for Ilya to come in, which he did, around twenty minutes later. I lay on my back, hands folded on my chest, regarding my older brother calmly.

'Why are you here?' Ilya began quickly. No pleasantries. No concern, at least not outwardly. He wanted the information straight away.

'It's been sixteen years,' I said, 'I was missing you.' My mouth tilted in a sardonic smile, 'that and... I ran out of money.'

'My money?'

'Yes.'

'You're back for good?'

I began to nod, but Ilya quickly crouched down beside me on one knee and said. 'Wait. Think carefully before you answer that question. You know that I can't just let you waltz back in and take control. There would have to be a reconciliation, do you understand what I'm saying?'

I closed my eyes briefly. 'Yes. I know. Yes, I am back.'

'You've changed so much. I can't believe that this-' Ilya touched the scar and I angrily jerked my head away. 'This has lasted so well over the years. You know, I think that's going to be permanent? What a shame.' Ilya stood up, 'Well, there are a lot of new faces around here... I won't introduce you to everyone now, I can see you're not in the mood to chat, you must be tired? But I'm sure everyone will come to greet you in their way. For now, Manpyre, please take my brother to his room.'

I marvelled at the change in my brother's attitude, his voice now cold with sarcasm. Perhaps he was distancing himself from what was about to happen?

The bearded David Manpyre slinked over to lift me under my arm. 'Come on, scarface, let's be having you.'

I shrugged my hand away, tossed my hair and walked slowly toward the elevator, refusing to look at any of the men as I passed them. Manpyre led me into the elevator. As soon as the doors slid closed, he moved close to me and took hold of my wrist. I watched, detached as he clipped a handcuff around one wrist and then the other. He stepped back, surveying me with an appreciative grin. 'Nice,' he said, 'Very nice.'

There was no way he would stand this close to me if I was not cuffed.

I leant against the wall staring dully at the red neon lights on the elevator panel, until my eyes began to sting. I had known Manpyre all my life. He was of Egyptian origin; lithe and thin with dark, creamy skin and narrow eyes. He was the only other gay man in the firm so we had something in common, but we never really got on. I think I fucked him once; I cannot really remember. He had changed little over the years. He still had his neat, black beard and insanity in his eyes.

Manpyre was, in my opinion, a psychopath. He was capable of bloody violence with seemingly no effect whatsoever on his emotions. I recalled an incident where he cut open a man's mouth, firm business. As we drove home from that disgusting, traumatic event, I was obliged to stop the car repeatedly, to vomit on the road, whereas Manpyre sat there in the passenger seat, picking his fingernails with the same knife he had just used.

On the third floor we got out and Manpyre led me along a corridor. Lord, the memories… they were coming back to me in waves as we walked in silence along the thick crimson carpet. We passed five doors. I tried to remember the rooms inside. My own suite had been in the family quarters on the first floor; I wondered who dwelt there these days.

'I know where you're taking me,' I said suddenly.

Manpyre said nothing as he stopped in front of the last door in the long corridor, confirming my fears. Through this door was a lounge with a bar and a fine view of the hotel grounds and the surrounding woods. I followed Manpyre behind the bar, through a well-remembered ugly, metal door, and up flight of stairs. This staircase was freezing cold and narrow, with brick walls either side. I remembered how Ilya and I used to race up and down this staircase, and how when I was seven years old, Ilya had locked me inside. I had only been trapped for a few minutes but I had screamed my lungs raw. Manpyre opened another metal door at the top and I stepped into an enormous warehouse space stacked high with furniture and boxes. I glanced at the small washroom off one side. There was a skylight in the washroom, I remembered, which provided the only source of natural light in the attic. Manpyre flicked a switch up and down; the electric lights did not come on. I turned to Manpyre, who was looking around.

'What do you reckon, mate? Biggest room in the hotel and it's all yours.' He spat on the dusty wooden boards.

'It's fabulous,' I said dryly.

Manpyre ignored me. 'C'mere.' He unclipped the handcuffs.

I massaged my bruised wrists. The handcuffs swung lightly in his hand. 'Eddie?'

I looked up as he unceremoniously swung the handcuffs across my face. I threw my hands up in shock and they turned slippery with blood. Manpyre grabbed my hands, pulled them down and hit me over and over again with quick movements until I sank to my knees, moaning in pain. I lifted a shaky hand to my nose; mercifully, my best feature did not feel broken.

'Ah.' Manpyre was a little out of breath. 'Ahh... aw, it ain't nice, is it mate? You'll be fine. You know that wasn't my best.' He patted my shoulder as he walked by.

I heard the door slam, keys rasped in the lock and Manpyre padded down the stairs.

Chapter 2

Colt

My name is Bryce Colt. When I was twenty, I fell hard in love with a terrible man. What made him so terrible? For a start… he looked terrible. His personality was often terrible and he had done something terrible. But, I loved him. That's the truth, I just out-and-out loved him. His name was Eddie Bodansky.

It began for me when I was working in a hotel, so I will start there. Hotel work was way, way better than medical school. I mean, I didn't, enjoy cleaning toilets, but at least I never felt suicidal doing it. I lived with my grandfather in a little town called Martin. Grandad was cut off from the rest of the family, which suited me down to the ground. He had nothing good to say about my dad, his own son.

'The man is a waste of space, lad,' he would say, 'You stick with me and you'll soon be right again.'

I came down to Martin from Scotland, after I tried to kill myself in my dorm at uni... don't want to talk about that and, I didn't die anyway. My Grandad rescued me instead and brought me down to Martin.

'I only wish we could bring your brothers down here as well,' he had said, in between cursing my father. I wished that, too. My brothers were in foster care in Edinburgh. Dad was too drunk to look after himself properly, let alone my kid brothers; at least they were safe now.

In Martin, I got a job in a bar called the Straight Rain, a place that was all black and chrome and trendy. I wasn't trendy but I was young, so I was in. There was a group of guys I got to know, who came in every Friday night. They all worked up at Lake Martin Manor House Hotel. I thought it was bit weird, as the all wore business suits and they never worked Friday nights. I didn't care because they tipped me really well. One guy in particular was always giving me crazy big tips, like ten quid just for serving him a pint. He flirted outrageously with me and when he found out that I was gay he ramped it up even more. He was called Dave Manpyre and it was he who invited me up to the hotel for a job interview.

'Better than this place,' he told me, 'Better money and the owner, Ilya Bodansky? He's my best mate. I can get you a job up there with us, mate. It'll be a laugh.'

So I took the job, and had been working at the hotel for almost a year before... well, before Eddie arrived. I did a bit of everything; cleaning rooms, bell hopping and waiting in the restaurant. Manpyre and the other guys didn't do much in the hotel, but they all lived there.

'We have our own private business, mate,' Manpyre told me. 'Don't worry your pretty head about it, yet.'

'Yet?'

It turned out that Ilya Bodansky was running an illegal business alongside his hotel. The firm handled stolen artwork from high-value robberies from all over the world.

Chapter 3

Eddie

The room had been my prison for a few hours, and the blood had now dried on my face. I had suffered further violence at the hands of Ilya's friends, and now lay on my side facing the door, fighting sleep. My hand was curled loosely around a hammer, the nearest thing to a weapon that I could find. I was desperately tired and my eyes felt stretched and hot.

A step on the staircase outside the door caused me to start. I tightened my grip on the hammer and sat up, planning to take the intruder in a low tackle. The door rasped open. It was the skinny young bell boy, bearing a tray. I let the hammer fall; I could take this one with my bare hands. The youth put the tray down on the floor. I allowed my gaze to flick towards the offerings; fruit loaf, hot tea and bread. I noticed that the young man looked frightened of me, and as though he was trying to hide this fact. I also noticed, sharply, that his hand now hovered near his back pocket.

'Brought you something to eat,' he stammered in his clear, nervous voice. His Scottish accent was so cute. He was a gorgeous, fragile little thing, not my usual type at all, but there was something interesting about him. What the hell was a classy little thing like him doing working for Ilya? I eyed him critically, and he continued.

'I'd also like to take a look at that head of yours.'

He finally put his hand into his pocket and to my astonishment, he drew out some surgical alcohol and cotton-wool. I was so bewildered that he gave a barking laugh.

'Oh, you would like to…? Would you?' Lost for words, I stared at the young man. 'What is your name?'

The boy flushed. 'It's Colt.'

'Colt… that's all? Well, Colt, give that to me, and I will clean it myself.'

'No. Let me,' said the youth, with more confidence.

He knelt down beside me and placed one hand gently under my chin, in a self-assured manner that surprised me further. He was such a little mouse, and he was obviously shit scared of me… but now he was methodically examining my eyes for further signs of concussion. It just did not fit with the overall skittish manner of this young man who seemed to blush at nearly everything I said. I almost felt sorry for him. I myself had never been shy… the only time I ever recalled feeling anything close to nervous was nineteen years ago, when Jason and I finally went to bed.

'This is a bad one,' said Colt, lightly touching the gash on my head. 'If it heals badly you could end up with another scar.'

I bristled, hating any mention of my disfigurement. I felt my accent shifting into Russian, 'Who are you, the fucking doctor?' I snarled, studying the young man's face.

Close up, the high cheekbones, thin mouth and huge eyes made him look even more girlish. God, he was so pretty. His small-animal fear still lingered about his eyes and the way he held his mouth. I felt a surge of irritation at his calm aspect and, on impulse, I seized his skinny neck. Colt froze, and though his eyes told a story of fear, he said nothing. Calmly, he fixed me with a reproachful stare. I was breathing heavily, there was blood on my bared teeth.

'How does it feel? Hm?' I heard myself rasp. 'I could snap your little throat right now.' I applied some pressure. Suddenly, all the fight went out of me. I saw myself as though from above; scarred, dishevelled, covered in blood, clutching a stranger by his neck while the boy stared evenly at me, his heart skipping like a rabbit's. I felt old. I let go, avoiding the anxious gaze.

To Colt's credit, he did not run screaming. He massaged his neck. 'Listen. I know it's horrible up here. Those guys were following orders. You'll get to understand how it works.'

'I do understand- this is my fucking company. So, is that what this is? Following orders?' I growled, gesturing at the surgical sprit and cotton wool. Anger flowed through my temples. Colt looked concerned.

'Hey, please. Listen, I work for your brother. I'm not a doctor, but I have studied medicine.' A proud light shone in his eyes. 'I went to Edinburgh Uni, got accepted and everything. Then I dropped out in my second year.' He hesitated, glancing at me apprehensively, as though expecting to be judged.

As if I give a shit about your fucking career, I thought but I simply sneered, 'I'm sure you had your reasons.'

My back ached deeply and my legs were stiff.

'But do tell me, why the hell are you working here?'

'I fell out with my father,' said Colt shortly. He did not elaborate. 'I left uni, left Edinburgh, and came down here. I was working in a pub then I met David Manpyre and I started working for Ilya, and things progressed from there. Technically, I work as a porter, but obviously I got to know... quite quickly... that this place isn't just a hotel.' Colt dripped some alcohol onto a thick pad of cotton wool. 'I was asked to bring you some food from the kitchens. I'm actually probably going against orders, cleaning you up like this. Word is that Ilya wants you to suffer a bit.'

His eyes turned curious, but he seemed to know better than to ask. He shifted towards me once more and began wiping the congealed blood with deft strokes. Close up, I could literally smell his fear. I had lost most of my

18

desire to kill him, and the fact that he chose to keep helping me despite his obvious terror made me feel some grudging respect for the kid.

'I wish I could stitch this, but obviously I can't go that far,' Colt was saying.

'Mm.' I was distracted. I thought I heard someone on the stairs.

Suddenly, the door swung wide open and two people stepped into the room; Will, whom I remembered and another, younger man with a shaved head, who I did not recognise.

'Whatcha doing, mate?' Will asked Colt, rubbing his hand across my hair. 'Did Ilya ask you to do this?'

'Yeah,' said Colt calmly as he cleaned my cuts.

His voice was even, but I saw how his hand trembled. The second man knelt beside Colt and watched him work with a childlike fascination. He sneered at me. 'I thought Ilya said everyone should kick his head in as long as he didn't die?'

I closed my eyes and hoped that was a fluid interpretation of any orders that my brother, my own flesh and blood, had given regarding my welfare.

'That was earlier,' replied Colt, examining the cut. 'You missed it. I was told to bring him food and to treat his wounds,' he lied. 'Ilya doesn't want him beaten anymore.'

When the men were gone, I thanked Colt for lying to protect me.

'You will get in trouble, no?'

'Nah. They don't really talk directly to Ilya, they're not much higher than me in this firm. I should be alright, it isn't a big deal. It's not the first time I've patched up wounds behind the boss's back.'

'Why are you helping me?'

Colt shrugged and smiled, 'I never got to finish school, but feel like I am a doctor all the same.'

I spread out my hands before me. 'Hey,' I said, 'you are the best doctor I know. My own personal physician! How good is this hotel? Five star luxury!'

Colt paused at the door. 'Has Manpyre been up here?'

I grimaced and waved my hand over my own face, indicating the worst of my wounds. 'He has.'

Colt nodded. 'Listen, you just… watch out for him. He and a guy named Bidden are Ilya's two closest friends. Bidden's okay but… Manpyre's a thug. He loves knives. Ilya uses him for every interrogation. Just… well, please just never, ever find yourself on the wrong side of him, or you will need a better doctor than me.'

'Kid, you don't have to tell me.' I brushed my thumb over my scar.

'They did that to you?'

I shrugged, 'Long time ago. Yes.'

I was lying. In actual fact, I put the scar on my own face. I thought back to that day, by the river, down in the mud. Eel lay dying. I closed my hand around his, wrapping our fingers together around the knife handle. I lowered my weeping face onto our hands and ripped it apart. Blood flowed down our wrists. Something to remember you by, never to forget. My pretty face died with you. My horror to be your monument.

When Colt was gone the room felt emptier, colder than before. I picked up my hammer and cradled it to my chest with both hands, resting my chin on its metal head. It felt absurdly comforting, this hammer, this talisman. I gripped it tightly with one hand and scooped up a big crumbling, chunk of fruit loaf. I would need my strength.

When the light quality through the skylight indicated that it was around 1am, I opened the door and limped a few steps. Outside the room the floor steeply fell away into the narrow staircase with red brick walls on either side. The boy, Colt, was sitting on the top step, reading by candlelight. He turned around in surprise, put down his book and stood up.

'I'm not escaping,' I said flatly, brandishing the hammer. 'There is something I need to do. Get out of my way.'

Colt glanced at the hammer and back to me, but he seemed nonplussed.

'Sorry, I have to guard you. I can't let you leave.'

I was genuinely amused by this. I leaned forward.

'How exactly are you planning to stop me?' I whispered.

Colt looked uncertain as he reached into his jacket pocket, and pulled out an enormous kitchen knife. He stood holding it out in front of him. I pinched the top of my nose with my thumb and forefinger and closed my eyes.

'Alright. I tell you what. You put that down, and I will be on my way.'

Colt did not move.

'Listen, you stupid kid, you think that because of that knife that you are stronger than me? Move out of my way.' I spat these words at him. I was inches from his face. He tilted his head away from me. His left arm was crooked upwards, holding the knife aloft.

'No? Then we do this the hard way.' I grabbed him and flipped him to face the wall, crushing his arm against the stone. With a cry of pain he dropped the knife. It clattered loudly down a few stairs. I pressed my body against his, grinding him into the brick wall.

'It isn't just me!' Cried Colt. 'Manpyre and Luke are just down the stairs, playing cards. You've got no chance.'

A door opened far below. 'Colt?' It was Manpyre's voice. 'Is everything okay up there, mate?'

I could feel Colt's heart thumping through his back. I hesitated, and then I pushed him away from me, hard. I turned and laid my forehead against the cool bricks, swearing softly in frustration. I kicked at the wall.

'Colt?' Manpyre had begun to climb the stairs.

Colt stared at me. He took a deep breath and yelled back, 'I'm fine! I just dropped my book.'

I looked up and quickly met his eyes.

'How's Edwina?' Called Manpyre. The footsteps stopped. He was not coming up.

'Fine. He's sleeping now.'

The door slammed shut again. Colt scurried down the steps and picked up the knife, but he placed it on the top step instead of holding it.

I rubbed my head. 'Why did you lie?'

Colt sat on the step. 'I'm sorry for you. I'm sorry this is happening to you.'

Silence lengthened between us then he added, 'If you went down there, they would bring you straight back up and give you another beating.'

I shook my head, 'Fuck that.' I stared at him wildly. 'This was my home. I used to paint in that lounge and have parties. I still own half of this fucking hotel.'

'I'm sorry…'

'So am I. I am fucking sorry, too.'

I went back into my prison voluntarily, shut the door. I heard him lock it and I sat up against it. I could actually hear Colt's gentle breathing out in the silence of the corridor. After a while I could hear the pages of his book rustling as he resumed reading. I huddled against the door and eventually I fell asleep listening to his comforting rhythm.

The next morning, Colt was back with some breakfast for me.

'Okay. I've got stuff to tell you. I found out that Ilya wants you back in the firm, but he's going to keep you up here for, like, a month as an initiation. He wants to take your pride away, and to punish you for being away for so long and… for stealing a load of money when you left?'

Ravenous, I fell on the toast.

'Yes, I stole quite a considerable amount of money. I spent it, too, and I know all about initiation.' I shrugged.

As they went, this one was rather light, and it would not, perhaps, be so bad. My gaze shifted to the young man and I tried not to smile. It may not be so bad at all.

It had been a very cold night. I ached and shivered so badly that I spilled some tea on the dusty floor. Colt made for the fireplace and began to search for useable bits of coal and twists of paper.

'No one's meant to talk to you,' he added, as he worked.

'So why are you? Just bring my food and leave,' I snapped, but even as I spoke I knew that the answer was loneliness. I felt a touch of sympathy for this friendly kid. I asked his age; he was twenty years old. I clucked my tongue. 'Heh. You are a child.'

Colt turned his head, smiled and shrugged. I thought, rather bitterly, I do not remember ever being as young as you are. Yet Eel and I were only one year older when I lost him. I did not say this, but instead, 'I am old compared to you.'

I wondered what Eel would have been like in his mid-thirties…

'So, what do you know about me? I am very interested to know how the others described me to a new kiddie like you.'

'I knew… that Ilya had a brother,' began Colt carefully. 'And… that you left with loads of money, and didn't came back for years.'

'Alright. Do you know why I left?'

'No. No one talks to me about firm business.' Colt looked peeved. 'I have a couple of friends, Bidden and Will. They tell me a little bit, but I'm not worth talking to, not really worth knowing, actually!'

'Wow. Mind that ego, boy. You're in danger of sounding a bit full of yourself!'

Colt smiled. Then he shifted uneasily.

'What else?'

'Well…' he squirmed. 'They say you are… like, a transvestite? Some of the guys, they call you 'Edwina.'

I looked away, trying carefully not to laugh. 'Hmm. Well, accurate. Glad they told you all of the most important facts first.'

Colt was blushing prettily. 'You're not what I expected.' He mumbled, 'I thought that you would be, like, actually dressed as a woman, not just wearing a little bit of makeup. And… I dunno, you're just not at all what I expected.'

'Sorry to disappoint.'

Colt shook his head and added, 'I know something else about you. You're a really, really good painter.'

'Oh? And who says I am a 'really, really good painter?"

'No one. Oh, I mean, I know for myself. Ilya has one of your paintings up in the library.'

I could not help it, I smiled. His pretty endorsement of my work was the review I have personally most enjoyed. Sometimes, certain people's opinions matter, even if they know nothing about art. If I could please this sensitive, emotional youth, then that was all that mattered. I was also rather touched by the revelation that Ilya had kept my painting in the hotel library all this time.

'Is the painting of a white horse?'

He nodded brightly. 'Uh huh. It's, like huge, did it take you a long time?'

'About two months. So Colt, do you like horses?'

He shook his head, 'Not really. I've never ridden a horse. They freak me out.'

I shook my head in mock disgust, 'Ah. Then you are not, as I first thought, my perfect man.'

My mind started to drift to Jason. I could picture him now; horse-crazy. Talking about them, obsessing over them. This place made my memories so horribly, horribly vivid. I looked at Colt, remembering that he was there.

'Well. Anyway… you ought to make the most of being so young. You should really do something about your hair…' I touched my own dishevelled hair. 'Almost the worst thing about this incarceration is what it is doing to my looks. I wish you would smuggle me some shampoo or shower gel.'

Colt shrugged. 'I would get into loads of trouble if I started bringing you luxuries. You don't really need them, do you? The only person who sees you is me.'

'What I really need is a hot bath, a hairdresser and a session with a good Botox practitioner.' I sighed heavily. 'But more than that, more than anything at all, I need paper and pencils. I need to draw.'

Chapter 4

Colt

It was an insanely hot morning. The sun was streaming through the windows as I cleaned all of the bedrooms and bathrooms on the first floor and washed every single pane of glass. When I had finally finished, I ended my morning duties by taking Eddie's lunch (sandwiches and bottled water) up to him.

I was parched and shattered. I flopped down and helped myself to some water. The cool, airy attic was a sanctuary from the heat of the day. Eddie ate his sandwich in silence, watching me. He never questioned why I was there, and I drew the conclusion that he wasn't actually interested; he seemed very self-absorbed. Still, he was a very comfortable person to be quiet with, and I liked the way that he never quizzed me or harassed me. We sat, as usual in peaceful, companionable silence.

I watched him out of the corner of my eye. He was really tall, and like, big. Massive shoulders and massive hands. He had light brown hair and a big, white scar running diagonally from his chin, through his lips and right up into his hairline. The scar tissue pulled the top lip into a permanent pouty sneer.

'Colt,' he said quietly, making me jump. 'Pass me that water, please.'

I noticed that he was using that perfect public-school accent again. I rolled the bottle towards him. 'What's happened to your accent?'

'What do you mean?'

'Well, when you first arrived, you had, like a foreign accent…'

'A Russian accent. Yes.'

'Yeah. But now you're speaking in cut-glass English, what gives?'

Eddie smiled slightly. 'I am Russian; I was raised in England. I am therefore entitled to speak using either accent.'

I stared at him, 'That doesn't make sense,' I said, laughing. 'Which one is your real accent? English or Russian?'

His smile had faded, and his expression became rather cold. 'My real accent is whichever comes naturally when I speak, and that varies, alright?'

'That doesn't make any…' I stopped. I realised that it was time to drop the subject, and I was left thinking, this guy is nuts.

Eddie took the last bite of his sandwich, 'You,' he said, pointing his middle finger, still chewing, 'have a terrible dress sense.' He brushed crumbs off his long, elegant fingers.

Despite myself, I laughed. 'What? It's a bell-boy uniform. I don't dress like this outside work.' I tugged self-consciously at the dumb red jacket with its daft gold buttons.

'I know, I know, I know. But the glasses? The curly hair? Stop blushing. You are a gorgeous-looking kid, under all that.'

'Gorgeous?' I laughed.

I had never been described as gorgeous before. I had always been very small for my age. Thick glasses, unruly curly hair and being gay hadn't exactly helped matters at high school, where I was bullied into insignificance then ignored, (except by any student who felt curious about his sexuality, and then I was inevitably experimented with and discarded). Quiet, shy and unremarkable, I had been pretty invisible at university. I sometimes went to the student union, and I was in a table-top roleplaying club, but I was always more interested in studying than socialising.

I offered some information about my life, and to my surprise Eddie was very interested indeed, even though he never probed for more than I was willing to reveal. I explained I had messed up my medical degree, dropped out of uni at the end of second year. I was surprised at how comfortable I felt, talking to Eddie. I found myself telling him that I hadn't spoken to my dad for over a year, since I dropped out of uni.

'You talk about quitting university a lot,' Eddie pointed out. 'What happened? Did you simply fail your exams?'

'I didn't take my exams,' I said. 'Some stuff happened with my family and the stress… I lost it. I couldn't do the work.'

I felt dark and heavy inside as the memories came back. I felt uncomfortable, but part of me wanted to tell Eddie everything. The older man seemed to sense this, questioning me further.

'Your family. Were they angry with you for dropping out?'

I smiled bitterly. 'Disappointed,' I said, quietly.

'As disappointed as when you told them that you were gay?'

Eddie probably meant this comment to be flirtatious, a playful way of confirming what he sensed about my sexuality. But it was too much for me, and I felt myself shutting down.

'If you knew me better,' I said tightly, 'You would understand why that is a bit of a touchy subject.'

'Touchy how? In what way?'

'My family… my dad didn't like it.' I swallowed and smiled strangely.

I didn't know how much to say. I opted for the basics; Mum, cancer. Dad, alcoholic. Clarke and Jamie ending up in foster care. I didn't feel able to tell him the rest.

'I could have taken care of my brothers. I was old enough. Our social worker was helping me and I would've had money and stuff from the government. But… I didn't. I just left them. They're still in care. They live in, like, a residential home with all these wild kids.' There was a short silence. I expected him to say the usual reassuring shit.

Eddie simply said, 'Sorry. That must have been a difficult choice for you to make.' He lit a cigarette and began to smoke it slowly, saying nothing further.

I hugged my knees. Eddie's company was so safe. He seemed to have an instinct for when to ask questions and when to be quiet. I sat there until I felt ready to speak.

'Do you get on with your parents?' I asked.

'They are both dead now, but yes, I was very close to both of my parents. I had a wonderful childhood,' said Eddie. 'My father kept racehorses. He loved horses and art, so we had a lot in common. I was very, very close to him. So was Ilya. I am sorry, Colt, that you did not have such a good experience with your family.'

He didn't know the half of it.

'My little brothers are lovely, lovely kids,' I mused. 'We all used to be really close.' I trailed off, thinking of Clarky, fifteen and Jamie, ten. They were both football-daft. I missed them so much.

There was a short silence, then, 'Whatever. Fuck them,' Eddie flapped his hand dismissively.

I looked at him in shock, then I relaxed. Maybe he knew how it felt to lose someone, and he knew that cloying sympathy was unhelpful and not welcome.

*****

It wasn't long before he asked to draw a picture of me. That's right. He wanted to draw. A picture. Of me. Eddie took a sip of tea, his eyes watching me. I was lost for words. Eventually I laughed and shook my head. Eddie persisted.

'Come on. I have no window in here to see anything. They have taken away my eyes. I love drawing people and I want to draw your face. Come on, I will impress you. Come on. Let me.'

I shook my head. 'Jeez… okay.' I smoothed a hand over my hair uncertainly. 'Sit with me out on the stairs tonight and draw my bloody face, if it makes you happy. But if anybody comes up, you move, fast. Ilya would fire me on the spot if he found out about this.'

'Yes! Tonight. We can sit on the steps together, or you could come in here...'

'No, we'll stay outside. That way we'll know if anyone's coming upstairs. Eddie, I'm really not supposed to even talk to you, please remember that. I could get into a lot of trouble.'

It struck me, as I unlocked the door to let Eddie out, just how much trouble I would get in if Ilya caught me. The door was opened wide, key sitting innocuously in the lock. The prisoner was sitting out on the steps, sharpening a pencil with his teeth. Eddie smiled at me, revealing lips and teeth stained with silvery-black lead. I tried to ignore the nervous cramp in my stomach. I settled myself against the wall, a book propped on my lap. The obligatory knife was tucked harmlessly in my uniform jacket, which in turn was in my room where I left it.

Eddie began to sketch, his eyes flashing from paper to face and back. I ignored him and tried to focus on my book, but the cramping in my stomach was getting worse and the words on the page blurred. Every noise in the hotel below made me jump.

'Stop!' I whispered constantly, at every noise, for the first five minutes. I abandoned my book altogether and sat listening tensely.

'Eddie, stop!'

'Argh! Stop!' Eddie slammed down his pencil. 'Stop, stop, stop!' he mimicked, 'is all I hear! Colt, relax! I have picture of you looking terrified now.' He held up the drawing.

'Hey. That's actually really good.' I reached for it and laughed. 'I do look scared. You could have done me smiling.'

'But you were not smiling. You hardly ever smile.'

For some reason, I suddenly thought about my little brothers. It was weird, thinking about them, out of the blue like that. Eddie was watching me closely and he said with irritation, 'When was the last time someone came up here on your watch? Hm? Never, I think?'

'Well… no, so far no one ever has. But they might!'

'No, they won't.' Eddie looked at the sketch. 'So, anyway, you like the drawing? You can keep it if you like.'

'Yeah, it's good. Well done.'

It was, actually. I handed it back and went to pick up my book again. Eddie continued to watch me.

'I will do another one, full body, in paint too. Then you would really be impressed, I promise.' His eyes flicked down my body. 'We should do it now. I have good thoughts about a position. Come in to my 'studio."

'No way! Are you mental?'

'What, you want to take off your clothes out here?' Eddie spat dull silver phlegm on the floorboard between us and grinned at the look of shock on my face. He seemed to absolutely love making me blush.

'Ah, no, I don't want to take my clothes off anywhere! Are you kidding me?'

'No, I am not 'kidding." I need to see the shape of your muscles, and your spine and everything, to do a proper painting. These stupid bell-boy clothes do not suit you, anyway!' Eddie's laughter was infectious.

'You'll have to be content with my face, I'm afraid,' I smiled 'Imagine if someone, say Ilya or Manpyre, came up here and I was naked? God, we would be in so much trouble! Is your art worth that?'

Eddie held my gaze and grinned at me. 'Imagine you naked? Easy! I am doing so as I speak.'

I blushed, but I was laughing. 'Stop it.'

Eddie turned a little more serious. 'No one will come up.'

I stood up. It was very late; yet again I had spent my whole evening with him.

'Well. We'll be very safe indeed, because I won't be naked, either.' I went to the door, 'Night, Ed. I'll see you in the morning.'

'You will be,' he smiled, as I shut the door. 'Believe me Colt, it is inevitable.'

I popped my head back into the room and studied his laughing face. He really believed I would strip off for his dumb painting. 'Not gonna happen, mate… g'night.'

'Sweet dreams.' He gave me a little wink.

My stomach flipped over as I shut and locked the door.

Chapter 5

Colt

I was clearing away the lunch dishes in the grand dining room. One of the tables of a family with young kids was covered with grated cheese. It was everywhere, all over the chairs and the floor. I was brushing it up when Manpyre walked into the room and strolled towards me.

'Alright?' he laughed. 'Cheese explosion?'

I looked up and pushed my hair out of my eyes, grabbing a bit of cheese in my fringe. Manpyre swept some cheese from one of the chairs, and sat down, watching me work. 'You don't half work hard,' he said kindly. 'Do you like doing this type of thing?' This struck me as a bit of a dumb question, but he didn't wait for me to answer. 'You won't have to do cleaning for much longer. Rumour has it that Ilya wants you to join the firm soon, properly.'

I put down my brush and dustpan and looked up at him. 'Really?'

He winked, 'Yeah, mate. But you never heard that from me.' I was thinking it over when he said, 'Have you got plans for dinner?'

I shrugged and tried to joke, 'Yeah, I was planning on eating dinner…'

'You're so cute,' he laughed. 'Come with me to this Lebanese restaurant tonight, if you want?' He began a long, boring description of what Lebanese cuisine entailed and why he liked it.

'You mean just me and you?' I checked, when I could get a word in.

'Yeah, you fancy it?'

I didn't quite know what to say. 'Alright,' I replied awkwardly.

I went up to tell Eddie that I wouldn't be coming to sit with him that night. I felt a real sense of responsibility towards him. I was actually apologetic about it.

'Okay. No, that is okay, do not worry about it… who are you going out with?' He asked despondently.

Instinctively I knew better than to tell him. 'Just… someone. A guy. It's not really a date. It's a bit of a date. I don't know.'

He didn't press for details. He seemed very depressed today, laying on his back staring at the sloping ceiling. He looked pale, too. 'Look after yourself, Colt,' he said seriously. 'Do not just go out with any old bastard. It is difficult to tell whether someone is genuine or not, at first. You are too quick to trust people, so please be careful, alright?'

This concern, I thought, was a bit rich coming from the man who was constantly begging me to get naked for him.

He needn't have worried. Manpyre behaved like a gentleman all evening. He was quite sweet in his own way, even though he talked too much and he bored me. Lebanese food? Not my thing. At the end of the night he drove me back to my flat and we sat out in the car talking. Or rather, he talked, at length, about the physics of why the top of the Eiffel Tower in Paris swayed, and by how much, and how a similar phenomenon occurred with streetlamps. I sat there, tired, stretching my eyes open and fighting to look interested. There was a black speck of food on one of his teeth. When there was a chance, I politely said I was tired. 'I had loads of fun. Thank you for dinner,' I said, 'Night!' I reached for the door handle as inevitably, he leaned over to kiss me. I moved away slightly.

'You're shy,' he laughed.

'I'm not shy. You- you've got something in your teeth…'

His mobile phone on the dashboard began to vibrate wildly. He was still laughing good-naturedly at me as he answered it. 'Hi,' he said, winking at me and casually taking hold of my hand. My fingers squirmed, enveloped in his hot, sweaty palm. 'What?' Manpyre dropped my hand and leaned forward, pressing the phone against his ear. 'Like, is he breathing? Yeah… yeah, he's here with me now.' Manpyre raised his eyebrows at me. 'Fuck. Fine, on our way now.' He slammed the car into gear. We were speeding down the street before he said, 'Eddie Bodansky's been found collapsed in the attic. Could have been there all day.'

'Oh no,' I gasped, 'What's wrong with him?'

'I don't know,' he muttered. 'Probably nothing. Fucking drama queen.'

Ilya kneeled on the floor beside Eddie as I examined him. 'Well?' he said, 'What's wrong with him?'

Manpyre was crouched by the attic door, smoking. 'He looks fine.'

Eddie raised his head a little and croaked, 'Aww, you look frustrated, David. Did I ruin your date? I am so sorry. You will just have to go and wank off.'

'Fuck you, Edwina.'

'Shh,' I said, 'Don't talk.'

Eddie smiled and closed his eyes, letting his head fall back on my hand.

I did my best to make Eddie comfortable. 'No hospitals,' said Ilya, as I opened my mouth to suggest it. I gritted my teeth and got on with helping him as best as I could. He seemed okay, insisting that he had just blacked out, but that he felt fine now. As I checked his eyes he suddenly gave a little gasp and sucked his breath in through his teeth.

I looked at him warily. 'Are your eyes hurting?'

He shook his head, but glanced meaningfully towards Ilya and Manpyre, and some others who were still around. 'It is not my eyes. I will tell you, just you,' he murmured, barely moving his lips. 'Just wait…'

I nodded my understanding.

I offered to stay with Eddie for a while. I waited until the others were gone, and then I was anxious to know, 'So? What is it?' I was leaning over him, quite close, staring at the really black flecks in his dark irises. His eyes were a combination of dark brown and green.

He took a breath and grimaced, 'I have a bad heart.'

'Bad?'

Eddie looked away from me. 'It is bad, Colt, it is fucking broken and defective. And I do not want anyone else to know about it. That is why I am telling you, I trust you.' I felt myself blushing as he said, 'You remember the first night I was here? I tried to leave, and you would not let me. Well, I was trying to go and fetch my heart medicine.'

'Oh. Talk about a guilt trip.'

'You should feel guilty! I need you to get it for me. I was renting a house before I came here and all of my things are in it. No one else knows about it. I need you to go there tomorrow morning, first thing, and get all of my pills for me. Will you do that for me?'

'Of course I will. Are you crazy? I'll go tonight.'

Eddie's little rented semi house was beautiful inside, like a plain box filled with bright candy. I walked all around it, fascinated by all of his belongings. There was a chair draped with silk scarves of every colour imaginable. I opened a drawer; it was full of lace gloves. In the wardrobes there were suits and silk shirts hanging alongside satin ladies' nightgowns. I touched the material and my hand quivered. There was so much jewellery. It must've been worth a fortune, proper diamonds and everything… I was fascinated by the amount of women's clothes. Corsets, tights, underwear… I began to wonder if a woman actually lived here, but then I saw the shoes, an extensive collection of men's styles alongside pretty, high-heeled ladies shoes. They were all the same size; it was weird seeing shoes like that in such a big size. Kind of funny but kind of sexy.

35

I found his medication pretty quickly; it was in the bathroom cabinet where he said it would be, but I admit that I carried on snooping. There was a bookcase lined with Russian literature and English books about Russia. Photos and drawings of horses adorned every wall. On the bottom shelf there was a big cardboard box of photographs and albums. I got on my knees and hauled it out, not even feeling guilty. Eddie just really interested me and I had to know everything about him. In his house, surrounded by his belongings, I felt immersed in his world. I actually felt like I was inside his brain.

I opened up a slim, black A3 folder. The cover page revealed that it was an agency modelling portfolio of 'Jason James Prescott.' He was a gorgeous young guy with really classic looks and arrestingly dark eyes. I had never seen him before, but as I turned each page and those eyes stared out at me from each shot, I began to feel that there was something a bit familiar about his face. There were two more portfolios from different agencies, all of the same person. Some of the shots were catwalk. I was studying one picture when a brown envelope fell out of the book and onto my lap. It wasn't sealed and it was marked, 'J.J. private shoot.' I was being really shamefully nosey now, and I should have been getting back to the hotel with Eddie's meds, but I opened that envelope and slid out the photos. I studied them briefly then I shoved them back, blushing. They were amateur and sort of personal; I had a glimpse of the blond man posing naked on a bed, touching himself. I began to feel cold chills, like I had gone too far, and I felt really creepy for invading Eddie's privacy like that. He asked me to come and get his meds, not rifle through his homemade porn.

As I put everything away I caught sight of one last portfolio. This one had Eddie's own name on it, 'Edvard Ivanov Bodansky.' I couldn't resist looking at it, and when I saw the first shot I actually gasped out loud, 'Oh my God.' He was so handsome. He was young, younger than me, and hadn't yet suffered his facial disfigurements. There was one black and white shot that I don't think I will ever forget… he was staring at the camera in a sort of drugged, dreamy way wearing this kind of female corset thing. It wasn't laced up, because his body was too muscular for that. There was something about the unlaced ribbons hanging down against his tight body, the power and masculinity combined with this feminine garment. I felt sick and exhilarated. I didn't know transvestism could be attractive. Maybe it was just him. He was breath-taking. I peeled one of the photos from its cellophane backing and pocketed it, feeling like a right little pervert.

'Got your meds,' I said later, back in the attic. 'Here.' I felt myself blushing faintly as he took the boxes, and his fingers touched mine. I dared to look at him and he was grinning at me.

'Thanks babe,' he said.

I nodded and looked away, not trusting myself to speak. Eddie opened his pills and swallowed two without water. He lay back down on the floor, on the pile of dusty curtains he was using as a bed and put his arms behind his head. 'I said thank you, Colt,' he repeated. 'You are being very quiet.'

I turned around and looked at him. I felt a strange desperation unlike anything I had felt before. 'I want you to do the... the painting of me,' I said, my throat inexplicably tight. 'I want to model for you. However you want, okay?'

Eddie regarded me, his face unreadable. Then he broke into a grin. 'Ahh. So, now I know, in future I should have more heart attacks to get my own way.' I didn't reply as he stood up and walked slowly around me. 'You want to model for me. What changed your mind?'

I got the feeling that he knew exactly what I had seen in his house. I shrugged. He was standing too close to me. He walked behind me and paused, just standing right behind me. 'I, myself, used to be a model, did you know that?'

'No.' I lied.

He laughed quietly. 'It is maybe hard for you to imagine because I am a monster now, but it is true. I only had a few jobs. Some of my friends were more successful.' Images danced in my head and he stepped away from me. I relaxed and he said, 'It would be an honour to draw you. Come up tonight and we shall do it, Colt.'

So, later that night, I found myself naked in Eddie's attic. The room was dark. There was a hand torch, a Maglite and a caretaker's torch, all aimed at where I stood stripping off in a pocket of light. Eddie lurked at the edge of the light. I unbuttoned my shirt. There was something compelling about Eddie. I can't believe I'm doing this, I thought, as I let the garment fall and I stepped out of my uniform trousers. In the years to come I would look back on this incident and recognise neither Eddie, nor myself. Eddie locked eyes with me. His gaze then travelled deliberately down my naked body, bisecting me like a laser. He took a deep breath, blew out slowly and said nothing. He just sat down, rested his weight on one huge hand and began to sketch with the other, the pencil, tiny in his hand, scratching loudly on the floor. I stood there naked, feeling ridiculous.

'What do you want me to do?' I said, wrapping my arms across my stomach. 'I can't just stand here doing nothing!'

Eddie looked up. 'You can,' he said simply. He dropped his head and carried on drawing.

I paused, and then decided to sit down, too. Standing up made me feel unbearably exposed. I hugged my knees to my chest and rested my chin on them. Eddie stopped and looked at me again for several long moments. There was intensity in his eyes.

'You can, because you look absolutely beautiful when you are like this. I am in shock that I have someone so perfect to draw.'

I was speechless. Suddenly I jumped to my feet. 'This is weird,' I declared.

'What? Stay standing like that. The position is good. The muscles in your legs are good.'

I picked up my trousers. 'It's freezing and weird, weird, weird that I'm naked. Why am I naked?' I grabbed my underwear and the uniform trousers.

Eddie pushed his paper away. 'Okay, so I won't even draw. To be honest, I just want to take you to bed. Not,' he added, glancing with distaste at the pile of curtains, 'that I have a real bed.'

I paused, my hand hovering over my shirt. I grabbed it and dragged it on quickly, shivering.

'I have to go,' I mumbled. My fingers fumbled repeatedly over the uniform buttons, missing them each time. I abandoned them, moving towards the door. 'See you later.'

Eddie bolted to the door and leant against it. He held up his hand and I backed away, my heart thumping and my legs turning to jelly.

'Stop,' said Eddie, 'Listen- I did not mean to scare you.'

'Please, I have to go.' To my horror my voice was shaking. I felt that things were slipping beyond my control, even my voice.

'Colt-'

'I have to go.'

Keeping one hand flat on the door, Eddie reached out and started to toy with the unfastened panels of my shirt, rubbing the material between two long, roughened fingers. His eyes sparkled and he impulsively grabbed my wrist, holding it tightly as his other hand left the door and moved across my back, stroking and exploring.

'Get off me.' I struggled. My wrist was twisting like a fish but his grip was fucking strong. My bones clicked, the skin of my wrist was being pinched. Now Eddie was hurting me, now I was failing to keep the panic out of my voice. 'Get off me.'

'Stay with me,' he pleaded in response, moving his hands gently across my belly, taking the warmth from my skin. 'I can't face another night in here by myself- you have no idea…'

'Please, just stop.'

Eddie looked down at me, a shadow darkening his face. His eyes went dead and I saw something different in there, something that for one moment made my heart stop. His fingers dug insistently into my hips, squeezing hard enough to bruise. I cried out in pain as his grip shifted to my face, squeezing harder still, the massive hand crushing into my cheeks.

'Manpyre!'

Startled by my hysterical shout, Eddie's eyes seemed to clear. He reclaimed himself and finally opened the door, looking abashed. I pushed past him and slammed it on him, the door biting down on a yell of apology.

I dug out my key and twisted it in the lock.

The door opened below and Manpyre pelted up the stairs. He shot a puzzled look at me, 'You okay, mate?' I turned around slowly and stared at him. After a moment I nodded, rubbing my jaw. Manpyre glanced at the door and frowned. 'Were you in there just now?'

'I… yeah… he said he was ill again.' I was thinking fast. 'I believed him, so I went inside and… he tried to escape.'

'Fucking hell, mate," Manpyre spat, 'you should've called me. Don't just go in by yourself. He can be a dangerous fucker.' He put his hands on my shoulders and looked concernedly into my eyes. 'I really don't want anything to happen to you, mate.'

He took my key from me and unlocked the door. Eddie was sitting by the fire, magnificent head in his hands. He looked up wearily as Manpyre strode into the room and I followed him, waiting uneasily by the door. Manpyre did not pause to talk to Eddie, he simply grabbed him and rammed his forehead against the stone fireplace. A long, low moan came from Eddie's lips as he rolled onto his side, closed his eyes and passed out.

'Done.' Manpyre looked at me and he walked over. He was studying my face, and he looked concerned. 'You go downstairs mate, get some rest. Ilya's had you up here guarding Eddie every single night hasn't he? It's not fair on you, kid. I'll watch him tonight.'

I was hardly listening to him. I was standing over the unconscious Eddie, staring down at him. Every muscle in my body was clenched. My jaw began to ache with tension.

I squatted down and stared at his face. His mouth was slightly agape, his breath coming in slow, deep rasps. The whites of his rolling eyes showed through slits; his Adam's apple slid up his exposed throat. He looked pathetic. I licked my teeth.

'Colt. You hear me?'

I stood up as the adrenaline ebbed away from my body, leaving me weak. I turned my back on Manpyre's quizzical look and hurried from the room, grateful to close the door on it all.

I went to the hotel bar and Sasha, Ilya's daughter, was in there, reading. She and I were friends, of sorts, she was only a couple of years younger than me and we had a love of books in common. Sasha was a lovely girl, always happy, but I just wasn't in the mood to see anyone. She put down her book. 'Bryce,' she called excitedly. I went over feeling awkward and reluctant.

'Hey,' I said softly.

'What happened to your shirt?' she smiled.

I looked down. My shirt was loose and partly undone. Sasha's smile faded at my expression. I started to fix the buttons, a deep blush spreading over my face and neck. 'I'm just a scruff,' I mumbled, lowering my face to hide the colour. Sasha pushed back her hair from her face with both hands and leaned forward, trying to look at my eyes, which I kept resolutely lowered.

'What's eating you, Bryce?'

'Nothing. I'm tired, is all.'

She sighed. 'I feel like something is going on, Bryce. Everyone is acting so strange, especially my dad.' She paused. 'Maybe it's about that crazy guy that came in… My dad seemed to know him… did you hear about that?'

'Nope.'

'Oh. I thought Mischa said you were there. There was a crazy guy in the hotel lobby! He tried to grab Mischa then he vomited on the stairs… gross, right?'

I had to escape. I made my excuses and, even though it was late, I headed straight to the hotel gym to clear my head. Unlimited, all-hours access to the gym was my favourite perk of living in the hotel. There was a fitness suite with full-length mirrors on every wall, a weights room and an oval-shaped swimming pool with a steam room and sauna. I loved it because it was usually quiet, often empty.

Having finished my workout I relaxed in the sauna, the baking air cleansing my skin. I worked out as often as I had time to. I was only too aware of the fact that I was the skinniest member of the firm and truthfully, it bothered me. Only Manpyre was as slim, but he was taller than me.

I stretched out my legs in the dry heat and breathed out slowly, examining my thighs. I was, at that time of my life, slight and small, yet well-proportioned. I knew that I could never become very well-built because I had a small frame to work with, but I was quietly pleased with the tight definition I had already achieved. I enjoyed keeping fit by doing a lot of cardio work.

The shower room was dark as the electric lighting was broken. I propped open the door with my gym bag, to let some of the light from the fitness suite in. I undressed, took off my glasses and laid them on top of my folded clothes. Almost blind, I then groped my way into the shower in the dim light. I began to shower slowly, the steam sucking and swirling out into the cold, dark room. I closed my eyes and tipped my head back. Rubbing shampoo into my hair, my hand slid around my neck and I paused, fingertips connecting with raised welts at my throat. I opened my eyes and quickly scanned my body with my fingertips. I hadn't noticed until now that on my waist, Eddie's fingernails had scratched deeply into my skin. I couldn't see well in the dark and without my glasses, but I traced my fingers along at least three blood-encrusted gouges. I tipped back my head and let the water run into my mouth, my eyes. I felt slightly shaken and emotionally exhausted. I knew how stupid I had been and no one needed to tell me how naive.

Eddie had frightened me and I prayed that no one would ever find out what had happened, what he had tried to do. I did know that I was partly to blame. I knew that Eddie was attracted to me. Why, I asked myself, had I played with fire? My cheeks glowed red as I stood there in the darkness, the hot water running all over me. I allowed myself, just for one minute, to relive that feeling of vulnerability. My mind drifted… what would have happened if I hadn't protested? My breath caught in my throat. Gasping, I opened my eyes. The water drummed all around me. I breathed through my nose, all the hairs on the back of my neck standing up despite the heat. I felt sure that someone was watching me. Stepping out of the shower, I shivered as my feet touched the tiles. The gym was silent. I hurriedly put on my glasses, dried myself and threw on my clothes. I sat down on the bench and began to dry my hair then I stopped, clutching my head in the towel. Suddenly I was shaking; shaking and crying so hard that I couldn't stop.

Chapter 6

Colt

I had been standing in the freezing stairwell outside the attic door for fifteen minutes. I stared at the door, knowing that Eddie was just behind it, waiting for me. I ran through my options. There was no way I could ask Manpyre to take Eddie's breakfast to him. One; that would make me look like a pathetic loser and two; it might lead to people actually finding out what had happened. God help me, I considered not taking the food at all but I realised that would be incredibly cruel. Anyway, I couldn't go on indefinitely starving the guy.

The knife in my pocket brought me some comfort. If I couldn't bring myself to use it then at least it would serve as a useful threat. I told myself, just go in, put down the tray and walk out. I kept repeating this, as the minutes ticked on and on. Finally I psyched myself up enough and I opened the door quickly. The room was empty. He wasn't there. I advanced warily, holding the tray in one hand and gripping the knife inside my pocket with the other. Shit, where was he? He might be ill again. His heart… or that bang on the head from Manpyre. Fuck, was he dead? I walked slowly into the centre of the room, feeling more spooked with every echoing step. I set the tray down in the middle of the floor and stood up quickly.

'Eddie? Hello?' In my shaking hand I held the knife tightly as I peered into the brightly lit bathroom. It was an oddly shaped, rather large room, with a sloping roof and one wall lined with tall white cabinets. There was a white laundry chest and a large cast-iron bath off to one side.

Suddenly there were footsteps on the wooden floor behind me. I spun around and found myself face-to-face with Eddie. He folded his arms and leaned against the door frame, effectively barring my only means of escape. 'Thank you for breakfast,' he said in his Russian accent; sadly, it seemed to me. 'It was brave of you to bring it, considering. So, thank you.'

My heart was thundering but I couldn't speak. I saw him looking at the knife in my hand, and his sadness seemed to deepen. 'I know you are scared, but I want to talk to you. Please listen, then you can go.' He settled himself more comfortably in the door frame. 'My actions last night were… unforgivable.' I just stared at him. I could not believe that I had gotten myself into this position; twice. Eddie was still talking, '… but I must try to convince you to forgive me. You are the only thing that has made my life bearable these last weeks. I cannot, cannot lose this friendship.' He unfolded his arms to gesticulate and I took a startled step back, holding the knife at arm's length in front of my body. He glanced at the knife and continued, unperturbed. 'So, how to make you trust me? I can think of only one way.'

I suddenly knew what was about to happen before it did, and I tried to simultaneously run past him, and lash out with the knife as he lunged towards me and we fell to the floor together… I landed on my stomach and knocked the air from my body. Gasping, I felt the weight of Eddie's knees crushing into the small of my back. He grabbed my head under my chin and raised it slightly off the floor, then, he put his hand over my mouth. Hysterical with fear, I heard his voice in my ear.

'You are completely helpless. I could do anything I want with you. I could rape you right here; there is no one to stop me, is there?' he shifted his weight and I involuntarily whimpered with pain and fear. 'But I am not going to. Remember, I had this opportunity and I did not hurt you.' Blood thundered in my ears and I begged myself not to pass out. It seemed like forever that I lay on the cold wooden floor, Eddie holding me tightly.

After a long time, he released me. He stood up and walked out of the room, leaving me lying there alone. Coughing gently, I rolled onto my back and stared at the sloping ceiling. I rubbed a hand over my hot eyes and found, to my surprise, that they were wet. I lay there by myself for a long time in a bit of a trance, gazing at all the imperfections on the white ceiling.

'Are you alright?' Eddie's voice was full of concern when I walked out of the bathroom. He was huddled in front of the fireplace, wrapped up in his dull green velvet curtains, holding his cup of tea. I sat down beside him and stared at the floor. 'Colt, I will never put you through something like that again. My wish is that you come to visit me always. I do not want to drive you away.' Eddie sipped his tea, looking wretched. I fixed him with a look, my eyes hot and itchy from crying.

'If you ever try that again, if you ever even fucking suggest that to me, I will go straight from here to Ilya's office. I don't care what happens to you. If you ever touch me again, I will feed you to him.'

Eddie sat huddled in his curtains, nursing his tea. After a moment he smiled sweetly and said, 'Wow. I made you really angry. That offer of going to bed with me still stands, any time you change your mind.'

I blushed furiously. 'Did you not hear what I just said?'

Eddie laughed openly at me and my blush deepened. 'Colt, don't worry. I had a drink last night and I got carried away. I am incredibly lonely. My mind is everywhere. I would have slept with you, though. I still want to. No, do not interrupt. I know you are not interested and I will never ask you again.' He held out his arm. 'Look. You little thug. You cut me.'

'You deserved it.'

I ran downstairs to fetch a bandage for Eddie's arm, and applied it under strict conditions that he kept it hidden. The cut wasn't deep; the knife had cleanly sliced the back of his hand and wrist without going deeply beneath the skin. Judging by the number of scars, his arm was no stranger to knives anyway. As I bandaged the wrist, I glanced up and saw Eddie watching me with pleasure in his dark eyes. I realised that his plan had worked perfectly in terms of getting me to trust him again.

'What is that?' I touched a small mark at his inner elbow, different from all of the other scars. 'A little tattoo?'

'Yes.'

I looked at it. It was old and crudely done, very deep and uneven, with blue ink bleeding unattractively. 'J.P. Looks like you did that yourself, did you?'

Eddie lifted his arm and studied it himself. 'I did,' he sighed. 'Not a fabulous job for an artist, is it? Why my right arm? Stupid. In love and stupid.' He shook his head and grinned.

'But who is J.P.?'

He would not be drawn. 'Ah. You do not tell me everything, do you?'

'Yes. I tell you absolutely everything. More than I tell anyone else.' Weirdly, this was true.

'Well. I am older, and my secrets are boring.' Eddie grinned. 'You really want to know, hm? Well, I have another one. This one I did not attempt to do myself!' He got up onto his knees and pulled his shirt over his head. I took a sharp intake of breath. Eddie's entire torso; chest, stomach, shoulders, arms, was a lacerated mess of scar tissue. He allowed me to look at it for a moment, while he unnecessarily folded his shirt over his forearm, never once looking at my expression, my reaction, to his mutilated body. He then turned and I drew my breath sharply. Emblazoned across his muscular, golden shoulder blades, in beautiful, antique-style script, were two words that left me in no doubt as to who J.P was. Jason Prescott. I remembered the photographs in Eddie's house and the stacks of modelling portfolios. Beneath the tattoo were some strange letters that I could not make into anything.

'It's Russian,' Eddie laughed quietly. 'It means- it just means, I love you; Ya lublu tebya.' He suddenly blushed, like a flame, and pulled his shirt back down.

'So, who is it? Who is he?' I kept picturing the stunning model.

Eddie's face went strangely blank. I felt a quick flutter of panic; maybe I had crossed a boundary. I was about to apologise when he suddenly turned to me, his eyes fierce. 'Jason was my boyfriend- he died.'

'I'm sorry. What happened?'

'Horse riding accident.'

I looked down. 'That's terrible, I'm really sorry.'

'Don't be.' His teeth were clenched. 'It was a long time ago.'

Eddie smoked two cigarettes in silence, and I sat hugging my knees, leaning my back against the marble fireplace. The shocking sight of his body was taking it's time to ebb away. It looked like he had fallen through a glass window, or something.

I looked at him and he looked back at me boldly, exhaling some smoke. His expression dared me to ask him more. When I did not dare, Eddie seemed both satisfied and disappointed. He grinned, stubbed out the cigarette on the floor and lit up a third before speaking.

'I got the tattoo just before he died,' he said. 'Maybe it is the reason why I have not had a long-term relationship since! I suppose it is a bit off-putting.'

I shrugged.

'Or maybe my lovers do not quite like my 'scratches'... did you notice them?'

'What?' I blushed, still feeling chilled from the sight of them. 'I don't know.'

'You don't know?' Eddie was still grinning. 'Maybe you missed them.' He stood up and literally ripped off his clothes, all of them, except for his underwear.

'Look at me,' he ordered softly. Squirming uncomfortably, I wouldn't look. 'Colt. This is part of my apology. I need you to look at me. If you do... I will feel every bit as exposed and vulnerable as I made you feel last night. Now, look at me. Look at me now.'

He was brutally scarred everywhere. All of the scarring was methodical, it all ran in the same diagonal direction and was all white or very pale, shiny pink. He sat down in his shorts with his feet on the floor, and I noticed further scarring on the inside of his thighs. 'It started the day he died,' said Eddie. 'I did it to myself.'

I was lost for words.

'That's mad,' I said finally. I was thinking about the photos I had seen of Eddie when he was younger. What would make the handsome youth disfigure his own body like that?

'Yes,' agreed Eddie. 'It is mad; literally. I suffered from a mental breakdown when I was...' he tipped his head back, making a show of remembering, '... ahh... twenty-one years old. Following my partner's death I damaged myself. And it is painful beyond endurance to have someone like you, someone perfect... staring at the damage and judging me.'

'No- I'm not judging you!'

Eddie wrapped the velvet curtains around himself. 'I ask that you leave me alone now.'

I stood up wanting to say more, but I couldn't so I left.

Chapter 7

Eddie

Alone again, I felt emotionally exhausted from my conversation with Colt. I was happy he was gone and glad to be alone. Slowly, I peeled off the curtain and took a long, hard dispassionate look at my body. I had not self-harmed for years, but I could well remember the emotion behind my actions.

It had been five weeks since my return from the hospital and I had not ventured out of my room. Dr Bell was keeping up his weekly visits and I welcomed the psychiatrist. Some of the medication he prescribed seemed to, at least blunt the sharpest edges of my emotions. Without the right medication I felt that I could not breathe, that I could not lift my head. I missed Jason so much, I could not believe that he was dead.

On one of those long afternoons, I was lying on the embroidered chaise lounge, my head flopping backwards. My left leg, encased in plaster to the thigh, was propped up on the seat, and my right leg rested on the floor, the foot only in plaster. I had been staring at a row of twinkling fairy lights draped along the wardrobe for over an hour. Their image burned into my eyes each time I slowly blinked. There was a sketchpad lying open on my chest. Someone had placed it there, I could not remember who. My fingers had been unconsciously scratching out the thing I always used to sketch, in the days and weeks following Eel's death. I hardly noticed when Ilya came into the room. 'How are you feeling?' he asked sympathetically. He strode to the window and opened the curtains wide. The light made me blink. I craned my neck towards Ilya and in doing so, inadvertently caught my reflection in the full-length mirror. My formerly golden complexion looked clammy and pale, and the ugly, disfiguring slash was not healing well. My eyes looked translucent in the bright sunlight, pupils narrowed to black dots. I winced from the image, while Ilya's smile faltered. 'Christ... you look awful. You should get outside.' He had a stab at being jocular, 'Your horses will have forgotten who you are!'

'I have two broken legs,' I pointed out, in a new monotone that did not sound like my voice. I knew I could never tend to the horses, not without Jason.

'Still. You can't sit here all day... again. Why don't I ask Will to wheel you downstairs in the chair? Go out to the stables. Feed the horses some carrots or something.' His gaze fell to the sketchpad lying on my lap, 'Or, you could take the chance to draw them.' He frowned and looked more closely at the drawing in the book, 'Edik... is that... what I think it is?'

I snapped the book closed and Ilya looked at me in complete disgust. 'You sick little bastard,' he said. I just stared at him, my mouth twitching.

'Illy,' I said. 'Is he truly dead?' Ilya must have known that I no longer harboured any hope; I was merely voicing the question.

He looked away. Then he looked me straight in the eye and softly, he said, 'Yes. You know he is, Edik .'

I turned my head to the window, my mouth still twitching. My heart was starting to pound, I wanted to hurt myself very, very badly.

Ilya began tidying around me, casually removing my sketchpad. As he did so he brushed his fingers over my arm, already badly disfigured. 'This,' he said loudly, 'is not going to bring him back or help you in any way.' I looked at him and he gestured to my arm. 'Don't do that.' He said.

Smiling very slightly, I lifted up my top, revealing my slashed, blood-crusted stomach. I dropped my top again, feeling almost bored. Ilya looked momentarily stunned. 'Edik!' He gasped. 'What have you done to yourself? You stupid little prick,' he spat. 'Pull yourself together. Slicing yourself up? Come on, what's the point?'

'I'm turning my body into a monument to grief,' I yawned.

Ilya hissed in disgust, missing the sarcasm. 'That is the stupidest thing I have ever heard. You're just another angst-fuelled kid. Your boyfriend died, I get that, it's sad. But-'

'He did not just die.' I swallowed. 'It is my fault.'

'But this? Disfiguring yourself for life? For Jason Prescott?'

I let my head flop back. 'I know I shouldn't do it, it just makes me feel- better.' As soon as Ilya left the room, I retrieved my Swiss knife from between the cushions. I had not even started on my left arm, yet.

Chapter 8

Colt

Most evenings, throughout the winter of Eddie's incarceration, I let him paint me. He told me that he used to have Jason model for him, but he found him too sexy, therefore too distracting, apparently. He never got any painting done. I felt a bit huffy about that... I didn't know how I felt about Eddie at that point. I was still scared of him and yet- I wanted him to want me. So, I didn't abandon him after his moment of madness. Why would I?

It pleased Eddie to lie in the porcelain bath while he painted me, this way we were both naked, for the avoidance of any shyness on my part. I brought some hot water upstairs with me, three or four trips running up and down the stairs with a kettle. I liked to see Eddie lounging there, his big, sinewy feet draped over the sides of the tub, his body striped yellow on sunny evenings or his nakedness a watery, translucent blue on darker nights; whenever the notion to paint me took him. The way his hair fell forward over his dancing eyes, the fat cigar with its reassuring upward finger of grey, black smoke calmed me as I watched him bathing, stealing every flaw and imperfection of my body and deftly making it his own. I often sat by the dirty bathroom unit or cracked, yellowing sink in this or that pose, reflecting the brooding storm beneath the hunched eyebrows.

One night, it was early evening, straight after dinner. We were in the cold attic, I had just lit the fire and I lay in front of it all sleepy, stretched and catlike. I loved the way the flames played back tenfold in Eddie's eyes. He was talking loudly, a drink resting in one long hand, a cigar pinched in the slender grip of the other. He announced that he wanted to draw me and even though I protested, I loved these spontaneous occasions.

I posed rather self-consciously before Eddie's tarnished bathroom mirror with my chin resting on my knee, curling and uncurling my toes as I watched Eddie without meeting his eyes. My body was nothing special, not handsome like Eddie's nor powerful like Ilya's. Yet, I knew that something in it inspired Eddie, evident from the stacks of tireless portraits, each began with an enthusiasm that knew nothing of its predecessors.

As always, Eddie was methodically preparing his 'studio'; prowling gravely around the dark narrow bathroom, he gathered his utensils, stooping slightly to prevent his head from grazing the slanted ceiling. He caught my solemn gaze, and frowned. 'No!' he growled, shaking his dark hair, crossing the room in one stride. 'No. Straight back, I showed you. Head down. Like this.' His thick Russian accent lent a grating quality to his pronunciation. I tolerated the feel of the big, patient hands manoeuvring my limbs and I stole a glance at Eddie's close-up and scowling face lined with a grave, professional thought. He ran a strong palm firmly down my spine and let his fingers rest right at the base. 'Stand straight,' he murmured, for the third time. The fingers rested there on the small of my back. 'Beautiful. Hold it. Straight...' Eddie growled softly. He stepped away, and his eyes moved darkly, critically over my body. My eyes flicked back into his with an almost accidental intensity, like a burning touch in the dark. Eddie's face tightened and he drew back a touch, fearful. Then he relaxed.

'Alright,' he said briskly. He dragged off his clothes without shame and

I immediately felt more at ease. We were, by now, so familiar with each other's nakedness, it was like looking at an awkwardly dressed chimp to see Eddie in one of his suits now. No, he was best nude; he looked majestic.

A grin from Eddie surfaced me from my thoughts. I straightened my back. Eddie, clutching a brandy, was folding his long body into the bath, the clawing shafts of bitter, dying orange sunlight fingering his muscular back. He turned, his expression strangely vulnerable. 'Here, Colt, hold my cigar,' he muttered distractedly, forgetting his model's pose. 'And now…' he set about pinning his canvass to the board, and balancing his oils in the brass soap dish. I sucked on the cigar, closed my eyes and waited. I was in for a long night.

Eddie

It was late, and the last of the light had died. I lay drowsily in a bath of cold, murky water, mingled with swirling oil, ash and alcohol. Fitfully, Colt was asleep where he stood in the semi-darkness, his head resting on his knee. Quietly I stood up in the bathtub and reached, shivering for my velvet jacket. I had not painted a stroke for over two hours. I wrapped my jacket around my body where it clung to my wet skin. My stomach clenched with cold, and my breath misted the filthy looking glass as I glanced at my appearance. Haughtily, my boldly etched features stared back, nostrils flaring.

My eyes slid down to where Colt slept, his pale, scant body breathing quickly. The drop of his head, the exquisite sensuality of his features, the strange fragility of the way his lips curved in a feminine arc… I strove to translate what I saw into my work. My colours could never be real enough to convey Colt. I attempted to, I tried; whispered hues, the pearliest, most translucent shades tried vainly to capture that inherent beauty. I dreamed of creating a painting that exhibited the vulnerable, foetal human, raw and exposed, too delicate for this world, like a flowering anther.

Sometimes, I just wanted Colt. He slept on, while I stared. Colt moved slightly in his sleep, his eyes opened and at that moment, something inside me broke.

'Can I see it?'

The canvass, stained with a lacklustre echo of my vision had been discarded on the floor.

'No, not for tonight, anyhow, no more painting. I am tired, Colt. I just need to drink.' Irritably, for my emotions had frightened me, I stepped fully out of the bath, chalked Colt's feet and hand and let him free.

Colt

It was one in the morning. I was feeling a little lightheaded as I left Eddie's quarters and made my silent way back along the labyrinth of narrow staircases that connected Eddie to the rest of the house. In one hand I held my candle, the other groping along the rough filthy wall. I could smell my own warm, grimy skin; the scent was comforting, as was the sugary gluey coating of brandy on my teeth and tongue.

I was feeling altogether pretty content, reminiscing about my evening with Eddie. We had passed the rest of our time warming up by the fire, and Eddie had been making me laugh telling me about his antics in Stockholm. I felt only a little tingle of trepidation at the idea of our illicit fun. It was thrilling to think that the two most oppressed, degraded individuals in the manor shared a secret life of camaraderie and joy.

On the surface of it, Eddie led an unenviable life indeed, but he never ceased to amaze me with his passion and vigour. The first day, for instance, on which I met him was prophetic, in that Eddie was utterly broken, yet he had been still able to draw upon a reservoir of strength and dignity. He was intensely emotional, a quality or curse bestowed upon him by his experiences.

'What are you doing prowling around at this time of night? It's cold tonight, Bryce.' Ilya's voice surprised me as it came suddenly, out of the darkness. He spoke softly with a cold light in his eye.

Drawing my blanket more tightly about my body, I tried to sound slightly irritated as I answered, 'I was in the bathroom?' I felt slightly drunk and hoped he didn't notice. I took a few steps away from Ilya towards my own door. 'Well…goodnight.' I laid a hand on the doorknob.

'Bryce.' He spoke so calmly that it made the hairs on my neck stand up. I glanced up. Ilya was leaning against the wall, his arms crossed. His partially shadowed face wore a look of haughty distain to rival his brother's. 'You shouldn't wander around at night. There are several unsavoury characters living in this hotel.' A smirk spread slowly across his face as he stared at me with his pale eyes, with their unearthly violet irises. 'However, don't worry too much,' he murmured, 'I'll be watching you carefully from now on... I wouldn't want anything happening to the youngest member of my firm.'

I frowned slightly. Those eyes were hard to read. Ilya had a reputation for lulling people into a false sense of security; he acted as though matters were resolved, but later he would dish out his punishment. He was a wicked joker who clearly relished his power.

'Okay... thanks, sir.' I swallowed and tried to smile. 'Goodnight.' I dived into my room and banged the door hard behind me. Shaking, I fumbled with the key, dropping it twice before successfully locking it. I switched off the light and jumped straight into bed, feeling completely unnerved. It was growing light before I finally fell into an uneasy sleep, tossing with the image of those wide luminous violet eyes hanging in the darkness of my fevered brain.

*****

'Watch you? Closely, from now on?' Eddie stared at me over his breakfast, which sat untouched on a tray between us on the floor.

I nodded seriously. 'That's what he said. I... I don't think I'll come up tonight, Eddie. Something's up, I think he knows.'

Eddie looked crestfallen. In his Russian accent he moaned, 'Do not say that. Come to me, I will go mad on my own. My brother is a real bastard. Come on, he doesn't have a clue. He is too fucking stupid!'

'No, I need to keep my head down for a bit. Maybe next week, once things have cooled down a bit.'

Eddie moaned in anguish and dropped his magnificent head in his hands.

'Eddie, quit the drama. I'll see you later when I bring your lunch.'

'I understand. You look like shit, you did not sleep?' Eddie leaned across, and placing his big hand on my head, he began to tease his thick fingers through my hair.

I sighed. 'Not too well,' I answered vaguely. I was cringing slightly at the close contact. 'Leave over, Ed,' I murmured softly.

Eddie smiled broadly as he continued to stroke my scalp. 'Why? This feels good, no? My mother used to do this for me when I was a little boy, if I was sleepy.'

'I'm not sleepy... stop it.' Now, I was never a particularly tactile person, so although I was well used to Eddie's ways, I always felt uncomfortable when he started to paw at me. However, the rhythmic motion was particularly seductive, and I submitted to being manhandled in this way for several minutes.

Suddenly, I felt Eddie's surreptitious touch crawling over my waist; my eyes flew open as he deftly unbuckled the catch of my belt. 'Hey,' I protested angrily, snatching for my belt as he whipped it through the belt loops and out of my reach. He tightened his grip on my hair, actually hurting me, and dragged me firmly to the floor. He then loomed over me and grinned down at me.

'Got you,' he laughed softly, mockingly. My face felt bright red and I felt a quick stab of panic. Images from the attic flooded my mind, of Eddie's fingers clawing into my flesh, the darkness in his eyes. Eddie laughed louder and released his grip. 'This will teach you- never trust me,' he joked, tossing my belt at me. I grabbed it and stood up, scowling.

'You bastard,' I gasped, only half-laughingly, half bitter. I walked out backwards, pulling the door. 'See you later.'

'If I am still alive! I am sick, might die with loneliness!' Called Eddie as the door closed.

Eddie

Stripped to the waist, I was shaving in the freezing bathroom when I heard the attic door opening again. I paused, my hands splashing into the water. 'Hello?' I called. The silence dripped.

'It's me.' Ilya appeared at the door frame. I turned away wordlessly and continued to lather up with the thin, gritty sliver of soap. Ilya sat down on the edge of the bath. 'How are you?'

Rolling my eyes, I said, 'Let's see… I have barely slept in a month. I had a heart attack last week. I am cold, and half-starved. How are you?'

Ilya smiled, despite himself and ignored the question.

'Interesting… you did not say lonely.'

'That, too.' I turned to look at him. 'As I am in isolation, I thought that would be obvious? What are you getting at, Illy? By the way, these razors you have given me are as blunt as shit.'

'That kid. Colt. What is going on there? I know you two are up to something.'

We were treading, I feared, on slightly dangerous ground. I began to shave, painfully, with barely any lather. I kept my voice light.

'The little, young chap, the one who brings my food? I do not know what you are talking about. He is quiet. I try to talk to him because he is my only human contact, normally. But he just brings my food and goes.'

'Oh, come on, Edik. I'm not an idiot.'

'Ilya, honestly. Would I lie to you?'

'Yes! Yes, you would!' As we talked, my eyes absently lingered on the laundry chest by Ilya's knees. Ilya followed my gaze.

'Tell me why you think something is going on?' I said loudly, turning away from the sink to distract Ilya's attention. It was too late; he undid the catch on the chest and flipped it open.

'What the fuck…? I am going to kill that little prick.' Ilya grabbed handfuls of chocolate bars and fruit. 'What's this? A fucking loaf of bread. And what is this?' Ilya held up several paintbrushes splayed out in his hand, incredulously lifted a box of acrylics from the depths of the chest. 'This is taking the piss, Eddie!'

I leaned against the sink. I knew that Colt was now in serious trouble but I suddenly wanted to laugh. Thank fuck for a bit of drama to liven up my life.

'I asked him to get me these things. Do not blame him.'

Ilya began to laugh.

'What now?' I asked warily.

'Oh my God. Fuck, Edik. Now you really are taking the piss.' Illy wiped his eyes and stood up, still laughing incredulously. He was holding a pile of my sketches of Colt. There were limits. I drew myself up to my height; I was proud of those pictures. Ilya was flipping through them. 'Quite well-built for a little guy isn't he? Listen Edik. I was going to do this today, anyway, and as it seems that I can't stop you from doing what you want, I'm ending your confinement; as of right now. You are reinstated in the firm. Housekeeping is fixing up your old living suite for you as we speak.'

I closed my eyes and breathed. 'Thank God.'

'Alright. Take your time, make your way downstairs. There are clothes and things in your room, and some cash in your desk. I'll see you at dinner tonight. Remember; you are my second in command. Do not take any shit from the other firm members; that's all over, now.'

'What about Colt?'

Ilya smiled with dead eyes. 'No harm done, eh? I'll give him a light slap on the wrist.'

I chose to believe him.

Colt

Ilya was coming up the stairs, and he smiled at me with the air of a hunter about to strike. 'Morning Bryce,' he said smoothly, brushing past.

'I was bringing Eddie his breakfast,' I said quickly, flustered. I risked a glance at Ilya's sceptical face.

'Yes, that's what I asked you to do, what else would you be doing?' Ilya paused as he made to enter Eddie's room, and raised one eyebrow at me. 'By the way,' he added carelessly, as if it was an afterthought, 'I need to have a talk with you. Could you go directly to my office, and wait for me there? I shouldn't be long.'

I stared at floor, frozen, thinking wildly.

'Oh, and- Bryce? Don't forget to put your belt back on before you go downstairs.' The corner of Ilya's mouth twisted into a knowing smirk as he eyed the belt dangling from my hand.

Numbly, for I had no choice, I turned and walked down the steps. I started to really panic as I walked along the corridor, pace quickening. I fretted at the thought of Ilya upstairs questioning Eddie. He might blab about us being friends... I, like everyone else, was expressly forbidden from talking to Eddie. I stormed past a couple of surprised firm members and straight into Ilya's office, slamming the door. The evening sun illuminated the large well-furnished room. Through the window, the grounds were bathed in beautiful amber light. I felt like weeping with fear and frustration as I sank slowly into a giant leather chair facing Ilya's desk. I clutched my face and moaned aloud. I looked at the antique silver clock, glowing bronze in the mellow sunlight. It was twenty past eight.

The door opened and Will put his head into the room. He looked at me in puzzlement and rubbed his ginger stubble. 'Hey, should you be in here, kiddo?'

I bit the skin on my thumb. 'Ilya told me to wait for him.'

'What's going on?'

I didn't answer. Instead, I stared out of the window, worrying. My other hand was on the arm of the chair, my sweaty palm slicking across the leather.

'Is this about Eddie?'

I pierced my thumb and it began to bleed. 'Ah. What about him?'

Will leaned further into the room, swinging on the door-frame. 'Everyone knows, kiddo.'

'Knows what.' I shoved my wet palms into my armpits and turned to Will. 'Knows what?'

'Everyone knows, Colt.'

At quarter past nine the door opened and Ilya entered his office. I was hunched low down in the leather chair.

'Sorry to have kept you waiting, little one,' he said with exaggerated politeness, gliding to the desk. He looked down, coolly at me; red-faced and sweating in the leather chair. 'Eddie and I have been having a long, interesting conversation. It was all about you, actually.'

I couldn't think of anything to say. I noticed that Ilya was holding a folded sheet of paper, or rather, parchment. No prizes for guessing what that was. Fuck.

'Let's get straight to the point, little friend, because there might have been a very unfair misunderstanding here.' Ilya smiled disarmingly at me and I looked warily back. 'So, what's going on between you and Eddie?'

'Nothing!' I gasped, shocked that he had come to the point so quickly, so bluntly.

'Really? That's what Eddie said, too. He tells me that he barely knows your name.'

I shrugged, my heart pounding. I felt my quickening pulse throb in my temple. 'We don't talk.'

'Huh. And yet… you seem to have made quite an impression on him, in the brief time it takes you to deliver his breakfast each morning.'

Sarcastic prick, I thought, just staring at the dark, shiny wood of the desk. My head felt light and I breathed quickly through my nose to stop myself from fainting.

'It's not just breakfast, is it Bryce? Somebody brought him all of the extra food he has up there, not to mention art supplies… which brings me on to my next point.' Ilya slapped the large piece of paper on the desk in front of me, smoothing the edges down very deliberately with his hands. I held my head in my hands as I stared at it and twisted my hair between my fingers until it hurt.

Ilya intently studied my reaction, then he walked to the window and stood looking out at the sunset, his hands in his pockets. After several moments of silence he went to the sideboard and lifted a crystal decanter. He poured two measures of brandy into crystal glasses, and handed one across the desk. I knocked it back immediately. My head felt lighter than before, I truly felt as though I would faint at any moment. Still shuddering from the drink, I struggled to focus on Ilya's wavering face as he finally sat down across from me. I fixated on his hand, swirling his oily brandy in its glittering glass, round and round. His voice sounded distant, unreal.

'This is an amazing likeness,' he said. 'Eddie's very talented and I have always been very proud of his skill… do you know he has a hundred other drawings? All of them are of you.'

I said nothing, my head in my hands. 'You are very quiet. What? I did not hear you.'

'It isn't what it looks like. He paints me. He just paints me. There's nothing else to it.' I was almost whispering. I felt a rising nausea.

'You're lying.'

'No.'

'Shut up. It's irrelevant anyway. Didn't you hear me when I said no one talks to Eddie?'

'I heard you, Ilya.' I looked at him wretchedly, 'I just felt sorry for him.'

'He was being punished for a reason! You directly defied me.' Ilya ignored me, his voice turning hard. All of the feigned pleasantness vanished. 'You've obviously been up there with him every night. I'm not going into any of the sordid details with you, the drawings are enough for me.' He grabbed the sketch and put it into his drawer. 'You admit to deliberately defying me. I ought to ask you to get your things and get the fuck out. I don't need a fucking supermodel in my firm.'

'No! Ilya, please don't do that. I-' There was a knock on the door. I clutched the desk in frustration as Bidden put his head into the room.

'You wanted to see me?' He looked curiously at me.

'Yes. I need you and…' he pursed his lips and sized me up. 'One of the others will be enough.'

My head snapped up. 'You're sending them to beat Eddie? His heart-' I bit my lip.

Ilya shook his head. 'No. I know Eddie, and I wouldn't expect anything less from him. You're the one to be punished.'

I felt the blood rushing to my face, but I gave a very small, resigned nod of gratitude. I wasn't going to lose my job, at least. Ilya continued, 'I wouldn't give you to Manpyre, I am not that sadistic.' He looked at Bidden. 'It's a nice evening. Take him out to the stables. Ten minutes and no lasting damage.'

I shoved back my chair and stormed out of the room.

Eddie

My old suite. The deep green bedspread was luxuriously large, sweeping to the floor on either side of the huge four-poster bed complete with sumptuous forest-green velvet curtains. I sank back against the nine pillows almost crooning with pleasure. I sat up. Nothing had changed; everything was exactly as it had been. There were exactly eight mirrors in the room, all diverted from the antique shop storeroom. I could barely believe that I had been reinstated in my old living suite. I gazed appreciatively at the heavy oak furniture and under the first bay window, a carved antique couch, upholstered in embroidered silk. Everything had been handpicked by me. I had enjoyed a fabulous time in Paris and in Stockholm, and I had lived in some beautiful apartments… but truly there was no place like home.

Eel's presence lingered everywhere in this hotel, yet in no room did I feel it more than in this one. I closed my eyelids lightly and the sunlight shone pink through my skin. My whole body sagged and I felt the rhythm of my heart, now quelled and calm.

Colt

I lay in the wet, muddy straw on the floor of one of the stalls. My right cheek, pressed into the straw felt completely numb. It was difficult to breathe. I tried to raise myself up on my forearms to give myself more room to breathe, but the pain in my ribs made it impossible. I felt myself being gently turned over onto my back and I gratefully breathed the warm, animal-musty air in short, painful gulps. I opened my eyes and flinched as Bidden's arm swooped towards my face.

'Easy. It's over now,' he said quietly, lifting my head and placing a bottle of cool water to my parched lips. I drank, and then stopped, intensely disliking the shame of being nursed in this way. I willed myself to be tough, to accept this punishment and move on. I tried to sit up, and managed to rest on my elbows, trying to look as dignified as possible while my vision adjusted to my surroundings.

Will was sitting near my feet, looking genuinely regretful. 'You alright?'

I shifted slightly, ignoring the searing pain in my ribs. 'Yep,' I managed.

'You'll be okay. Listen, the thing is…you really pissed off Ilya…'

Bidden stood up. 'And… sorry kid, but you're out.'

My heart began to pound. 'What? No.'

They left me, taking the torches with them. I just sat there on the stable floor in the middle of the dirt, in the darkness. My job. My grandad. Eddie. I wanted Eddie.

Cold air rushed across my back and the back of my neck. The stable door opened behind me and closed. I was slow to turn my head because everything ached, and before I could see who had come in, my ribs suddenly exploded. I screamed and collapsed, clawing at my chest. In the darkness someone was pacing slowing around me. A shaft of moonlight struck the floor in front of me, and through my tears I saw black cowboy boots with steel heels and toecaps. They paused in front of my face and I whispered, 'Please don't.' The boots paced behind me. I was helpless. 'Please!' I shouted with all the breath I had. The boots slammed into my back, over and over again. I was dying. I scrabbled at the floor in front of me. 'Stop.' This guy was kicking me to death. He stopped, and I opened my eyes slowly. I had them screwed shut. My vision was blurred. Eventually I focused on this thing in front of my face. He was holding it there, taking his time, making sure I could see it. A belt. A belt with a buckle on it.

Chapter 9

Eddie

I had not seen Colt all day, which was unfortunate. I needed his support. Tonight, for the first time since my return to Lake Martin, I would be eating dinner with Ilya and his eighteen-year-old twins. This was going to be a struggle. I dressed for dinner with great care. I spent an hour in front of the mirror, brushing and styling my hair and applying my customary thick layer of primer, concealer, foundation then eyeliner, mascara and blusher. Using a mirror for so long was painful, but it was important to me to get the makeup right for tonight. I looked directly into my own eyes, keeping the rest of the face in soft-focus until my skin was covered up. Each stoke of the tiny brushes felt like applying a layer of armour.

Sunday dinner was important to Ilya, a family time; a time to be together. He usually dined with his kids, some of his firm members and any special guests of the hotel. I sat down on Ilya's right and gazed with interest around the table. There were two empty seats on his left, but they were about to be filled. I looked up and my heart stopped, then began to beat quickly as they walked into the room.

Oh, I had let myself picture it, painfully, like turning a razor blade slowly in my mouth with my tongue. I thought about it frequently while cutting myself. And what had I imagined? Both of their faces blended mockingly into one. I knew that it was just a matter of biology, but… The girl, Sasha, stretched her hand towards a breadbasket in front of me and our eyes met. I smiled. I knew I was staring, but I could not help it. A deep, profound sadness came over me as I caught and held the gaze of those reflective, almost black eyes that she had inherited from Eel. Hers were lined carelessly with black eyeliner and thick teenage mascara. I took a sip of water and looked away, but I sensed her curious stare was still on me. Irresistibly, I looked at her again as I drank. Then, I shifted my gaze to her twin brother.

'Eddie.' Ilya's voice was too loud. I looked at him coolly and saw that he looked slightly panic-stricken. 'Another drink?' My glass was still full, but I agreed, realising that I was deeply unsettling my brother. The rest of the meal passed peaceably enough. I risked an occasional glance at the young twins as they ate, feeling Ilya's anxious eyes on me the whole time.

After dinner Ilya approached me, lightly touching my arm as everyone made to leave the room. He seemed about to say something, but I spoke first. 'It would be lovely if you would introduce me to your kids.' I looked at him unsmilingly, realising that I could probably ask him for anything right now, any favour, and Ilya would give it to me. Anything to keep me away from Jason's children. I breathed out through my nose, slowly. I had him over a barrel. This was power indeed.

Ilya regarded me, then he closed his eyes briefly. 'Fine. Of course… Mischa, Sasha?'

They came over. They both looked rather sceptical, for which I could scarcely blame them.

'Mikhail, Aleksandra. This is my younger brother, your Uncle Edvard.'

'Hello.' I kissed the girl, Sasha, on her small hand. As I took the boy,

Mischa's hand in both of mine, Ilya twitched. Not so as anyone would notice, but because I knew him, I detected the involuntary lurch of his shoulders. I pressed Mischa's hand between mine briefly, then let him go. The kid was scowling at me.

'Dad,' he said, in a bored, public school accent. He looked at me doubtfully, then at Ilya. 'Is Uncle Edvard feeling… better, now? He got sick on the stairs…'

I laughed before Ilya had the chance to answer, 'Mischa, I am feeling one hundred percent better. You are so grown up now! And you look just like your father.'

My brother looked like he wanted to murder me on the spot. 'Yes. He does… the twins are going back to school next week. They board.' He said, defiantly. I looked at the twins and grinned widely. Sasha grinned back, the old charm was obviously beginning to work on her, and she was starting to forget the insane, concussed version of me she had witnessed when I first arrived.

'Then we have a whole week to spend together!' I laughed. 'Tell me, do you two ride the horses? I used to have six horses when I lived here… I need someone to introduce me to all of the new animals, remind me of all the best trails…' Sasha broke into a big smile, and Mischa's eyes sparkled in a way that was both familiar and quite painful to me. Bingo, I thought. Ilya stirred uncomfortably.

'No. The twins have a lot of schoolwork to finish, they don't have time for horse riding,' he said.

'What are you talking about Dad?' Broke in Mischa, 'We ride every day anyway. And we finished all of our work for school.' He looked interestedly at me and I grinned broadly.

'In that case, kids… It's a date. How does tomorrow morning sound?'

'No!' Barked Ilya. We all looked at him.

'Dad?' Sasha's eyes were large. 'We were going to ride out tomorrow anyway… Why can't we go with Uncle Edvard?'

'Because…' There was no good reason. I raised my eyebrows at him.

'Kids, your father never liked horses. I think he's scared of them,' I teased.

'Please, Daddy,' begged Sasha. 'It would be so much fun.'

'My dear, you could not be more right,' I grinned, looking at Ilya, 'It will be sooo fun. Right, Mischa?' I winked at Ilya and could not help laughing a little. My brother looked like he was going to be sick.

I got my own way and took the twins out riding the following morning. They seemed quite immature for eighteen, but they were charming, especially Sasha. Mischa was just... beautiful; I kept having to stop myself from gaping at him. His resemblance to Jason was singular and it absolutely threw me. On seeing him in his riding gear, I literally had to turn my head away. For a moment, I thought it was going to be unbearable. But I managed to master myself. Mischa's resemblance to Eel, after all, was physical only. He was a fairly sullen, and at times, nasty, young man. He warmed up as the day went on, and I began to suspect that his initially cold demeanour was a combination of teenage angst, and having been badly spoiled. They chattered incessantly, probing me with personal questions.

'Why do you wear earrings?'

'Why do you wear lipstick?'

'Are you gay?' Giggled Sasha. I felt my mouth twitch into a smile.

'Is that just a lucky guess?'

She giggled again, breathlessly. 'No. Everyone says it.'

'Ah... Well, they're right. I am.'

'Do you have a boyfriend?'

'No-one special, not at the moment.' Not since your father, I thought. I smiled, thinking of Colt. 'I am working on it, trust me.'

Mischa spoke in his bored, posh voice. 'Please don't rush to get a boyfriend until we go back to school.' He stared straight ahead at the path, his expression matching his voice. 'No offense, Uncle Eddie, but I don't, like, want to see two men kissing, or whatever.'

'Mitch!' Sasha laughed. 'It would be weird, Uncle Eddie, but I don't mind.'

I shrugged, smiled. Glancing at Mischa's profile, I thought to myself, your Daddy taught me everything I know about sex, you little brat.

'So, what about you two? Are you in any little relationships at school?'

Sasha tossed her hair. 'We don't go to mixed schools; Mitch has a girlfriend, in pony club. I like someone, but he's not interested.'

'In pony club?'

'No. Here.' She looked around, even though we were surrounded by miles of countryside, and Bidden was lagging far behind on chaperone duty. 'Okay,' She said conspiratorially, dark eyes gleaming. 'So, you know Bryce?'

'Colt?'

'Yes, Bryce Colt. Know who I mean?'

'I know of him… yes.'

'Well, him. He is the most amazing guy, Uncle Eddie.'

I shrugged, Mischa snorted. 'Amazing? He's the lamest guy ever.' He cast his eyes over to me. 'Uncle Eddie, this guy she's talking about, he's the bell-boy. He's got stupid, massive glasses and he goes bright red all the time, he's the biggest loser ever…'

'Hey, hey,' I protested. 'What has he ever done to you?'

'Yeah, Mitch. Stop it!'

Mischa continued, his face twisted, 'But he is so lame! He started studying medicine, then he flunked out and now he's my Dad's porter.'

Sasha broke in. 'He didn't flunk. He left because he wanted to take care of his grandad, you know that, Mitch. He lives in Martin, Uncle Eddie.'

'Yeah, in the shittiest part of town,' added Mischa.

I rode along, mulling over their childish conversation. Mischa suddenly burst out laughing. 'Isn't it the most pathetic thing you ever heard, Uncle Eddie?'

Taken aback, I threw him a cold look. 'I would not say that, no. I would say it was rather damn compassionate of him.'

'What, to throw away the chance to become a doctor? To care for an old dude who's clearly gonna die soon, anyway? What a dumb fuck! Why doesn't he just stick his grandad in a home?' Mischa's voice was harsh. 'Why would he rather be a porter than a doctor?'

'Mitch, just shut up! He's so lovely, Uncle Eddie. Maybe he can go back to uni someday.'

'I am sure of it.'

We stopped for lunch up on the hill at the edge of the woods. I lay on the grass, propped up on one elbow. I was using my sunglasses to stare openly at Mischa; what he did not know, would never hurt him. I let myself become lost in his gorgeous face, his familiar mannerisms. Christ, he even had Jay's half-smile, as did the girl. Why am I doing this to myself? I smiled wryly at my own foolish masochism.

Mischa was clearly looking at me too, and he wiped the smile from my face with his next comment. 'What happened to your face?' He asked suddenly, chewing his sandwich.

I paused, tapped some ash from my cigarette. I licked my lips. Truthfully, I was trying hard to keep my temper.

'Sorry, you don't like talking about it? It looks like you've been in a fight. It looks deliberate. My Dad said I shouldn't ask you about it, he said it might hurt your feelings.' Mischa did not look in the least bit concerned about anyone's feelings. I threw back my head and laughed loudly. The twins looked startled.

'Ah, Mischa. Your Dad would say that, wouldn't he?'

I took a long drag on my cigarette, said nothing for a while. I was thinking about how I got the slash on my face, wondering what the twins would make of my other scars. The thought amused me. They were such pampered children, they would almost certainly never have seen anything like my body; not in movies, possibly not even on the internet. I kept my voice steady and impassive. 'I was in an accident with my boyfriend… Jason.' Saying the name, I half-expected some kind of a reaction. Instead, they just looked at me. Mischa swatted a fly. 'I may tell you about it someday. Not today, though. Okay?'

When we returned to the hotel I searched for Colt. I could not find him anywhere but as it was Friday, I knew that he would be in the bar or at the Straight Rain later in the evening. I was looking forward to seeing him, but he wasn't there either. I glanced all around for him before I sat down for the usual Friday evening meet with the rest of the firm. Manpyre was sitting directly across from me, glaring at me. In fact… they were all glaring at me. I ignored it. I leant across the table. 'Hey.'

Bidden looked up and frowned at me.

'Where is Colt?' I asked, keeping my voice down. Bidden sighed.

'The kid's gone. Ilya dropped him from the company. I thought you knew.'

I sat back in my seat, wrestling to keep my composure. I looked at the table, attempting to seem not overly concerned.

'Oh, right… I see. Do you know why?'

'Yeah, I know why and you know, too.' Bidden looked around, then he leaned closer to me. 'Listen, Colt's a good kid, and now thanks to you, he's gone. We all know why.'

Chapter 10

Eddie

I dressed with particular care. After all, I was going to meet Colt's family... I chose a lovely velvet of deepest blue, and a black silk shirt. I kept my make-up low-key; I did not want to embarrass Colt in front of his grandfather. Just a little eyeliner and obviously, plenty of concealer and scar minimiser.

Mischa had been correct about one thing, that Colt and his grandfather lived in the run-down end of Martin. It had always been run down but had become worse over the past few years. The only businesses left were betting shops and second-hand furniture stores with fluorescent paper signs in the windows and graffiti on the metal shutters. I got out of the taxi and climbed the steps to Colt's flat. A cat ran past me in the opposite direction. As I reached the door of the flat, it opened. Colt stood in the doorway, cheeks flushed, thin shoulders heaving. When he saw me he dropped his head slightly. What a beautiful, helpless gesture; it made my heart ache and

I fought an urge to touch him. He had never seemed so far away. He raised his big eyes and I saw that despite himself, he blamed me.

Colt mildly and politely introduced his grandfather, who was standing behind him.

'Mr Colt,' I said respectfully, taking the old man's hand. 'It is a pleasure to meet you.'

Davy Colt was in his early eighties. Though elderly, he was far from frail, his compact figure was wiry and solid and his blue eyes glittered with contempt as they measured me. 'Mr Bodansky,' he answered civilly, his words careful and clear. 'Come in to our home.'

I stepped in, Colt shut the door and turned limping; limping, I noticed with horror, my heart in my mouth, into the living room. I barely noticed my surroundings. What had they done to him? My eyes followed him as he walked lamely to the seat and sat down heavily, wincing. I was invited to sit. The old man insisted that I take the second armchair while he seated himself on a low stool. I sat down, scarcely taking my eyes from Colt. The lamplight warmed his soft features and illuminated two blackened eyes; a badly bruised cheek. At the collar of his shirt, where his shoulders tapered to the slender neck, further bruises were visible. My eyes burned with inconvenient sympathy, and I coughed twice before speaking. I found that I could not, and in response to the expectant stares of Colt and his grandfather, I stared helplessly back. Davy leaned forward and gestured with a helpless hand towards his grandson. 'He's lost his job, and he won't tell me why.'

Colt rested his head on his hand. 'Grandad, I told you, it was this whole crazy thing. I got into a fight with some of my colleagues. It doesn't matter now,' he said softly. He looked at me, his large eyes meaningful. He was perfectly still, as though too tired to argue with anyone and in too much pain to move. He looked incredibly world-weary for someone so young.

'Well whatever it was, this fight, the boy obviously came off worst. Have they not hurt him enough without your brother sacking him and evicting us as well? Just look at what they did to him! Bryce, show Mr Bodansky.'

I winced. It could not have been plainer if Davy had substituted his

74

choice of the word 'they' for the more fitting 'you', what his opinion was of the matter.

'No, Granddad. He doesn't need to see.'

'He does, Bryce. I don't know what kind of place your brother is running up there, Mr Bodansky, with all due respect.'

Colt was reluctant, but in response to his grandfather's urging he stood up and gingerly peeled off his black waistcoat and white shirt, without bothering to undo his cuffs. I fought to keep my cool head; I smothered my features into an expression of passionless nonchalance, with intense difficulty. Colt had been severely beaten. There was scarcely an inch of his thin white skin not perverted with violent bruising, and he was clearly having trouble breathing. He avoided my eyes, casting his own up to the ceiling. My heart was beating quickly. Then I noticed the worst of all. Some of the marks on his body were clearly defined outlines of a belt buckle. I looked more closely at the mark on Colt's face and sure enough, I picked out the shape of the same buckle. On his face.

'Those are buckle marks, Mr Bodansky,' Davy Colt was saying, 'What could my grandson have done, at work, to justify being beaten with a belt buckle?'

I felt hot, and my eyes began to swim with madness. I tore my eyes from Colt and looked at Davy, who seemed surprised at the dark shadow that had descended across my face. In a Herculean effort, I shrugged. My throat ached. 'My brother... my brother reserves the right to discipline his staff.' My vision cleared, I was the master of myself again. 'Perhaps on this occasion, he went a little overboard... but I cannot comment on his methods.' I stood up, deliberately avoiding looking at Colt lest I could contain my passion no longer. 'Once again, I am sorry you have lost your position, and your flat... and I will do my best to talk the boss around, not that I have much influence.' I felt that I was babbling so I stood up, brushed off my jacket and excused myself. 'Good day, both of you.'

Outside in the harsh unblinking daylight, I stormed, brooding, down the street. I took a random direction, I could not think straight. My heart was black. The image of my idol, violated, had me literally shuddering with hot spasms of rage. A voice behind me caused me to stop. Colt was jogging gingerly behind me. Having caught my attention he waved and stopped. Placing a hand to his ribs he panted softly. I bounded back up the street, almost skidding in my haste. Roughly, I grabbed Colt's face and studied the wounds in the daylight, dragging my thumb angrily across a weeping scratch below the left eye. Colt winced and jerked his head away. 'Leave it,' he complained. 'It kills. I hope it doesn't scar, I might end up looking like you.' He tried to smile but my face was no doubt humourless. Colt changed tack. 'Thanks for coming,' he said quietly. 'It means a lot, you helping me.'

'Who did it?' I felt useless and awkward; I was possessed with an urge to do something for Colt and came up with only revenge.

He sighed. 'It's done, and it doesn't matter now. If that was all they did, then I would say fucking great.' He took a deep breath and winced. 'But I'm more worried about losing my bloody job and the flat.' He threw me a look. 'You know, he only fired me because of you, what he thinks we've been...' Colt blushed, for he could not say it. 'I took the beating because I thought that would be it all over and done with, then Ilya goes and fires me, too.' He spat on the pavement and gazed at the traffic behind me, his cheeks glowing warmly. 'What's going to happen to my family now?'

I grabbed Colt's small hand and looked at his bitten fingernails. 'Nothing. I promise you that. I will think of something to do.' I waved my free hand dismissively. Colt looked at me desperately, disappointed. I knew I was giving him the impression that I could not care less, that I did not give a fuck. He was wrong, but just at that moment, I could not think clearly. All I wanted was to take him somewhere private, wrap us both in a blanket, and lick his wounds all afternoon. Of course, that was not about to happen, but that was what I wanted, and that was what I was thinking about. That, and splitting my brother's skull. Christ, I had not felt this protective since Jason.

I looked at my watch. 'Let's go for coffee somewhere. Now I am my own master again! No one can stop us, no one, from doing just what we want.'

'Aye, sure. Coffee...' Colt spun to face me. 'Eddie, you will talk to Ilya for me?'

'Yeah.' I nodded hungrily. 'I will, I will… where can we go round here? Do you have Starbucks?' I draped my arm around Colt's shoulders and we began walking.

'It's just, I really, really need my job back. For my family.'

Fuck, but would he never let the subject drop?

'You do not,' I replied curtly. 'You could work anywhere else. Go back to school, or whatever. My advice? You are out, so cross your heart, thank the angels and do not look back.' I glanced at my friend's troubled profile. The bruises stood out dark against his pale skin. 'I will find you a new flat, okay? But just forget the job. Look at you. You've had a little taste of what will happen if you stay. I warned you that they would chew you up and spit you out, and they have. Lesson learned, no serious damage done. Other people have not been as lucky as you, galupchick.' I pulled him to me and called him by a little Russian pet-name.

'I'm not your friend 'Eel." I faltered but kept walking.

To hear the name from his lips was very strange… If anyone else had said it, I would have ripped out their tongue. When Colt said it, I felt an odd ripple of nervous, taboo enjoyment.

'No… True. You are less strong and also less smart than he was. You know your books and your science or whatever. Shit, baby, but you are so dumb about real life it is untrue. You are not wise. I tell you, if Eel had had your choice, he would have run.'

'Eddie, just talk to Ilya for me, please. Promise me.'

'Ah, baby, baby, baby.' I hugged him towards me and spoke into his ear, my mouth brushing against his skin. 'Trust a wise old man to know what is good for you.'

Colt was exasperated. 'Please! Just make him believe that I will work for him from now on, no more messing around.' I smiled bitterly.

'Are you going to be a good boy from now on then, Colt? Are you going to work hard at your muscles and become a tough guy?'

'Fuck off, Eddie. You're in the firm, and you're sure as hell no tough guy.'

'Baby, please. I just got my stripes back. You ain't seen nothing yet.'

I did not ask Ilya right away, and for a while it did not matter. Colt's grandfather contracted pneumonia, and Colt was caring for him in their new flat. I visited him twice, and on both occasions I gave Colt some money.

'I can't,' he said, colouring up. 'You've done so much already, paying for the flat... I can't even pay you back for that yet, let alone take more from you.' Still, he held on to the bundle of notes.

'Shh.' I closed his small hand around it, 'It is only money.'

Colt blushed harder, but kept it without any further protest, promising to pay it back.

'Please don't mention it to my granddad,' he begged in a whisper, 'He would be really mortified. We're not charity.'

I reassured him. I glanced past him, into the living room where his grandfather rested on a makeshift bed. His lungs, said Colt, were too weak for him to manage stairs.

'He is fortunate to have such a good doctor looking after him,' I said. 'Take care, Colt.'

Two weeks later, Colt left me a message to say that his grandfather had died peacefully. The funeral was small and simple. I attended and Colt introduced me to the few other mourners as 'My boss, Mr Bodansky.' His two younger brothers were there, accompanied by a social worker from their children's home in Edinburgh. Clarke, the older one, had an edgy, hostile manner and Jamie was like a cute mini-Colt. Colt, himself, looked fragile and pale. He seemed to sway slightly where he stood, and his voice sounded faint and breathless. He sat with his brothers at the wake, arguing gently with Clarke. 'Not here, Clarky. We'll talk about it another time,' he was saying quietly. Clarke was shredding a napkin, flicking it into a glass of coke.

The social worker said that it was time to get going, they had a long drive back to Edinburgh. 'I want to stay with Bryce,' said Jamie, the younger brother.

'You see?' Said Clarke, and they started arguing again, in hushed tones. Colt, the social worker and the younger boys went outside and I stayed at the bar, but when Colt didn't return after twenty minutes I went out looking for him. He was alone, leaning on the wall outside the pub.

'They left,' he said dully, 'Jamie freaked out a bit… Clarke didn't say goodbye.'

I offered to take him home, and I was surprised but relieved when he nodded and murmured his assent.

'Go and change out of your funeral clothes. I will take care of everything,' I said. The flat was a mess of dirty plates and clothes. The makeshift bed was still set up in the living room and the whole place was a monument to illness and death.

'I'm really sorry about the mess,' said Colt faintly as he started to slowly climb the stairs.

'Sweetheart, do not worry about it for one minute. Go upstairs; I will clean this place up for you.' I picked up a few plates and moved them to the overflowing sink, then, I gave up. I had never truly cleaned a room in all of my life so I made him a black, instant coffee, as there was no milk.

He had changed into a hooded sweatshirt and tracksuit bottoms and was curled into one corner of the couch. 'Thanks,' he smiled when I gave him the coffee. 'Mm… Strong.' He set it down politely. He was rather lucky, it was the first time I could remember making any kind of drink for anyone.

Colt laid his head against his arms and began sobbing.

'Sweetheart-'

'I hate him,' he mumbled. He was crying hard. I dislike being around people crying so I sipped my own coffee and waited for him to stop. He wiped his eyes. 'Sorry. I just can't believe my dad never came today. This was his dad's funeral…' his mouth trembled again. 'They weren't speaking cos of me. He hates me. I fucking hate him, too.'

Seemingly, this father of Colt's was a heavy drinker. He had blamed the children, especially Colt, for stressing out his mother and exacerbating the illness which eventually took her. 'He said a lot of it was my fault for

79

coming out as gay,' said Colt dully. 'But my mum was totally fine about that. When I told her, she said she already knew, and she loved me.'

'Does not sound like she was bothered, Colt,' I said. 'And if I may say so? Your father sounds like a prick.'

He smiled and closed his eyes, resting his head on the back of the couch. 'Yeah, you've got that right.' He was right there, and he was so very pretty.

We were alone in his house in the afternoon and it was quiet and sad. I started by holding his hand, capitalising on his grief and the fact that he needed comforting. I thought about kissing him but I feared I might frighten him. I hugged him instead. I was conscious of my size and his comparative fragility. I brought my face to his soft dark hair, it smelled deliciously of almonds. I needed to see him all the time. I decided, there and then, to do everything in my power to get Colt's job back.

Ilya clasped his hands together and looked at me with feigned exasperation. 'Edik, why do you care so much about this boy? He flouts my rules, so I have him whipped. He can't follow my rules, so I have him fired. Where is the issue? Why are we still talking about this?'

I shook my head and slipped into Russian, as I grew more incensed. 'You really are a piece of shit. His grandfather just died, after you made them homeless. He needs his job... Ilya, this whole mess was my fault, anyway. Not Colt's. Give him a second chance."

Ilya shook his head, 'Edik, no. He is an insubordinate little prick. He showed me zero respect. I just don't have any use for a headstrong, green kid.'

'He is green, but he is very clever. Give him a chance, Ilya... come on.'

Slowly and deliberately, Ilya mouthed, 'No.' He smiled at me. 'Now, I'm bored of this, can we drop this subject once and for all?'

I started to turn away. He had given me the answer I wanted. I did not want Colt back in the firm. I wanted him back at university, his curly head bent over his notes in an airy lecture theatre, a pencil being traced absently along his pretty lips. That was where he belonged. But I had promised him. More than that, though, it was my selfishness, for yes, I needed him... that made me turn back around, the hem of my emerald-coloured velvet jacket swirling. 'I know why you're doing this, and can I say that this is not about me. I don't want this guy for me.' A shameless lie. 'He needs his job. I tell you, he's a good kid, and he will do anything you say.'

'He's a liability. See you at dinner, brother.' Ilya stood up.

I shook my head disgustedly. Ilya spoke again, in Russian, as I started to flounce out of the office. 'This isn't about getting at you, Edvard. Quite the opposite, in fact. Friends are worse than enemies in this place. You should know that; you, more than anyone else.'

Ilya must have seen my back bristling, my fists tightening.

'Say his name,' I growled warningly. 'Say his fucking name, just once.'

'I won't. Edik… the score is settled between us now. You're back in the firm, I'm your brother and your boss, and occasionally I grant my staff a favour. I just granted you and your boyfriend one. Recognise that.'

'It's a shame you didn't grant me the same favour sixteen years ago,' I replied.

We looked at each other.

'Mm,' groaned Ilya. 'Why must we always be fighting with each other? You only just got back. I was looking forward to managing the firm with you again. Let's not start on such a bad note.'

'Give Colt his job back, then.' I was starting to smile. I, too, had been looking forward to working with my brother again. I could see that Ilya was about to give in to my demand.

'Christ, I could manage a pack of wolves more easily than I can manage you. Alright, Colt can come back; on one condition!'

I grinned warily, 'What?'

'I manage him, me, okay? Not you.'

'Obviously.' This did not concern me even slightly, as I knew I could still influence things in Colt's favour easily enough.

'And that means I initiate him, too.'

I paused. 'Yes… I suppose… as long as you are fair to him.'

Chapter 11

Colt

So, I was back in the firm. I was actually even living in the hotel now, as my grandfather's flat was gone. Looking around the hotel bar at my criminal colleagues, I felt an odd mixture of relief and serious anxiety. The firm scared me to death, but at the same time, I needed to be here. I looked up and felt a jolt of anxiety as Ilya entered the room. He walked through casually, stopping every few steps to exchange words with someone or other. Eddie was with him, dressed in one of his dark green suits. He looked different these days, I reckoned; healthier, with bright eyes and a little bit more flesh on his bones. He didn't look across to where I was sitting. Ilya was moving closer. I bent my head and studied the waves of wood grain on the table. Was I really in the firm? Surely there had been some mistake, I realised, my heart pumping. This was a joke, everyone laughing at me. They were going to kill me. Everyone was laughing at me… 'Bryce?'

I looked up. Ilya smiled down at me interestedly, an odd hardness in his eyes. 'Welcome back.'

I exhaled. I felt like I was about to wet myself. 'Thanks,' I breathed. Ilya smiled once more. He leaned down and I tensed up all over again, even though I tried not to. Ilya's breath felt hot against my ear.

'As I implied yesterday… being fired is no longer an option. You are in this for the rest of your life.' He backed off and looked into my eyes. I was silent until Bidden's sharp kick prompted me to reply,

'I know, sir. Thanks again for taking me back. You, ah, won't regret it.'

'Alright, I have a job for you, but we'll discuss that later. Just relax and enjoy yourself for now. Relax,' he repeated. 'Help yourself to the bar. You toe the line and this firm will be very, very good to you.' His smile thinned, he was already moving away. Beside me, Bidden was unimpressed.

'Toughen up, Colt,' he warned, 'You can't turn to a pile of shivering shit every time the boss talks to you. No-one's going to want to do a job with you unless you grow some nuts.'

I went behind the bar, and began inexpertly pouring myself a whisky. Suddenly Eddie approached. 'Hello… told you I could get you your job back, galupchick.' He leaned right over the bar and grinned. 'That is about half a pint of whisky you have there, my friend. Give me half of it in there.' He passed his empty glass over the bar.

'Thanks a million for talking to the boss; Seriously. Hey… um, should we be, like, talking to each other?'

'Everybody is now allowed to talk to me,' laughed Eddie. 'I am no longer the leper.'

'Yeah, but… I mean you and I, should we be talking to each other?'

'It's fine, fine. I think talking is allowed. Talking yes, fucking, no,' he joked.

I blushed furiously and Eddie seemed to realise that I was too sensitive to joke with. He changed the subject, 'So here you are. And how did Ilya reinitiate you into the firm?'

I looked down at the bar, the shiny mahogany reflecting the lights above it. I knew that I would never tell anyone about how I had been reinitiated.

'Please, I… don't want to tell you,' I said, my voice almost a whisper. 'Look at me.'

I lifted my head and instantly, I saw that Eddie understood me perfectly.

'You do not have to tell me, just because I asked. You do not have to tell anyone. Ever.'

I nodded. 'Listen to me,' said Eddie quickly, 'Jesus, I did not want to have to say this tonight, but you're so bloody naive about everything. You are a member of a criminal organisation. No one is going to watch your back for you, Colt, you have to learn to be in control of yourself, to take care of yourself.' Eddie looked extremely serious. 'I did not want for you to come back here, but against my advice, you have. So now my only option is to look after you. You are going to say you do not need my help, but you do.' Eddie glanced up; Ilya was at the other side of the room, paying us no attention, so he continued. 'Colt, if you find yourself in any trouble, you need to ignore your pride, and tell me… I am going to make you invincible. I am going to protect you, until I teach you to do it yourself. You are ridiculously young, and, like it or not, I am going to watch out for you.'

'I'm not a coward,' I said.

'I know. I know that, absolutely. But you are young. This…' Eddie looked around the room. 'It is not right for you. I know that you do not believe me.'

I made my way back to the sofa, getting used to walking in a new way in my new clothes. I felt bigger, somehow, as if I were taking up more space. I dropped onto the sofa, my drink sloshing out of its glass a little. Lighting a cigarette I sat back and surveyed the room. I felt Eddie's eyes on me, now.

'Excited about your first job?' Asked Bidden.

I nodded slowly, heart rate slowing, the smoke calming me right down. 'Aye, I suppose. I don't know what it is yet.' I sipped my drink and felt an odd stab of wellbeing and excitement in my belly.

Bidden shrugged. 'Who knows? You'll be going with Edwina, probably, he's keen to get back into the game.'

I lowered my voice. 'Between you and me… is Eddie actually any good at this? The rough stuff? I mean…'

'I know what you mean, kid, and let me tell you something. Don't be fooled.' Bidden paused for effect, taking a long draught of lager.

'Meaning…?'

'Listen. Eddie may come across as a bit effeminate, and it's true, he doesn't really like getting his hands dirty. But when he does… Colt, he is the one person in this firm I would least like to be on the wrong side of.' As soon as Bidden said it, I could see it.

'I've never seen that side of him before,' I lied, thinking it over. I lifted my eyes and Eddie was now leaning forwards against the bar, turned slightly away from us. Something told me that he had overheard the whole conversation. A question was still bothering me. Half-wanting Eddie to hear, and desperate to know the answer, I put it to Bidden.

'So, why did he just lie down and take the beating you all gave him when he first came back? Why didn't he fight back?'

'Because he deserved it, and he knew it,' said Bidden, squinting as he imparted his knowledge to me, the younger man. 'He needed to clear his slate before he would be accepted back into the firm. You understand?'

'I think so.' I looked up and Eddie was gone.

'Just like you had a little re-initiation of your own,' added Bidden knowingly.

I felt my face getting hot, I tried to ignore it. 'That's my business,' I tried. Bidden just laughed at me.

Later, in the gym, my muscles burned as I worked the weights machine. I was using smaller weights than usual but I couldn't even manage six reps, it hurt my ribs too much. With a grunt of defeat I dropped the weights and sat back and let my battered muscles relax.

'You should be taking it easy, mate.'

I looked up. Manpyre dropped his gym bag on the floor. 'Take it easy,' he repeated.

'You're probably right.' I smiled at him and stood up. 'I think I will call it a day. Enjoy your workout.' I hadn't really spoken to him much since our aborted 'date' and I wanted to keep it that way. He trailed after me, talking to me as I headed to the shower. I ended up sort of half-undressed, reluctant to be totally naked in front of him. It was so awkward standing there in my underwear while he droned on about his latest car trouble.

'Wow,' he said suddenly, looking at my body.

'What?'

'Your bruises. Poor little guy.' He stuck out his bottom lip in exaggerated sympathy. My bruises were fading, but my body was still all shades of yellow.

I shrugged. 'It's okay… Anyway, I'm gonna get a shower. Talk to you later.'

'I'll join you.' Manpyre peeled off his shirt.

'Showering before you work out? What's the point in that?' I was getting a nervous flutter in my stomach.

'I always do it,' shrugged Manpyre. 'It's nice to be fresh before and after. What's the big deal? Come on.' He backed me up against the wall. 'Hey. So, did you actually enjoy having dinner with me that night, or what? I couldn't tell if you enjoyed it or not.' He had both hands on the wall, either side of my head. I was really freaked out because of what had happened with Eddie.

'Yeah. It was fun. Dave, don't,' I said, trying to laugh it off while actually panicking. 'Come on, stop it, get off me, man.'

He tip-toed his fingers up my arm. 'You didn't let me kiss you that night.'

I laughed nervously. 'Well, it was only… um, you know it wasn't… hey. Back up, man.' I was painfully conscious of being almost naked. I seemed to be constantly being pinned to walls by men.

Manpyre brought his face up close to mine. His beard scratched my skin. 'One kiss, and I'll let you go,' he teased.

I knew he was only kidding but, I was having real problems with the fact that he was pinning me against the wall. I wasn't laughing anymore. 'Dave… come on mate, leave me alone.'

'Is there a problem here?' Eddie and Ilya were standing there holding sports bags, staring at us. Together, those brothers looked huge, formidable.

They put down their bags as Manpyre backed away from me.

'Colt, is there a problem?' Eddie repeated.

I shook my head, 'No. We're just messing about.' My heart was banging.

'See you later kiddo,' Manpyre murmured, and as he oozed out of the room Eddie spoke to him in a cold voice.

'Manpyre? The next time Colt tells you to leave him alone, you leave him the fuck alone, alright?'

'Fuck you, Edwina. Mind your own business.'

Ilya started to laugh. 'Oh, Bryce, what's this? Two members of the firm fighting over you, eh?'

'Not me, I am not fighting about anyone,' growled Eddie, suddenly Russian.

I escaped to the shower and a few moments later Eddie stormed in after me. 'Listen,' he said fiercely, grabbing my shampoo from me and stealing some for himself. We were both naked under the hot showers. 'Do not get involved with Manpyre, he is serious trouble. If you need help, come to me. Do you need help?'

'No,' I said. 'I can handle it. It's just Dave.'

Eddie threw back his head and let the water run on his face. I stared at his beautifully muscled body, in awe, particularly at certain parts of him. He opened his eyes and I looked away, blushing. He totally caught me checking him out. When I dared to look at him again he was watching me with a slight grin, and he shot a deliberate, playful glance at my own nakedness.

'See you later, Colt.' He ducked out of the shower and I turned my shower to a colder setting.

Chapter 12

Colt

That summer at Lake Martin started out as the best time of my life. It wasn't a wild summer, or anything, I was just happy. Everything felt easy. Maybe everybody has to have a really good, coming-of-age summer, and that was mine. I wasn't ready to get together with Eddie. I was keeping him at arms-length until I was totally sure about him. But... we were getting closer and I knew that it would happen, eventually and so did he, and that was sweet and exciting.

We would hold hands in the cinema and say nothing about it when the movie was over, or we would fall asleep in the same bed, holding each other all night, but I was always up and out before he woke up. I used to lie awake on hot nights thinking about him, aching about him. Then, the next day I would see him at work and I would be tingling with excitement. He was really naughty and bolshy in meetings and he pissed off Ilya all the time and would do things like take me for a drive just before an important meeting.

'Won't Ilya mind?'

'He can eat his heart out, baby. Stick with me.'

We laughed all the time that summer. I remember one hot, airless night there was a big wedding on at the hotel. I was wearing my waiter outfit- a white starched shirt, black trousers and black bow-tie. Eddie and I were sitting in the middle of one of the fountains. It wasn't switched on of course. But if you jumped, you could get to the middle. He had stolen me from the wedding and we were drinking champagne, also stolen from the wedding. The night air smelled of burnt sugar. They were testing the fireworks and every so often one squealed joyfully into the dark blue star-spangled sky. Eddie was laughing so hard about something that he smashed his champagne flute on the stone fountain. Sweeping the remains into the water, he grabbed the bottle and took a big swig. 'Baby, I swear, I haven't felt like this in years. You make me feel twenty years younger.' I held out my glass for him to refill and he put his arm around me. I snuggled in and without him knowing, I smelled him. Maybe I'm weird, but I always have to smell people if I'm really attracted to them. I held on to that masculine smell, mixed with the burnt-sugar in the air.

'I came back here for revenge,' he said suddenly. I sipped my champagne as he continued, 'But now, I do not feel that way. I love someone who is dead, I always will, but... he would want me to live like this. This is the way he would have lived if he were in my position. If anything, I have wasted years thinking of revenge, so now I have to start living, properly, right, baby?'

'Right.' I raised my glass tipsily. As I drank, the fireworks started going off like guns and I dropped my glass, too. Eddie laughed and poured some straight from the bottle into my mouth, soaking my crisp white shirt.

'Do you believe in angels, Colt?'

I swallowed. I was quite surprised by his question. 'Well, I'm Catholic, so yeah, I do. I do, of course.'

'So do I.' Eddie leaned his head back against the fountain, 'I am not

89

religious, so my beliefs differ somewhat from your own… I think that if you love someone… and then you die, you stay with them. You become their 'angel'.' I looked sideways at him. I really didn't expect him to have beliefs like that, somehow. I smiled, because I liked hearing him talk that way.

'I know that Eel is watching over me. I just know that he is not gone. Does that sound… insane?'

'No, of course not. It's nice.'

Eddie's hand was at the back of my neck, his fingertips brushing my skin. He pressed his forehead against my cheek, just for a second before he went to kiss me. I flinched away and banged my head on the stone fountain.

'Fuck. Ow.' I blushed furiously. 'It's not that I don't want to.'

He regarded me, his eyes sparkling. I wanted to trust him. I thought I could trust him, I was around eighty percent sure.

'What if I swear I will not touch you,' he laughed. 'I will put my hands behind my back, see?' He leaned across, hands behind his back and kissed me really gently. His lips were soft and warm.

When he broke his promise and started touching me everywhere I was hardly even scared. I didn't feel ready to go too far with him.

'Enough,' I said, and my breath came in ragged gasps. Eddie was sort of half in the water of the fountain, leaning over me with one hand on my thigh and the other on my waist.

'No. It is not enough for me,' he replied gruffly. But he did stop. He stood up dripping wet and grinned at me, 'We take things at your pace. It's natural for you to be nervous.'

My face felt as flushed as his looked. I wanted to tell him I wasn't nervous of sex, not at all. It was him, personally. He was so bloody scary, huge and unpredictable, but I had never felt such lust for anyone. I didn't want to offend him, though. Better to let him go on believing that I was some nervous virgin. As I looked at him I was feeling something like elation. We had kissed. I was still in one piece. He stopped when I asked him to, and he wanted to 'take things at my pace'.

Eddie

The garage was stacked with art. It was something of a treasure trove, though badly disorganised. I sighed and raked a hand through my hair. There was enough work to keep me in this bloody garage all week. And the company was not my favourite.

Manpyre murmured something. I asked him to repeat it. Head down, staring at his hands, lips almost touching the table, he said, 'Can't you leave Colt alone?'

Doing a stock take with him was bad enough (standards had really slipped since I had been away, I would hardly even classify half of this rubbish as art) but now Manpyre was turning pathetic on me. I sighed; this could get very ugly.

'Fucking hell, Dave. What are you asking me... urgh, please can we not have this conversation?' I made a note, heavily, on my lined yellow legal pad, and flipped through a stack of printed photographs. Whoever had last catalogued the firm's art collection deserved to be shot. 'You realise how many gaps there are in this catalogue?' I complained, 'Who the hell has been in charge of this?'

He refused to let it drop. 'Bodansky, I like him.'

I sighed, adjusted the hem of my skirt and leaned back against some crates. Manpyre was irritating me, now, and I did not want to talk about Colt with him. 'No, you don't like him, Dave; you would like to fuck him. Actually, ugh, I do not even want to think about what you want to do with him.'

'No.' Manpyre shook his head slowly, 'No, it really isn't like that... I genuinely like Colt. I met him, I got him the job here... because I like him. He's become pretty special to me. I think I might fucking love him.'

'Oh, Christ, Dave... stop. I beg you.'

'And I was getting somewhere with him, until you came along. You could have anyone. Anyone else...' I turned away; it was all getting very 'Jolene'.

I sighed and turned back, 'If you must know... he is not just a fuck for me, either. You are right, he is special.'

'You've got feelings for him, really?'

I shrugged. Manpyre took a few steps away from me and said, 'Then I feel sorry for him.'

Cold prickles danced up my spine, 'What do you mean?'

He was walking away, after saying that to me, he was walking away. 'What do you mean, prick?'

He stepped into the lift, furiously pushing the buttons, 'You know what I mean. I know what happens to guys you fall in love with.'

I rushed at the lift, roaring as the doors slid closed in front of his smug face. I punched my fist against them and left a deep dent in the metal.

Manpyre could taunt me all he wanted; I still had Colt. I had the pleasure, that same evening, of taking him with me to collect a piece of art from one of our clients. It was the most unprofessional job I have ever been on. I drove there one-handed, feeling him up with the other.

'You scared?' I teased as we went up into the flat. 'Here, I will hide you.' I folded him gently inside my fur coat. He pulled away, laughing. We got the painting to the bottom of the stairs without incident. I unfolded the blanket carefully while he watched. 'Now,' I told him, 'We check it. We do not want any fakes.' I touched the rough acrylic, I smelled it, and I damn near tasted it. 'It is so, so beautiful,' I groaned, 'Oh, I love this job.'

'What's it worth?' Asked Colt, nervously.

'Oh- endless amounts, if it's real. You don't want to know, really.' I re-arranged the blanket in swathes around the painting. Colt chewed the skin around his thumb. 'Is it making you nervous babe? The value?'

He shook his head. 'No.' Suddenly, he turned and went back into the apartment building, down the narrow staircase.

'Babe? Colt? Where are you going, that is just the basement, there is nothing down there...' I followed him. It was pitch black. I swore as I stumbled over a mop bucket and almost smacked my forehead into the wall. 'Bryce?' I did not have to search any further. Suddenly his hands were on my face and his tongue in my mouth. I could hardly believe that it was Colt there in the dark. So forward, so decisive. I wondered, fleetingly who had taught this boy how to kiss. He slid his hand into my trousers and I drew my breath in sharply. 'Slow down a little,' I whispered. 'In fact... let's go back to the hotel. You should not rush this.' He was being naive. I had made plans in my head for his first time, and I knew it would be better to take things slowly.

'Wait! Wait,' I protested as he unfastened my trousers, 'Slow down. Before I... wait! Have you done this before?' He had come prepared; he had condoms, he had lube and he wasn't shy in using either of them, on me. I was bewildered by his unexpected confidence.

He touched me, gently, taking his time now. I could not make out his face in the darkness, but I heard him breathing out, slowly and tremulously. Then he laughed slightly. 'Yes,' he said bluntly. 'A lot.'

'Wha... really?'

'Yeah, really. So... don't worry. This is our first time but it isn't, like... the first time. I'm used to it.'

That was a relief.

Fucking him felt so good. There was a height issue at first, and he said, 'Take your shoes off.' I kicked off my heels, and that was all he said the entire time. Afterwards he walked calmly outside into the street. 'Thanks,' he said quietly, giving me a little smile over his shoulder. He turned around to face me. 'That was awesome. My knees are still shaking.' I was still getting my breath back.

'You're welcome,' I said tightly. My heart was worrying me as it was banging in my throat. I began to feel that familiar drawstring tightening across my chest. I tried to ignore it and kept walking towards the car.

'Hey are you okay? You look grey!'

I shook my head. 'Fine.'

'It's your heart isn't it? Sorry, I should've thought...' He blushed. 'You just need a puff of your medicine, physical exertion can make angina flare up.'

'Colt. This is extremely embarrassing. I am sorry.'

'Ah no, don't worry...' We looked at each other in the orange glow of the streetlights.

'I love you,' I said helplessly.

'I love you too,' he told me, gently. 'Now, get in the car, old man. I'll drive back.'

When we arrived back at the hotel, David Manpyre was in the back garages waiting to meet us. 'You took your time,' he commented, opening the boot of the car. Neither of us said anything. I looked at Colt but he was busying himself with helping Manpyre to lift the painting out of the trunk. I lit up a cigarette and leaned against the car, watching Colt and thinking how pretty he was. Manpyre threw me a look, 'You could help,' he admonished.

'No, Eddie don't lift anything,' said Colt quickly. 'Dave, I don't need your help either, it's not that heavy.'

Manpyre and I watched him as he started to walk out of the garage with the blanketed painting. I gave in to a wicked idea.

'Babes, wait one moment.' I went over to him and kissed him deeply, lavishly, groping him as well. He let me, then dipped his head away with a shy glance at Manpyre. I let him go. 'Go on, I'll see you later.'

'Sure. Bye.' Colt looked mightily pissed off with me as he left, but I didn't care. A naughty kind of glee tickled me. I turned to face Manpyre's glare of impotent rage as he slammed the trunk of the car.

'You're being really inappropriate,' he tried finally, helplessly. He had nothing, nothing else.

I grinned, 'Inappropriate? David...' I could not speak any more, I laughed so hard my belly ached. 'Inappropriate... yes. Well, as we both know, I am a very fucking inappropriate person.' I wiped my eyes and burst out laughing again.

'What are you laughing for? You think you're fucking funny, Bodansky?'

I shrugged. He marched around the car and launched himself right up to me, stood about two inches away from me, veins popping out of his forehead.

'Oh, don't be so dramatic.' I muttered, suddenly bored. I went to take a drag of my cigarette and he smacked it out of my hand, my bracelets jangling.

'Ow,' I said mildly.

'You're not fucking funny. I could kick the shit out of you. I should kick the shit out of you.'

I absolutely did not want to fight him. For one thing, it would be so undignified. For another, I was bloody worn out. So, I extracted myself.

'Sorry. No fighting. My doctor says I should take it easy. Have you met my doctor? He's a honey.'

I left him to rage on his own. Whatever it was that he smashed, as I walked upstairs, I hoped that it was one of the shit paintings.

After a rest and some medication, my heart was fine. I suppose the old man was merely shocked at having to keep up with a young lover all of a sudden. Luxuriating in the bath the next morning, I sank lower into the bubbles, enveloped by the hot steam. I smiled incredulously as I relived the previous night. I had assumed, wrongly, that Colt was sexually inexperienced but I could not have been farther off the mark. Interesting… I went over the whole thing in my mind, again. As much as I appreciated him, I thought his approach was much too casual. As he said, he was used to having sex that way, but I wondered how often he had experienced romance. Next time, we would do things my way, in comfort and luxury. I was getting a bit too old for basements and alleyways. Yes, Colt was quite a lot younger than me, so I did not want to let the age gap become a problem. I made a mental note to get to the gym more often, build up my stamina.

I stepped out of the bath, wrapped a towel around my waist and squeezed out the damp ends of my 'hair'; I was wearing a waist length, blonde wig that I loved, but tended to only wear when I was alone. I shrugged on a silk dressing robe, sprayed a little Chanel, slipped into fluffy pink heeled slippers and headed to my room to dress, only to find Mischa was sprawled on my couch. 'Hey,' he said quietly.

I tugged at the blonde wig and it slid off my head. 'Ah… Mischa… what are you doing in here, kid?' I shoved the wig into a drawer and kicked off my shoes.

'You don't gotta take that stuff off, Uncle Eddie,' said Mischa gently, 'It's cool.'

I knew that he was mocking me. I shot him a glance. He was staring at my scarred legs in obvious revulsion... he was the only person who could make me feel anything close to uncomfortable. I tried to stay calm as I quickly removed some trousers from my wardrobe and put them on. 'What are you doing here?' I repeated. When he did not answer, I looked over at him and my heart softened. He was so like Jason. It was like skipping back a decade or two, having Jason sprawled on my couch, just like that. Just like him.

'Your door wasn't locked. I just stopped by to say hi, that's okay, right?'

'Mischa, it... it is nice to see you, but I am getting dressed. Why not come back later-' There was a knock on the door. Mischa leapt up and answered it.

'Hi Dad,' he said.

Ilya barged into the room, wild-eyed. 'Mischa! Eddie, what the fuck is he doing in here?' He was verging on hysteria, as he looked at me in my state of half-undress.

'Ask him,' I said tightly, turning away. 'Look, I am getting dressed, here. Is there such a thing as privacy in this hotel?'

Ilya turned to Mischa. 'Why are you in here? What are you doing?'

A shrug, 'Just hanging out with Uncle Eddie.'

'You... know, you don't ever hang out in private rooms, okay? If you want to socialise with your uncle you can see him in the family rooms, or downstairs. Don't ever hang out in bedrooms, do you understand me?'

'Chill out, Dad.' Mischa was smirking. Maybe he did not fully understand why I was in trouble, but he certainly seemed pleased to have caused upset. Ilya shooed him out the room. Once he was gone, Ilya sat heavily on the couch, dropped his head into his hands.

'What are you trying to do to me, Edik?' He moaned.

I folded my arms. 'Nothing. Ilya, please, he's perfectly safe from me.'

'But... you called him Jason. The first time you saw him, when you came back. I know he looks like Eel but Christ, Eddie he's my kid in every other way. Please don't use him to replace Eel because he isn't-'

Now fully-dressed, I sat down beside my brother. 'Illy? Stop.'

He looked at me. He was almost in tears.

'Listen,' I said firmly. 'I would never do anything inappropriate to Mischa. You have my word on that. I love you, I love them. You can trust me.'

Ilya breathed out. 'I know. Sorry.' He slapped me on the back. 'How well-stocked is your drinks cabinet?'

We had a couple of early-evening vodkas together, discussing business. I thoroughly enjoyed his company. He could be a prick, but I had missed my brother very much.

'Guess what?' I said, sloshing more spirit into his glass. 'I am seeing Colt.'

Ilya stared at me. 'What? Oh, no, no and no. Not a firm member.'

I grinned at him and sipped my vodka.

'You're going to do it anyway, aren't you?'

'Yes.'

'Even though I'm saying no?'

'Especially.' He threw up his hands.

'Fine. What can I say? Look after him. He's terrific with my accounts.' I took a draw on my cigarette, thinking about Colt.

'Do not worry,' I said, 'I intend to look after him very well.'

Chapter 13

Colt

I was spending my tea break sitting in the conservatory, reading a book. Eddie was with me, studying the arts section of a broadsheet. I peered over the top of my book at him; the words on the page couldn't hold my interest while this man sat opposite. He was wearing a dark, red, long-sleeved velvet dress with dozens of little brooches pinned to the front. His hair was tied back neatly and his red lipstick was the same shade as the dress. I thought he looked fantastic. He wasn't the slimmest of guys I had ever been with, he was definitely the oldest and frankly, he was a bit scary. I wondered why I loved him but, then realised it didn't matter. He looked up at me and I grinned at him.

'What?'

'Nothing.' I grinned again, 'I'm just happy.'

Eddie raised his eyebrows. Suddenly, Mischa stropped into the room and made a beeline for us. Actually, I was becoming increasingly worried by the way Mischa treated Eddie. It was unpleasant to see how Eddie submitted to the boy. I had resolved that if it didn't stop soon, I would have to say something to Eddie about it.

'Hey, Colt, Uncle Eddie.' Mischa stood beside Eddie's chair, towering over him, his broad shoulders casting a shadow on to the table. 'Uncle Eddie, have you got any money on you? I'm going out tonight.'

Eddie automatically reached for a black velvet clutch bag beside him, took out his wallet. 'Of course! How much do you need?'

I put down my book and watched as Eddie's red-painted nails opened up his wallet and Mischa began to smile in a most self-satisfied manner, his tongue between his teeth.

'Just whatever you have.' He looked at me and very subtly, he winked.

'Fifty pounds?'

A shrug, 'I dunno, Uncle Eddie... I'm taking my girlfriend out to dinner first, and then I need to go to one of the good clubs, just to make sure I stay safe... the more I think about it, I'm going to need a couple of hundred tonight. Call it two-fifty.'

Incredulously, I watched Eddie handing it over, then Mischa turned to flounce out of the room. 'Hey, Mischa,' I burst out. He turned around.

'Did you just say 'hey', Porter, you should really be calling me 'sir.''

I felt my cheeks flush. 'Okay; fine, 'sir?' Your uncle just gave you a lot of money. Aren't you even going to thank him?'

Mischa looked at me, then at Eddie. There was a wicked gleam in his eye. 'Thanks Uncle Eddie,' he cooed sarcastically. He walked up to Eddie, wrapped his arm around his neck and gave him a theatrical, exaggerated kiss on the cheek. Eddie froze and stared down at the table, his hands clenched into fists. Mischa slapped him playfully on his cheek, laughing, 'Heh. There you go, you old homo. That's what you wanted isn't it? Hope it was worth two hundred quid.' He laughed and left us alone.

Eddie flipped open his paper. 'Thanks, Colt,' he said tightly.

'Sorry. The wee bastard just riles me. Why do you give him everything he asks for? He's a cheeky git.'

Eddie shrugged. 'He is my nephew. And it is only money.'

'No, it isn't. Why do you let him talk to you that way? He hurt your feelings just then, I can tell.'

Eddie shook his head. He stared out of the window, looking troubled.

'Tell me honestly,' I ventured, 'Is it because he reminds you of yourself, when you were younger? Something like that?'

He shook his head and was quiet for a long time. He looked at me, seeming so much more vulnerable than usual. 'Have you ever seen a photograph of Eel? I mean, Jason?' He reached into his wallet again, flicked a photo out onto the table. I glanced at it, feeling inexplicably jealous again; jealous of the dead guy, how pathetic. He was bloody good-looking, though.

I plumped for honesty, 'Well, yeah… I looked through your stuff when I was at your old house. Saw his modelling portfolios… and, uh, stuff. Other pictures. Sorry.'

Eddie raised his eyebrows. 'Thanks for that… well anyway, don't you see? Does Mischa not look somewhat familiar?' He picked a speck of dust from the photo and replaced it in his wallet. I looked at him blankly.

'He's Jason's son. Jason and Ilya's wife, Alex? They… had a relationship. A brief relationship.'

'Wait- your Jason?'

'Mm hm.' He looked tense, obviously he hated talking about this.

'And the twins are… Jason's.'

'Yes,' said Eddie.

'Does… everyone know?'

'Everyone knows, yes, except for the kids themselves… Ilya loves those kids like they're his own. It is complicated… at the time, it destroyed Ilya's marriage. My boyfriend and Ilya's wife. It was awful, and devastating. Eel chose me in the end, of course. I made him prove it, too.'

I felt a sinister prickling up the back of my neck. I couldn't resist asking, 'How?'

Eddie smiled coldly. 'Well. You know the tattoo on my back? He had a matching one, of my name. Only his was… bigger.'

'Bigger?'

'Yes,' said Eddie mildly. His voice had a dreamy quality. 'He did not want to have it done, but I… made him.'

He took a final drag on his cigarette, dropped it on the floor and stubbed it out with his black heeled shoe.

'It seemed so important at the time. Stupid. It's nothing but my name carved into the rotting dead flesh of someone's chest.' Eddie looked angry, growing angrier, 'And she has his fucking kids walking about, the bitch mingled with him, living flesh. Mischa, Mischa is the fucking image of him; my heart almost stopped when I saw him. Bitch! That bitch, she has more of him than I can ever have, and I thought that forcing him to get a tattoo would make him irreversibly mine.'

I put my hand over his. It was shaking. He gripped my fingers and he began to calm down. I could see now why Mischa had his uncle wrapped around his little finger.

Hours later, we were in the lounge when Mischa reappeared in a sharp black suit over a black t-shirt, a white-gold chain around his neck, blond hair artfully constructed. He sat on the leather sofa, and although there was plenty of space, he sat down right next to Eddie. I narrowed my eyes slightly. Mischa looked at me and smiled, before turning to Eddie.

'I got another favour to ask you,' he said, mock-shyly. 'Can I borrow your car?'

Eddie laughed in surprise. 'My car? Ah…' He shook his head, grinning as he said in his Russian accent, 'You are going drinking. I do not want you to get smashed up, you know?' Eddie glanced at me uneasily, and I gave him a meaningful look. He shifted his gaze back to Mischa, and I could tell that the boy just melted him. It was hard not to feel jealous, even if Mitch was just an obnoxious kid.

'You mean,' teased Mischa, with his lopsided smile, leaning forwards and subjecting Eddie to the full force of his charm, 'you don't want your Jag to get smashed up.' He put his hand on Eddie's leg, 'I know you, Uncle. You love your car.'

'Ah… you got me.' Eddie laughed shyly, and I noticed that he moved his leg away. He was blushing faintly, though. He was like a schoolgirl. It was so maddening.

'Okay,' said Eddie, 'How about this. I will drive you there. You can phone me, have me pick you up later.'

'Sound.' Mischa sat back in his seat, leaning away from Eddie. 'We have to pick up my girlfriend Debbie on the way.' He grabbed the television remote and flicked on to a music channel, Kiss FM.

Eddie stood up. 'I will get my keys.' He left the room.

I couldn't help glaring at Mischa. 'Do you mind? I was actually watching Mastermind.'

Mischa swung his legs up on to the sofa. 'Shut up, geek. It's my house. My rules.'

I bristled. Mischa was lying on his back, one hand absently massaging his own chest, the other fondling his groin as he hummed along to the music. He was admittedly, gorgeous, but he knew it, and he adored himself. He had Eddie running after him like a manservant, My Eddie.

'So, couldn't get a taxi tonight?' I asked him sarcastically. 'You should be able to afford one.'

'You're joking, right? I already, like, spent that money. On E.'

I felt a hot prickle of renewed fury. 'You spent Eddie's money on drugs?'

Mischa opened his eyes. 'Hush,' he said simply. 'One word about it and I'll have you fired.' He closed his eyes again, still smiling, 'You're just, like, crazy jealous, aren't you? Well, I know exactly how to play the old pervert to get what I want. Watch and learn, loser.'

I was throbbing with anger. I stared at him, experiencing a disturbing intensity of dislike that I had never felt before. Just then, Eddie strolled back into the room jangling his car keys. 'All ready?'

They left together. I put Mastermind back on but my own mind was firmly on Mischa. The wee bastard.

Apart from Mischa Bodansky, the only thing that continued to trouble me was worrying about my family. I phoned my brother Clarke and, as usual, he wasn't happy. 'When are you coming back?' He asked. Sitting on the edge of the peach-coloured bed in the room I was meant to be cleaning, I sighed and rubbed my eyes. I was tired of this conversation and tired of feeling guilty for the same damn thing.

'Not anytime soon, I told you. I'm just calling to check if everyone's okay.'

'Aye. We're alright I suppose.' He was a good kid, and he didn't sulk for long. I asked him about school, and his football. It hurt, because each time we talked, it seemed like we had less and less to say to each other. After a few minutes of awkward small talk, I said goodbye.

'Look after everybody,' I added, and he mumbled, 'I do. I do it all the time, but.'

'Clarky…'

'It's meant to be your job, but. We hate it here. The other kids are mental, I'm trying to keep Jamie from getting in with the wrong crowd. You're our big brother, you should be helping us…' He didn't know how much he was hurting me. I held my stomach, my eyes clenched shut.

'I'm always here if you need me. You've got my mobile number.'

'Right then, fine- I need you.'

'Ohh… Clarky, it's not that easy.'

'Why? Because you're scared of Dad?' He sighed. I sighed, too. We had been down that road a thousand times. He apologised, I apologised and we said our unhappy goodbyes until next time.

I shoved my phone in my pocket, sighed and returned to my stack of sheets and towels. I was in the family quarters preparing a bedroom for Ilya's ex-wife Alexandra, the twins' mother. She was due to stay at the hotel for a few days before and after the twins' eighteenth birthday party. Apparently she and Ilya were still on cordial terms. I finished making up the bed and moved on to the bathroom, stacking fresh towels on to the rack. Then I heard voices on the other side of the door. 'You are looking wonderfully well, Alex,' said Ilya, in his low voice.

'Thank you. I must have tried on every outfit in my wardrobe,' she laughed.

I froze. The bathroom door was almost closed; they obviously didn't know I was in there. I should have walked out right away, but for some reason I panicked and stayed where I was, thus making it more impossible to come out with every passing second.

'Well, you made a lovely choice. That colour,' Ilya cleared his throat awkwardly, 'it suits you.'

'Thanks, Illy,' she said gently. 'John says hello, by the way.' She dropped her handbag with a thud on the dressing table; I hoped to God no one would come into the bathroom.

'Oh, yes… likewise. I mean, send him my regards. How is John? How is the plumbing trade?' Ilya's voice held a touch of scorn, and I could picture his sardonic smile. Ilya always became sarcastic when he felt under pressure.

'Lucrative,' said Alex. 'More lucrative than the hotel trade…' Her voice was teasing. 'John's fine; and you, still single?'

'Oh, you know. I don't have time for relationships. My last one didn't work out too well, if you recall.'

'I was your last relationship?'

'Pathetic, isn't it?'

'Kind of, honey, yeah.' Alex looked at him appraisingly, her eyes sparkling. They both smiled and looked away.

They talked for a while. I was sweating, panicking. I wondered if I could get out the window, but we were up on the second floor, so probably that wouldn't be too sensible. In the room, the conversation had turned to Eddie. Alex didn't sound happy. 'Illy, why is he back here? Does he know something?'

'No.'

'He mustn't find out. Not ever. He would ruin everything.'

I moved a tiny bit closer to the crack in the door.

'Alex, he will not find out. Do you think that I would risk the kids finding out?'

'No. No, I guess not.' Alex sighed.

'Our secrets are safe. My brother is too self-absorbed to work anything out. He's busy with work, and… Ah, Manpyre persuaded me to employ this kid, Bryce. Supposedly he's some kind of maths genius… that remains to be seen, I think Manpyre was exaggerating to get me to hire him… anyway, my brother has decided to make him his latest toy. So, you see, he is very distracted. He won't find out.'

'Okay.' Alex exhaled, 'That's good, Ilya. I was freaking out when I first heard he was back… How did he react when he met Mischa?'

'Don't remind me! God damn Prescott's strong genes.'

'Ah… y'mean, God bless Jason's beautiful genes,' laughed Alex.

'It's still too soon to joke. How is Jason, anyway? Do you still see him?' Ilya asked. In the bathroom I frowned, unsure if I had heard correctly. Jason?

'I still try to see him most weekends,' replied Alex, 'When I can. Every time I get a new photo of the kids, or when they win anything with the ponies, I take it to show him. I'm actually going to pop up to see him tomorrow…'

'How is he?'

'Do you care?'

'Not really. Just curious.'

Alex sighed. 'He's… fine. Just fine, Ilya. John and I had dinner with him last Sunday.'

I could swear that I heard Ilya snort with laughter.

'Ah.' His voice was rich with amusement, 'So, what was for dinner, liquidised Sunday roast? Or has he moved on to solids?'

'That's not really funny, Ilya.'

I was totally bewildered. Brow furrowed, I kept listening. Alex was speaking, 'Honestly, how can you still be jealous of Jason? All things considered you'd have to be pretty damn insecure to be-'

'Oh, come on. I'm not jealous. I am sorry, Alex, I was only trying to lighten the mood.'

I cowered in the bathroom for several agonising minutes longer but thank God, they left, with Ilya saying he wanted to show her the refurbished gym. I came out of the bathroom and sat on the bed next to Alex's suitcase, feeling dazed. I had a bad feeling about this. What were they keeping from

Eddie? I didn't like what I was hearing. The next morning when Alex's jeep pulled out of the hotel gates and turned left, she was being followed at a discreet distance by me in my Fiesta.

Chapter 14

Colt

The place we ended up at felt like some kind of hospital or rehab centre. Huge red brick walls, covered in ivy surrounded the grounds. There were several wheelchair-accessible vehicles in the car park. I parked my car in a bay marked 'Visitors only', and hurried in to the building. A small marble sign by the automatic doors read, 'Harbour Residential Centre. Acquired Brain Injury Rehabilitation'. I hurried inside. The warm reception area was hushed. I approached the desk.

'Excuse me.' I spoke in a low voice, feeling paranoid. 'A woman with short, blondish hair just came in. I'm with her... could you tell me where she is?'

The receptionist pointed behind me. 'Right over there,' she smiled, 'With Jason.'

I turned slowly. I had walked right past her. She sat with her back to me and hadn't yet noticed me. Opposite her, facing me, was a man. His big, very dark eyes were fixed on me; his face was expressionless; his steady gaze across the room, unnerving. I stared right back, unable to believe. Following her companion's gaze, Alex turned in slow-motion and jumped to her feet. 'You... from the hotel? The bell-boy... What are you doing here?' She hissed, rushing towards me. I couldn't tear my eyes away from the man, and only did so when she grabbed my arm and yanked me out of earshot of the receptionist. 'Did Ilya send you to follow me?'

I shook my head, 'I- no. I'm Bryce- Eddie's boyfriend. I just'-

'You shouldn't be here.'

'Neither should he,' I countered, anger suddenly surging. 'Is that Jason fucking Prescott? What the fuck is going on here?' I glanced over her shoulder. The man who was apparently Jason, dead Jason, was looking out of the window, tightly hugging himself with his skinny arms. 'I don't understand.' I felt as if my mind was about to explode. 'Isn't he dead, like, years ago? Did I miss something?'

Alex turned away. 'Oh, God,' she groaned. 'Oh, my God. Why did you have to come here?' She steered me even further away. 'You know what happened to Jason?'

'Sure. Horse riding accident.'

Alex and I studied each other carefully, warily. Finally, she said, 'Okay. The night that- that Jay got hurt, the boys were both taken to hospital. Jason fell into the river. He was without oxygen for so long that his brain was damaged. Ilya, well, all of us- told Eddie that he had died, because absolutely everyone thought that he would. Eddie was kept in hospital for a while, raving about Jason, and Ilya was extremely worried. He didn't know what to do for the best- Jason was still alive but hadn't regained consciousness. There was every chance he would die. Ilya decided to take Eddie home once he was discharged, and keep him in the dark. Eddie basically went crazy, once he was home. It was... like he was possessed or something. He inflicted a lot of damage on his body; cutting his arms, his legs, his face... Ilya was beside himself. Then after a few weeks, he left, taking a lot of Illy's money. He left Ilya a note but no contact details whatsoever, and he never gave Illy any way of contacting him for three years.

In the meantime, Jason didn't die. Illy always hated Jason, but he did what had to be done, making sure he was treated in a private hospital near home. He was in intensive care for weeks. Ilya made sure that he had all the CT scans, private MRI scans and consultations with specialist neurologists. To be fair to Ilya, he did everything right by Jason. He did all that for Eddie, I think, because in the early days he expected him to come back any day. He didn't, of course. He thought that Jason was dead, so he had no reason to come home.

Jason's condition stabilised but it became obvious that he was going to be severely disabled. He stayed in hospital for just over two years, then he was moved here.' Alex shrugged. 'He improved a lot in the first few years, but he's been pretty much like you see him now for about... ten years. He needs help with eating, getting dressed, bathing; everything. He has severe epilepsy now, too...' She pushed her hands into the pockets of her denim jacket. 'Sorry to focus on the negatives. He's pretty content most of the time, happy, even. I'm only telling you how disabled he is, because I don't want you to tell Eddie about him.'

'Well... he deserves to know.'

'Deserves...' she was quiet for moments, then, 'but, why tell him? Who would benefit from it? It would confuse Jason, he wouldn't even know who the hell Eddie was after all these years. It would hurt Eddie so much, and then what? Guilt, burden, that's what. A few visits, maybe; but what would Eddie want with him now?'

I looked across at Jason, who was resting his head on his arms, staring out of the window. He was skinny and ugly, except for his eyes. Alex was still talking, persuading.

'Bryce, don't get me wrong. I love Jason to bits, he is the sweetest man. His smile lights up the room. But he can barely talk. He needs help with everything. Eddie remembers him as this gorgeous, vivacious twenty-one year old model... but that kid is gone. He's in love with the memory of

Jason, that's all.'

I nodded along with what she was saying, then confused, shook my head slowly. A million thoughts were clamouring in my head.

'Come and meet him,' Alex said, with an air of wanting to make a point. Jason was doing a dominoes puzzle that involved matching wooden pictures of different types of transport to their corresponding words. He was moving the pieces with one hand, the other, wrapped protectively across his waist. Every so often, his big dark eyes flashed curiously at me. Those eyes really were the only feature that remained of the handsome model that he once was. He had been studying a word, ('motorcycle') for several minutes and was obviously having trouble matching it.

'Here,' I said, pushing the picture towards him. He clicked it in place and flashed me a little half-smile.

'Don't help him,' tutted Alex, 'He can do it by himself.' I shook my head, looking at Jason.

'Man… What would Eddie say if he could see me right now? He wouldn't believe it.'

'No, don't mention that name…' Alex hissed.

Too late! I sensed Jason's reaction right away. His head snapped up and he stared hard at me with narrowed eyes. I shifted uncomfortably under his intense stare.

'Jay-Jay,' said Alex quickly, 'Look, a bus. Find 'bus' for me, darling.'

He kept on staring at me, his eyes burning. I felt myself blushing at my huge mistake.

'Bus, Jason?' I whispered. He picked up the card and twiddled it thoughtfully in his hand before clicking it into place. It was the final piece of the puzzle. He looked at me again, so hard; it was as though he was trying to draw information out of my eyes. I broke into a light sweat, feeling like I was trying to beat a lie detector.

'He said 'Debbie', Jay,' said Alex gently. 'Remember I told you that Mischa has a girlfriend now, named Debbie? That's who Bryce was talking about.' Jason curled his legs up under himself on the chair, wrapped both arms around himself and stared out of the window.

After the visit, Alex and I walked out to our separate cars in heavy silence. Alex turned to me, 'You seem like a nice boy. I can't stop you from telling him, but please just stop and think about it first. Jason is happy enough as he is, isn't he?'

I glanced back at the red brick building, thinking about Jason's reaction to hearing Eddie's name. 'I don't know.'

Leaving me to think it over, Alex got into her car and drove away.

After a confused drive back to the hotel, I was heading to my bedroom when I ran into the last person I wanted to see.

'Hello babes,' smiled Eddie, 'Where have you been all afternoon?'

'Nowhere special. I went for a drive.' Great, now I was lying to him. I was horrified to find that I couldn't meet his eyes. I felt myself going red, as I always did when I lied to someone I loved. Mercifully, he seemed preoccupied and didn't notice my distress.

'Are you coming to dinner? Alex is here, Ilya's wife. I have to eat with her and I need some moral support.' He sighed dramatically, then paused. 'You look a bit flushed, are you okay?'

'Yeah… yeah, sorry, I'm fine. 'Course I'll come to dinner with you. I just need to go and wash up first.'

'Okay. Oh, put on a tie, babes. Ilya makes a big deal out of Sunday dinner. See you downstairs.'

'Eddie!'

'Yes?' Eddie looked at me expectantly and a wave of misery washed over me. 'Babe,' he said, 'Are you sure you're okay?'

I nodded, and swallowed hard.

Eddie smiled at me kindly. 'Whatever you are worrying about, just stop. Okay? It has taken me a long time to learn that no problem can be made any better by worrying.' He touched my cheek. 'You are tired, I know. You have been working too hard. Let's do something together tonight, we could go to the gym then watch a movie. And if you still feel bad, we can talk about it afterwards?'

I nodded.

'Okay. Take it easy. I will see you in a few minutes.' Eddie loped off down the stairs with an easy grace, leaving me feeling utterly wretched.

Dinner was a taut, tense affair for most of the diners. There was Ilya, Alex, the twins, Eddie and myself. On seeing me, Mischa Bodansky literally stopped in his tracks. Wow. Having met Jason, I could appreciate the resemblance more than ever.

'Why is he here? Why are we eating with the bell-boy?' he protested.

Sasha murmured something to him, no doubt filling him in on the situation, and the look of disgust on his face wasn't a surprise. His father shushed him distractedly as he showed Alex to her seat. Mischa beckoned me to one side and hissed, 'Are you being real right now? Like, really for real, you're dating my uncle?'

I shrugged, 'Yeah.'

'No, but like- for real? Not, like, for a joke?' His face.

'No, no joke. We're actually dating. He's my boyfriend. Yeah.'

'Shut up. Shut up! Why? Because he's rich?'

I rolled my eyes and shook my head in disgust. The look of incomprehension on his face was pretty priceless.

Eddie was dressed eccentrically, probably to irritate his brother and disrespect his guest. He was wearing a dark blue suit, metallic blue eye shadow, navy blue eyeliner and blue mascara. A single peacock feather was artfully strapped to his head, 1920's flapper style and the look was completed with pearl earrings and choker. I loved the way he looked and I loved his humour. He was not serious and the combination of his size and power with the playful feminine accessories was something I would normally have found pretty sexy; had I not been feeling sick with worry.

'Take off that fucking feather,' snapped Ilya as we sat down. Eddie ignored him, pulling out a chair for me like a gentleman.

'Hi Edvard,' said Alex. She was fiddling awkwardly with the tablecloth and her voice was charged nervously. 'Welcome back to England!'

He chose not to look at her as he sat down. 'Thank you.'

Alex and Eddie didn't exchange another word throughout the meal.

I felt Alex's anxious gaze on me for the whole time, but I couldn't look at her. Eddie squeezed my hand under the table and gave me a beautiful smile which I returned as best I could. He seemed really happy to have me there and I could tell that he sort of wanted to show me off, too, by the way he tried to include me in his conversation with Ilya. I had no social skills that night, though. He tried to bring me in on everything; books, films, the news headlines, anything, but I just helplessly muttered a few words, I couldn't think of anything funny or interesting to say. I knew that my dumb act was embarrassing him in front of Ilya and I was pretty sure I wasn't impressing Ilya, either as my boss or my boyfriend's brother. I couldn't help it though and eventually Eddie just threw me a puzzled look and left me to my thoughts.

Thankfully, the twins kept up a flow of conversation, interrogating their father about their birthday gifts. I was so glad when it was over and we were excused.

After dinner, Eddie and I went upstairs to his suite. We were lying on the rug in front of the fire, where we had watched the first twenty minutes of 'O Brother, where art thou?' Without speaking. I felt the heat of the fire on my belly and Eddie's strong arm around me. I was sure that he must be able to feel my heart pounding through my chest. There was a knot of dread in the pit of my stomach. Eddie did not seem to notice anything was wrong. He pulled the feather out of his hair, tucked it playfully into my belt and absently began to kiss my neck, while still watching the film. I lay still in his arms. Eddie unbuttoned my jeans and slid his hand down the front of my trousers, beginning to caress me expertly. Normally I would have loved it; normally, I would have been in heaven. But tonight, I couldn't cope with it at all.

'Babe,' he murmured. 'Baby.'

Yeah. It would've been easy to lose myself in the colourful trance of sex. But I kept thinking about Jason and the clinical hush of the hospital. I mean, he was there right now. So, as Eddie started to bite my ear and turn my face in order to reach my mouth, I found myself murmuring, 'No...'

Eddie dropped his hands as though I was red hot. He stood up and stretched, no questions asked. I knew that he was really sensitive about pushing me into anything, because of the incident in the attic months before.

'Do you want a drink, babe?' He asked, flicking on one of the lights. 'Think I need one, anyway, maybe a cold shower too.' He laughed at his own quip, as I paused the movie. We looked at each other and I knew I had tears in my eyes. Eddie shook his head, 'Okay, this has gone too far. I said we would talk. What is on your mind? You said nothing at dinner. You are beginning to worry me.' He sat down and wrapped his arms around me as I stared worriedly into the fireplace.

'You won't believe me. I shouldn't tell you. Oh, I don't know.' It was torture.

'Colt, you are beginning to annoy me, now, what is it?'

'Okay, okay, I'll tell you. But first, I have a question for you,' I said, a lump in my tight throat.

Eddie tightened his reassuring hug. 'Yes?'

'Did you love Eel?'

I felt Eddie's whole body stiffen. I had tears in my eyes as I stared into the flames. It did not matter, Eddie couldn't see my face.

'You know this… did I love him? Jesus… yes.'

He was right, I did know it. I closed my eyes, and gently, I told him.

Eddie pushed me away from him to look at my face. His eyes were large and suddenly wet with tears that blurred the light reflected from the flames. 'What?' he asked quietly, in amazement. I felt that I had never been stared at so intently before. I looked at the floor, choosing my next words carefully. While I was thinking it through, Eddie leaned forward and grabbed my face hard, with one hand. 'Look at me. Look at me, Colt; is this a joke?'

'No.'

'No, no, no?' Eddie mimicked. 'I saw him die.' He broke eye contact for a moment then looked straight back at me. The look in his eyes sent prickles running all over my arms and neck. 'I was three-quarters dead myself. You are lying to me.'

114

'No.'

'You are lying to me.' Eddie jerked the steel poker out of the grate and pointed the white-hot tip directly at my mouth. 'Admit that you are lying, or I will make you eat this. I will burn your lying tongue out of your head, understand? Who put you up to this? Who?'

'Eddie, it's true.' I was crying. 'I'm not lying. I'm sorry.' I felt the powerful grip on my face loosening, and Eddie broke down in tears, his head in his hands.

Chapter 15

Colt

I promised to take Eddie to the centre first thing in the morning. He was desperate to go that night, but somehow, I managed to persuade him to wait. Eddie did not sleep at all that night. The only thing that calmed him down was going out to the stables, where he stroked and talked to the horses, pressing his face against theirs. He asked me, over and over again about Eel's condition. I told him repeatedly all that I knew about hypoxia, brain damage and epilepsy.

'What have the doctors tried? I mean what; operations, what drugs? What?'

I sighed. 'I don't know.'

'But Colt, you have to tell me.' Eddie scratched the ear of a big grey horse. 'I need to know everything that he has been through.'

I ran my hands through my hair, and tried to stifle a yawn. It was four in the morning. 'I don't know. How could I know? What do you want me to tell you? His prognosis is severe and permanent brain damage. Eel was injured sixteen years ago; it's a long time. I can't imagine he will be getting any... better, after so long.' I knew that I sounded blunt, but we had been over the same ground more than once already that night. Eddie did not seem to be taking in anything that I was telling him. He laid his head against the horse's face and closed his eyes as it nuzzled him.

'You say that,' he said, in his matter-of-fact voice. 'But I can pay for any doctor, any treatment, anywhere in the world. There must be new treatments for... brain stuff, getting developed, all the fucking time. I think I saw a programme on TV about shit like that. Scientists are always coming up with new things, right? Okay, so, Eel will get better. I will take him to America or something. To one of those... specialist clinics, you know, that they have there.' I said nothing. What was there to say? Eddie sounded irritated. 'Hey, Colt. Do you agree?'

'With what?'

'With what I just said... do you agree that some clinic in the States will be able to fix him?'

'Eddie, I...' I shrugged helplessly. 'To be honest, I doubt it.'

He closed his eyes again. 'No offense, but you're not even a qualified doctor. They have those clinics, I have seen them. They can fix all the... you know. I don't even know why I am asking you.'

Morning broke and at six forty-five, sat in the passenger seat of his own car, Eddie drummed his long fingers on the door. I glanced sideways at him, noticing the inward, hungry look in his eyes. He was dressed perfectly and he had done his make-up immaculately; "For Jason." My heart was heavy with sorrow for him.

'Eddie,' I began carefully, running my hands appreciatively over the steering wheel as I settled into the smooth glide of the beloved Jaguar. It was a lot of fun to drive. 'You know last night, when I told you about Eel; about what he is like now?'

'Mm.'

'Just…' I nervously licked my dry lips. 'Just try to be prepared. He is going to seem really different.'

'Mm hm.'

'Oh, please listen to me. I know what's going to happen here. I don't want you to be shocked.'

Eddie picked a speck of lint from his sleeve. 'Colt, I appreciate your concern. But you do not know what you are talking about. It's Eel; I do not need to be 'prepared' as you put it, and you are driving this car like an old lady; drive faster!'

The centre was a large, red-brick, one-storey building, surrounded on all sides by quiet, attractive gardens. Eddie complained that the perfume from all of the flowers was giving him a headache.

'Eel will be so ready to leave this place,' he added, irritably swatting a passing bee. I glanced at Eddie's tense expression, a knot of trepidation tightening in my own stomach. He was still talking about walking in there, collecting Jason and leaving. We walked in and I approached the reception desk while Eddie critically surveyed the empty lobby. The atmosphere was muted and bland. Eddie turned away with a little snort of disgust from the cheap, faded Monet-style prints on every wall. I heard him sigh impatiently as I talked to the nurse on reception.

'I was here yesterday,' I was explaining. 'We're Jason Prescott's friends; this is his best friend, from years ago.' The nurse glanced at Eddie; he glared right back at her. She hesitated, taking in his huge and imposing figure, and turned back to me. I smiled apologetically, but I was half-hoping she would refuse to let us see Jason.

'Gentleman, it's early… Jason is just about to have breakfast,' said the nurse. 'I really don't think-'

'If you please,' I broke in, very politely, 'Eddie and Jason used to be really close. I'm sure that Jason would love to see him again, and it would only take five minutes.'

The nurse replaced the cap on her pen.

'We have come a long way to see him…'

She sighed and shook her head. 'I shouldn't, but well, alright. He doesn't get many visitors. He's in his room. It's the last room on the left, down at the end.'

'I remember from yesterday. Thank you so much.' I gestured to Eddie and started down the corridor.

'Wait.' Eddie slammed his hands on the desk, making the nurse jump a little. 'Are you not going to tell him that I am here first? We have not seen each other for sixteen years.'

The nurse's eyes were large, and she glanced at me. 'I… I don't think that he would understand,' she said falteringly.

'What? Of course he will. Why not?'

'Because, he…' she studied Eddie's face, and seemed, like me to suddenly realise that Eddie was cornered and terrified. He was covered in sweat. Her expression became rather kind and she rolled her eyes. 'Come on, I'll take you down and 'reintroduce' you. Try not to worry.'

We stepped into the simple, comfortable little room. There were photographs pinned to the wall above the dresser; school photos of Mischa and Sasha, some of Jason on various outings with his care staff. In some photos he was in a wheelchair, in others not. Jason was sitting on the bed, his knees drawn close to his chest. He raised his head as the door opened. Eddie had both of his hands over his mouth. He was smiling, his eyes bright.

'Jay,' he whispered. 'Eel. It's you. It's actually you.' He reached involuntarily towards Jason. Jason stared at him, his dark eyes flicking all over Eddie's face. He looked terrified. Eddie took another step towards him and stopped. 'Jay…' Eddie turned, bewildered, to the nurse and I, who were standing quietly to one side. For me, the scene was almost too painful to watch. Something deep within me had begun to ache, and I dropped my gaze to the floor. Eddie laughed a little.

'Is… Is he okay?' His eyes darted from me to the nurse. He was still smiling but his eyes had taken on an expression of panic now. 'Colt?'

I swallowed and forced myself to look at him properly. 'He's fine. This is… normal. For him. Now.' I cringed at my poor choice of words. There was an awkward silence. Eddie put his outstretched hand deep in his pocket. Jason continued to stare at him, hugging his knees ever closer to his body. He seemed absolutely fixated on Eddie. The nurse broke the silence. Approaching Jason, she affectionately clasped his chin, turning his head gently to face her. Despite this, his eyes never left Eddie.

'Just look at all these visitors. Aren't you lucky today? Say hello to the nice men, Jay Jay,' she said warmly.

'Stop touching him,' snapped Eddie. 'Stop talking to him like that!'

'Sorry…' I automatically apologised on his behalf.

The nurse looked taken aback, but she nodded. 'I'll leave you alone for a few minutes,' she said quietly. She hesitated, her hand on the door frame. 'I'll be right outside. Five minutes only, okay?'

Jason shook his head quickly and continued to stare hungrily at Eddie. The minutes ticked by. Eddie was acting as though, in the stillness of the room, there was only Eel and him. He clasped his hands together, pressing his index finger to his lips, as he leaned forward in his chair and stared hard at Eel. I felt a kind of rising anxiety as I stood there, helplessly looking on. Jason was kneeling on his bed, one arm wrapped protectively across his body. His free hand picked absently at the quilt beneath him. He was staring down at the quilt as he picked. Fifteen years in an institution had not done his looks any favours, but Jason retained a sort of fragile gracefulness. He had short, fair hair greying softly at the temples, and those arresting brown eyes. He was slight and thin. Eddie's face darkened and his eyes flitted rapidly over Jason's face. I thought that he looked almost disgusted. There was a cold, desperate light in his stare.

'Jay,' he said suddenly, making me jump. His tone was angry and too loud for the small room. Jason stopped handling his quilt. He was breathing slowly, saying nothing. 'Talk to me Jay,' said Eddie, in a low tone. It was not a question. His voice sounded flat, hopeless. He was not looking at Jason anymore, but at the floor. I swallowed.

Eddie pushed back his chair and kicked it aside. He shoved past me and stormed out of the room, almost knocking over the nurse who was waiting outside.

'Is everything alright?'

Eddie turned on her. 'What have you done to him?'

'Keep your voice down this is a medical centre.'

'What have you done to him? You obviously have not cared for him properly. How did he end up like that?'

The nurse held up her hand. 'Excuse me! I've known Jason for years, when he first came here he couldn't walk. Jason has made excellent progress here at the Harbour Centre.'

'Oh yes, excellent. He looks fantastic. Good job.' Eddie turned and marched up the corridor. I caught up with him near reception; he was shaking violently. He couldn't look at me.

'It is not him. I need to get out of here,' he mumbled.

'It's not him. Literally?'

'No… It is him, of course. Oh, fuck, I cannot do this… Come on. I cannot stay here.'

'You're just… leaving?'

'Immediately. Come.'

I stood, bewildered. 'Eddie. Eddie? It's Eel. You are unbelievable.'

'I do not care. Move it.' He turned round and stared at me because I had not moved from where I stood. 'Hey. Don't.' His face turned angry and tears suddenly stood in his eyes. He pointed at me, 'Fuck you. Don't you judge me!' He spat, and walked out.

We drove home from the hospital in complete silence. I tried to talk to him, but he wouldn't have it. He just shook his head, tears boiling in his eyes. He had been badly shocked, I knew. When we arrived back at the hotel, Eddie went straight to the stables and was out riding by himself for the rest of the day. I went about my work, constantly glancing out the windows in the hope of seeing him returning on his horse. There was no sign of him all day.

That evening, as I slipped into my chair at the long table with the other firm members assembling, Eddie was still nowhere to be seen. I straightened my tie and glanced around anxiously. Firm meetings were intimidating and Eddie was my safety net, discreetly fielding any difficult questions, and subtly deflecting the most difficult and dangerous work away from me. Suddenly the door opened and in he walked, as smoothly as ever. His face was absolutely impassive as he glided into his seat, dressed in an immaculately simple black suit with black shoes, black tie and his hair slicked dark with oil and scraped back. He was wearing hardly any makeup, only a hint of black eyeliner. He leant forwards, in the dim lighting it was difficult to make out his features. 'Sorry I am late,' he said loudly, staring at Ilya, his eyes dancing. I closed my eyes briefly; I could sense trouble. Ilya looked at him, frowned, and turned back to the group.

'Alright. Gentlemen,' he began.

'It is just that I, ah, was visiting someone today; an old friend.'

Ilya paused again, fists clenched, then continued without acknowledging the interruption. 'Will, would you like to update the group on your findings about the Mill exhibit?' He continued calmly.

Eddie leaned farther across the table towards his brother. 'Of course, I had to wait in line to see him. You know, your wife has visited him every week for the past fifteen years, Illy?' Eddie laughed and the group sat in a tense silence, Ilya seething. 'You know what the strangest thing is? I was quite sure he was dead! I positively remember you telling me to my face, that Eel was dead. You, Ilya, you yourself described his funeral to me, in great detail!' Eddie laughed again, harshly, 'And yet there he was. There he was.'

Suddenly Ilya looked at him. 'Is that supposed to trouble me? My ex-wife visiting him?'

The two brothers looked at each other across the table. Eddie's face was alight; he had pushed Ilya to say whatever he was about to. Ilya's eyes narrowed, 'In case you have forgotten, we're divorced. Secondly, as I understand it, Prescott's a dribbling, brain-dead freak now. Hardly a threat to anyone's marriage. Am I right? I am right, aren't I, Eddie?' There was a long silence. Suddenly, Eddie pushed back his chair and walked quickly from the room without a backward glance.

Ilya cleared his throat. 'Okay, so, if there are no further interruptions? Will, could you update the group, please? We haven't got all night.' Ilya threw a glance at me and I looked pointedly away. I wasn't going to give him, nor the rest of the group, the satisfaction of watching me hurrying after Eddie, as much as I wanted to.

Nevertheless, I barely heard another word throughout the rest of the meeting. My mind was on Eddie, and his mental state. Ilya's comment had been really cruel.

Underneath the table, I sent a quick text to Eddie. 'U ok? Don't worry. C U after meeting,' I wrote. A few moments later, my phone beeped loudly. Ilya glared at me, guessing.

'No mobile phones in meetings, Bryce,' he chided. 'Switch it off.' I did, but not before sneaking a glance at Eddie's reply. My heart sank, and I thought about it for the rest of the meeting. Eight words, 'My brother is a bastard. But he's right.'

Eddie

I left the hotel and walked, in inappropriate shoes, to the place where it all began. I sat by the river leaning my back against a tree. My back felt stronger now than it did back then, and my body taller; harder. I wondered if the place remembered me when I was twenty-one. I wondered if anyone could see me as clearly as I saw myself now.

My mobile vibrated in my pocket, a message from Colt. I tapped out an answer then switched the phone off, tempted to throw it into the river. Fuck them, I thought, fuck all of them. My brother's ugly words played over and over again in my head. A dribbling, brain-dead freak. A brain-dead freak. Oh, Jason. My Jason. I pulled my jacket around myself, my crisp suit offering no protection against the damp air. My hair was unwashed yet gelled to perfection and I felt like a shell, left in the sun for months. The pressure had deepened my cracks so much that a finger touch would crumble me. The pain had made my skin fragile; one more harsh word would blow me to dust. 'Jason,' I said aloud. It felt good to say the name. I hardly ever said it out loud to anyone. 'Jay, are you there? Are you listening to me? Darling, I am down to my last shred of strength. I'm reaching out for you.' As I spoke, loneliness stole into my heart. I used to talk to Jason all the time, in my sad and private moments. I had believed that Jason could hear me, was somehow with me spiritually, like an angel. But, now I knew the truth. An angel? In reality, Jason was incapable of understanding anything that I chose to say to him. I felt strangely and newly bereft of my dead lover, faced as I was with what he had become.

I sat there until I became very cold; inadequately dressed for riverbank meditation. The air that whipped from the surface of the river was freezing, and it had become too dark to see. My tears had dried by now, and I stood up, feeling the solid trunk of the tree behind me. A gust of wind whispered past the back of my neck. I shivered. 'Why did this have to fucking happen? I would give… anything… for this to be a nightmare.' I laughed bitterly in spite of myself, still talking to Jason. It was still wonderfully comforting, for reasons unknown. But I knew it had to stop. It had to stop tonight, because the fantasy was well and truly over. 'Goodbye, Jason,' I said simply. And it was. Up until that point in my life, I thought I knew what it was like to feel lonely.

Chapter 16

Colt

I hadn't seen Eddie since the meeting. As soon as it was over I had raced up to his suite and knocked on the door, for what seemed like an eternity before he called out, quietly, 'Whoever that is… I am in bed.'

'It's me,' I had said. 'It's me, open up.' I rapped on the door. 'C'mon.' There was a very long pause.

I inhaled to speak again just as he said, 'Baby? I am already in bed. I will see you tomorrow.'

'But… don't you want to sleep with me?' I blurted out, before I realised how pathetic I sounded. He didn't answer anyway.

It felt weird sleeping alone, knowing he was just down the hall in his own bed. Wasn't he cold without me? Didn't he, after tonight's trouble, want some comfort? I know I did. I guessed that… he just needed space.

He would be fine in the morning, I was sure. But, the next day I couldn't find him. Everyone was really busy getting ready for the twins eighteenth birthday party. I was doing a million jobs; carrying tables to the poolside, setting up the bar, hanging lights. Even though I was a firm member, I was still the hotel dogsbody when it suited Ilya.

I wasn't working at the party but I was invited, along with all the other firm members. I didn't feel like it, but maybe Eddie would show up. I turned up early, almost before anyone else, found myself a leather armchair by the pool, and made up my mind to sit in it all night, drinking free champagne.

The guests arrived, the seats and the poolside quickly became busy. I brought three glasses of champagne back to my chair and drank them slowly; moodily. No sign of Eddie. I felt kind of sick. People walked by me, occasionally someone caught my eye or smiled and I just glared. I was in a proper mood.

'Hey, handsome.'

I looked up. It was Manpyre. 'Where's your man?'

I shrugged irritably.

'Well.' He perched on the arm of my chair, 'I guess someone will have to get you a drink. Whatcha want?'

'Anything,' I said. 'Manpyre? Make it a big one.'

'Okay-doke. Cheer up, it's a party.' He grinned at me and made for the bar.

There was some commotion at the far end of the pool. Screaming and cheering. A group of people had just arrived including Eddie who was making a grand entrance; dressed in a gold sari and nothing else. I stared in fascination and horror. Like his friends, Eddie's skin was covered with elaborately painted body art. The colourful, luminous designs artfully concealed all of his scars. One of the painted women slid into the pool. Her body paint oiled all around her in streams of purple, gold and red. Eddie's body paint was all gold and silver. He was kneeling by the pool, animatedly discussing his designs with some of his friends who were lounging in the water. He twisted around to show the designs on his back, and as he did so, his eyes met mine for one split second across the glistening aquamarine pool.

There was no trace of the tattoo, just elaborate gold markings and a large gold horse across his back. He was ignoring me. He seemed entirely at ease chatting and laughing with his friends, his gold-gilded face showing no outward signs of the previous day's trauma.

Manpyre landed on the arm of my chair again. 'Here you go, mate.' I accepted a vodka and coke distractedly and we both watched Eddie as he joked around with his mates. He seemed to be knocking back endless Cosmopolitans. Not once did he look in my direction.

'He's completely ignoring me.' I murmured to myself.

'Indeed he is,' said Manpyre, settling himself more comfortably on my chair.

'No wait, he's coming over.' I sat up as Eddie and a friend breezed past us, without a glance.

'Yeah… he's ignoring you alright,' laughed Manpyre. 'Mate, who cares? You've got me…'

I jumped up, shoved my drink back into Manpyre's hand and followed Eddie to the bar. I elbowed my way to the front and squeezed in beside Eddie and his friend, who were chatting. The friend turned away and he was effectively alone for a moment. 'Eddie,' I said.

He smirked coldly without looking at me. He was trying to catch the barman's attention. 'Alright?' he murmured.

'Alright, yeah. You?'

'I've never been better, babes,' he replied dryly.

'Nice paint. Whose idea was that?' He smiled a little more warmly at that, actually looked at me, probably relieved that I hadn't mentioned Jason.

'Mine, of course! Lesson one; how to creatively attend a pool party without your body freaking everyone out.' He winked as he moved away, 'Enjoy the party, babes.'

'Hey, Eddie. Um, are you okay about… about Eel? If you want to talk…'

'Well, listen.' As Eddie tasted his champagne I noticed that his lips were golden too. 'I preferred him when he was dead. Does that answer your question?' I said nothing. 'No, I not want to talk about it, but I will say this, try to understand. You did not know Eel before.' Eddie licked his lips; he was trying to find the right words, trying to make me understand. 'He was funny, Colt. He was fucking hilarious. He was sexy. I... he was my role model. In many ways, I looked up to him. He did not even know me today-' I stopped him there.

'He did know you. He couldn't take his eyes off you!'

'Ahh... you do not get it, do you? I feel sorry for him, I really do. Believe me, I am sick for him. But you have seen him, he cannot even talk. He is fucked.'

I was stunned. I sat back down on my chair as the party swelled around me and the noise rushed in my ears. Eddie was holding court in the centre of his friends. A man was sitting at his feet, his head resting on Eddie's lap, and Eddie was absently stroking this man's bright ginger hair as he laughed with his friends.

'Bryce!' Sasha bobbed into view. 'Hello? You're quiet! I didn't even know you were here!' Her voice a happy squeal, she grabbed my hands.

'I'm not here. I mean, I'm going inside, Sash,' I apologised. I looked over at Eddie and a fist crushed my heart.

'Why? Stay out, it's my birthday. Don't be a bore.' She threaded her arm through mine and put her head on my shoulder. 'Have you seen Uncle Eddie with Paul Russell?' She giggled.

I glanced discreetly at Eddie again. 'Wow, yeah, I didn't even realise that was Paul Russell. The journalist, right? He's really famous.' This famous young gentleman was now straddling my boyfriend and licking his tonsils. I shifted uncomfortably and looked away.

'And really drunk.' Sasha laughed. 'We always have a few famous people at Daddy's parties.' Sasha leaned back and looked at me quizzically, 'So... I guess that you and my uncle aren't... anymore?'

'I guess not.'

'Ah, Bryce, wanna talk about it?'

'No, no. I'm fine, sweetie. Enjoy your birthday.'

I managed to disengage myself from the party and went into the hotel, through the side entrance by the kitchen. I closed the door and the noise of the party was immediately muted. I took a deep breath, relishing the sudden calm. I headed through the kitchen, it was busy with waiters hurrying everywhere around, refilling and balancing huge silver trays of canapés. I weaved my way through and headed straight through the dining hall and into the big hotel lobby.

'Colt!' I turned around to see Manpyre hurrying across the lobby.

'Mate... are you okay?'

I nodded.

'Aww, I saw Eddie with that journo wanker... don't be too hurt. That's just Eddie, mate. He's very fickle. And he likes fucking with people's feelings... what do you see in him, anyway? He's weird. And he's fat and ugly, don't you think so? He's fucking minging.'

'Dave! Leave it out, I'm hurting here, man.'

Manpyre took hold of my hand. 'But you're too good for him, mate.'

I shook my head, tears brimming in my eyes. 'I thought he liked me.'

Manpyre put his arms around me and said, into my hair. 'I like you, mate.'

I shrugged him off casually, but it wasn't so bad having company. Better than being alone, in some ways. We took a seat on one of the red leather benches in the lobby, chatted for a bit. I asked him if he knew Jason Prescott, before the riding accident.

'Riding accident?' He frowned.

'Yeah, like, his accident? How he got hurt?'

Manpyre looked carefully at me. He started to say something, then, stopped. 'I did know him,' he said slowly, thoughtfully. 'Yeah. Of course, because he was in the firm. He was nice. I can still remember him sitting there in firm meetings with that blond Mohican...' he smiled and shook his head, '... mouthing off about something. Anything. Everything. He was very opinionated, a bit arrogant maybe. But he was decent. It's... ah, really terrible what happened to him. Poor kid. You saw him at the hospital, I believe?'

I nodded.

'How is he these days?'

'He's...' I didn't know how to describe it. 'Like, I dunno. He can't talk and stuff.' I didn't want to talk about it, anymore.

Manpyre rubbed his chin thoughtfully. 'Sad. Very sad... Colt, can we go somewhere more private to talk? I have to tell you something. It's important.'

I was thinking about Jason and a wave of misery washed over me. I didn't want to cry in front of Manpyre. I mumbled my excuses and headed for my bedroom, alone.

As I stepped into the corridor I heard voices and laughter. I considered turning back and taking another route to my room, I wanted to be alone so much. It felt too late to turn back so I kept on walking quickly down the corridor, past Eddie's door.

Eddie was laughing, pushing the journalist into his room as I walked by, head down deliberately averting my eyes. Eddie spun around and seized me with his powerful grip.

'Why are you alone?' He demanded, blocking my route down the corridor. Inside the room, there was a crash as the drunken journalist stumbled into something. Eddie looked around and laughed a little too loudly. Then he turned back to me.

'I just am,' I said irritably. Eddie still made me nervous when he had been drinking.

'Suit yourself. Me? I am going to have a little fun with this guy; I can tell. He is wild,' he smiled, stretching. 'And tomorrow, you can 'read all about it!' Goodnight, babes.'

I couldn't stop myself. 'Goodnight?' You're just about to sleep with some other guy! What the hell are you doing?' He swayed on the spot. He was so drunk.

'What about us?' I asked.

To my amazement, he just shrugged. 'Join us. We can both fuck him.'

'Ugh.' I turned away in disgust, but anger spewed out of me and I rounded on him again, bursting out, 'And! And how can you stop thinking about Eel, just like that?'

Eddie's face dropped. 'Would you rather I did think about him? You're sick,' he sneered. He stepped into the hall and shut his door behind him. His face was bright red. I'd never seen him look angrier. 'You self-righteous little bastard! You have no idea.' His face was livid. He shook his head, 'I thought you knew me. Fuck, Colt. Fuck.' I was speechless and Eddie continued, 'Now that we are on the subject, I have a question. Why did you tell me that he is still alive? Why did you do that?'

'Because it felt like the right thing to do.' I felt myself beginning to question my own judgement, and I shook my head. 'No, it was the right thing to do.'

'Was it?' Eddie snarled. 'Have you never heard the phrase, what you do not know cannot hurt you?'

'I never trusted that saying. It's dishonest.' I looked at him. 'Come on, man, you're not really saying I shouldn't have told you.'

'You told me,' whispered Eddie, 'That Eel was alive. He is not. You introduce me to some poor, broken creature in a mental hospital and you tell me that is my Eel? And then you expect me to rejoice?'

'I never expected you to 'rejoice', I expected you to... I don't know,'

'What?' Eddie exploded. 'What do you want me to do? Bring him home with me, bathe him, spoon feed him? What can I do for him? What do you want from me?'

I began to speak but Eddie held up both of his hands. 'You know what? I don't have to explain myself to you.' He slammed the door and I was left to stare at it.

I felt like a dick. The worst part was that I did understand how he was feeling, at least a little bit. After all, I had left my own brothers in foster care, so it was kind of a similar situation. Maybe not... I did that because I was scared and felt incapable, not because I didn't care about them. Did Eddie care about Jason or not? What the hell was going on inside his head?

Over the next few weeks, Eddie stopped speaking to me almost altogether.

I carried on with work, and so did he. He seemed to be dating that Paul Russell, and I won't lie, the whole thing hurt. Breaking up was shit, but it felt especially painful to be cut off from him like that.

Even though our relationship was dead, Eddie never stopped protecting me in firm meetings, in his usual way. Thanks to him, the dangerous work never came my way. 'I would very much value Bidden's insight on this project,' he would say, seamlessly allocating this work to anyone but me. 'Manpyre, you have contacts in this area… this is definitely your bag.'

About two months after the party, an important job was being discussed. Someone was needed to drive to Bristol to collect eight paintings, stolen in a high-profile robbery from a fairly distant relative of the royal family.

'Colt should do it,' said Bidden. Manpyre, Eddie and Ilya all leaned forward uneasily while everyone else looked at me. I was watching Eddie, but he didn't speak.

'Such a delicate collection,' began Ilya, 'Ought to be handled by someone more experienced.'

'Yeah, and it's too dangerous for the little guy,' frowned Manpyre, 'Come on, Bidden, what are you thinking? Why Colt?'

'I'll tell you why,' said Bidden, 'And I know the others will back me up here. It's not right that only one person in this firm, hasn't ever done anything illegal. It puts the rest of us in a vulnerable position. He knows everything about everything, but he's completely clean. Now, I'm not saying that Colt would use what he knows against us, he's a smashing kid, a really good kid, but he's never risked himself.'

Eddie had his hands clasped calmly before him. He was looking serenely down at the table, listening to what everyone had to say. Ilya looked at him, then at me. 'Perhaps, Bryce, no offense, little one, but perhaps you could take the next job,' he suggested. 'I think that this one is slightly too intense, and it's rather important… Eddie, what do you think?'

'I think…' Eddie raised his head and looked directly at me, his eyes bright with meaning, 'That Bidden makes an excellent point. Colt will do this… and he will do it alone.'

'Alone?' Ilya looked baffled.

'Yes,' murmured Eddie dreamily, 'Colt has to take full responsibility for something quite flamboyantly illegal. The only difficulty, as I see it, is that eight oils will not fit in his Fiesta…' He said the name like a curse, 'So, Bidden, he will take your car. You just got that new BMW, did you not? Give him the keys now, please.' With that, Eddie whipped out an emery board and began gently filing his manicured fingernails.

My hands were shaking as I programmed the Sat Nav. Breathe, I told myself. Knowing I could go to prison for years chilled my insides. The car door opened and I jumped as Eddie slid into the passenger seat, bringing the rain with him. He slammed the door and I stared at him, speechless. He looked beautiful, dressed all in grey, a string of light pink pearls sat in the hollow of his throat with co-ordinating pearl studs in his ears. He didn't look at me.

'I am coming with you,' he said softly, 'Because, I do not want anything to happen.' He did not elaborate. Eddie switched on the radio and turned it up to a volume that would make conversation, while not impossible, difficult. He also turned his body slightly away from me, staring out of the window. I got the message.

That drive to Bristol was one of the most stressful and awkward journeys I have made with him, and there have been a few like that. We arrived at the warehouse and a man in a black raincoat waved me around the back to park. I killed the engine and sat there for a moment. I looked over at Eddie. He caught my eye briefly, then subtly, he twitched his jacket up a tiny bit. I saw the gun for a fleeting second. The wind and rain were crying outside, and then someone rapped their knuckles sharply on my window. I looked at him in panic and he met my eyes properly. 'Go on,' he murmured, 'I have got you.'

Lying in bed that night, unable to sleep as adrenaline pulsed around my body, my thoughts were on Eddie. I kept hearing his words, 'I have got you…' I reached under my pillow and drew out my stolen photo of Eddie in his modelling days, held it up and studied it in the moonlight.

His dreamy, druggy eyes stared back at me, heavy-lidded and bruised with makeup. I groaned and turned my face to my pillow, as I imagined his lips, his fingers and his tongue… That night I dreamed that he was straddling me, cutting and slicing me all over my face and body. I woke to find I wasn't choking on my own blood, it was my tears. That summed Eddie up, for me; he was my fantasy and my nightmare, all rolled into one.

Chapter 17

Eddie

I flipped through the phone book until I found the number I was looking for. I drummed my fingers as it rang out; impatient. 'I visited one of the patients recently,' I said quickly. 'Jason Prescott.'

The nurse was friendly, and mentioned how pleased the staff had been that Jason had some new visitors. I listened as she told me more details of Jay's condition, and his dispiriting prognosis. "Brain injury." "Disability." "Permanent." Harsh, cruel words, but it was oddly comforting to hear the answers to many of the questions that had been torturing my mind. I gripped the phone tightly and felt thankful that no one could see me.

'Listen,' I said, after a while. I cleared my throat, which was feeling oddly hoarse. 'Whatever he wants; anything he needs. Get him some decent clothes, for God's sake. Buy him anything, and send the bills to me.' I gave my name and details of my bank. I could not bring myself to end the phone call. Everything felt to be of vital importance, as it was to be my last influence on Eel's life.

'About his magazines,' I said, half-whispering now, for I could hear voices in the hall. 'I saw them in his room, and they're not right. He's not into cars, none of that stuff. Jason loves horses, do you know that? He is crazy for them. Subscribe him to a proper racing horse magazine. Write this down.' I heard someone calling my name from the hall. 'Music is another thing,' I added hurriedly into the phone. 'Jason has the most horrible taste in music. Get him as much punk as you can lay your hands on. His favourites are Patti Smith and the Dickies, and he likes a bit of Velvet Underground; are you writing this down?'

The nurse interrupted me, 'Maybe you could bring some music with you next time you visit Jason,' she suggested. 'Or a list?'

I paused. 'No… I won't be visiting him again, but as I said, bill me. Don't be shy. Go wild with my money.' I hung up the phone and turned around just as Ilya put his head around the door.

'There you are,' he smiled.

'Hello.' I stretched my arms above my head. I hate you, oh, I fucking hate you, you told me he was dead, you took him away from me, I thought, yawning. I winked at Illy. 'Good day?'

Ilya did not answer. Instead, he closed the door behind him.

'You look tired,' he said, finally. 'You sleeping?'

I rubbed my eye. 'Like a baby.' Like hell.

'Nightmares?'

I swallowed. I knew why he was asking; when I lost Eel the first time, my breakdown started with vivid, violent night terrors. I almost wanted to tell Ilya what was happening now, that those dreams were back. But… I knew that he could not help me. 'No,' I said.

Ilya cleared his throat, 'I just want to say I'm… sorry, for what I said about Jason. That was out of order, I'm sorry.'

I stared at him. 'You think I am angry about that? It- I do not care about what you said!'

'But you seem… things haven't been right between us, ever since you saw Jason.'

I was incredulous. He seriously did not know why I was upset? 'Ilya,' I said quietly, 'You told me that Eel was dead. You let me think that I killed him. There is nothing you can say to me.'

His voice was high, pleading as I walked away. 'You were only twenty-one. I was trying to protect you.'

I closed my eyes. I could not cope with this much horror, not a second time. The memories I had so carefully smothered were rasping for breath again.

Later, upstairs in my room, my thoughts tumbled faster. Indistinct, overlapping voices droned and murmured in my head. 'Stop,' I whispered. The voices began to shout. I sat on my bed, pulled open a drawer in the bedside table and as I was rummaging, the door opened.

'Hi,' said Mischa, quickly closing the door behind him. He leaned against it and smiled. 'Hi,' he repeated. 'You okay, uncle?' I stared at him. It was like seeing a ghost. A beautiful, blond ghost.

I shook myself out of my trance. 'You should leave,' I murmured. 'Your father would-'

'I know.' Mischa started strolling around my room, picking things up and setting them down. He rubbed his thumb over a bronze statue of a horse that I bought for Jason, once upon a time…

'My Dad would go mad if he knew I was here, but, don't act like you don't want me here, uncle.'

He was wearing black. Jason always used to dress in black. I looked away because frankly, watching him was becoming unbearable. I said nothing at all, I simply willed him to leave. To detach myself, I began counting, slowly, in my head.

'You want me here, don't you?' Mischa persisted, as he flopped down beside me on my bed. I jumped up and made for the door. 'Hey,' he said. 'Hold on. I'm only joking. I just need a bit more money, if you have any… what are you doing, are you freaking out or something, uncle?'

I was leaning my forehead against the door frame, my eyes closed and

I was starting to hyperventilate slightly. 'You are Jason,' I whispered, into the wood. I thrilled myself, through my mad haze. Because it was almost like talking to Eel.

'What? I can't hear you.'

I stumbled into the bathroom and took some deep breaths.

'The thing is, uncle,' he continued calmly, following me into the bathroom, 'I kind of owe some people some money. I've got a situation, I need a bit of money and…'

'Mischa. You're Mischa. Ask your father.'

'Uncle, I can't.' He spread out his hands, 'It's to do with drugs. Okay? I was given a load of pills. I was meant to sell them all but I took millions of them myself and gave them to my friends and yeah, it was stupid but… I wasn't thinking, and now… some people want more money than I've got.'

'Tell your father.'

'Uncle, I can't. I need it from you, and…'

'Leave me, Mischa.'

'… and if you don't give it to me, I'm gonna tell my dad what you've been up to. With me.'

My blood ran cold. 'I have done nothing-'

'But you want to, right? And he knows that. It's not that unbelievable, your last boyfriend was like, practically the same age as me. Who's my dad gonna believe? Me…' he looked into the bathroom mirror and smoothed his hair, '… or his freaky brother? Who likes dating guys my age and obviously fancies me?'

I sank onto the floor, my back to him. 'There is… I keep cash in the top left drawer of the dresser. I do not know how much is there, but have it. You did not have to say those things, I would have given you whatever you wanted, Jason.' From the bedroom where he was already rummaging in the drawer, he called, 'Who's Jason?'

I did not answer and seconds later, the bedroom door slammed. Mischa was gone. I stood up, threw open the bathroom cabinet and grabbed a pair of nail scissors. I held them open between my finger and thumb, on the fleshy part. I snipped. I bit my lip, my cheeks puffed out. I had forgotten how much cutting hurt. I flexed my thumb and the skin gaped, blood welling and dribbling out. I dug the scissors in and whining softly, I scraped deeply into the wound.

When I met Paul for lunch I was wearing black lace gloves. He reached across the table and touched them. 'Nice gloves,' he said shyly, 'You've got a mental dress sense. It's cool.'

'Thank you,' I replied. I flexed my hand subtly and all the wounds between my fingers opened up, sending an itchy trail of pain and discomfort up my arm. I did that every few minutes, it calmed me.

'French lace. They match my underwear.'

'Really?' Paul grinned excitedly, 'Not sure I believe you. You may have to show me.' How dull… I smiled anyway. I grabbed his hand under the table and pushed it up my skirt. While Paul pawed at me I stared across the room, bored.

'You okay? You don't seem very into this.' Paul was staring at me, stupid eyes drilling into me. 'You okay?' He repeated.

'Yes. Come here.' I grabbed him and kissed him, just to avoid looking at his face any more. My mind hammered a string of thoughts dribbling with anxiety… Jason… Jason… I kissed and kissed him, one gloved hand gently round his throat. My heart was drumming erratically.

'I love you man,' Paul mumbled between kisses. He did not notice that I was crying. I scrubbed my eyes viciously and something in my hand split open again, spewing fresh blood between my fingers.

'I am going to the bathroom,' I gasped. I jumped up and hurried into the toilet off the dining room, straight into the empty stall. I whipped out the little razor I was carrying, hiked up my skirt and made a quick slash, slash, slash on my thigh. One, two, three, quick like that. Blood curled down my leg. I watched it as my breathing evened out, and told myself very calmly but very firmly, Edvard, stop this right now. No more cutting. That is enough.

Chapter 18

Colt

It was Friday night and we were sat around the big table as usual. 'Is Eddie late again?' Complained Bidden.

'He's definitely not here yet,' said Manpyre, 'You would smell him coming.'

I threw Manpyre a look, but unfortunately he had a point. It wasn't hard to notice that Eddie's personal hygiene had rapidly deteriorated over the past few weeks. Strange, since he had always been so clean. I even remembered him taking cold baths in the attic when there had been nothing else to wash in. His dressing habits had changed, too. Eddie normally changed his clothes two or three times a day, but not anymore. He had been wearing the same grey, cashmere jumper for several days now. I suspected that he was sleeping in it. They were still laughing about him round the table.

'Boss,' said Luke, 'Can't you get Eddie to take a shower?'

'My brother's bathroom habits are none of my concern,' said Ilya crisply.

'Colt, then, you tell him.'

'Yeah,' laughed Bidden, 'Tell him his manly smell is giving you headaches and his stubble chafes when you kiss.'

'Shut up, Bidden,' said Manpyre.

I shook my head, 'Yeah, shut up... I don't know why you think I've got any influence over Eddie...'

'Oh, that's right.' Bidden grinned at me, 'He's got a new boyfriend now. You're not this month's pin-up, are you?'

I rolled my eyes, 'No...' as they all laughed. I didn't mind the teasing, really. They had all seen the infamous paintings of me and it remained a running joke.

'Damn right he's not,' said Manpyre, the only one who wasn't laughing.

At that moment he walked in. He was wearing that bloody same grey jumper, Versace sweatpants and carpet slippers that he had been wearing all week. He looked really bad, to be honest. He hadn't shaved and his eyeliner was smeared all around his eyes. He sat down next to Luke, who shifted his chair slightly away and made a face at Manpyre. Eddie wasn't looking at anyone. He was in a world of his own. In meetings, Eddie normally brought his sketchpad and sat doodling, but he would always listen sharply to everything being said. He missed nothing and he always contributed at the right places. Tonight was different. He just sat there staring dully at the table, his arms hanging limply by his sides. Ilya started the meeting and Eddie literally did not speak for the first hour. Ilya kept shooting anxious glances at him until finally he said, 'Edvard.'

There was a silence and everyone looked at him. He just sat there as if he hadn't heard, staring off into space.

'Edvard?'

I felt slightly desperate. 'Eddie?' I said quietly.

He looked up slowly and stared at me in confusion. Then he slowly turned to Ilya.

'That's it,' snapped Ilya, 'You're acting like a zombie. I think you need to go upstairs and lie down.' Eddie nodded sleepily and stood up unsteadily.

'Alright,' he said, then he looked me in this weird, unfocused way and said, 'Jason, are you coming with me?' I blinked in shock and Bidden muttered, 'Fu-cking hell…'

It was the first time he had really spoken to me in weeks. All I could think of to say was, 'I'm not Jason, mate. I'm Colt.'

His eyes cleared slightly and he looked around the table. 'Okay,' he said. 'Okay, yes.' He rubbed his unshaven face, 'Urgh. Sorry. I think I will go to have a lie down, actually.' Ilya went with him. As soon as they were gone, Manpyre sat back in his chair and said, in a satisfied kind of way, 'He's going mental again.'

'He probably just has a fever, high temperature,' I said, chewing the skin around my thumb. 'That can make you, ah, hallucinate. Get confused.'

'Nope. Mental,' said Manpyre. 'Don't forget, we know what it looks like. We saw it first time round.'

'Yeah,' said Will, 'He is mad. It doesn't go away. It's always there in your brain, ready to blow up into another meltdown.'

'Once a psycho, always a psycho,' agreed Bidden.

'That just isn't true,' I said. But I was worried.

After the meeting I went to the hotel bar with a book I was reading. A few of the other guys were heading out to the Straight Rain, but I didn't fancy it. I liked spending my Friday nights curled up on this big red leather armchair with my nose in a book, half-watching the TV by the bar. It was just busy enough that I could enjoy a bit of people-watching, but it was also a nice solitary way to wind down after a hard week.

Someone waved at me from the bar; Eddie's boyfriend, Paul Russell.

'Hi, Colt,' he said. He knew all of us who worked in the hotel and was a nice enough guy. 'What are you drinking, mate?' He came over to sit with me. 'I'm waiting for Eddie,' he explained, 'We're going to the theatre to see some Russian language play.'

'Sounds like his kind of thing.'

We chatted for a while, passing time. Paul told me about a crime novel he had written, and he invited me to his book launch in two weeks' time. I gave him a non-committal "yeah, probably."

Paul looked at his watch, 'He's cutting it fine, to be honest. The play starts at eight.' He smiled, 'You know Eddie, he's probably agonising over the right pair of earrings.'

Not likely. 'Paul?' I said. 'Eddie was a bit... ill, at a staff meeting earlier. Maybe he's too sick to go to the theatre.'

'Oh? Well... is he alright? Ill in what way?'

I shrugged, 'I dunno, he got dizzy or something... he's been acting a bit funny lately. Haven't you noticed?'

Paul thought for a moment, 'I suppose he hasn't perhaps quite been himself... oh, here he is, now.' Eddie had stomped in. He was wearing this fur coat, and I bet that I could guess what he still had on underneath. He had brushed his hair but his makeup was still a mess. I felt so sorry for him. He was obviously trying to pull himself together, but he was clearly in such a state that he just couldn't manage it. Paul stood up.

'We'd better go. Nice speaking to you, Colt. Have a good night.' He touched the sleeve of Eddie's coat. 'Won't you be hot in this, love?'

Eddie gave him a cold look and just said, 'No.'

Paul raised his eyebrows and shrugged. 'Okay.' He glanced at me, 'See you then, Colt.'

Eddie whipped around and his eyes found me, as if noticing me for the first time. He stood there just staring at me. I stared back warily, my heart speeding up. 'I know what you are doing. You little cunt,' he said quietly. My mouth fell open.

'Jesus, Eddie- what was that for?' Cried Paul, bewildered. Eddie bared his teeth at me.

'He is reading,' he seethed. 'He is mocking Jason, Jason cannot read anything and this little bastard is sitting there reading some fucking... he is fucking with me, Paul-'

'Come on.' Paul had his hands buried in the sleeve of the fur coat, gently trying to tug Eddie out of the bar. 'Come on, let's go. I don't know what this is about, I dunno who Jason is, Eddie...?'

Eddie threw me another look of pure disgust and left the bar. Paul looked at me, held up his hands. 'Sorry. I don't know what that was all…'

'Paul!' Screamed Eddie from outside.

'Colt- I have to go. I'm sorry. I'll talk to him.'

I looked at the same page of my book until the words blurred together. I felt shaken and oddly, I started to wish that Manpyre and the others would come back from the pub.

Chapter 19

Colt

The day had started normally enough. I spent the morning washing the inside windows on the second and third floors. It was a big job, and a messy one. I had just started on the window in the music room, a small room beside the library. It contained a piano, a harp and a shelf of music books. I sloshed water over the window, careful not to splash the piano, then I got my squeegee and started to wipe down the glass. As I was wiping, I heard a weird noise. I lowered my squeegee and listened. All I could hear was my own breathing. I raised my hand again and paused. That noise… a human sound, a shout. It lasted for the briefest of seconds, coming from the next room, the library. I dropped my squeegee into the bucket and walked tentatively into the corridor, listening. I hesitated outside the library with my hand on the door. Raised voices, followed by a loud scraping sound of heavy furniture being moved. Another terrified shout; I pushed open the door.

The heavy curtains were drawn, and the library was in darkness. As my eyes adjusted to the shadows I saw dozens of books swept from their shelves and scattered everywhere. Several chairs were knocked over. A voice was raised and pleading. 'Stop it. Please, it's not funny. Get away from me. Stop!'

I ran into the middle of the library. For a few moments I simply stared, struggling to process the scene before my eyes. Paul Russell was pinned up against one of the stacks of books. Eddie was standing behind him ripping at his clothes and laughing a little as Paul struggled pointlessly against him. His laughter had a weird, distracted quality. He seemed to be in some kind of physical frenzy but his eyes were dark and calm.

'Eddie!' I was genuinely shocked. 'Stop!'

Eddie turned slightly, one arm around Paul's waist. He turned his head towards me, his eyes large and unfocused.

Paul struggled. 'Get him off of me,' he shouted. 'Animal!'

Eddie's eyes narrowed. 'Animal…? I will show you an animal,' he growled, and ripping Paul's shirt open from the collar he sank his teeth deeply into his pale, freckled shoulder.

Paul screamed loudly, 'Oh God… oh Christ get him off me! Ahh!'

'Enough!' I yelled. 'Enough, stop! Eddie!'

Eddie pushed Paul away from him. Blood poured from his lips. Paul ran to where I stood, a safe distance from Eddie. He clutched his shoulder and felt the blood there.

'Psycho,' he declared hoarsely. He pointed his bloody fingers at Eddie in disbelief. 'You're a psycho, man.'

'You were just getting what you asked me for,' snapped Eddie. He pulled his hand down his face and flicked sweat from his fingers.

'Not like that, you nut job. We were having a laugh, fooling around in here, then he goes… berserk, starts attacking me.' Paul squeezed his shoulder and sucked his breath through his teeth. 'Ah. You bastard, Eddie.'

'Well this is me, Paul,' he said bitterly, pacing up and down the stacks, dragging books onto the floor, 'This is what I do, so if you don't like it you can fuck off.'

'Don't worry about that, mate,' Paul snapped.

I kept staring at Eddie apprehensively. He was like a dangerous animal, pacing back and forth. He grabbed some more books and flung them onto the floor.

'Fucks sake, Paul, it's just a bit of fun,' he said quietly, angrily. 'What's wrong with me giving you what you asked me for?'

Paul snorted in disbelief, and I spoke for him. 'You can't treat people like that. I'm sure he didn't want you to hurt him; to be so rough with him.' I swallowed an inexplicable lump in my throat. 'What's happening to you?'

Eddie's eyes narrowed. He was beside me in two strides, bearing down on me. He took my hair gently in both of his hands and held on, pushing his face close to mine. 'Stop talking,' he whispered.

My knees wobbled. 'Stop it. You promised you would never hurt me.'

'Do I look like the sort of person who keeps promises?' Eddie laughed bitterly and pushed me away from him, tears in his angry eyes. 'Go on- get the hell out of here. Both of you.'

'Eddie! I can help you. You're not well.'

'Get out! I don't want to hurt you.'

'I can help you. Calm down, and let me help you. Talk to me.' I held out my hands soothingly. Eddie glared at me, then he suddenly he grabbed my wrists and yanked me forward. I didn't flinch, but looked steadily at him, my heart pounding. Eddie's chest heaved with emotion.

'You kids- think you are so superior to Jason. You-' he jerked his head towards Paul. 'All you do is go to parties and write trash. You think you're better than Jason. You are nothing.'

'Who the hell is this Jason?' Cried Paul, bewildered. I was trembling in his grip.

'Eddie, no one thinks that. Calm down.'

Eddie glared at me, his teeth glinting as if he meant to bite me, too. 'You.' he whispered to me, spitting, 'You are the worst of all. You are

147

wasting everything that Jason lost, and I hate you for that.' He hit me hard in the mouth with the back of his fist. There was a silence. I felt my legs give way a little, but I was being held standing. I stumbled, and Eddie steadied me. Small white lights were erupting all over my field of vision. I could feel blood sucking through my teeth. I was vaguely aware of Paul, backing into the doorway.

'Bloody hell- I'm sorry, man.' Paul turned and ran. Alone now, I struggled to focus my eyes.

'Don't, Eddie,' I said groggily. Eddie hit me again, harder, and I fell, first to my knees then backwards against the stack, losing consciousness.

I struggled to lift my head; it felt heavy. I opened my eyes and blinked, my vision was all red and green flecks. Everything looked all blurred and indistinct; it took a few moments before I realised that my glasses were smashed. Removing them with trembling fingers, I noticed Eddie sitting against the opposite stack, watching me, tears running down his face. In his hand he held a long silver blade; a letter-opener. He was digging the pointed blade into his own arm.

'Get out of here,' he wept. 'Go on, get out.'

I managed to drag myself into a sitting position. 'Eddie, let me get help. You're not well.'

He dropped his head, crying. The bright daylight streaming through the window hurt my eyes as I stumbled out of the library. I cradled my forehead on one hand, feeling sick and a little dizzy. The flavour of blood in my mouth sharpened my senses. I leant my head on the banister, shaking violently, willing myself to take deep, shuddering breaths. What I had witnessed had frightened me. That dead, blank look in his eyes. The blade; the self-inflicted wound.

'Bryce?'

I looked up wearily.

'I've been looking for you. What's the matter? Your nose is bleeding. Your mouth is bleeding!' Ilya looked sharply at me. Two guests appeared behind Ilya and made to go into the library. I sprang to the door and stood before it.

'I'm sorry,' I croaked, dizziness pulsing in my head, 'The library is closed just now. It... It's being cleaned.' I felt a trickle of warm blood from my nose. I smeared it quickly as the mortified guests hurried away.

'Bryce!' Ilya snapped, 'What is going on?' More hotel guests were appearing in the corridor. Ilya grabbed me by the neck and made to push me into the privacy of the library. I honestly felt like I was about to black out.

'No!' I gasped.

'What do you mean, no? Get in there; people are looking,' shushed Ilya.

'No, sir, it's Eddie.' I hesitated. My boss's face turned expressionless. Immediately, he drew out his master key and locked the library door.

'Tell me,' he said.

I was sent to clean myself up while Ilya went in to the library to tend to his brother. I washed my face as quickly as I could, popped a couple of paracetamol and hurried back to the library. The door was wide open. Ilya was directing two chambermaids in tidying up.

'Just throw away all of these spoiled books,' he was saying. 'Thankfully, he has not chosen to bleed on anything irreplaceable.' The maids, wearing plastic gloves, were tossing the books into a plastic bag. I stared.

'There's so much blood...' At the sound of my voice, Ilya looked around.

'Bryce.' He led me out into the corridor and spoke in a low voice. 'Yes, it is awful. He was damaging himself with a letter knife, and he found some scissors, too. He will need...' Ilya coughed gently and looked away, '... stitches.'

'Oh no.'

'I know... he is in his bedroom now, resting. Bidden is guarding his bedroom door, I don't want him coming out of there and scaring the guests.'

Manpyre appeared on the landing. 'Sorry to interrupt,' he said. 'You asked to see me, boss?'

'Mm. Need you to take care of something; Paul Russell.'

'Eddie's guy, the journalist?'

'Yes…' Ilya held Manpyre's gaze and something significant passed between them. 'My brother is not in his right mind… Christ knows what his pillow talk has been like. Paul Russell may have seen some things, heard some things. He ought to keep those things to himself. If he writes anything, he loses fingers, all of them. Make sure he won't write, scare him, show him I am serious.'

Manpyre nodded. 'Consider it done.' His gaze fell on me, 'Oh shit, look at you. You alright, mate?' I bit my lip, nodded and looked away. Before he could fuss anymore over my battered face, Bidden suddenly appeared, a little bit out of breath.

'Sir,' he said, then paused. One look at his expression told me that something was seriously wrong. There was horror etched across his face and his shoulders sagged. 'It's Eddie.'

I ran past them, to Eddie's room. The door was open. Will and Luke were standing in the doorway open-mouthed, staring into the room. Will turned to me wordlessly and I pushed past them.

'Eddie, no, no, no,' I murmured, my heart free-falling as I dropped to my knees beside him, my jeans crunching on shards of a shattered mirror. He was kneeling too, his face white and pattering blood onto the carpet. I put my hands on his face and pressed my forehead to his, I didn't care that Will and Luke were watching.

'What have you done to yourself?' I whispered. I prised a greasy, blood-dulled slice of broken mirror from his shaking fingers and threw it onto the bed.

'His arms are completely fucked,' observed Will, from the doorway.

'And his face,' added Luke shakily, 'He did that to his own… face…'

'Yeah? Call a fucking ambulance, then,' I snapped. 'Don't just stand there.' I tried to look at Eddie's face but he continued to avert his eyes. He just kept staring at his own lacerated arms, slippery with several ribbony cuts.

Chapter 20

Colt

We were standing in the corridor outside Eddie's bedroom. Ilya was behaving practically, yet tiny signs indicated that he was every bit as worried as I was. He repeatedly drummed his long fingers on the banister. Occasionally, he touched his temple, then quickly took his hand back down. These tiny clues were all that he would reveal. 'Eddie's psychiatrist is coming here,' he murmured.

'Psychiatrist? Ilya,' I tried to level my voice, 'Eddie is raving. We would be lucky if a psychiatrist doesn't section him.'

Ilya looked distracted. 'No. No, you do not understand. Eddie has put me through this before.' He paused and corrected himself, 'I should say we, as a family, have been through this before. The doctor that is coming, knows Eddie, he treated him when he was younger, after, you know, his accident. He is a good doctor.'

I swallowed. 'I'm sure he is. I'm sure he's a great doctor. But Eddie doesn't need a psychiatrist. He needs someone to stitch up his arms, and I can do that.'

'Bryce-'

'We don't need to involve a shrink!'

'Bryce! Listen to me, you are not a doctor. I know you know the basics and can patch people up, but this is my brother. He just tore his face open. You couldn't possibly stitch his face anyway, that type of thing is too delicate.'

I shook my head, frustrating mounting. 'Okay. So I'm not an expert. Worst-case scenario? He might be left with a few scars,' I said nastily. 'A fancy psychiatrist is going to take one look at him and pack him off to an asylum. Do you want that?'

Ilya looked at me, and looked away.

I swallowed. 'Sir, I can do it. I'll do it quick, and clean. And I'm sure I can calm him down, I'm his best friend. Give me a chance, please.'

Eddie was in bed, lying there in the darkness. I perched on the edge of his bed and looked down at him. The scarred left side of his face was visible, the newly slashed right side turned to the pillows. Blood stains were streaked all over the pillowcases. I felt guilty, as though I was prying, looking at those disfiguring scars so closely. For one thing, I was unused to seeing Eddie without makeup, looking so plain and vulnerable. He was unshaven, deep grooves pulled down the corners of his mouth, and his forehead was heavily lined. He looked tired, old. His arms lay on top of the blankets, a raw mess of ragged, open flesh. At the sight of the wounds I had a momentary crisis of confidence in my own ability to repair such damage. While I was thinking it through, Eddie turned his head and opened his eyes fully, showing that he had been awake the whole time. 'You should not be here,' he whispered.

'I thought you were sleeping.' I was fighting an urge to jump to my feet and run.

His face looked horrific; Horror-movie horrific. He had put the mirror in his mouth and given himself a fish-hook cut, splitting his cheek wide open. I wanted to cry. I was glad that the room was kind of dark. Eddie looked at me blankly. His right eyelashes were clumped with dried black blood.

'You should go.' His speech was a little slurred, which was understandable. I forced myself to stay sitting.

'Let me put a couple of stitches in your arms, just to close up those cuts.'

'No.'

'Come on. Come on, Eddie… you know they have to be sorted out.'

'I know. I am saying I do not want you to do it.'

'Listen.' I leaned into him and spoke in a lower voice. 'Some psychiatrist is on his way over here, and-'

He looked at me interestedly; eyebrows raised a fraction. 'Bell?'

'Yeah- something like that. But anyway, if you let me tidy up your arms and just relax a little, we can send him away. We can tell him you're resting?'

Eddie closed his eyes and nestled his head back against the pillows. 'No, I want to see him. Tell Ilya to send him to me the moment he arrives.'

I paused in confusion. Clearly, he didn't understand. 'I don't think it's a good idea at all, mate. You are ill, but you're going to get better. And I'll be right here to help-'

'Shut up,' croaked Eddie. He opened his eyes and stared unblinkingly at me. 'You- you do not know what I have done. You have no idea what I am capable of so, stop being so fucking nice to me.' When he said 'fucking' it came out sounding like 'sucking' because of his cut mouth. He held my frightened stare, and finally looked away, his eyes damp. 'I have been hurting men. Paul… and others.' He stared straight ahead as he spoke. 'I go out, I meet men and I hurt them. Every time I feel lust for someone- I compare them to… him. And I want to harm them. I want- to hurt you.' His wet, tortured eyes shifted back to me. 'I've been fighting it. I don't want it to be you, or…' he fell silent. He didn't need to finish his sentence; we both knew exactly who else he meant. 'Get away from me, please. I am going to lose control if you do not. I cannot help it, and you are tempting me.' He was still speaking in a harsh whisper. I sat there dumbly, my mouth dry. Although I heard what he was saying, I could scarcely process it and I began to speak again, falteringly, but Eddie's face darkened.

'How much fucking clearer do I have to be?' He threw back his bedclothes and jumped out of bed, veins jutting from his pallid skin. I jumped up, not quick enough to get out of harm's way. Instinctively I threw my arms over my head, however Eddie seized me by my upper arm. I felt myself being literally marched to the door, which Eddie duly flung open.

'Will someone just get me my fucking psychiatrist?' He roared as he shoved me bodily out of the room, so hard that I hit the banister and fell to the floor at the top of the stairs. Manpyre rushed forward to help me up.

'You mad bastard,' he spat at Eddie, doing a theatrical double-take at Eddie's face. Eddie's arms were still dripping with blood, which he had accidentally smeared on to his forehead. Everyone in the vicinity took a step back, just as Ilya and Dr Bell reached the top of the stairs. The psychiatrist regarded him over the top of his glasses.

'I hope this is my patient,' he said, 'Otherwise I shall be in for a busy night.'

Dr Bell did not section Eddie, of course. Ilya was paying him well for his services, and besides, Eddie calmed down greatly after his two-hour consultation with the specialist. One of Bell's colleagues had come to the hotel and had just finished stitching Eddie's wounds. I was sitting in the card room with Ilya and Manpyre. To my irritation, Manpyre kept touching me. He had one hand on my knee, which he was rubbing in slow, annoying circles, and the other was stroking my face, 'Poor little guy,' he said.

'Shh. I'm fine,' I shushed him, shifting my leg away. I was trying to listen to what the doctor was saying about Eddie.

'I have increased Edvard's dose of anti-depressant,' said Bell, handing Ilya a signed prescription. 'I will come back in two weeks to see how he is getting on. There are one or two other medications I would be willing to try if we have no success with this one.' Ilya folded the prescription into his inner pocket.

'Thanks, Doctor. And thank you again for coming so quickly.'

'Hang on,' I interjected, 'Since when has Eddie been on anti-depressants?'

'Since he was twenty-one?' Ilya looked at me strangely. 'I thought you were his buddy, did he not tell you he was on medication?'

I bit my lip. 'No.'

Bell was looking at me now, too. 'Ah, yes,' he said softly, 'Am I right in thinking that you are Bryce?'

I nodded dumbly, and the doctor placed a hand on my shoulder, looking not at me, but at Ilya. 'Edvard has specifically requested that this young man be kept away from him while he is ill. And, while I would never break patient confidentiality, I will say that... based on my long conversation with Edvard, I agree with him. It is important that Bryce does not go near Edvard, for his own safety.'

'Fine,' said Ilya briskly. 'Bryce? I mean it this time. I had better not catch you anywhere near him.'

Manpyre draped his arm around my shoulders. 'Don't worry boss, I'll look after him.' He snaked his arms around my waist and weirdly, even though it was Dave, I didn't want him to let go of me. I'd had a fair few shocks that day and it felt nice having someone give me a hug.

Manpyre walked me back to my room, and he asked if he could come in to have a word with me. I threw myself on my bed, craving sleep.

'What is it, Dave?' I yawned. I was so tired from all that had happened. Manpyre sat in my armchair. He picked up the photo on my bedside table, (my brothers at Disneyland) and examined it.

'Right,' he said, setting it down, 'There's something I need to tell you. Eddie's a lot more dangerous than you give him credit for.'

I ran my tongue round the inside of my cut lip. 'Yeah,' I said, thinking, well, duh.

'He's ill,' continued Manpyre, 'He is mentally ill. He could really hurt you, mate, you understand?'

I shrugged, then looked in surprise at how stressed he seemed. 'I know,' I said faintly. 'What's the big deal? I know.'

'You don't.' Manpyre rubbed his face. 'How could you possibly know what he's capable of?' He sat back in his chair. 'Eel Prescott didn't get hurt in any riding accident. Eddie beat him. He beat him so badly that… well, you've seen him. Eddie did that to him, Colt.'

'No way,' I said flatly.

'He did, mate.' Manpyre was speaking softly, taking hold of my hands. 'I know that it's a shock for you but… it's true.'

I was shaking. I brought my hands up to my face, 'He wouldn't do that,' I trembled, knowing full well that Eddie would, that he had. I pictured him with Paul's blood on his bared teeth. 'How could he do it?' I dissolved into tears.

'Because he's mad and dangerous. They had a fight and Eel came off worse. I didn't want to tell you, mate. But I can see you getting closer to him, which is one thing… and now that he's ill again… he could kill you, easily mate. If he lost his temper with you… I don't want…' Manpyre stopped abruptly. He swallowed and added, 'I don't want anything to happen to you.' I was squeezing Manpyre's hands, tears pouring down my face. Maybe I was in shock, but I just kept picturing Jason Prescott doing his jigsaws in hospital for sixteen years and right at that moment I never wanted to see Eddie again.

Chapter 21

Eddie

It had been quiet for a long time, maybe days. I rolled over in bed, my fingers closing around a small plastic bottle. New anti-depressants. So, I was still crazy. Nothing was new. My eyes felt sticky from falling asleep in tears. My mouth felt dry and my arms were stinging. I reached up and gently touched my cheek, tracing my fingertip along one of the six new cuts I had made across my own face. I decided there and then that, if possible, I would never look in a mirror again.

I sat up slowly, my head throbbing, and risked a look at my arms. I had no idea what time of the day or night it was. My arms resembled sewn-up meat. Bright blue stitches jagged through the swollen, bruised flesh. I sighed and let my head drop back on to the pillows. 'Bryce,' I said aloud. My voice was a dry croak. I needed water, but I needed Colt more than anyone could ever need water. I sat up, stared out of the window and began forming plans in my mind. I knew that I had to leave as soon as possible. But first, there was someone that I quite desperately needed to see, one last time. I made myself get out of bed, put on a silk dressing gown and sat holding my head in my hands. There came a light knocking on the door, and as I croaked, 'No, do not come in,' the door opened. I looked up. 'Sasha... oh, darling, not right now, please.' I clutched the gown to the lacerated side of my face and stood up.

Sasha came into the room and closed the door gently behind her.

'It's okay. Uncle Eddie.' She came right up to me and wrapped her arms around my waist. The top of her head only came up to my chest. 'Bryce told me what happened. Don't be mad at him for telling me. He's really worried.' After a moment, I found myself gratefully hugging her back. This warm young person in my arms was incredibly comforting. I felt her small hand reaching up to my face, sweeping my hair back. 'You poor thing,' she murmured.

She did not seem horrified or afraid. Even though she was only a little girl, I reasoned, she was also partly Eel, my bold, brave hero. She stayed with me for a couple of hours and I appreciated that she did not ask me questions about what had happened. She was just a comforting presence. First, she washed away all the bits of gore from my hair and eyelashes that the surgeon had not bothered to clean. Then she brushed my hair and got out my makeup. As she applied it for me, I stared helplessly at her, feeling like a child being tended to by his mother. It was not an unpleasant feeling. 'Look up,' she said, and I obeyed as she swept on some mascara. 'There. You still look gorgeous. You always do.' She smiled.

'You are a good girl,' I murmured, thinking about Jason.

Sasha made to leave, promising to come back up later in the day. Before she left, I simply could not resist asking her, 'Where is Bryce? What is he doing?'

'He has the afternoon off... I think he's with David Manpyre, I saw them together earlier in reception.'

I began to tidy away the makeup, careful not to look at her. I knew how

158

upset Colt would be feeling, how easy it would be for Manpyre to take control of the situation, to manipulate Colt's vulnerability. It did not bear thinking about, so with effort, I stopped dwelling on it.

'And where is Mischa?'

'Still at school. His school doesn't break up for half-term until next week.'

I stayed in my room all day, and Sasha had not come back by evening. I was hungry, but I did not want to speak to any room service staff. I tried to phone my brother to ask for a meal to be sent up. He did not answer the phone in his suite, nor in his office. Perhaps unwisely, I staggered into the corridor in my dressing gown, with a scarf wrapped around my face. Ilya's rooms were only at the other end of the corridor and I made my way by feeling along the wall for support.

'Oh-' Suddenly Colt was there, stepping out of the lift. He flinched, looked as if he meant to run. Instead, he shoved his hands in the pocket of his blue hooded sweatshirt and looked up in anguish at my face, torn apart as it was. I looked down at the floor. Then Manpyre appeared behind him. He put both hands on Colt's shoulders and threw me a haughty look.

'Crawl back to your room, Freddy Krueger,' he sneered.

I waited for Colt to say something in my defence, but he did not. Manpyre resolved my confusion. 'I told him what you did to Prescott. He's fucking terrified of you, so just do one, right?'

Oh God. Oh, no. I felt dizzy. 'Colt?' I whispered.

Colt looked uncomfortable. 'You lied to me,' he murmured. 'You said it was a riding accident.'

He had only heard Manpyre's version of events and I had no energy, no heart, to give him mine.

'Yes,' I said. I tugged down my scarf to show him the full extent of my injuries in the light of day.

His face paled, while Manpyre studied me mockingly and whistled, 'Oh, fuck... no more modelling for you, eh?'

'Oh, Eddie...' said Colt. His eyes filled with tears of sympathy.

'Come on,' I said, feeling like crying, myself. 'Tell me, what do you think of me now?'

He shook his head. 'I don't know what I think of you.' He looked wretched. He was not being malicious at all, I could see that.

Manpyre pulled him gently away, away from me. 'Come on,' he said softly. 'Come on, mate.'

I staggered back to my room and lay on the floor, sobbing. The look in Colt's eyes... true, he knew nothing of the circumstances, but still. I saw reflected in my best friend's eyes what I already knew; that what I did to Eel was truly unforgivable.

There was a soft knocking on the door and my head snapped up.

'Eddie,' said a gentle voice, 'Eddie, it's Colt.' I clamped my teeth into my hand to stop myself from answering. 'I know you're there,' he said, just loudly enough. 'I'm sorry about before... I know there must be more to the story than what Dave said. You loved Jay, what you did must have been part of your illness, I guess?'

My teeth snapped through the skin on my hand.

'We can talk about it all when you're better... I just want you to know that I'm still... I don't think you're a monster. I forgive you for everything.' At that, I stood up. He did not know anything. A surge of cold rage made my skin prickle. I had damaged Jason's brain. It was an insult to Jason for anyone to stand there and to 'forgive' me for it. Forgiveness? That was about Colt's own Christian sense of righteousness, nothing to do with Jason, or me. The sanctimonious little cunt, who was he to forgive me? The darkness seized my heart. I lurched across the room, wrenched open the door... he was gone. Thank God he was gone, because my rage might have killed him. Oh, God help me. The heat of my anger melted from my bones and I fell against the door frame, knowing that for Colt's safety, I must leave Lake Martin at once.

The next morning I dressed myself slowly. I put a few precious items into my bag, and then I made myself walk out of my suite, down the main stairs and out into the white hot daylight, the heat prickling my skin. My medication made my skin photo-sensitive. I jumped into the shade of my car and drove off.

Radiating false confidence, I approached the reception desk. A red-haired young lady looked up and her smile faltered at the sight of me. 'Hello, I wonder if it would be at all possible to disturb Mischa Bodansky from his class. I'm his uncle… I'm afraid there is a family emergency.' I flipped my driver's license to her. The secretary nodded quickly, stealing a horrified glance at my face as she handed it back. She was, no doubt, wondering about my stitches and why I was so hideously disfigured. I gestured to my face. 'I just had an operation,' I offered by way of explanation. She picked up her telephone. 'Of course, Mr Bodansky. Please sit down while I telephone Mischa's form tutor, to find out which class he is in just now.'

I took a seat, asking myself what I was doing. I need to see him again. I need to see Eel in him, I need to pretend that he is Eel; for an hour, for an afternoon. Better than that, I would take him to Stockholm, to my little gallery. He would adore Sweden; Eel had been looking forward to going there so much. He just never got a chance before I smashed his head in.

I opened my eyes and breathed more slowly, noticing the secretary staring at me. I grinned at her and she returned my smile very uneasily. Closing my eyes again, I let myself drift into thought. Mischa was Eel. He was him, and that meant he belonged to me.

The phone in reception rang, jerking me out of my reverie. 'Mr Bodansky?' Called the secretary. 'Your nephew is on his way down now.' I nodded, then suddenly it occurred to me that whatever I was doing was ridiculous. What was I doing, transferring my obsession for Eel onto his eighteen-year-old, heterosexual son? I stood up and walked out of the building, hands in my pockets, head down, past the astonished secretary. I was in my car, smoking. Or trying to smoke. It was agony on my mouth and I could not get an adequate seal around the cigarette. Suddenly, Mischa walked out of the building. I hunched down in my seat, even though the car was out of his sight. I took another messy drag of smoke, watching

Mischa. He scanned the car park, his lovely eyes raking over every car. I was so tempted to get out, to go out and get him. He looked confused, turned to go back into the building.

Impulsively, I jumped out of the car, 'Mischa!' My cigarette fell from my lips, in catching it, I burned my finger. 'Ah. Fuck,' I swore, shaking my hand. He was crossing the car park towards me; hands shoved low into his blazer pockets, scowling as usual, with his shoulders self-consciously hunched.

'What are you doing here, freak?' He spat at me. He looked at me properly for the first time and did a double-take. 'What the hell happened to your face?' I could not speak, I was watching his lips, thinking that he was such a harsh person. Physically, he looked just like a perfect version of Jason. 'Well?' He said, forcefully, his lip curling as he studied my latest disfigurements. 'This had better be good. I'm phoning Dad anyway, he'll kill you for coming to my school.' Mischa jerked his head towards my cigarette, held out his hand. 'Give me one of those,' he ordered. I did, and watched him light it. I was… entranced. He sucked on it quickly and blew out the smoke right away, into my face. 'So? Why are you here?' His chin jutted out confrontationally, his dramatic eyes hostile. My heart was thudding. He was beautiful beyond words. I could live with the rest. Yes, Mischa was a poor substitute. But he would have to do. I was craving Jason now, and one way or another, I was going to get my hit.

'Come sit in the car with me, and I will tell you why I'm here.'

He sat there in my Jag, smoking, coughing, and flipping through my CDs with distain. 'Lame; lame; gay,' he sighed. 'You are such a loser, you know that?'

'Your father never used to think so.'

'My Dad hates you. You're an embarrassment to him.' Mischa looked at his watch, a Rolex. 'You know, I'm only sitting here because I'm missing my Physics lesson. You have, like, twenty minutes until my next class. It's music production. I like music. Good music; you wouldn't know.' Mischa promptly switched on the car radio. 'Radio 4? Whatever.' He began tuning it then, glanced at me out the corner of his eye. 'Stop staring at me. What are you doing here, anyway?'

I did not answer because I simply could not. We sat there, listening to the radio. It started to rain.

I watched his hand, fiddling with the radio controls. He had large hands, like Jason's. Jason used to wear lots of silver jewellery, and I wondered vaguely what had happened to it when he went into hospital. It was probably in a box file somewhere, labelled with his name. What an image; a personality in a box. What about his piercings? He used to have so much metal in his beautiful face. It was not my thing, but that was Jason. They must have picked it all out when he first went in to hospital.

I hated that thought; a nurse, carefully removing his eyebrow piercings and gently tugging the metal ring out of his unconscious lip. What about his other piercings, the ones in his body? They must have removed those, too, leaving him plain, the way nature intended, but not the way he intended himself; his autonomy, sloughed away. They were only piercings, I knew that, but, oh, God, he was a person! He did not even like car magazines. I felt like screaming until my throat burned raw… oh, Christ…no. Enough. Breathe.

Mischa's hand looked just like Eel's, with that well-remembered dusting of fine, blond hair on the fingers.

'Let go. Let go of my hand.' He sat frozen still. We both stared at my hand, clutching his so hard that my knuckles and his fingers were white. I barely remembered how I came to be holding it.

'Let go,' he whispered. 'Now. Now, please.'

I looked at him, as though I was in a trance. He was pale, and his lip trembled.

'Just listen,' I said. My voice seemed to come from far away. 'Shut up and listen for once in your life. I need to tell you this. Just listen. Do not waste what you have. You are special, you hear me? You have something special. Please do not waste your life. You could be a wonderful person.'

He looked terrified and I continued desperately, 'Ilya is not your real dad. Your father is someone else, someone wonderful and what I am saying is, you do not have to be the way you are. I know what else is inside

163

you; I know what you could be. You could be just like him. You could be Jason…' I had my hand on his face now, stroking his skin. 'Baby,' I said, my voice cracking as he pulled away from me, 'I love you. Jason, baby, I missed you so much. I love you.'

'Let go of me you freak! Help!' Mischa screamed hoarsely, and he hit the car horn with his free hand. I let go of his hand, covered my face with my own. What was I doing? Mischa jumped out of the car and I watched him running towards the building, blazer flying. I spun my wheels as I got the hell out of there.

I was a mile down the road before I realised I was crying; all these big fucking tears just streaming down my face.

Chapter 22

Colt

Ilya took the hysterical phone call from Mischa, and the whole place went into an uproar. Ilya wanted both twins brought home immediately, so I was being sent to Sasha's school to fetch her, while Ilya decided that he would drive to collect Mischa personally. I was summoned to Ilya's office to get the directions to Sasha's school. When I arrived, Ilya was speaking on the phone. He glanced up when Manpyre brought me in, and motioned for me to sit. He looked dreadful.

'Do not let him out of your sight until I arrive. I don't pay you for him to come to any- I don't care. I don't care what your policy is… stand outside of his room, then. Do not let him out of your sight or I will sue you so fast, your feet won't touch the ground.' He hung up, and began quizzing me about where Eddie might have gone. He had apparently turned up at Mischa's school and then tried to drag him into his car. He had scared the life out of the kid. I hated to admit it, but it sounded completely plausible, given Eddie's state of mind.

'Mischa's terrified. Not only that, but Edik's been telling him things, making up things about our family... oh, I could kill my brother, Bryce. I know he's sick, but why must he poison the whole family?'

'So, he told Mitch about Jason Prescott.'

Ilya looked up at me mournfully, his eyes searching my face. 'How much do you know?'

I didn't answer, and he looked away from me.

'Everything,' he surmised bitterly.

He sent me to fetch Sasha from pony club and, once she was in the car and I had reassured her that Mischa was alright, I didn't know what to tell her. One look at her told me I couldn't lie. Honesty had done me no favours thus far, but I decided with Mischa knowing everything, there was nothing for it but the truth.

'Sash.' I stopped the car by the side of the road and just told her everything, about Eddie, Jason, their relationship, her father, her mother. I told her the whole story, and telling to someone was like a release for me.

'Just give me a minute, Bryce,' she said, holding up her hand. 'Just give me a moment to think.' She held her head up. 'I want to see him.' I looked at her, doubtfully but she was staring at the road ahead. Wordlessly, I put the car into gear and turned in the direction of the Harbour Centre.

Alex was standing in reception in her heeled leather boots, holding a cup of coffee and talking to one of the nurses. She looked up, saw Sasha and I. 'You,' she cried. She handed her coffee to the nurse, 'Hold this, or it'll end up all over him. You stupid little fool,' she exploded. 'I told you not to tell him. What did I say would happen?' I dropped my head. 'Bryce, what did I say would happen? I said that Eddie would visit him maybe once, mess with his head a little, then fuck off and abandon him. I know that bastard, I know him better than you do.' She broke off, glancing at Sasha. 'Hi, honey. This must be awfully weird for you, sweetie.'

'Yeah, just- please stop yelling at Bryce,' said Sasha.

'Sorry.' Alex took out a pack of cigarettes with a shaking hand. 'You thought you were doing the right thing. It's just, I wish you had listened. I know Eddie.' She went to light a cigarette.

'It's no smoking in here,' I said automatically. I bit my lip as she shot me a murderous glance, and shoved the cigarette and lighter back in her bag.

'Jason is just… in bits. Seeing Eddie has unsettled him; really unsettled him. Poor guy.'

The nurse recognised me. 'You're here to see Jason?'

I nodded. 'Yes. I brought someone else with me, if that's alright.' The nurse looked harassed.

'What are your names?'

We told her.

'Okay, Bryce. Since your last visit Jason's been having some problems. He has been incredibly anxious, okay? The only reason I'm going to let you see him today, is because I am willing to try anything to calm him down. Maybe he enjoyed your visit so much last time, he was sorry to see you go.'

She led us down towards Jason's room, explaining that they had had to remove most of the furniture, for everyone's safety. I felt a knot of trepidation as she reached for the door handle.

'Honey,' Alex said to Sasha, 'You stay back at first.' The room was bare. A plain mattress lay in the corner, and that was all. Jason was crouched in an opposite corner of the almost-bare room, rocking gently.

The nurse explained, 'He refuses to eat almost every meal. Screams hysterically in the night, just like he did when he first arrived all those years ago. Lately, he's been trying to leave, to run away, at every opportunity.'

I knelt down beside him. 'Jason?' He lifted his head. 'Remember me? Hey, it's alright, buddy. It's okay.' Jason took a deep breath, his eyelashes all clumped together from crying. He looked past me, all around the room, and began to shake his head slowly.

I looked round. 'How long has he been like this?'

'Since you visited with that other man, the one with all the scars,' sighed the nurse. 'Goodness knows what you triggered, but I don't think it was happy memories.'

Casting a meaningful look towards me, Alex put her arm around Jason and he curled into her for reassurance, trembling.

'Oh, Jay,' she sighed. Looking at the nurse, she shook her head, 'I haven't seen him like this for years.'

'Nor have I,' said the nurse. I looked at Jason again, feeling miserable. Suddenly, Sasha was there, kneeling beside him.

'Hi Jason,' she said nervously. 'I'm Sasha.' She touched his knee with trembling fingers. Jason lifted his head from Alex's shoulder, and looked at Sasha. I searched for a flicker of recognition in his deep black eyes, and although I didn't see anything, it could not be denied that he was watching her, and that he had stopped crying. Sasha looked spellbound.

'What should I say?' She whispered to me, holding Jason's gaze.

'Um… just tell him it's going to be alright.'

'It's,' she swallowed. 'It's going to be okay, Jason. We're your friends, Bryce and I. We want to help you get better, we want to come and see you again.'

We stayed for a while. Sasha was really good with Jason and he seemed a little more settled by the end of our visit. 'Bye, Jason,' she said brightly, taking his hand as we made to leave. 'I will come to see you again really soon, okay?'

Outside, she broke down. 'I can't believe he's my dad,' she gasped. 'And he's been like that all of my life. It's so, so, sad that he used to be normal.' She wiped her eyes. 'He looks just like Mitch, doesn't he? Exactly like him.'

'I know. What will you do?'

'I'm not sure. Let's not tell my Dad, until all of this drama with Uncle Eddie has blown over.' She looked at me. Bryce, let's visit him though. Let's go again tomorrow.'

'Okay.'

'Bryce?' She frowned. 'You said that Uncle Eddie… that he was very much in love with him. If that's true, then why does he not even visit him? Why doesn't he live with Uncle Eddie?'

'It's hard for him… Jason's very different, now.'

'I guess… I understand.'

It was around eight when we arrived back at Lake Martin in a convoy with Alex's car. We saw the police car parked right at the front entrance, and we hurried inside. They were all in the drawing room; Ilya, standing behind Mischa's chair. Mischa was sitting huddled in an armchair wrapped in a blanket, and two policemen sat opposite. Ilya's tense expression collapsed when we walked into the room.

'Lastochka. Thank God.' Ilya called his daughter by a Russian term of endearment that I had heard him use before; those brothers sure seemed to like calling their dear ones after little birds and pigeons. She ran up to him and he hugged her tightly, looking at the policemen. 'My daughter,' he said helplessly. 'Oh, where have you been? I thought… I called the police…' he pressed his face into her hair. One of the police officers stood up.

'Glad that she is home safely,' he said. 'Young lady has your uncle made contact with you, is that why you are so late?'

'No… Bryce and I got talking. We didn't realise how late it was,' she said. Sasha disengaged herself from Ilya, and turned to hug Mischa, too. He returned her embrace, but he was glaring at me over her shoulder. Ilya was also staring at me, his eyes glittering with anger. Made me nervous, truth be told.

'Officers,' Ilya said, ripping his eyes from me. 'Thank you once again for your time. If there is nothing more you need, I will show you out. My children need to rest now. It has been… a trying day.' The officers both stood, but they were not quite ready to leave.

'Mr Bodansky… it's important you let us know if you hear anything from your brother.'

'There's really no need.' Ilya's smile was friendly, if a little tight. He was clearly exhausted. 'My kids are absolutely safe with me. We tend to deal with things within the family, I am quite sure you understand.'

'Be that as it may, we'll still need to talk to him as soon as possible. He has assaulted your son. Young Mr Bodansky assures us that he wants to press full charges.' Everyone looked at Mischa, sitting in his chair clutching the blanket to his chin. I noticed that he seemed a little embarrassed to meet his father's eyes. He couldn't really look at anyone, but his expression remained irritatingly nonchalant. Ilya went to show the officers out. I couldn't stand it anymore.

'Mischa. How exactly did Eddie 'assault' you? Because you look okay to me, and if he had… well, you wouldn't. You would look like me.' I gestured to my own facial wounds.

The teenager drew himself up and fixed me with a look of distain. 'It's difficult to talk about, but as you're being so insufferable, I'll tell you. He pulled me into his car, wouldn't let me out. He was, like, gripping onto me, wouldn't let me go. I managed to get away from him.'

I narrowed my eyes. 'How?'

'What?'

'It's a valid question. If Eddie was holding on to you, how the hell did you get away?'

Mischa glared at me and huddled into his blanket.

Closing the big double doors, Ilya turned to me as the police car started down the drive. 'Come with me,' he said quietly, without looking at me. He strode past and walked very quickly to the card room. Reluctantly, I followed him. He closed the door behind me, and as soon as I turned to face him he hit me full in the face with the back of his hand. My mouth filled up with blood and tears boiled in my eyes. For the second time in two days, I had been hit by those huge Bodansky hands. I put my hand over my mouth and looked at him, feeling that initial gush of hot tears wetting my hand. I quickly wiped my eyes on my sleeve.

'That was for keeping my daughter out for five hours,' he growled. 'Where were you? What did you tell her?'

'Ilya!' Alex stood up, 'Sasha was with me…. And Jason. It's not his fault! Don't bombard him with questions.'

I lowered my hand from my mouth. He hadn't hit me quite as hard as Eddie.

'Then just answer me one question. Just one.' He dropped into a seat, his head in his hands. 'Is Eddie coming after my kids?

'I don't think so.' My heart was beating fast. I had never seen Ilya like this; utterly broken. 'What does he want with Mischa? Oh, Christ, my son.'

Chapter 23

Colt

Early next morning, Eddie's car was delivered to the hotel, minus Eddie himself. 'Mikhail Badin- Bodin,' said the delivery driver laboriously, reading from the delivery sheet.

'Bodansky.' I snatched the piece of paper from him and read it. It was a notice and receipt; Eddie had arranged for his car to be delivered to the hotel. A note in his spidery writing was scrawled at the bottom of the receipt, which read, 'To Mischa, please accept this with my sincere apologies. Edvard.'

'I don't want it,' said Mischa abruptly, when I went in to tell him about it. 'Just scrap it. I don't care.' Ilya reached for the delivery notice and read it slowly, his brow furrowed.

'Mischa,' he sighed, 'That car is worth a lot of money. If you don't want it, we can sell it.' He sighed again, heavily, and passed the paperwork back to Mischa. 'Well, wherever Eddie is, he obviously doesn't need his car.'

'I hope he's dead,' said Mischa. 'Hope he did himself in, did us all a favour.'

I looked at the floor, my heart beating quickly. Oh Eddie. Where are you? Ilya told me to take the car around the back of the house, to the staff car park. He told me to wash and cover it until Mischa decided what to do with it.

I felt really sad while I was washing Eddie's car. His suicide seemed quite likely. That was my worst nightmare. I opened the door, got into the car. It smelled like him. I stroked the steering wheel and I opened the glove compartment, all the while whispering feverishly, 'You stupid fucker. Come back. You fucking dick, please don't kill yourself, you stupid, stupid fucker. Please.' I pocketed everything personal I could find; a comb, face powder, a pen, a bracelet. I went to the stables to get some car wax. When I got back, the windscreen was shattered.

'What?' I cried, dropping the wax. Mischa walked around from the other side of the car holding a crowbar. With an angry grunt he slammed it into the back window.

'Mitch! Stop it! What are you doing?'

He strode around the car and smashed it through the window on the other side, then he wrenched open the door and began attacking the panel. He was grunting with effort as he bashed the interior with the end of the crowbar, cracks radiating on the walnut dash.

'Mitch. Mischa.'

He stopped, panting. 'I'm not going to drive his bloody car,' he spat, looking frenzied. 'Do you know what he did to me in this-' he whacked the paintwork with the crowbar, 'In this car? Why the hell is he giving me this car? I just want him to leave me alone. I just want to smash it into little bits!' He dropped the crowbar and leaned back against the wrecked Jaguar. I was shaking a little.

'Mitch,' I said, gently kicking the crowbar under the car, out of his way. 'Eddie's a good person, honestly. He was mixed up. Don't hate him.'

'Don't hate him? Are you being real right now? You don't know what it's like. He was…' he rubbed his hair, 'He was scary. You haven't seen that side of him.'

'Yes I have.' I put my hands in my pockets. 'Trust me, I have.'

Mischa stared at me, his face working with emotion. Then, predictably he went back to thinking about himself. 'Do you know where he is? I bet you do, you're protecting him.'

'No.' I swallowed. 'I wish I did.'

Mischa looked angry then he turned away, his shoulders shaking. Without thinking, I touched him lightly on his arm, meaning to be comforting. I startled him. He almost fell over and shouted, 'Do not touch me! You dirty, little fucking homo. You're all the fucking same!' He screamed the last word right in my face as he stormed past me.

A week had passed since Eddie left. I was in his suite where I had been sent to tidy the room and pack up his belongings; Ilya had decided that he wasn't coming back any time soon. It was sad, handling all of the things that he used to wear and use. It sounds morbid, but it honestly felt like… he really had died. The wardrobe was worst of all, because his clothing held so many memories for me; the gold dress from a crazy night at the drag club; a green jacket that made his eyes dazzle; A scarf with anchors on it that he had been wearing the night he first kissed me. I sealed most of these memories into cardboard boxes, but the scarf I stole for myself.

Opening the bureau drawer, I paused. There, among pencils and charcoals, was a letter. Although I was alone in the room my cheeks flushed with anxiety. My first thought was that the letter was for me, and that it was a suicide note. Eddie always called me a pessimist, and truly, my mind did always jump to the worst conclusion. The note wasn't in an envelope. I picked it up and began to read.

Eel,
I want you to know that I am sorry. I left you because I am a coward.
It is not because I do not want to see you. I cannot see you. I cannot bear

to see you.

Enough. I do not even know if you can read. Get someone to read this to you. I miss you. I miss everything about you.

The letter ended abruptly and the pencil had been scored angrily through the whole thing.

The bookstore was very busy, even for a Saturday afternoon. I followed the signs; large, glossy posters featuring an airbrushed version of Paul Russell's smiling face, downstairs to the back of the store where a bunch of chairs were grouped around a desk. Just seeing his face on the posters brought back unpleasant memories.

The book signing was almost over so I joined the end of a very small queue. I approached Paul as he sat at the desk, spinning a pen between his fingers and staring off into the distance. His eyes cleared as I approached and hardened. 'Colt. How are you? I'd shake your hand, but…' he shrugged and looked at me bitterly.

'I'm totally sorry about your hand, Paul.' I spoke quietly, but I meant it. What happened to Paul's hand was hideous and shouldn't have ever happened. I felt sick about it. He flinched visibly at my sympathy.

'Is that the official company line? Is Ilya sorry about my hand?'

'I don't know. I'm sorry, that's all I know.'

Paul shook his head in disgust at me. 'For the record? I didn't know anything about your… company, your gang or whatever it is. I didn't know anything. So, this was all for nothing. I did nothing wrong, I just dated that psychopath. Biggest mistake I ever made let me tell you.' He shifted in his chair and my stomach churned with dread. Please don't take that hand out of your pocket. I don't want to see it, I don't… I picked up a copy of his book from the stack on the table.

'I'm sorry,' I repeated. 'I just came to buy your book.'

'Take it. Shit, have it as a freebie. Enjoy it. You won't find anything about your goddamn gang in there.'

'I'm sure I won't,' I said. I started to turn away. 'Bye, Paul… good luck with the book and... everything.' As I walked away he called my name and I turned around slowly. He was holding his hand out to me. Sickness soured my throat as I stared and stared at it... Jesus.

'This is going to happen to you, next,' he said seriously. He looked at his hand and then at me. 'I'm saying this because I like you. Get the fuck out of that hotel.'

Weeks passed and still no word from Eddie. As time went on, things were going from bad to worse. I was to blame for everything. I had inadvertently caused Eddie untold grief, leading to a full-blown psychotic meltdown. Because of me, he was gone God knows where. And Mischa? He was living in fear behind a bodyguard, too afraid to leave the hotel, too afraid to be alone, even at night. As if these casualties of my stupid, naive, honesty weren't enough, now Jason was suffering too.

Out of a sense of responsibility, and partly because I rather liked him, I visited Jason as often as I could. After Sasha returned to college in September I kept up the visits on my own. Jason's health was not improving. His weight was really low and constantly dropping, and because Alex was worried about this she became very embittered with me.

'Look at you, the little saint,' she goaded me one day at the Harbour Centre. 'The Florence Nightingale act doesn't change what you did.'

'I know.' I was sitting with Jason, patiently coaxing him to eat some yoghurt. 'I know that.'

Alex sat in silence for a moment, then she added, 'Sorry Bryce. I know you never meant to cause any harm. You did what you thought was right. You probably had no idea that...' she glanced at Jason, 'That you-know-who would abandon him.'

'He didn't 'abandon' him,' I said quickly. I was surprised to feel myself becoming rather heated. 'Eddie loves him, he just can't handle this. He has his own problems. Oh, shit, sorry Jase...' At the mention of Eddie's name, Jason whimpered and started to bite his own hand.

'This is ridiculous,' I groaned, gently pulling Jason's hand out his mouth. 'I can't do anything right, can I?'

One thing I was doing right, according to Ilya Bodansky, was accountancy for the firm. I now lived full-time at the hotel, and worked exclusively on the accounts for both the hotel and the business. I threw myself into the distraction of my work, hating every minute without Eddie. I wanted to scream as I was given ever greater responsibilities with the money; Eddie would never have let me get into it so deeply.

Life just felt like hell without him. I began to wonder how I ever managed to get by on my own. The first business meeting I went to without him, I somehow ended up being given a bad assignment. One of the firm's associates was, apparently, unhappy with the way we (or rather, I) had calculated his cut of earnings from an art sale.

'He wants an explanation,' Ilya sighed, 'So I've arranged to meet him next week. Colt, you're the money. You can join me.'

I was in a foul mood, already. I shook my head, 'Is this guy stupid?' I snapped, 'The calculation is really simple.'

'Still,' said Ilya tightly, 'He wants to go over it. And please, try not to call him stupid in the meeting, or he may shoot both of us.'

Manpyre slinked over to me as the meeting broke up. 'Hey. You hungry? I was thinking of heading back to that restaurant. Coming?'

I swept all of my paperwork together. 'The Lebanese place? No.' I wasn't even polite with him. My stress level was through the roof.

'No problem.' Manpyre passed me a loose sheet of paper, tucked it into my stack. 'By the way, don't worry about that Kellerman meeting.'

'Mm.'

'Seriously. Don't worry. Your figures are correct, so, just present them again. Then let Ilya do the rest of the talking. You don't have to do or say anything. You're just the money, your best bet is to just keep it factual. Okay?'

I looked at him. 'Okay.' I actually felt a little better.

He smiled. 'And I'll be there, so you really don't have anything to worry about, mate!'

'Yeah?' We started walking out, together. 'You're coming, too?'

He rolled his eyes, 'Yes, mate. Did you think Ilya would go into that meeting without his bodyguard?'

'I guess not.' I stopped, fastening my shoulder bag. I was beginning to realise that David Manpyre did have something to offer me. Was it wrong to think of it in that way? Were relationships really just a transaction, an exchange of needs? I wasn't sure, but at that moment, even the thought of eating dinner alone made me nervous.

'Um,' I said. 'I'm not so much into Lebanese food, but... I could be a little hungry.'

He smiled, 'Okay... let me guess, you are... a hamburger person.'

'Perfect.' We went to a drive-thru then back to the hotel, sitting in the car park eating hamburgers. This time, when he went to kiss me, I had a Coke in one hand and a hamburger in the other, so I couldn't really stop him. I opened my eyes halfway through and saw myself in the rear-view mirror. What the fuck was I doing?

Manpyre pulled away and said, 'I've wanted this for a really long time.'

'Yeah,' I said. 'I know.'

'I mean, I don't mind telling you Colt... I've been lonely for a long time.'

I was feeling so low and lonely, that I pretty much gave in to Manpyre's advances. He was delighted and treated me like a prince.

We got serious very quickly, we were always together and were sleeping in the same room almost every night but I was hesitant about having sex with him. I just kept saying I wasn't ready but... truthfully, it just didn't feel right. The last person I had sex with was Eddie, and I felt weird about moving on from that, accepting that it was past. He was alright about it at first, but then he began to get slightly impatient. I knew I couldn't fend him off forever, by saying I needed more time, and I began to feel fairly pressured and trapped.

Despite his lithe, dark good looks, I wasn't especially attracted to Manpyre... I felt ashamed of myself for my dependency on being close to a more powerful member of the firm but, as I was finding out, that was me all over. A coward, the thing I hated the most. One morning, after I had spent the night in his suite watching movies, and then faking sleep after giving him my usual chaste kisses, he was trying to persuade me.

'You're driving me crazy, mate,' he said, as I stepped out of the shower. 'Come on, honey, baby, please.'

I put on all of my clothes, feeling quite guilty. I'm not a demonstrative person; I'm not even very romantic and I was afraid of this relationship because it felt so wrong. Possibly, because I knew how regularly Manpyre's work demanded him to be violent and immoral, and how naturally that stuff came to him. He was very two-sided; there was the sweet, clingy side that he lavished all over me, and the ruthless torturer. I hoped the two sides would never merge.

That morning I kissed him deeply out of guilt, and he held onto me gratefully. I parted from him, with effort, and he gave a little sigh, 'Uh. Honey, honey, when are you going to let me fuck you?'

I looked at him and we both laughed. 'I gotta go to work, like, right now. Ilya's totally on my back about this new acquisition.'

'That's killer… so, can we fuck tonight?'

I blushed at his choice of words. 'I dunno. Maybe.'

Manpyre looked at me with something in his eye that I didn't like. 'How wonderfully vague. Love it. Sounds enough like a 'yes' to me. See you later.'

I escaped. I had been given my own little office on the same floor as Ilya's. As I was unlocking it, paperwork shoved under my arm, Mischa appeared behind me with his bodyguard Luke.

'Hey, Porter.' Mischa had not returned to college for the new term, claiming to be too scared. He spent his days hardly leaving the hotel and as a result his skin was pale and greasy, and he had gained a lot of weight. 'Why are you going in there?'

'It's my new office,' I said. I felt quite sorry for Mischa, as much as I disliked him. At that moment, Ilya came out of his office.

'Son, leave Bryce alone today, he is very busy.'

'What's he doing? Can I help him? I should really be learning about all this stuff. The business and everything.'

Ilya pursed his lips. 'Not yet. You should be finishing college, Mikhail, not dragging about this hotel. Now, leave us. Bryce and I have work to do. This whole thing…' he gestured to Luke, '… is becoming ridiculous.' Ilya was clearly very harassed. He turned to me, and as Mischa began to speak again his father turned and snapped at him, exasperated.

'Mikhail, if you ever want to be part of this business you had better grow up, fast. Edvard was running half the company at your age. Tell me how I can take you seriously, when you are hiding behind a bodyguard? As far as we know, Edvard is abroad. He is gone.' Ilya glanced at me.

Mischa pouted and whined, 'You don't know that for sure. Besides, you don't know what it was like, Dad. He's about three times bigger than me and he wanted to rape me.'

'Enough. That is enough,' barked Ilya. 'Alright? Just… go to your room.'

Mischa scoffed. 'I'm eighteen, you can't send me to my room.'

'Oh, then just get out of my face, Mikhail! And Luke, you can stop with the bodyguard thing.' Luke nodded gratefully, smirked at me and hurried off. Mischa's eyes burned with furious tears. He stormed off. Staring after him, Ilya's jaw twitched with emotion.

'I was hard on him,' he murmured.

'Hm,' I shrugged doubtfully, thinking of my own father.

'Hush. I was not asking a question. We have work to do.'

We worked hard all morning. Ilya was very business-smart, but he didn't really have a head for figures, which is where I came in. My mobile beeped loudly and Ilya shot me a look of irritation. Manpyre again; he had been sending me messages all morning.

'Can't stop thinking about you today! Meet you at lunch?' I deleted it.

Ilya sighed and sat back in his chair. 'Well, Bryce, it's 12.30 and all of these figures are giving me a headache. What do you say we break for lunch? It's lamb cutlets in the restaurant today…'

I didn't feel like running into Manpyre again and I really did have a lot of work to get through. 'Thanks, boss… I'm not too hungry,' I said. I chewed my pen and flicked it between my thumb and index finger, as I rechecked a calculation.

Ilya strode back into my office and tossed a sandwich on my desk along with a stack of papers. The top sheet was a handwritten letter addressed to Mr Bryce Colt.

'Sorry about that,' said my boss, 'We thought that he would contact you eventually, so we've been opening all your mail.'

I grabbed the letter.

Dear Colt,

Where should I begin? With an apology; I am sorry for laying my hands on you, believe me that I have never felt more shame. More than that, I regret that you saw me in that state. I asked you not to, darling, but you did. You burrowed to the very hellish core of me and now you have seen it. I know what you must think of me. The truth is, I took myself away to protect you, but I was still particularly unwell and remained thus for a long time. It is only recently that things have changed. I am fragile, but almost well again. I have friends here in Stockholm, and I am working.

The only way that I can function is by knowing that Eel is safe and receiving the care that he needs. I know that his life is empty, but I literally cannot bear to think about it. See how my pen shakes? I apologise for the mess of that last line. I repeat it like a mantra, 'He is safe. His needs are met. I can do nothing more for him.' And with that in my mind like a lucky coin fingered in a pocket, I can breathe again.

The letter didn't exactly convince me of his sanity. At the end of the strange letter was a paragraph of writing that I now recognised as Russian. I asked Ilya what it said and he smirked. 'It is a message for me. It talks about Mischa and… it's a bit of an apology for me, really.' He smiled at me, 'I won't translate it word-for-word. Some things are meant to be kept just between brothers. Look, he put his address on the top, Bryce. I think you should go to him. Take a week or two, visit him.'

My heart flipped. 'Can I?' I said. Ilya started to smile slightly and I blushed. 'I mean… yeah, if you want me to I will.'

'I think… that it would be good for him. And it would be good for me, if you could go, and let me know how he is. He's my little brother, you know?' Ilya gave a small, sad smile. 'He is a bit crazy, but he literally can't help it. I lost him for sixteen years, I worried about him for that entire time. I don't want to miss a chance to check that he is okay, this time around.'

'I understand. I… I've got a little brother, too.'

I checked the airline website. There were flights out to Stockholm the next day, so I booked myself on an early one. I was feeling excited, but I was already nervous too, wondering how Eddie would feel about seeing me, or anyone from the firm. I spent the day packing my stuff, and ahead of my early flight, I was just getting ready to go to bed when someone tapped on my door. I pressed my eye to the spyhole; Manpyre. I swore under my breath and opened the door but I kept the chain on the latch.

'Hey,' I said, yawning slightly for effect. I rubbed my eyes. 'Man. I'm sooo tired.'

'Alright, mate? Ilya says you're going to Sweden tomorrow. To see Eddie… hey, open up.' Gently, he rattled the chain.

'Mm… Dave? I'm like, really tired,' I yawned. 'I need to get to bed, my flight's really early…' Even as I spoke, I felt bad. I knew what he had been hoping for tonight. He looked hurt.

'Mate… I'm going to miss you next week like crazy. I only want to sleep next to you, that's all. Can I come in? Please?'

I bit my lip, feeling really guilty. Someone passed behind him in the corridor and wished him goodnight.

'Night!' He called. He turned back to me and lowered his voice. 'If this is because you don't want to sleep with me… then let's forget that for now. Don't push me away, mate. I'll wait for you. I'm bonkers about you… who else would I stand out in the corridor for, begging to let me in?'

I opened up the door and he rushed in and covered me with kisses. He was really sweet in some ways, he made me think of a puppy. We went to bed and got comfy with his arms wrapped tightly around my waist.

'I don't want you to go,' he whispered.

'It's okay,' I said. 'Eddie's all better now.'

'Never let your guard down with him. Honestly, mate, I'm terrified for you…'

'I'll be okay.'

He was silent for a bit, and then he said, 'Bodansky had better not try it on with you.'

'What?'

'Just saying, honey. It would be just like him to have sex with my boyfriend before I get the chance to. So, I'll rip his guts out if he fucks with you.' His voice had hardened. I lay there, recognising stirrings of excitement at the idea of Eddie trying anything with me. I shifted onto my stomach to hide my feelings.

'Don't be daft,' I assured Manpyre. 'We're over, really over.'

He kissed me. 'You sure?'

'Yeah.'

Manpyre sat up and turned to face me. 'Here,' he said. He twisted off one of the rings from his finger, and I just felt dread, thinking, please don't do this. I don't really care for you, stop investing in me. Just stop. My jumbled thoughts made no difference to anything. Manpyre took my hand and pushed the ring on my finger. 'Too big,' he said, with a nervous laugh.

I should have said, 'Aw, well, never mind, mate. It wasn't meant to be.' What I said instead was, 'It might fit on my thumb.' It was still a little too big for my thumb, but it would do. I stared at it. It was gold, with a black stone in the middle and two tiny diamonds either side.

'So you don't forget about me,' he said shyly.

I kept staring at it. What the hell was happening? What was I doing?

'Is it okay?' He asked gently. I knew he meant, was it okay to ask me to wear his ring, to symbolise our relationship. In truth, it wasn't okay. I felt too committed, too quickly, to someone that I wasn't sure about. Somehow, it felt like I was signing a contract. Maybe I was paranoid.

'Sure. I like it,' I said, staring at it.

'Make sure you wear it all the time,' he said, his simple words laced with something that I didn't like. 'I'll be waiting for you, mate. I'll be waiting.'

Chapter 24

Eddie

Endless days spent in daylight darkness. I slept in my hire car for almost a week before I remembered that I had friends in Stockholm. When I found my friends, I collapsed on Ava's gallery floor, raving about Jason. I rented the apartment just above her gallery. She kept it on to rent to her friends whenever they were in Stockholm. My sanctuary. I smelled the wood, opened the wardrobes and wrapped myself in sixty-year-old moth eaten Elk fur. Jason Prescott had never been inside this apartment. It was a refuge from him and oh, so gratefully, I shut him out.

I began to carve out a new existence and slowly, my heart began to ache less. Eventually, peace came in an unexpected form; a Swedish man, a sometime recovering heroin addict named Robban Malmstorg. He worked in the Irish themed bar on the street where Ava lived. Robban was thirty five, yet he looked several years older. His quick, narrow eyes, radiantly creased from his near permanent grin, somehow made it hard to believe that he was still so young. His slim body was wiry and tight. His hands were rough and brown; his fingertips, yellow. Most of his teeth were either rotting, or missing, yet he smiled constantly as he worked behind the bar keeping up an easy rapport with the customers.

Although he was supposed to be straggling along on a methadone programme, he was still topping up with heroin. He was supplementing his income and funding his diminishing habit by selling his body. Rent boys were all that I could be bothered to find, and it was unfortunate because they truly brought out the worst in me. It was the way in which they were wrecking their young minds with drugs that maddened me. Eel simply did not have that choice.

I took all of my pain out on the young addicts by beating them, but in doing so I never felt a skewed sense of justice, or anything like it. The whole sordid situation only served to make me sad.

Eventually, they began warning each other about me, and I knew I had hit rock bottom when I struggled to pick someone up one cold, wet night. I walked, slowly at first, past so many boys who simply turned away from me and fell to talking in groups. I picked up my pace, sensing their growing hostility. 'Fan ta dig, Engelska,' called someone behind me as I hurried on by. Only the most desperate of all would go with me, and I resented those people more than anyone. Eventually, they too, decided that my money was no longer worth the risk. Soon, I was trailing the wet lamp-lit streets, unwelcome and lonely and desperate for someone to distract me.

I hit Robban the first time we were together. It had simply become my habit. After I met him in the bar, I took him with me back to Ava's. His attitude, his willingness to follow me up to the dark, cold apartment and into my bedroom, when he had almost certainly been warned about me, annoyed me, very much and his lack of self-respect made me sick. I punched him almost as soon as we finished negotiating price. He was not expecting it, and his head snapped back. He touched his hand delicately to his cheek. He was looking down, and I watched him breathing through his nose, controlling his instinctive anger.

'Is that it?' He asked calmly.

I looked at him.

'Maybe,' I replied.

'If you want to hit me,' he said calmly, 'Three things; give me a little warning first. Don't leave marks because, my other clients don't like the beat-up look. And pay me half extra.' The consummate professional, he began to take off his clothes. 'Okay, so. Where do you want me?'

I did not hit him again. Afterwards, I barely looked at him, simply leaving him lying in the bathroom where we had been together. I felt nothing, if I ever felt ashamed I had learned just to drink a bit more to blot it out. I heard him singing tunelessly as he sorted himself out in the bathroom, and I let my head drop into a fitful sleep, face down on the dirty bed, a cigarette smouldering between my fingers.

When I woke in the morning, Robban was gone. He had stubbed out my cigarette and thrown a blanket over my back which was thoughtful because it was a fucking freezing morning. Sweet. I checked my wallet; he had only taken the 2000 Kroner I owed him. He had not even taken his half extra… I gave him no more thought.

As I entered the hot, steamy bar the following wet Saturday evening, I caught sight of Robban, cheerfully bantering with the customers. His old, laughing gaze caught my stare across the bar and he motioned for me to come to the bar.

'Only the bravest have come out in this weather. How are you tonight?' He smiled, pushing my usual double vodka into my hand as I sat down at the bar.

'The bravest? No, just the most alcoholic. I am alright, thank you.' My eyes flickered to his high cheekbone; it was red and promising to bruise. I cringed, remembering how it had felt to punch him. Not good. What was the point? What was the point in anything? I was slipping into a dark place. Robban leaned across the bar, his face open, smiling.

'Glad to hear it,' he grinned.

He bounced off to serve other customers, leaving me feeling confused and unable to take my troubled eyes away from his elegance, his air of dignity. I noticed a paperback novel jammed into his back pocket, and, the next time my glass became empty, I asked him about it.

'I haven't actually read it,' confessed Robban, pouring a large measure into the glass. 'I'm teaching myself to read English, properly. I'll get there in the end.'

'You can't read English? And you thought you would start with James Joyce?'

Robban shrugged and grinned. 'I like a challenge.'

'Is that why you are still talking to me?'

He laughed out loud. 'Eddie, I work here. It's my job to talk to you!'

'Yes, but you do not have to be nice to me.' I sighed and looked up into Robban's face, frankly. Judge me, I was thinking.

He simply winked at me. 'It's not difficult to be nice to you.' He started to walk away.

'Hey, Robban! Hold on.'

He was already pulling a drink for another customer. He smiled at me to show he was listening. I watched his dirty hands as they worked the beer pump.

'Why do you not treat me like everyone else does? Like a monster?'

He set the pint on the bar and quickly wiped his hands on his apron. He leaned across the bar and spoke in a low voice, for my ears only. 'I've met monsters, Eddie. Monsters don't have sad eyes. They don't normally cry in their sleep, either.' He gave my shoulder a squeeze and went off to serve other customers.

I invited Robban to come home with me again that night, and to my surprise he readily agreed. We walked back to mine, slowly, in the snow. He was wearing a thin jacket and was hugging himself against the cold. I thought about offering him my gloves, then realised I needed them the most.

'You didn't hit me this time,' teased Robban, as we lay in bed together later that night, 'Congratulations!' He looked at the ceiling, 'Or am I tempting fate here?'

187

I clenched my teeth, embarrassed. 'Robban, I'm sorry.'

'Seriously, don't worry about it. I've had worse.'

'You do not deserve worse. I... ah... I do it to anyone that comes too close, these days.'

Robban sat up in bed and stretched. 'In that case, I am in a dangerous place right now,' he smiled teasingly. 'Good thing I am not afraid.' He took hold of one of my curled fists and pressed his lips to it, as though to prove his point. I watched him, perplexed.

'Why are you different from everyone else? And why have you not asked me about my body?' I asked bluntly. 'Normally that is the first thing people say, 'Oh my God, what the hell happened to you? Were you in some kind of accident...?" I droned. My gaze fell on Robban's bare forearms, scratched with track marks from years of needles. I was not the only one with self-inflicted scars.

'None of my business. Obviously, you're a cutter... but you're paying me for sex, not a counselling session.'

'Then I will pay you more. I want a counselling session.'

'So, see a counsellor, brother, I'm a rent boy and a junkie; don't take life advice from me.'

I needed someone just like Robban; someone who was not afraid of being close to me and someone who could cope with a few violent outbursts when I felt low and cornered. We were soon in a relationship, and I flourished. This did not happen overnight. Robban had to be extremely patient and tolerant of me; luckily these virtues came naturally to him. I told him about Eel. I rather poured my heart out to Robban, and despite his assertions that he was no counsellor, he was a wonderful listener. He listened while I confessed what I had done to Colt, and finally, crying with shame, I told him what I had done to young Mischa.

'But remember, you didn't hurt him, you let him go,' said Robban soothingly, stroking my hair, my head lying in his lap. 'Be kind to yourself. Remember the good things.'

I was still prone to violent and aggressive behaviour, as much as I fought to control myself, and I still occasionally attacked Robban. Usually, I directed my aggression only towards myself, angrily damaging my own body. Robban handled things in his unique way. If I hit him, his shoulders were broad and he brushed it off as unimportant, as part of my illness. When I injured myself, he did not panic or beg me to stop, like Colt would have. He simply waited until I had vented my emotions, then he would help me to care for my wounds. He offered no advice, no comfort, and no judgement whatsoever. Instead, he was calm and practical. I felt that he had been sent to me from above. Maybe I could reprise my belief in angels after all.

One evening, a month into our relationship, after I stopped paying him, I was sitting at the kitchen table in the bluish half-light. I was drunk and dreaming about Eel. It bothered me particularly that I had not been there when he woke from his coma, and I began to dwell obsessively on this fact. I kept picturing him there in hospital, waking up. How terrifying, to wake up alone and to be unable to make sense of his surroundings, to be unable to speak or even know what he wanted to say. How frightening and I had not been there.

I was cold, dressed only in my underwear, and the bottle sat at my elbow. Robban stirred at the corner of my vision and I flinched. If I could help it, no one ever saw me quite like this, out of control. Robban moved to the side of the table and sat down calmly. Though his expression remained calm, his eyes quickly scanned the scene and took in the details; knife in my hand, blood staining the wooden table and bloody finger marks smeared all over the bottle. I looked up dully as Robban wiped the bottle with his sleeve and took a sip. I felt wretched; guilty, defeated and strangely expectant. He continued to meet my gaze steadily. When I did not say anything, he simply smiled and took another small sip from the bottle.

'Well?' I finally said.

'Well nothing. Are you alright?' He seemed completely unfazed.

'I… I am cutting myself.' The alcohol caused my words to melt together. I looked at the back of my own hand, at the wide cuts running down the wrist. My hand; my arm. Robban nodded.

'Yes.'

'I am a…' Mischa's word reverberated in my head, the same word Ilya had used to describe Eel. 'A freak. I am sorry.'

'No.' Robban turned serious. 'Listen. You do what you got to do. You hurt that much, I guess this is the only way you know how to make it stop. You know best. I'm not going to fucking judge you. No one can judge you, because only you know what it was like to be in that relationship, and what it was like to lose him.

So go ahead, do it. I'm here. You'll be alright, I won't let you go too far. I'll keep you safe so you can just do… what you feel. What you need to. Don't be afraid.'

I turned my hand over and flexed my fingers. As a painter, my hands meant everything to me, which is why, over the years, I had attacked them so savagely.

Robban watched as I stuck the knife tip in to the palm of my hand, and sliced it across an existing scar, directly through the heart line. I curled my fingers over the wound and, as the blood flowed between my fingers, tears of relief ran from my closed eyes. I touched my finger to my lips. It tasted warm, sharp, and it comforted me in every sense. Robban poured me another drink, but he kept himself stone cold sober.

Chapter 25

Colt

I stopped in front of the shop window. I peered through the thick, smoky-grey window pane. There were the pictures, resting on red velvet, framed in matte gold. Paintings of me. I should've known. There were plenty of horses too and surprisingly, also some of Jason. Those were the nicest in a way, all white and gold and angelic, but in each painting of him, the eyes were scratched out and blurred.

I pushed my hands deeply into the pockets of my grey overcoat, gazing at Eddie's work feeling a deep core of warm familiarity in my belly. Just then, a middle-aged couple stopped in front of the arresting display in the gallery window and began to discuss which painting of my naked body would look best in their study. Suddenly self-conscious, I turned my face further into the folds of my upturned collar. In reality, I kind of knew that the paintings were too abstract to be recognisable; I probably identified every aspect of my own body only because it was mine. Even though it was irrational, I felt exposed, as though I were standing naked right there on the snowy pavement. I pushed open the heavy door, the bells tinkling softly as I hurried into the shop.

I stood there for a second shaking the snow from my grey woollen coat, my eyes adjusting to the dim light. I looked up, and there was this tall figure in a black wig that fell to his waist. With absolutely no preliminaries he swept me into his arms.

Eddie held me for the longest time, pushing his face gratefully in my hair. His sweet-scented nylon wig caught up in my mouth and I pressed my face harder against him, my throat tight with emotion. He seemed elated to see me too. I had never seen my friend so animated.

'I'm sorry I didn't call you. I thought you might not want to see me,' I began quickly, my mouth against his shoulder. I started talking nervously, explaining myself, but Eddie shushed me.

'Shh. I want to see you. Of course I want to see you.'

I loved this about him. With anyone else, you would have to sit and tell them everything straight away. With Eddie I never felt rushed and I found that I could rest, in perfect peace, sipping a coffee amidst all the beautiful paintings while he watched me with a rapt gaze. 'Unbelievable.'

'What?'

'You, my friend. I have never felt so happy to see anyone, ever, in my life. And you look more beautiful than ever before. I like your hair longer; you look like a Renaissance angel. I am aching to draw you; dark against the pale and the pink, yes, you can still blush, my darling.' I was indeed blushing, yet for once, Eddie's comments didn't bother me.

'Thanks,' I grinned.

I couldn't return the compliment for his appearance. He was thinner and there were dark circles under his bloodshot eyes. His face was starting to heal, but… the damage was bad, and permanent. He was now disfigured to the point where he would certainly attract staring in public.

'Um. Your face looks better.'

'Does it? Oh, gosh… I am wearing layers and layers of makeup.' Ruefully, he touched the scar tissue at the edge of his mouth, 'I cannot smoke properly anymore…. Or kiss.'

'You been kissing, have you?' I grinned.

'Trying.'

He took my coat. Eddie lit a cigarette and passed one to me, for once I accepted it. He leaned forward, invading my personal space; he had always been given to studying me intently. He was staring at my eyes.

'You are wearing contact lenses.'

'Yeah.'

'I liked the glasses better.'

'You hated my glasses. And you broke them, remember?' I smiled nervously but Eddie didn't seem to see any humour in the situation.

'It might surprise you, but I am a lot calmer, here,' he said, after a while. He certainly looked more relaxed. My eyes drifted to his arms, where fresh cuts glistened along his tanned, weathered flesh. Eddie noticed me looking and he rubbed his forearm self-consciously.

'Don't,' he murmured. 'It looks so awful, I know. When I first arrived, I really could not get over what I did to you. I kept re-living it… every time I thought about it I just… ah.' He shuddered and mimed slashing his arm with an imaginary knife, his eyes in shadow. I kept on smoking, my eyes narrowed against the slow stream of smoke that I wasn't used to. I felt suddenly serious.

'It's alright.'

'It is not, though. I hit you. That is not alright.'

'It is. I'm tough now, remember?' I smiled.

'You may be a little tougher than you used to be… but not against me.'

It was time to change the subject; I didn't want him getting upset.

'Okay. Anyway, what the heck are you wearing?' I asked.

'Oh, you like it? It's a vintage wedding dress.' He was wearing it with big black workman boots.

'How did you even get that in your size? That bride must have had pretty broad shoulders…'

Eddie laughed. 'It does not fit. It does not lace up at the back, see?' He showed me, and I could see the 'Jason Prescott' tattoo right there on his back, partially covered by the lace of the dress. The 'I love you' part wasn't visible, but I knew it was still there.

With Eddie's arm around my shoulders, I stepped into the room and took in my surroundings. The apartment above the gallery had a musty, antique smell. The red-carpeted room was crowded with old furniture and the wallpaper was covered in a pink and gold pattern, dulled by time. An older, bohemian lady was sitting down, studying an unframed painting which was on the coffee table before her. She peered up interestedly.

'Colt, this is my landlady Ava Saskgaard. I could not do a thing in Stockholm if I did not have Ava.' Ava had powdery orange hair and pale, rouged cheeks. She smiled kindly at me and I smiled back. Eddie pushed me forward, 'Ava, allow me the pleasure of introducing the love of my life.'

She lifted her thinly-pencilled brows. 'This boy? My dear, he is not how you described.' Her English was prettily accented.

'No? How did I describe him?' Eddie flashed a grin at me.

'Ah. You have a short memory. You tell me that the… his brain is destroyed, that he cannot talk? You sit here and tell me these things, not two nights ago. You sit here, and you cry. Now, you show me that he is here, that he has travelled to Sweden alone?'

The smile dropped from Eddie's lips, and I felt desperately sorry for him. 'No, Ava, I was talking about Jason. Who is, of course, the love of my life. I was only joking before; this is Bryce Colt, my dearest friend. Perhaps he can be more accurately described as my muse.'

A slow smile spread across her face. 'Oh, the one from your paintings. Then he is most welcome in my gallery. Most welcome! Edvard, bring us some coffee. Come and sit by me, young man.'

I took a seat beside Ava and she showed me some of her own sketch work, turning the pages of a small sketchbook with trembling fingers like leaves in the breeze. She peered up at me in concern as I looked politely at her drawings.

'How long did it take for you to recover from this brain injury?' She asked.

'I never had a brain injury,' I said patiently, 'that was Eddie's other friend. He didn't really recover, he's alright though. He lives in a hospital now.'

'Ava,' said Eddie, with an expression of exasperation, walking in with coffee. He rolled his eyes at me, 'Sorry babe, but Ava's got you pinned as brain damaged now, for as long as she knows you.' Eddie grinned and kissed Ava on the cheek, and she batted him away good-naturedly.

At that moment, a man strolled into the room, wearing one of those tacky Swedish 'Blondes Have More Fun' t-shirts. A curious smile lit his dramatic features when he saw me sitting there. He had classical Scandinavian looks; blond hair and very bright, sparkly, pale blue eyes but his teeth were very bad. I returned the man's friendly grin with a rather nervous smile.

'Colt, this is Robban Malmstorg. He lives here too.' Eddie turned to Robban and began to speak in jubilant tones. Eddie's Swedish was very simple and elegant, and I was inexplicably annoyed with myself for being unable to understand what was being said. I heard my own name, and saw an 'Ah,' of recognition on the other man's face; evidently, Eddie had mentioned me before. Robban smiled with those awful teeth and said something very quickly to Eddie, while looking at me. They both laughed. I felt myself blushing.

'It's lovely to meet you, Bryce,' said Robban suddenly, in smooth, perfect English, extending a hand. I looked at him in surprise. He noticed this and waved his hand, saying, 'Oh, everyone in Sweden speaks English, Bryce. Swedish is a secret language, only a few million people speak it. But I am out of practice so I am sorry for my terrible, bad English, do not think me stupid, promise?' He winked at me. Christ, he was confident.

'Just call me Colt, everyone else does,' I mumbled, blushing harder. Robban grinned, his eyes creasing.

'Ahh… Eddie. He is adorable. Alright, then, Colt. And in return, you call me Robban, okay? By the way, brother, I love your accent, it's Scottish, yes?'

I nodded and he added, 'So, Colt. Colt. You're the one with the serious, no, terminal case of drag fetish, yes?'

I just stared at him, speechless. How could someone be that rude and personal? He was certainly amusing himself, though.

'Don't tease him, Rob,' Eddie chuckled, briefly laying a casual hand on Robban's forearm.

Eddie showed me around the apartment.

'Is that the one you've been kissing?' I asked him casually. 'Robban?'

'Yes,' said Eddie simply. Oh... we were history, but it still stung. I tried to sound jokey, 'I should've known you would find yourself a good-looking Swedish guy...'

'You think he is good-looking, hm?' Eddie grinned at my blushes. 'He is nice. I am not in love with him, or anything like that. Robban's just nice. He is good for me, keeps my head level.'

I nodded, suddenly consumed with a deep, aching jealousy.

'And,' continued Eddie, 'He is strong, which is fairly essential for me. He saw me through the worst of my breakdown and he did not run away. Unlike poor Paul Russell! I probably traumatised him for life. Whatever happened to him?'

'Manpyre chopped his fingers off.'

Alarmed, Eddie raised his eyebrows. 'All of them?'

'No...' I held up my own hand and folded over my fingers. 'Just these three.'

Eddie shivered theatrically. 'Poor Paulie. Poor baby, he did not deserve to be caught up in my mess. Ah. Well. Poor, stupid, little, party boy. My brother was harsh on him, no? Manpyre probably enjoyed that little task.'

Oh, yeah... Manpyre. I felt a weird urge to make Eddie jealous. I looked at him and dropped the shell, 'Speaking of... well, I gotta tell you something. I'm seeing somebody too, it's, well... it is, actually, Manpyre.'

Eddie did a double-take, his eyes popping.

'I will assume that I misunderstood you. Colt, look me in the eye and tell me that you are seeing Dave fucking Manpyre.' He looked quite ill and

I wanted to burst out laughing but I contained myself.

'Yeah. He's alright you know, he's not that bad. I'm not, like, sleeping with him yet, if that's any-'

'Yet? That is disgusting. He is vile. Trust me, I have known him for over years and he is filthy-minded. He has some strange ideas about... have you ever had very rough sex before?'

My face was on fire. 'Jeez... Eddie. You shouldn't ask stuff like that.'

'I don't mean to embarrass you. Do not sleep with Dave Manpyre, trust me. He-' At that moment, Robban came in and, thank goodness, the conversation moved on to other things. I wanted to tell Eddie about Jason being unwell, but with Robban hanging around all afternoon there was never a good time. Eventually, he went to fetch his cigarettes from the kitchen and I found myself alone with Eddie at last.

'Eddie?' I said in a small voice. 'There's something else I have to tell you.'

'Oh? More good news?' He laughed quietly. He shook his head, 'Dave Manpyre... Jesus.'

'It's about Jason,' I began. 'He isn't... very well, right now, and I just thought that you would want to know.'

Eddie froze. 'Oh, no. No, sweetheart, I do not want to hear it. I cannot hear about it.' His face was white with distress. He stood up suddenly and turned his back on me, and at that moment Robban walked back into the room holding his cigarettes. He looked at Eddie standing by the window, clutching his head in his hands, and then he looked sharply and accusingly, at me.

'What happened?' He asked.

Suddenly Eddie turned round in tears. 'Why did you have to say that to me? What can I do? He has doctors and nurses, what can I do? I am getting better, damn it. I am getting better!' He raked his hands through his hair, muttering quietly. Suddenly his arm lashed out, swept a bunch of stuff from the table. A cup and a lamp both smashed on the floor. Robban stepped between us and spoke Swedish to Eddie in a low, soothing voice. Eddie was shaking badly, but he was listening to Robban, nodding and taking deep, shuddering breaths.

I stood there, feeling frightened at his reaction, and ridiculous for having caused it. Robban turned his head and murmured, 'Go upstairs, Colt.'

There was nothing for me to do other than turn and trudge slowly upstairs to the kitchen. I sat on the arm of a chair and listened anxiously, but I couldn't hear anything. I felt terrible. After a while someone came upstairs. Robban was holding an armful of blood stained towels.

'Oh my God,' I gasped, jumping to my feet.

'It isn't as bad as it looks,' he said calmly, pushing the towels into the washing machine, 'It's just a little cut on his arm but it bled a lot.' He switched on the washing machine, 'He's calmed down now, go see him; he wants to apologise. Just try not to upset him again, right?' Robban looked down and noticed a bloodstain on his top. He tutted, and pulling it over his head he went through to the bedroom and shut the door.

Eddie

Colt was typically shocked by the nature of my relationship with Robban.

'He's nice, Colt. You know he is.' I wanted to laugh at his prudishness.

'He's fine and nice and all but he's a prostitute.' Colt whispered the word so indignantly that I actually did laugh at this point.

'There is no problem, baby. I like him.'

Colt huffed. 'How do you even know somebody who is a prostitute?' He asked me, in all innocence. I smiled inwardly, loving him for it.

'Oh, well, you know. He is a friend of Ava's,' I fibbed. Some truths were too gritty for Colt's delicate ears. He became rather supercilious about the whole thing.

'I don't think it's healthy that he lets you cut yourself, is all.'

I almost laughed. 'Oh, sweetheart. I am a big boy. 'No one 'lets' me do anything.'

'Fine, okay, then he encourages you.'

'He does not 'encourage' me, Colt; that would be madness.' I sighed. 'It is all black and white with you, is it not, baby? And so it should be. I like your innocence, and your neat, clean little morals.'

'Don't patronise me.'

'I did not mean it as an insult. You are lovely. I would not change one thing about you.' I looked at him and smirked. 'Well, maybe one thing; and then you would be all mine.'

Colt ignored that.

'Don't joke. Let me help you. Robban maybe means well, but he's making you worse!'

'He isn't. Besides, I don't want you to be dragged down here with me. I am, oh, so happy that you came to Stockholm to visit me but I want you to enjoy your time here. Let Robban deal with my ugly side, you have seen enough of that now.'

Seeing how frustrated he looked, I touched my friend's face, but he flinched away. 'Colt. Just relax. I have so much to show you. You will have fun in Stockholm if you let yourself.'

He looked at me. His eyes were wide and pleading. 'Please Eddie. Don't do it.'

I shook my head. 'No. I can't promise that.'

Colt turned away from me, taking a newspaper from the rack, and sat down. I folded my arms and leaned back against the table, watching him. He was frowning as he stared at the newspaper, biting his thumbnail, his breathing quick with anger.

I reached into the drawer behind me. 'Sweetheart,' I said, as I took out a packet. 'Don't you think I am happier than I was? Put down the paper, sweet. I know you cannot read Swedish.'

Colt put the newspaper down, still biting his thumbnail.

'Don't you think I am happier?' I repeated gently.

'Yes.' He replied grudgingly

'Okay. Look at this.' I held up a blister pack of pills and tossed them to Colt. 'Antidepressants. I stopped taking them.'

Colt studied the packet. 'It takes weeks to withdraw from these. You may still need them,' he said worriedly.

'Relax. I stopped taking them three months ago. I wanted to feel, again.'

I went over to him and perched on the arm of the chair. 'When I first came here, I was torturing myself about Eel, making myself feel every detail of what he has gone through, alone. And I was missing you, my moral barometer.' I took a deep breath. 'But now… you have forgiven me. I hurt you, and you know everything I have done, and yet you are here. That helps a lot. I also know that Eel…' I sighed. 'You shocked me, mentioning him right out of the blue. It is difficult to think about him. He is the only thing, now, that makes me want to cut. But I tell myself, be reasonable. He is alright. I know he is being well cared for, and he is happy enough.'

Colt looked down, and nodded slightly.

'I am feeling better every day.' I rolled up my sleeve and ran my fingers down my own arm. 'Eventually, this will stop. Just not yet. Can you understand?' Handing me back the blister pack, Colt stood up.

'No. And I don't want to have any part in it. I'm never going to sit and watch you hurting yourself. Robban's an idiot.'

I should have known he would react like that. I rolled down my sleeve. 'Then we will have to agree to disagree.' I smiled wryly, 'I will refrain from it whenever you are around. It is Robban, not you, who has to look at my ugliness, anyway. Now, can we forget about this and have a nice day out?'

Colt turned as he made to leave the room. 'You're not ugly,' he said. 'I hate every single mark on you because you're hurting yourself and there is no reason for it; not one reason, but you could never, ever be ugly. I think that you're-' he stopped. I looked at him warily.

'You think I am what?' I thought he was going to walk out without saying it, but he did not. He looked me in the eye and just said, 'You know I think you're beautiful, you twat.'

Chapter 26

Colt

I soon became accustomed to life at Ava's apartment. It was by no means ideal. It was not particularly comfortable. But it was fun. There was often nothing but wine for breakfast and there was also no bed for me. Ava had her own private apartment on the second floor and in Eddie's, on the first-floor, there was only one bedroom. Eddie, and usually Robban, slept in the expansive four-poster, while I had a makeshift bed on the floor; a rejected pile of last season's clothes covered by a blanket.

The floor was very dusty and not comfortable in the least. I managed a couple of hours sleep a night, if I was lucky, but strangely, I felt really relaxed nonetheless. Most nights I lay awake, arms behind my head, watching the car lights from the street outside swooping across the ceiling.

I felt vulnerable lying so close to Eddie all night. A small but very insistent part of me still feared him, but, I reasoned, this was probably healthy. The strange thing was, even though I was still afraid of him, I was feeling really mixed up in other ways. As Eddie was getting better, he was becoming like his old self again. We were having a laugh like we used to and I felt myself becoming really attracted to him again; I suppose I never really stopped.

Manpyre had nothing to worry about, though. There was the awkwardness of Robban being there at what felt like all times. Robban used drugs, and obviously I didn't approve. I mean, heroin? I was scared of it, scared when I saw all of his drug paraphernalia in the bathroom cabinet. I slammed the cabinet, then opened it again, slowly and just looked at the cellophane-wrapped needles and tape and wool. Medicinal-looking, but the opposite; poison. It belonged in movies, not in my life, not in Eddie's cabinet. I closed the cabinet and met my own judgemental face, still looking disapprovingly in the mirror. Maybe Eddie thought Robban was cool. He was lovely, and calm, and funny. He was just too bohemian for me, I guess. Because he worked at night, during the day he was always in bed; stoned or sleeping. As Eddie always slept late with him, I never saw either of them until late afternoon.

A nightly ritual had developed… every night, Robban finished his work at the bar and would return to the apartment at around three am. He always stepped over me to get into bed, and I always pretended to be asleep. Sometimes they had sex. I tried hard not to listen to them, and I appreciated that they probably tried to be very quiet, but inevitably my pillow, clutched over my head, had a limited soundproofing effect. I was especially keen not to hear, because listening to Eddie with someone else seemed to squeeze my chest with a crushing pain. Furthermore, I was beginning to suspect that Eddie derived no little excitement from the fact that I was right there on the floor. One night I woke up to hear him saying my name.

'What?' I groaned sleepily, then I froze in the middle of a yawn. Eddie was gasping my name in between moans of pleasure. I blushed hotly in the darkness and I heard Robban protesting indignantly in Swedish. Eddie just laughed at him.

'Sorry,' whispered Robban, as he accidentally stepped on my arm on his way into bed. It was the early hours of the morning.

'Robbie? What happened?' Murmured Eddie blearily.

'I stepped on him. I stepped on Colt.' Robban climbed into bed.

'You oaf.' Eddie leaned concernedly over the side of his bed, looking down at me. 'You okay babes?'

I bit my lip, turned away and said nothing, irritated. Not so much by the fact Robban had hurt my arm, but because he had spoiled the cosy pretence that I was asleep. With discomfort and embarrassment gnawing at my insides, I balled the sheets up in my hand. Robban said something to Eddie, who laughed. Then there was a long silence. I began to imagine all kinds of things; somehow, maybe because they had spoken to me I couldn't access the 'off' switch that night. Then a cushion fell off the bed, onto me, and something inside me snapped. I threw back my sheets, scrambled off the floor and hurried into the kitchen.

I warmed up some milk in a saucepan. The apartment was full of heroin and booze, but I wanted hot milk. I sighed; even I could sort of see the funny side of that.

Sipping my milk, I frowned slightly. Bloody Robban... I was no longer tired, so I wandered downstairs, into the gallery. The room was striking in the pale moonlight. Through the shop front windows the snow swirled in the street, falling thickly with silent drama. There was no one out there in the cold. I stretched out on the chaise lounge opposite from the window and watched the snowfall like it was a cinema.

I was not in the least bit tired. I rested my head on the back of the chair, and images of Eddie with Robban came flooding in. The wooden stairs creaked slightly, and someone pushed open the door.

'There you are,' said Robban, 'Are you okay? I didn't really hurt you, did I?'

'No, I'm fine. I couldn't sleep.' I wished that he would go. He stood there.

'Pretty,' he commented, looking at the scene outside. 'Budge up,' he added, and I was forced to move my legs to accommodate him on the chaise lounge. Robban got straight to the point. 'You seem jealous.'

'Of you?'

'Of me with Eddie, yes.'

I sighed heavily. 'Robban, no offense, but… I don't want to talk about any of this. I'm tired. You woke me up, then you guys were keeping me awake. I just want to sleep.'

Robban shook his head. 'Listen. I don't normally get involved in other people's affairs. But you two need help. Why don't you tell Eddie how you feel about him?'

I looked at him, trying to work him out, his motives. 'What? You're his boyfriend. Why would you say that to me?'

'I don't live under any illusions, brother. We're not in love, it's not forever. I care about Eddie as a friend. I want him to be happy, and you're the man for that job.'

I looked down at my hands. It felt weird to be talking to Robban about this… he had just come from Eddie's bed. Still, I understood that Robban, more than anyone right now, knew what was in Eddie's mind. I didn't have many friends and certainly, I had no one to talk to about my feelings for Eddie… maybe that was why and I found myself opening up to him.

I talked, like an idiot, about Eddie's courage and confidence. How much I admired him, how proud I felt of the way he was overcoming his mental health problems. I went on to talk about his beauty, the way he dressed, his attitude, the way that some days, he yelled at anyone who gave him shit for cross-dressing and squared up to them, making them either apologise or run when they saw how big he was and realised what they were dealing with… or some days he would just blow them a kiss and say, 'Puss puss.'

I loved the way he looked at me. I truly loved his voice; his deep, gravelly voice with the exaggerated Russian accent, or the cut-glass English depending on how he was feeling. Robban listened to everything I said, and his smile said it all.

'Colt,' he said. 'Don't ever talk like that in front of him. His ego is big enough already.'

When it was over I felt breathless. 'What am I going to do?'

Robban pulled me towards him and gave me a kiss on the side of my head. 'Whatever you do cutie, one thing is clear; you don't need me around.'

The next morning Eddie started work early, so when I woke from a deep sleep on the chaise lounge he was sitting next to me, sketching me.

'Shh,' he said. 'I finally get you lying still; do not spoil it by whining.'

Robban came downstairs at that moment holding a rucksack. Eddie stood up and gave him a hug, 'Have a safe trip. Call me when you get there.'

I sat up and rubbed my eyes, 'You going somewhere?'

'Robban's going to Gothenburg for Christmas,' said Eddie.

'Ja. My sister lives up there,' smiled Robban, 'I haven't seen her in ages. Shit, I have a seven-hour bus journey to get through now!'

'Well,' said Eddie, 'You know you are going to be lying stoned along the back seat of that bus. You will not notice seven hours.'

Robban hit him gently, 'I'd like to see you lowering yourself to travel on a fucking bus… Colt, I didn't want to leave Eddie alone at Christmas time but seeing as you are here now…' He met my eyes and gave me a little wink, 'I know he will be in safe hands for a few days.'

'You are sweet,' said Eddie tenderly, smiling at him as he tucked his hair behind his ear smearing charcoal on his face. 'Come, I will walk you downstairs.'

They left, and I felt a rush of fear and paranoia. Part of me wanted to shout for Robban to come back, but an equal part of me was tingling with excitement. A few minutes later Eddie came back upstairs. He leaned in the doorway and folded his arms, grinning at me. He was wearing a pink silk dressing gown and nothing else; it was clingy and left little to my imagination.

'So, galupchick. Now, it is just you and me.'

'Yep,' I said. I couldn't look at his eyes, so my gaze drifted to his body and I blushed and looked at the floor. Eddie just kept on staring at me, a playful grin on his face.

'Are you alright? You seem uncomfortable,' he laughed.

'It's… I have backache from sleeping on this damn couch,' I said. This was partly true.

Eddie said nothing. He waited until I looked at him again and then he said quietly, 'Well now, we would not want that, would we? Perhaps I can make you more comfortable tonight.'

Chapter 27

Eddie

I lay in bed listening to a siren outside. Whatever the emergency, it was far from me. The calm was like a blanket. In the absence of Robban, Colt had taken to sleeping in my bed with me. While this was pleasant, his behaviour was beginning to irritate me somewhat. I lay there, thinking about what had happened earlier that night. Of course, I was not blameless. Knowing how much cross-dressing turned him on, I always made sure to wear something pretty to bed. Tonight was no exception and as ever, he acted as though my negligee annoyed him.

'Don't wear that. Why are you doing that? Who are you trying to impress anyway?' He huffed, trying not to look at me as he got into bed and pulled the covers right up to his chin.

'What do you mean? This is what I wear,' I laughed at him. I was sitting in front of the vanity mirror, brushing my hair before bed. 'If you do not like it, you do not have to share my bed. Sleep on the floor, or on the couch.'

'No,' he said tightly, 'It's bloody cold down there and it's wrecking my back.'

'Well, then.' I unhooked my earrings, dropped them into a little dish on the table. I fluffed up my hair. 'You will just have to put up with me.' I got into bed and he tensed up even more, curling up to avoid touching me.

'Goodnight,' I whispered. He did not answer.

I woke up a little later to find him nervously pulling me close to him, his hot mouth on mine. I responded eagerly, pulling him on top of me and gratefully stroking his smooth skin as he kissed me on my scarred mouth. His erection pressed against me through his tracksuit bottoms. It was quite deliciously torturous, but I stuck with my decision to be passive and let Colt take the lead. I did not want to make his decisions for him. Eventually, his hands began to explore tentatively, sliding under the silk of my skirt and tugging at my lace underwear; as predicated, it was driving him mad.

'You want to touch me?' I asked softly, bringing his hand back up, 'Come on then, ask me.'

He continued kissing me with less certainty. He began to touch me again, but this time I grabbed his hand and resisted altogether. My self-restraint was failing, but making my point was important to me.

'No. Ask me first, baby. Talk to me. I need you to acknowledge that this is me, and you.'

At that, he rolled away and ignored me, pretending to be asleep. I propped myself up and looked over, I could barely make him out in the darkness of the room, but I could hear him breathing quickly.

'You…' I began, and faltered, biting my tongue. I had been about to say, 'You cannot keep doing this to me.' I knew that was unfair, so I laughed a little and said, 'You are back to sleeping on the floor tomorrow night.'

Colt had continued with his pretence.

I had an appointment the next morning to visit an art dealer in the city. A lot of money, perhaps commissions, depended on the meeting, but I was not nervous, I was looking forward to it. I began planning in my head which paintings I still needed to take photographs of and I realised I had better check my digital camera, so I rose from the bed and wrapped myself in my dressing gown. Colt stirred and turned over in bed.

'Where you going?' He asked sleepily.

'Hush… go back to sleep. I am checking something for work, babe.'

He closed his eyes and settled into the blankets. 'We could be together,' he said drowsily.

'Could we?' I was bemused. Colt never seemed to want to talk about our relationship.

'Yeah.' He snuggled further into the blankets. 'I mean, I don't know.'

'You are dreaming. Go to sleep.' I picked up my camera and sat down at the dressing table, searching through the photographs. I picked up a pen and began to scribble notes to myself about the paintings.

'I love you, I'm just scared,' murmured Colt. I paused, staring at a photo of the royal palace. I looked over at Colt. From the rise and fall of his body I could tell he was fast asleep.

'You are dreaming,' I repeated softly.

The Seven Eleven was busy, warm and scented with cinnamon buns. Colt was perched on a stool at the window, his head bent over a book. I watched him for a moment without attracting his attention; admiring his elegant legs in skinny jeans and his feet in bright orange canvas sneakers tucked gracefully under his high stool. I startled him by plucking the novel from his hands.

'Trash, trash, why are you reading this trash?' I sang, peering at the cover. I tossed the book back onto the table, 'Paul Russell is almost as bad a writer as he is in bed.'

Colt laughed guiltily. 'Oh, that's mean… I think the book's okay, actually. Ilya told me to check it over for any veiled references to our firm. Because someone might have spilled information to him while someone was all crazy.' I laughed good-naturedly. I ordered coffee and joined him.

'So, how did it go?' He smiled, referring to my big appointment with the art dealer.

'Extremely well. Very interested,' I told him. 'She wants to buy some of what I already have, and she wants to commission me to take some photographs and do sketches of her own house.'

'That's great. Congratulations!'

'Yes, well, it's money.'

We decided to eat a late breakfast somewhere nearby.

'Wait a minute,' said Colt, catching sight of a telephone box across the street. 'I just have to phone Manpyre, he texted me yesterday asking me to call him.'

'Tell him I hate him. Oh, Colt, don't be long, he is a dickhead and I am starving hungry.'

Colt ran across the street and fed endless coins into the telephone; apparently, there was no reply. I watched him as he ran back across the street, looking like he belonged on the cover of Vogue. The food was arriving at the table; I had ordered pastries and bowls of hot chocolate, swirled with cream and cinnamon.

'A rather funny thing happened last night,' I said, ripping a pistachio bun with my teeth.

Colt sipped his chocolate, 'Aye?'

I grinned at him, chewing and swallowed, enjoying his expectant gaze. 'You said… that you loved me.'

Predictably, he blushed and picked up his bowl of hot chocolate again, in an obvious effort to hide his face. A few minutes passed in silence, and once Colt had composed himself he changed the subject.

'So, tell me more about your commission. That's so exciting, how much will you be paid?'

I sat back, leaning my arm on the back of my chair. I studied him and decided not to let this one go.

'No… I do not think I will tell you about my commission. Why is it that you think you can kiss me every night- no, do not run away.' I grabbed Colt's wrist as he made to get up from the table, and pulled him firmly back into his seat. 'Why do you think you can do that with me, and then

210

refuse to talk about it? Do you think it does not have an effect on me? I always stop before things go too far, I protect you, despite wanting you so much.' I was leaning earnestly across the table. I released Colt's arm. 'You said you loved me. You were half-asleep, but you-'

'I know, keep your voice down. I know. I remember saying it.' Colt's face was bright red.

'Then you may also remember saying we could be together. Can we?'

He shook his head. 'No.'

'Why not?'

He shook his head, lips clenched.

'Is it because of my face?' I knew it was not because of my face, I simply needed to get him telling me the truth.

As I predicted, he became worked up, bloomed a deeper shade of red and cried, 'No! What, are you crazy? Of course it isn't because of your face. How can you say that to me after everything we've-'

I interrupted him calmly, 'Well, what is it, then?'

Colt looked at me. It was in my nature to be direct and to ask outright for the things I wanted. It was in his nature to be honest, and I should have been expecting it. Nevertheless, it was hard to hear.

'I'm afraid of you.'

My lips parted slightly, I felt breathless as though from a blow to the stomach. Christ, who could blame him? He had known me at my darkest, cutting my own face up, biting Paul and he knew what I did to Jay. No wonder he was scared of me.

'Fair enough.' I drained the last of my coffee and signalled for the bill.

'Eddie.' Colt touched my hand; even this familiar gesture seemed tentative and nervous. 'Just reassure me. Tell me that it won't happen again.'

'Oh, I can't promise anything. Anyway, even if I did, you would still be afraid.'

Colt looked down at the table. 'It's not so much afraid. I used the wrong word. I feel...' he sat back in his chair, clearly racking his mind for the right words. 'I feel kind of helpless when I'm with you. Like, fragile. Breakable.

You're somehow too… big; your body, your personality. I think I would break if we were together. Not physically but… emotionally, you would wreck me.' He pushed his hair out of his eyes. 'And I just don't want to feel like that. I want to be strong, I want to be myself. I don't want to just be 'Eddie's boyfriend'; just some sidekick, serving your needs and ending up worse off. Like Paul Russell, or…'

'Jason.'

'Yes.' Colt spoke softly. 'No, look, I'm sorry. I don't know what I'm saying.'

The Swede behind the counter was ignoring me and looking uncomfortable because of our heated conversation. I lost it and impatiently slammed 500 Kroner on the table and swished my jacket from the back of my chair.

'It is alright, you have said quite enough. Thank you for your honesty.'

I left.

Chapter 20

Colt

Over the next few days, despite our heated exchange in the cafe, relations were as friendly as ever between Eddie and me. He started sleeping on the couch in his gallery. 'You have my bed, babe, I want my guest to be comfortable,' he said, that first night after our discussion, winking at me as he headed off to the gallery holding a stack of blankets. I couldn't exactly argue. I had behaved like a total dick; I was giving him mixed signals all over the place. That night, I missed him terribly. I kept tossing and turning, and thinking about him constantly.

It was Christmas Eve. Eddie was already working in the gallery when I woke up, and unusually, he declined joining me for breakfast in our favourite cafe in the old town. He barely looked up from the small, bleak piece he was working on, and he politely asked me not to disturb him until the evening. Eddie was quite morose throughout dinner. We were at a cheap Chinese restaurant. He ordered two beers for himself, didn't drink them, and then ordered coffee instead.

'Don't you want any food?' I asked, ordering tons of everything for myself. He shook his head, staring into a tank full of depressed, bound lobsters.

'You're a cheap date,' I said. 'Are you gonna drink those beers?'

He shook his head again.

'Aren't you speaking to me?'

Eddie turned to look at me, a faraway look in his eyes. He shook his head and his eyes cleared. 'Sorry, babe,' he said softly, fiddling with his dangly earring. 'Sorry. I am miles away.'

I took a bite of rice and gazed around the restaurant, accidentally making eye-contact with a guy at the next table. He was with a group of three other guys and they all seemed to find Eddie very interesting. It was probably his outfit, his scars or his makeup. I wished that they would stop staring so confrontationally, it made me feel angrily protective over him but also, useless, because there was no way I could've stood up to a table of guys in defence of him.

'What's Swedish for 'stop staring?' I muttered, to Eddie.

He replied in Swedish, then said dully, 'Why?' He followed my gaze to the next table and shrugged, 'Babes… I do not give a fuck about them, and neither should you.'

Taking his lead, I ignored them.

I had been speaking to Manpyre on the phone earlier in the day, so I gave Eddie all the news from Lake Martin Manor.

'The hotel is completely full over Christmas.'

'Thank God I am not there, then.'

'Oh, don't you like Christmas?'

'I don't celebrate it.' Eddie accidentally pulled his earring loose. 'Eel died…' he paused, corrected himself. 'Well, you know what I mean. The 'accident' happened in early December; Christmas season. I do not… I mean, I do not associate the two things, really. But, if I was at Lake Martin, it would be too close to the bone. When I think about that time, his death, I still see Christmas lights, that fucking tree twinkling at the end of my bed and the fucking Christmas presents that they brought me while I was lying there with two broken legs and a broken heart. I could hear the carol concert in the entrance hall. It sounded so beautiful… I cannot listen to Christmas carols.'

I leaned forward and pursed my lips, my brow furrowed. When Eddie mentioned Eel on his own terms, it was a window of opportunity to talk about him, but I never knew what to say. I wanted to ask so many questions, and these occasions, when he was in a decent mood and talking about Eel, were so rare that the pressure was on.

'So… were you going to spend Christmas with him that year?' I cursed myself for yet another idiotic comment. Eddie looked at me through narrowed eyes.

'Yes, Colt… we were planning a delightful Christmas… until I fucked up our plans by nearly killing him.' He scowled and fell silent, lighting up a cigar.

'Look here, I'm sorry, okay?' I suddenly felt myself getting heated. Eddie looked at me in surprise as he tapped ash from his cigar. 'I'm sorry if I don't know what to say, I'm shit at this, alright? I dropped out of uni before we did the 'Bereavement Support' module.' I looked nervously at Eddie, who had a completely unreadable expression. 'That… that module was going to be in Year Three.'

Eddie began to laugh quietly, which completely startled me.

'Baby. I am so glad you did not do that 'module'. What the fuck are they teaching at those classes?' He laughed again.

I felt slightly defensive. 'Well, I suppose… the theory of bereavement? It's important for doctors to know how to support people in that way. To counsel them.'

Eddie shook his head. 'Okay, let us assume you have the 'theory'. But do you have the 'theory' of me? Do you know the 'theory' of Jason; of our relationship?' He leaned forward, waving his hand as he delved into the subject. 'Baby, some things in life cannot be taught in school. I know that

215

you can be clumsy when you ask me questions about Eel, and sometimes I just do not want to talk about it. But I know you are only trying to help.' He shook his head and took a quick draw on the cigar. 'Besides, even if you had a theory for me, it would be useless. I am not really bereaved, am I? I'm quite the opposite, now.' He pushed back his chair and stood up. 'I am going to the bathroom.'

He was probably going off to cut. I took a sip of beer, watching him as he walked away. Then someone jabbing me on my arm startled me. It was the guy from the next table, leaning way over in his seat and grinning at me drunkenly.

'Hej. You speak English right? I hate to tell you, but I think your girlfriend might be a man.' His friends howled with laughter. I couldn't be bothered with these pathetic losers.

'Oh, my God,' I gasped, mock-horrified, 'Do you think I can run out before she comes back?' I threw him a dirty look and resumed drinking my beer.

The atmosphere at the next table changed fast. One of the other guys got involved, slurring, 'Are you winding us up?' It was obvious that this lot were just looking for any chance to start trouble with us. I kept my head down and ignored them but they were constantly making remarks, trying to needle me.

'Want me to kick your head for you, English?'

'Whatever. My girlfriend could beat all four of you into the ground.'

'Colt?' Eddie was back. He looked really tired as he stared at the four angry drunks. He was leaning on the back of his chair in a certain way, a particularly disarming, feminine way. He sat down quickly and smoothed back his hair and twisted a lock around one finger.

'Come on,' he said, keeping his voice quiet, light. 'No one wants to fight tonight. It's Christmas!' The way he inclined his head, moved his hands, everything was submissive, feminine; and being seated, he wasn't provoking them with his size. It was a good tactic, but I was disappointed. I had seen him when in a different mood, beating up a couple of homophobic guys, and frankly I had enjoyed it. Sadly, tonight it wasn't to be. The drunk guys cooled off, left us alone. I watched Eddie across the table. He looked miserable. Beautiful, but miserable.

He looked around the restaurant then he looked at me and said, in a small voice, 'Colt? Can we go home? I want... I want to talk to you about Eel. I need to talk about it tonight, please.' For once, I felt like the one who was in control. I gestured to the waiter, ordered my food to go and took my best friend home.

I was lying on my front before the roasting fire, nibbling spring rolls. He was smoking another cigar. Eddie breathed his smoke, open-mouthed and relaxed, laying his head on the back of his armchair. He spoke slowly with his eyes closed. 'I am going to tell you what happened to Eel.'

'Jason and I had just finished making love on the riverbank, at the edge of the woods. I rolled onto my back and pulled him up on top of me. He sat straddling me while our heartbeats slowed together. Sweat glistened on his beautiful muscular body. I stroked his piercings, touching them, all in turn; ears, eyebrow, nose, tongue, lip, nipples, navel and penis. I myself had no piercings, they frightened me; I was nervous of blood, of needles and knives.

I rotated the silver bar in the soft tip of his penis; my favourite. I liked the way the metal felt inside me, a cold hard knot that made me shiver but felt sweet as honey.

I knew that I had to ask him about... the thing; the thing that Ilya had asked me to ask him. My heart felt like lead. It was getting dark and I could see bats flitting in the tree tops against the creamy night sky.

'Jay Jay,' I said quietly. His eyes looked pure black in the twilight. I stopped playing with his cock as it seemed inappropriate. I cleared my throat.

'Are you stealing money from my brother?' There was silence for a long while. His face was an unreadable mask in the darkness.

Then softly, calmly, 'Yeah... I am, as it happens."

'What happened then?' I was careful not to look at him.

'Jason seemed reluctant to explain, at first. He got up and put his clothes back on, a pair of black jeans and a leather jacket sewn all over with music badges.

'I need the money,' he said.

I shook my head. 'Why? I have money. I look after you.'

'I don't want to be stuck in this place forever,' he burst out. 'I want a life. I want to see things, do things. I don't want to end up in jail, or just staying in this hotel. I have to go. I've been saving the money, I've got enough now.'

I wriggled into my trousers, zipped them and stood up, too. 'Eel-' I began, but he interrupted me.

'No, listen, babe. It's not just all that. Ilya's gonna kill me if I stay, anyway.' He gave a short laugh, 'I really don't like the way he looks at me. I know, if I stay here, I'm gonna have an accident. Maybe I'll choke on a gun in my cornflakes one morning...'

'Jesus, Eel. I would never let that happen.' My mind was already racing, thinking; fuck, why did he have to steal from Ilya? What was I going to tell Ilya? How could I protect Jason, the stupid, impulsive...

He was still talking, 'And! I don't want to watch him raising those babies, either. Aw, he went and gave them crazy Russian names... no offense.'

'What do you care about that?' I stared at him, we never talked about those kids. Only Jason could sleep with someone twice and get them pregnant... with twins. Only Jason could fuck up so royally. He was never lucky.

He came over to me, put his arm around my shoulders while he dug a picture from his back pocket, 'It's just, look at this. How fucking cute are they? Look?'

I turned away.

'Anyway. It doesn't matter. At least they'll be rich. Me? I'm getting sick of watching my back all the time. I am gonna leave, babe. Probably this weekend. Okay, I'm gonna tell you- now, don't panic when I tell you this.

There's this American guy I used to model with. He's helping me out, he's got a place I can lie low. It's a punk bar in Atlanta… baby, don't look at me like that, he's just a friend.'

And I started to panic.

'You're leaving me?' I suddenly found my hands around his throat. 'Are you trying to leave me?'

'No.' He pushed me away. 'I obviously want you to come with me, you madman. Once I'm all sorted, you can join me.' I stood there and Eel glared at me. 'I love you, why would I leave you…'

I did not believe him.

'You are lying. Why have you never mentioned this before? I could have gotten money far more easily than you stealing it. You were going to leave me.' I shoved him in the chest. 'You're not leaving me!'

He tried to grab onto my arms and I pushed him again, hard and he stumbled back, towards the river… he fell. I did not even stop to think, I just jumped after him, smashed my legs on the rocks.

Hours passed as I lay there in the mud with him. He was cold. I knew, or I thought I knew, that he was dead. It was freezing cold. I kept flitting in and out of consciousness. I had hallucinations. I kept waking up, screaming… then I would see him and I knew that the truth was worse. At one point I took my knife and…" Eddie touched his face, fingering the old scar.

'Shh,' I said, 'Don't get upset. You don't have to tell me any more…'

'Then,' he continued, staring at the fire, 'I would not let him go. When they found us, I fought them; I was delirious. But, I knew I would never see him again. They had to inject me here,' he tilted his head and ran his fingers over his neck.

'So you see what I did; my temper cost Jason his mind, his life. Knowing that makes it hard for me to feel… little other than revulsion for myself.'

I swallowed hard. It was a terrible story and I was frightened, and not really any more reassured… but I still didn't feel any differently about him. I still loved him, the whole fucked-up package. I looked at him thoughtfully and noticed that he was digging his fingernails into his palm, leaving deep red crescents.

'You want to cut yourself…' I said, suddenly realising. Eddie was biting his lip.

'It would help,' he said, breathing in. 'Though I am not going to, not while you are here. I will do it later. It is all this talking about Eel… it is hard, you know?'

I nodded. He was in obvious discomfort; I felt so uneasy.

'Do it now,' I said rashly.

Eddie shook his head, 'Shh. No.'

But, I stood up. 'Come on. What do you use?'

His eyes were haunted and circled with grey. Wordlessly, he took out his wallet and drew out a straight razor blade wrapped in a piece of green velvet. He handed this to me.

'Okay.' I unwrapped it fully and I faltered, but collected myself. 'I'm going to sterilise this.' Eddie nodded hungrily, looking grey and sick. I quickly disinfected the blade by dropping it into a mug of boiling water, then, with shaking fingers I passed it back to Eddie and sat on the floor by his feet.

'What do I do?' I whispered. 'What does Robban do?'

Eddie rolled up his top and positioned the blade just above his navel. 'You are not Robban. Go away if you want, babe. It is not pretty.'

Instead, I took hold of Eddie's trouser leg, clutching the material in my fingers. My heart was beating fast and I felt a rising panic as Eddie rested his head on the back of the couch, stared up at the ceiling and dug the point of the blade into his skin.

'Be careful,' I blurted. Eddie closed his eyes and steadily drew the razor across his stomach. Blood welled out of the cut and ran down, seeping into his waistband. Eyes closed, his breathing lengthened.

'Thank you,' he sighed. To me or to a higher being, I wasn't sure.

Eddie opened his eyes and laughed weakly, 'Look at your face! You are as white as marble.' He sat up. 'Oh… you are shaking too. Sweetheart.'

'Stay still while I wash your cut,' I stood up feeling lightheaded.

Eddie grabbed my arm gently. 'No. You sterilised the knife, didn't you? Well, then. When will you realise… this whole world is dirty, we just have to learn to live in it?'

'But…' I knelt in front of Eddie again, pushed up his top and skimmed my fingers over the new stomach wound. It wasn't so bad, not very deep. The blood smeared across his skin and I found myself kissing Eddie's scarred stomach, my tongue tracing the uneven skin, the tangy edges of the razor cut. The vulnerability was erotic to me. Eddie's weakness made us, in my mind, more equal. My hand found his hardening erection. My heart was pounding; I wasn't thinking, just acting on instinct.

'Please,' said Eddie hoarsely, as I pressed my forehead against his taut stomach, 'Do not be afraid of me.'

Blood in my mouth, I looked up at him and lied, 'I'm not.' I was scared. I could feel his muscles and strength and I was scared.

There was a picture of me hanging up on the wall right behind Eddie. The picture showed me my own masculine body; the power in my shoulders, my back, my thighs.

'That's how you see me, isn't it?'

Eddie craned his neck to look upside down at the picture.

'That is how you are,' he groaned, exasperated. His hand was in my hair, twisting it slightly. It hurt, and I felt dizzy with a combination of lust and fear. He looked down at me and I really couldn't tell whether he was going to hit me, cut me, bite me or just fuck me. Break me, I thought suddenly, angrily. Damage me, destroy me, and take over my body. I know you will but I don't care, I love you, God help me, I love you.

He didn't break me, of course. We ended up in a world free from pain, a place I only ever went to with him. In the cold bedroom, I got out of my clothes and lay on the bed while he kissed me quite forcefully, pressing my wrists lightly against the pillows. He stopped and looked down at my face.

'You alright?' He checked briskly. I nodded, speechless. I was, actually, more than alright.

'I missed this,' he told me, and he carried on. He just did things, shocking things that felt unbelievably good. I realised with a flush of embarrassment that I was moaning out loud. This was so not like me!

'Oh my goodness,' said Eddie. 'Hearing you gasp like that... you sound so uninhibited. You are also quite high-pitched, you know, you sound like a girl.'

I was blushing furiously. 'S... sorry,' I stammered.

'For what? Please, do not apologise, I love it.'

'Ah... you're laughing at me for being noisy...' I couldn't help it. Whatever he was doing, was making me flip out. It felt really good. By the end I was shouting and bathing in unbelievable pleasure blossoming all over my body.

'Fuck,' I was panting. 'Eddie, fuck.'

Afterwards, I was stunned. I was in awe of my feelings for him.

'I love you,' I said fiercely. 'I love you. I love you.' Overwhelmed by everything, I put my forehead against his shoulder and sobbed. Eddie kind of laughed, stroking the back of my neck.

'You love me, do you? Okay, show me.' He lay back on the bed, pulled me up on top of him and with gentle commands; he encouraged me to make love to him. It was my first time topping a guy and it wasn't exactly a world-beating performance; I was crying the whole time and I was so overexcited that I only lasted about fifteen seconds. But it felt amazing. Eddie was laughing at me as he held me afterwards, but I didn't care.

Chapter 29

Eddie

Colt managed to negotiate staying in Stockholm for the next eight weeks, persuading Ilya that I would benefit from having his support for a while longer. He said that he was going to spend the eight weeks thinking about what to do next. I decided for him.

'You are not going back to Lake Martin; ever. You ought to go back to university.'

'Hm… Don't know about that. You can't make me.' I grinned at that.

'True.' I loved it when Colt became slightly defiant. I was rather enjoying the fact that his prediction of our relationship dynamic had come true. I felt as though I had won something. The prize was, almost certainly, Colt himself. Things were different between us now, what with everything that had passed between us, we knew each other so well and I believed that his fear of me was a thing of the past. He seemed to have lost most of his self-consciousness and he just stunned me.

Making love one afternoon, I gazed up at my shy, beautiful boy pinning me down, his eyes closed in abandonment, his skin glittering with sweat.

'Bryce,' I breathed. He opened his eyes and held my gaze steadily while he fucked me. He was more confident, even, than Robban. He was just giving everything to me; everything that he had to give. I had to remind myself that this beautiful creature was both very vulnerable and very trusting, he certainly was not Robban, and I could not treat him in the same way. I was careful not to take advantage of his trust and I never hit him. If I needed to self-harm I did it in private.

Robban, bless him, was so happy for me.

'Aw, nice one, you guys!' He grinned, genuinely delighted when I told him about Colt and I, on his return from Gothenburg. Colt was watching him nervously, and Rob could not resist teasing him.

'You little bitch! Stealing my boyfriend while I'm away!'

I rolled my eyes, 'He is not serious, as always he is teasing you, darling.'

Robban moved back to his old place. I offered him money, which he refused. 'As tempting as that is, and it's so nice of you, brother, it's better that I earn every cent myself,' he explained, 'I'm less likely to spend it badly.'

When he moved out, a part of me was apprehensive about losing his reassuring presence, I felt suddenly, like I was off-balance at the top of a flight of stairs… but he was never far away. He joined us for dinner, often, and he was always there on the phone if I needed to talk.

My need to hurt myself was diminishing, daily. I had called myself happy when I was with Jason, but looking back I saw things as they truly were. My love for Jason had been more than passion, it was obsession. I swung from desperation to maniacal joy; painfully intense. He cheated on me, and we argued and physically fought one another, all the time.

The break ups were intense, the making up… was passionate, but still awful. I felt that I could not hold onto him, by seduction nor violence. Now, I was discovering the virtues of loving someone deeply, mutually. I woke up every morning and Colt was there, comfortable, perfect and safe. I remembered how I used to wake up, stare at Jason's sleeping face and be afraid to wake him up. My throat had ached as I stared at Jason, praying that the moment could last forever, wondering how it was possible to love someone so much.

I found myself able to reflect on such things without fear. I thought about Jason a lot, every single day, but now I was able to think more calmly and clearly. Knowing that he was alive meant that he was always in my mind, and sometimes, perhaps every few days, the pain would suddenly engulf me like someone had touched a raw nerve. At these times I would sit sobbing on the bathroom floor, misery and guilt clawing at my heart, muffling my cries with a towel jammed into my mouth.

'Baby… my baby, Jason,' I whispered. 'Oh, my love.' I realised that Jason would never fully leave my thoughts. I began writing postcards addressed to him at the Harbour Centre. 'Dearest Jason,' they always began. I kept the language very simple, and wrote about things I had done. I hoped that the nurses would read the letters to Jason.

'Today, I visited the Gamla Stan, the old town. It is minus 15 degrees here Jay, my fingers are still frozen as I write this. The picture on this postcard is of Alfred Nobel. I love you. Eddie.'

I could not resist sending a letter every other day, noticing with interest that I never mentioned Colt, nor did I make a point of telling Colt that I was writing to Jason… I laughed wryly at myself, did I think either of them would get jealous?

Colt

I stood leaning on a bridge in Stockholm city centre. I was meant to be handing out leaflets for the gallery shop but I was taking a break. Bicycles breezed past me, bells ringing. In keeping with the fashion of the city, I was wearing a tight white vest, a loose navy blue cardigan, drainpipe jeans and unlaced black boots. Sunglasses on my head held back my long dark hair. I was enjoying time out of the apartment. It was literally the first time I had been out for two weeks. I was spending my days deliriously happy, albeit almost always drunk due to Eddie's fondness for red wine, marijuana and poppers in bed.

I bit my lip and felt myself blushing slightly, recalling the night before. I had been lying on the couch in the studio, naked and completely stoned, wearing lots of eye makeup and letting Eddie take lots of photos of me. Then he had literally painted me. I mean, he painted on my skin. The apartment was now covered in dried paint and I was still scraping flakes of it from under my fingernails. It wasn't all sex though. Eddie was talking about setting up home together, looking at flats on the internet. He wanted us to live in my native Edinburgh because, apart from wanting me to return to the university, he said he liked the art scene and the city itself. I was up for it. To be honest, I was ready to follow him anywhere on earth.

I absolutely loved being with him. He was controlling and he could be frightening, but everything felt natural; everything felt good. Edinburgh would take me closer to my dad… standing on that bridge, I became lost in reflection about him. I wondered if I was being unfair to him. That awful fight, the last time we saw each other. My dad had said terrible things to me; that my mum would have been disappointed in me, that I was a failure, a quitter. He said that I was weak. I remembered sitting in front of my laptop in my dorm room, weeping over another late essay with Dad, standing behind me, pissed and screaming at me to pull myself together.

'I can't,' I wanted to shout. 'My mum just died. I can't think properly.' I did not say it, just sat there breaking my heart.

'Can't you do anything right?' He was saying. 'Can you do anything at all?'

I was really crying, like someone had opened the floodgates. Humiliated in front of him, I stood up to go to the bathroom. As I passed him, head down, I felt this huge whack on the side of my face. After that he just lost it, hitting me with both fists until my roommate managed to drag him off.

I wasn't badly hurt. While security threw my father out, I stayed in my room, sitting against the door, shivering and shaking as though I was really cold. It became dark, and I remember I didn't bother turning on the lights, just sat there in the darkness. There was a light knocking on my door.

'Bryce. You okay dude?'

I rested my chin on my knees. I felt numb, my eyes were dry. Minutes passed, I could still hear them out there.

'Bryce,' voices said again. 'Bryce.'

'It's okay,' I said quickly. I stood up and opened the door, 'I'm okay, everybody just… Everything's alright now.' I closed the door on their worried faces. 'I have to finish my assignment now.'

I took a bunch of pills that night; a whole bunch of pills. My roommate thought I was dead when he found me in bed covered with pills and vomit, deeply unconscious. I'm glad that I was still out when my kid brothers came to visit me up at the hospital, I wouldn't have liked to see their wee faces. Dad didn't visit.

I asked myself, honestly, if I had demonised my father in my own mind. He was brutal, but the man had only just lost his wife.

I wondered what my dad would think if he could see me now. I was unemployed and I had absolutely no idea what to do with my life, how was that for a failure? Eddie didn't know about my overdose, but I told him everything else about Dad.

'I want to meet your daddy,' he had said to me on a number of occasions. 'I think I know you better than anyone, and I could tell him a thing or two about you. If that bastard thinks you cannot do anything right, babe, he does not know you at all.'

I felt warm thinking about Eddie. What would Dad think of him? Of all the potential partners he might've imagined I would end up with, Dad probably hadn't predicated a six foot, heavily scarred, practically bi-polar, Russian transvestite. I laughed. The laughter came right from my belly and it felt good. I spread my arms out and felt the sun on my face. I had no idea if it was Wednesday or Sunday; the days all merged together.

Chapter 30

Eddie

I still did not quite grasp how Colt could be both Catholic and gay, but he informed me that there were many practising gay Christians. Personally, I did not even believe in angels anymore, not since my very own angel had come crashing to earth, broken and changed. No, I had faith in nothing but human beings; the good, the bad and the ugly.

I was thinking about his religion because living with Colt, it became obvious just how much the boy prayed. Morning and night, he went off and sat quietly with his little rosary beads, looking out of the window and whispering. He started talking about St Eric's Cathedral and he dragged me there one afternoon.

'It's gorgeous,' he said. 'Can we go in?'

I smiled, 'Do whatever you want, babe.'

Whilst I paced around looking at the art, Colt knelt down at the altar and crossed himself. Closing his eyes, he bowed his head, his lips moving in silent prayer.

He looked absolutely charming, kneeling down there. I moved closer to him until I could actually hear his soft whispering… oh, dear, he was praying for me. I smiled, feeling an enormous wave of love for him. He asked God to watch over his brothers and, to my surprise he spent quite some time praying for his father, who frankly, deserved it even less than I did. Finally, Colt took a breath and began to speak about Jason. I froze, listening.

'Can we help you?'

I glanced up and two men in black robes were standing watching me uneasily. Probably wondering why I was standing behind one of their flock, staring at him in horror as he prayed. Perhaps they took exception to my outfit? My vintage Dior dress was prettier than theirs.

No,' I said, my voice sounding loud indeed as it echoed round the silent cavernous room, 'I do not think you could.'

Colt looked up, then dropped his head back to the cracked and ancient tiles, silently completing the rest of his prayers. I backed out of the Cathedral. When Colt finally emerged from the church, blinking in the bright sunlight, I was sitting on the steps waiting for him.

'Not my scene, babe,' I said. I took his hand and thought that if I were given to prayer, how many of mine seemed to have already been granted.

That night, Colt kept complaining that I was unusually quiet as we sat watching a Swedish film. I was on the couch and he sat on the floor between my legs. Every time I wanted another beer I would dangle my empty bottle in front of him, and he would dutifully go to the kitchen to get me another.

'What's on your mind?' He asked, opening another and handing it to me. I looked down at him. He seemed sweetly tipsy, which I loved, though tonight I was distracted.

'Nothing,' I answered, sipping my beer. I was actually thinking about his overheard prayers in the church, his sweet, earnest voice whispering simply for God to 'comfort Jason in his suffering', to 'protect him and give him strength'. Now, I could not stop wondering about this 'suffering' Jason was going through. Perhaps Colt had simply been referring to his condition, but somehow, I knew it was more than that. I remembered Colt trying to tell me that there was something wrong with Eel, but at the time, I could not bear to listen. Personally, I did not believe that God was going to help Jason in any way, as much as Colt's innocent prayers were very beautiful.

As I fell asleep that night with him in my arms, the true words of the prayer reverberated drowsily in my mind, 'Please Lord, bless Jason. Please help him to regain his health and strength, and to find peace again, without Eddie.'

That night, I dreamed. Eel was crawling across the mud, his head twisted unnaturally, bright eyes fixed on me. He was crawling too fast. 'Help me,' he whispered. His face stretched, turned furious, 'Help me! Help me now.' I woke in agony, screaming.

'It's okay! It's alright…' Colt had jumped out of bed and was standing quite close, but maintaining a safe distance, just as I had told him to do. I knew from experience that I could easily attack and hurt anyone who attempted to comfort me in the confusing, terrifying moments between nightmare and reality.

'It's okay,' repeated Colt. He, himself, looked visibly shaken. 'Look at me, it's okay.' Shivering, I lay back down and my pounding heart gradually stilled.

Colt said nothing about it until he came out of his morning shower, where he had obviously been thinking it over. 'You haven't had such a severe nightmare for weeks,' he said reproachfully, wrapping a towel around his waist. Grabbing another towel he began to dry his hair. 'I'm worried about you.'

'Don't worry,' I said shortly. I was lying on the bed with my arms behind my head. 'It was only a dream.' As much as I tried to forget I could not rid my mind of the image. I wished that Colt would drop the subject.

'Still…' Colt rubbed his hair and I thought how attractive he was, close to perfect. I watched as his brow creased with concern, and his perfect lips formed the words.

'I mean, you were absolutely terrified. What were you seeing?'

'Stop asking questions,' I said. 'Come over here, baby. Take my mind off it.'

He came over and I laid him on his front, crawled on top of him and fucked him very slowly. I swept back his hair and buried my face in the back of his neck, trying desperately to concentrate on his body. Just connecting, just trying to lose myself. It was no good. I spent the whole Sunday in bed with Colt; even so, my mind sparked constantly with images from the nightmare.

In the late afternoon, I woke with a start from a shallow, disturbed sleep. The bright morning was long gone, the room was dark and Colt was asleep, or pretending to be. I was gripped with a terror of being alone, and I roughly shook Colt's shoulder to wake him up. 'Mm?'

'Hey, I know you are not asleep. I need you.' Distractedly, I began to manhandle him and then I stopped, seeing the look on his face. I felt suddenly awful.

'Ah… babe. I am so sorry. You are exhausted.'

Colt sat up. 'Honestly, I'm okay. I'm okay,' he said. In actual fact, he looked ill. I realised that I had been treating him roughly without thinking, focusing instead on trying to numb the painful images in my own head.

'Ah… have I been hurting you? I have. You need to tell me if I am hurting you. Do not just… I did not even realise I was doing it.' I swung my legs out of bed, sat on the edge and rubbed my own face.

'Christ. What is wrong with me?' I stared at the ceiling, stretching my neck. 'Think I am going crazy…' I caught the look of terror on Colt's face.

'No! I do not mean literally crazy, like last time. I simply mean… I do not know. I feel as though something is wrong. Something dreadful. Sorry, I know I am talking nonsense. It is just this nightmare, this… horrible nightmare.'

Colt looked sweetly concerned. I noticed huge bruises on his exquisite pale arms, where I had gripped him so tightly earlier. I felt like a huge brute, and even worse, when he said gently, 'Dreams can be really freaky. They can chill you for the whole day. What was the dream about?'

'Nothing, babe. Listen, I want you to get some rest. I will sort out dinner for you.'

Having grown up in a hotel with award-winning chefs and thereafter living off Parisian restaurants since I was twenty-one, I am afraid my concept of sorting dinner was to buy it from a restaurant and bring it home.

I caught the tunnelbana to a certain Italian restaurant, two stops from the apartment. We had dined there a few nights before, and I remembered how much Colt enjoyed the angel hair pasta.

Jason was on my mind. Jason, the nightmare and Colt praying for him.

On my way home I passed the internet cafe by the station. I stopped as though compelled, and stood looking through the window as I absently weighed the foil containers in my hands. The image from my nightmare was still locked in my head. I could simply phone up and enquire as to Jason's health; for reassurance. I asked myself if I was ready to do that. I felt so much stronger than before. As if Colt had given me life and strength. Surely one tiny phone call would not break me down again? It would be all that I needed, to hear that Jason was safe and well.

Within seconds I was in the cafe, on the pay phone. 'I am calling to ask about one of the patients, Jason Prescott. I am a friend,' I said.

The line was bad. I cradled the phone between my ear and shoulder, holding the hot foil cartons of food. 'How… is he? Is he well?'

'Sorry,' I was told. 'I can't give you any information on the phone.'

'But I… ah. I have called before. Is something wrong?' Fear clawed at my heart. 'Is something wrong?'

'Look, I'm sorry. You need to make an appointment to speak to one of the doctors. What's your name?'

'It does not matter what my bloody name is!' Suddenly, the line went dead.

I realised I was shaking as I redialled, a different number. It took a few seconds to connect. 'Come on!' I shouted impatiently.

'Hello.'

'Alexandra. It's Edvard.' There was a long pause. I did not hesitate. 'I phoned the centre, I know that something is wrong.' I held the telephone with both hands, feeling warm and sick. 'Please tell me that he is alright.'

'Believe it or not,' said Alex finally, 'I'm glad you called. Jason's not okay. He's really not okay, and it is your fault.'

I closed my eyes, a sick prickling feeling in the back of my throat.

'Eddie, he is heartbroken. He stopped eating and he's lost loads of weight. He's dying. You caused this. '

'Oh, God. Oh God.'

'Ever since you visited him that one time, his behaviour completely changed. He tried, escaping from the gardens, climbing out of windows. The hospital tried everything but in the end they couldn't keep him there.'

I heard myself ask, monotonously, 'So where is he now?'

'He has been transferred to a private hospital. It's... a more secure place.'

As I considered what a secure hospital might entail, all of my original doubts swelled in my chest. I felt a familiar cramping ache my heart, and I gasped.

Alex continued, 'Did you think your visit wouldn't have an effect on him?'

'It had an effect on me. I lost my mind. That's why-'

'And your stupid postcards? He is hysterical; we had to stop giving them to him. Glad you're having fun in Stockholm, by the way, at least somebody's bloody happy.'

'I will come to see him. That would help him, would it not?'

'Probably.'

'Then I will. I will come.'

'Eddie, you can forget it. There's still a warrant for your arrest. Come anywhere near and I'll tell the police where you are. My only hope for Jason is that he'll forget all about you again. I am not,' her voice trembled with anger, 'going to subject him to another meaningless visit from you.'

'It will not be meaningless. I will stay. I will stay forever.'

'Just leave him alone!' She was crying, but she stayed on the line. I clung on to that fact; that hope. I had a chance to make her understand.

'It is me he wants,' I hissed, my voice growing louder with every word, 'It is me that he needs. He will die without me, I will die without him. Understand?'

A waiter came over, tapped on the old-fashioned glass booth and made 'shushing' gestures. 'Get the fuck away from me, I am talking,' I spat, slamming my hand against the booth. The waiter backed away, hands held up, and I turned my back on the whole cafe staring at me.

'Did you just yell at someone in Swedish?'

I ignored her. 'Alex, he is wasting without me; you said it yourself. He is dying. I have been deluding myself that he is alright.' It was coming so clearly to me now. How I could ever have dreamed that Jason and I could live without one another… 'Tell me where the hospital is.'

Alex composed herself. 'No, no. I'm not going to let you see him. You stay away, Eddie. You'll hurt him again and he's been through more than enough shit, he doesn't deserve that.'

'I will never leave his side again. Not for one minute.'

'I can't hand Jason over to you. You are sick, you can barely look after yourself. You did this to him, and tried to kidnap my son, for God's sake. You are an animal, aggressive and weird. You've always been the same. I don't trust you with Jason. He's like… a toy to you. You don't care about him; you used to draw pictures of his dead body!'

I shook my head. I was not even going to try to explain that to Alex, she would never understand how it felt to have an image of something so powerful and horrifying, and to be unable to force it out of your mind. The only way I knew how to rid myself of such an image was to sketch it out onto paper, to physically push the image out of my body and onto the paper. I used to draw Eel's body all the time, almost unconsciously. My psychiatrist had been fascinated.

I pushed the bad memories away.

'Alexandra. You know I can help him. Save him, even.'

'I don't know… I don't know.'

I changed tack. I stopped trying to be nice and said what I really felt.

'He is mine. Give him to me,' I hissed. My phone credit was about to run out. 'Alex, I am coming to see him. Have me fucking arrested, okay, then Jason will die. That is your choice. See you in a few days.' I hung up the phone.

I walked slowly back to the apartment in falling snow. My mobile phone vibrated in my pocket and I looked at the text message that would change my life.

'Phillip Wren Hospital. Don't let him down. Alex.'

The wheels were in motion; all I had to do was pack up my life in Sweden. The light in the streets of the city that healed me, were quietly fading as evening fell. A sudden pain gripped my chest and I staggered, clutching the front of my coat. Colt was my comfort, he was my home. He was almost too much to sacrifice. I fell into a darkened doorway, pain clawing in my chest like a sharp scratching. I reminded myself that I would sell the souls of everyone on earth for Jason's.

When I entered the apartment Colt was relaxing in the armchair, freshly showered, his head bent over a book. He looked up thoughtfully and smiled when he saw me.

'Aw hey, you went to Nello's! You're the best. I'm starving...'

'Jason is dying.'

Colt stood up.

'He needs me. I am going to him.' I heard my own calm, slow voice. Simply, there was nothing to agonise over anymore. I had no choice; I did not want or need a choice. I watched Colt carefully. I could see that as always, my darling was processing the information, carefully calculating what it meant. After a moment, he nodded.

'Wow. Okay. I guess I... I'll go to the internet cafe, book us onto the first flight.' He paused, then turned away and lifted his coat from the chair. I felt a quick stab of pain in my chest, as I watched Colt masking his emotions with brisk practicality. This was exactly how I predicted he would react.

'Colt- sweetheart, I have just come from there. It is already booked. My flight is on Friday. Yours too, of course.'

'Yeah?' Colt pulled on his coat, avoiding eye contact. 'Whatever, I need a minute on my own, okay?'

This, too, was typical. Colt hated anyone to witness him at times of extreme emotion, and his instinct was always to hide.

'Babe,' I said. 'Do not run away. Stay here, please, I need you here.' Colt stopped. He looked confused, troubled. I felt a desperate tightness in my throat. Colt had invested so much in our relationship, and I felt responsible for his obvious pain. I felt a rapid pulsing in my neck, and my chest suddenly scrunched with a ferocious pain. I sat down heavily, hitting the base of my spine on the floor which sent a shivering ache up my back. Colt was by my side in an instant.

'Breathe slowly,' he said, loosening my coat and shirt buttons. He felt in my pockets, 'Where are your tablets?'

'I don't know,' I answered crossly. 'In the bedroom. On the bureau.'

'Not much good there, are they?' Colt fetched the tablets and fed two into my mouth. 'No, don't swallow them, you're meant to let them dissolve slowly.'

'Oh- baby, stop. This is unbearable, embarrassing. I feel like an old man.'

'Sh. This is what you get for being with an almost doctor. Anyway, this is all a ruse to get me to stay, isn't it?' He teased.

I groaned. 'Ha. Yes, I knew you would not leave me dying.' I sat up a little.

'Feeling better yet?'

I rubbed my chest. 'Yes. Not so tight.'

'Good.' Colt was reading the label on the box of medication. He looked up, 'You need to be fighting fit for Jason. You wouldn't want him to see you like this.'

Colt tried to separate strands of congealed angel hair pasta.

'Obviously, you're thinking we can't be together anymore, once we get home. Can we?'

I crunched thoughtfully into a hardened bruschetta, picturing how life would be. I intended to rent a place in the village near the facility, to visit Jason every day. I would spend whole days with Jason if I could, then work at night on my drawing and painting. There was no room for Colt in this vision. He was only twenty years old, there was still so much for him to do and experience. I felt my mouth twitch slightly. This was difficult.

'No, babe.'

We were silent for a long time. Colt was shivering although the room was warm. I finally spoke, 'I don't know what is going to happen. But one thing; do not worry about your future. My advice is this; resume your studies. You must not waste that big brain of yours. If you want, I will pay for whatever you need to go back to school; fees, accommodation. I will buy you an apartment.'

'Ilya would never let me leave,' said Colt bitterly. 'I'm not leaving the firm without you to protect me.'

I smoothed back his hair. 'You know something?' I said quietly, 'Not once have I questioned whether Jason is worth this sacrifice. Not once.'

Colt wiped his eyes. 'Then you're doing the right thing. Then you love him. But, Eddie, what am I going to do without you?'

'Shh. You will fine, galupchick.'

Colt

After Eddie collapsed, I made him lay down and rest for a while. Lying up against the pillows, he asked me to tell him what I knew about Jason Prescott's condition. Nervously, I did… and instead of his usual rage whenever Eel was mentioned, Eddie was rapt. He lay facing me, his long legs folded elegantly beneath him, resting his head on his curled fist. He watched me as I talked, drinking in every word. It was nerve-racking, talking about Jason; I worried that Eddie would flip out at any moment… but no, something had changed. He seemed strangely… I don't know, peaceful, as he listened. So, I included as much of the gory details as I dared.

'He's on protein shakes to keep him going but when I saw him last he weighed about… seven and a half stone.' My voice was low in the darkness and the quiet of the room, 'He's so malnourished that he's actually lost a few teeth. That's pretty serious.'

Eddie didn't flinch. Perhaps there was a flicker in the darkness of his eyes, some huge shadow surging fathoms deep, but on the surface, he remained calm. Speaking slowly, without breaking eye contact even for one second, he said, 'He will be alright once he is with me again. Of that, I am certain.'

He did look certain and I really felt the change in him. From the moment he made his decision to become responsible for Eel, I had been slightly in awe of his level of resolve; that sharp, blazing focus of his. Nothing would come between Eddie and Eel now… certainly not me.

Chapter 31

Colt

It was three in the morning: Eddie had gone to Robban's apartment to tell him what had happened, and to say goodbye to him. This was just an excuse, really. I knew that he needed reassurance and cheering up tonight, and Robban was always better at that than me. He had been gone all night. There was no answer on his phone; I knew, because I had tried calling him about twenty times. I was lying in bed in the dark, staring at the T.V, cradling a beer between my knees. My head ached with tension and I felt the pressure behind my eyes of hot tears stinging. Blinking, I picked up the remote and starting clicking randomly between channels.

It was the first time I had slept alone since I got together with Eddie. I tried to focus on the T.V, but instead I saw myself, broken and discarded. Eddie had taken just about everything from me, and I felt robbed. I turned up the volume and tried to focus entirely on the screen, forcing my mind to detach. It was impossible, my eyes burned, my throat became tight. I coughed and grabbed the remote again, keeping my finger pressed on the volume button as a laughter track echoed around the room. The door suddenly swung open and Eddie clicked on the light. I quickly muted the volume.

'Are you going deaf?' He enquired, tearing off his coat and gloves. 'I could hear that from down in the gallery.' He sat down heavily on the bed and began to unlace his boots. 'Sorry I am home so late,' he added, 'I lost track of time talking with Robban.'

As he spoke, he carelessly laid his hand on my arm and I kind of jerked away. 'Bryce... you flinched.' Eddie's voice was full of surprise and hurt. 'Your eyes are all red. Have you been crying in here?'

As I picked up my beer and took a swig, I was aware of Eddie looking, searchingly, at me. You took my future, I thought, swallowing hard. I don't have a future.

'Well?'

'Well, what?'

'What do you have to cry about?'

I fiddled with the neck of the beer bottle. 'Nothing. It's nothing.' I looked at him helplessly. 'I guess... I'm worried about everything.' I shrugged, 'I'm stressing about what to do- if I don't go back to Lake Martin, they're gonna- find me and kill me. But I don't want to go back. You talked me out of it, and now I'm too scared to go back. On my own.' I added meaningfully.

Eddie looked steadily at me, his eyes dark. I took a sip of beer, my eyes still on Eddie.

'That, and... well, this is possibly the last evening you and I will ever spend together.'

Eddie's mouth twitched slightly. He fingered the pearls around his neck, and gave a slight, elegant shrug. 'Yes.'

'So I guess... I'm alone. And scared, and...' I couldn't say what I really felt; rejected, humiliated. I had given everything to Eddie; Everything. I felt that he didn't understand. Eddie took the beer from me, took the last sip, and was silent for a long time. When he finally spoke, his words were not what I expected.

'Depressingly, you are right. We are both alone, now.'

I glanced at him, surprised.

'But you'll have Jason.'

Eddie's mouth twisted into a sad smile.

'I love that man better than anyone,' he whispered, his voice hoarse. 'I love him more than I do you, for Christ's sake.' He looked down. 'But I am going to be alone in many ways.'

I nodded, sort of understanding what he meant. Eddie seemed to recollect himself. 'I just thank God he is alive. I hope that I can do something to help him. As for your situation with the firm, I- what are you doing-?'

I kissed him again, pushing myself hard against him, almost biting him. My hands grasped his clothing, his shirt. Eddie barely moved, and I felt all of the blood rushing to my head.

'I'm yours. You wanted me, you have me. Please don't leave me on my own.'

I was desperate, dragging at Eddie's clothing, my kissing becoming more aggressive. I felt like a kitten scrabbling at the sides of a huge building. 'Please,' I whispered, desperately. 'Eddie.'

Eddie remained humiliatingly still. Finally, he gently pushed me away from him, and stood up without looking at me, his face unreadable. I stared at his expressionless profile, disbelief mounting.

'No,' I said angrily, pushing back my hair. 'No, you can't do this to me. You can't gut my entire life and then just leave me. I'm a human being.' I stood up and tried to embrace him again, but Eddie kept pushing me carefully away.

'I know you love Jason,' I said frantically, 'but, even so, we could still be together. I get on well with Jason, we could visit him together. We could look after him together. It would work.' I felt sick. My hands trembled with desire to lash out and hit Eddie. He turned away.

'You do not understand,' he said quietly. 'I do not want anyone else but

Jason. I am sorry if it sounds harsh, but you must understand why I no longer want you. With Jason in my life, you mean almost nothing to me.'

'Oh, thanks. You dickhead.'

'Call me whatever you like. It is not that I do not care about you, I just love Jason so much that he eclipses everything. He is everything. I do not have the capacity to love anyone else, not even you. You come closer than anyone, take that as a compliment.'

Tears brimmed in my eyes. 'I'm gonna go back to Manpyre,' I said tearfully, threateningly. 'Watch me.'

Eddie closed his eyes briefly, and I could see that he hated that thought. But I wanted to hurt him, right back. I buried my face in my hands.

'I said you would wreck me,' I mumbled bitterly. 'You have, you've broken my heart. And now you don't want me anymore.' I broke into rough sobbing. 'Why did you work so hard at getting me to fall in love with you? Why didn't you just leave me alone?'

'I could not leave you alone, Bryce. Do you regret being with me?'

I didn't answer. Eddie sat down, put both arms around me and held me close.

'I am so sorry darling,' he murmured, while I wept brokenly. 'I am so sorry.' He was brushing away my tears with his thumb while he held me. I couldn't take it anymore. That was too much.

'I have to go,' I said. 'I'm leaving.'

'Oh babe. Do not be stupid, darling. Where would you go?'

'Anywhere.' I pulled a jumper over my head. 'I'm sorry, I'm not angry with you, okay, but I can't be around you. It's too hard.'

'It is three o'clock in the morning. You have nowhere to go. Colt, sit down.' He tried ordering me, which would have worked yesterday. I ignored him and rushed out.

Chapter 32

Colt

Robban answered the door wearing checked pyjama bottoms, holding a bowl of pasta. 'Hey,' he said, forking some into his mouth. He chewed thoughtfully, while I stood leaning against his door frame, shivering with cold, exhausted from crying.

'Come in, then,' he said calmly. 'Eddie's not here,' he added, leading the way into his sitting room. His apartment was dark, bare and musty. The kitchen, sitting room and bedroom all seemed to be in one medium-sized space containing a black leather sofa with worn patches, and a super-king size bed taking up most of the room. Robban perched on the end of the bed, dug around with his fork and shovelled more pasta into his mouth.

'I'm not looking for him,' I said, sinking onto the sofa, which felt sticky and smelled sweet. 'Can I stay here tonight?'

He shrugged. 'Yeah. You're only little, you shouldn't take up too much space… You want some food? There is pasta on the stove. Help yourself.'

I looked around the room and felt myself welling up again. I was in so much pain; I just wanted it to stop.

'Robban,' I said, and I pulled out all the money I had on me, about 600 Kr. 'I need… please, I need something to take the pain away, do you have anything? I just need to forget. It hurts.' The money was shaking in my outstretched hand. He looked at it and licked his lips.

'Oh, brother,' he sighed. Then he gave a sort of tired laugh. 'You little darling. You think that because you've smoked pot and done poppers with Eddie, that you can handle proper meds?' He was laughing at me as he reached out and took the money. 'I know it hurts. I know you want it to stop; you can't breathe real well, you can't go to sleep, and you wonder how you'll ever make it through tonight, right?'

I nodded hungrily.

Robban came and sat next to me. He pulled out his mobile phone and rested one reassuring hand on my shoulder as he made a call. I assumed that he was phoning a dealer, but then he said, in English, 'Hej- yeah, he's here with me. He's fine. You really fucked him up, he's asking me for drugs… no of course I won't. Listen, Eddie, if I had any I would take the entire stash myself, after dealing with you two all night.'

Robban was rubbing my shoulder as he talked to Eddie. I was panicking and my heart was racing, because I felt so distressed. I just did not want to feel like this for the rest of my life.

'Colt's fine. I'll look after him. Talk to you soon.' He hung up. 'He is worried about you.'

'I don't care.'

Robban told me to get into bed, so I kicked off my shoes and climbed in, fully-dressed, my teeth chattering. His sheets were black satin, unwashed. I curled up in the middle of the big bed, exhausted. At the other end of the room Robban was messing about in the kitchen.

'Here you are little brother, sit up and take this.' He perched beside me and handed me a glass of water. In his other hand was a pillbox with scratches on the lid. He flicked it open to reveal a few tiny pink pills on black velvet. 'Don't tell Eddie that I gave you this, okay? It won't hurt you, it'll zonk you out. Make you sleep.'

'Is it... heroin?' I asked in a small voice.

Robban laughed delightedly. 'No, no,' he said. 'God you're cute. It's not heroin. It's nothing nasty, it'll just make you sleep and forget.' Robban licked his middle finger then pressed it to the pill. 'The brilliant thing about these,' he said softly, 'is that you won't dream on them, either. Eddie used to take them for nightmares. Here.'

I opened my mouth and he placed it on my tongue, then I drank the water. It tasted really funny, not much like water at all.

'Sleep tight,' he said.

I laid back on the dirty bed, my darkness and sadness still banging in my head. A few minutes passed and then I felt the powerful chemical rush, a wave that was stronger than my feelings. I couldn't fight it. I didn't want to fight it. My eyes swept closed and the drug finally let my exhausted mind lose consciousness.

I woke up suddenly. Sunlight was pouring through the window, warm on my face. My neck was cricked, I obviously had not moved an inch all night. I knew I shouldn't have taken the pill, but I had slept so soundly. I sat up, yawning and pulled my knees up to my chest. My skin was crawling from being in that filthy bed. Robban's apartment looked worse by daylight. I gingerly stepped out of bed and my toes curled as they sank into cold, soggy carpet. I looked down in horror and saw it was a spilled bottle of Coke. The carpet was littered with bits of food including some twists of the pasta he had been eating last night. On the sofa, Robban lay on his back with arms and legs draped over the sides, fast asleep and snoring. I tried to sneak past him to the bathroom, but he woke with a snort and opened his eyes.

'Colt,' he said, in a growly morning voice. 'Hey...' He sat up slightly rubbing his eyes. 'Did you sleep well? Did my little magic pill knock you out?'

'Yeah,' I said. 'Thanks, and I'm sorry for keeping you awake so late last night.' He grinned.

'I'm a night owl. I'm always up all night, I sleep in the day; it's right now you should be apologising for.' He laughed loudly, 'Aw, look at you, blushing. I'm only joking kiddo. It's cool. You feeling a bit better today?'

I frowned. I was no longer feeling the acute distress of last night, but today I felt empty. I just missed him. Mornings in bed, sharing a shower then getting breakfast at the local 7-11. I really missed the simple domestic things like that, but more than anything I missed living with the prospect of sharing my future with him.

'I'm okay,' I told Robban. He looked at me, studying my face with his kind, calm expression.

'Okay. Just... take it easy brother. Be nice to yourself... oh, I'm vibrating.' He arched his back and pulled his phone out of his back pocket. 'Yeah. I don't know...' Robban looked at me, 'Want to talk to Eddie?'

I shook my head quickly and escaped to the bathroom. There were no towels in there so I just stood by the sink, basically hiding. I didn't want to touch anything, there was drug paraphernalia beside the sink. After ten minutes Robban tapped on the door.

'Look,' he sighed, when I opened it. He was still holding the phone, 'This has nothing to do with me but I'm caught in the middle. Eddie just wants to know that you're safe and okay. You're welcome to stay here, but what do you want to do?'

I knew that I couldn't face Eddie. 'I'll stay here,' I decided.

'Fine,' Robban put the phone to his ear, 'He's staying here.' He listened for a long time, then he hung up.

'Eddie's going to bring your stuff round later.' He gave me a friendly clap on the shoulder, then he went to the other room, got into bed and dragged the stained duvet over his head.

Friday came and went. Eddie had booked us both on the flight home, but I couldn't face being on the same plane as him. He dropped my ticket off at Robban's, but I let it go to waste, chipped into my savings and booked myself on the next available flight a month later.

I spent my time at Robban's, literally doing nothing but lying on the threadbare couch watching DVDs on his laptop. I was lonely. Robban slept mostly during the day, he would get up at around six, ready to start work in the Irish bar at eight. On his nights off, he dressed in leather jeans and tight fitted tops and disappeared all night. Sometimes he brought his clients back to the flat and at those times, I would go and hide in the bathroom, trying to sleep. I would sit there against the door with a towel wrapped around my head, trying to ignore the strange noises of uninhibited, kinky sex going on in the next room.

I found it stressful living there because it was cramped, uncomfortable and busy. His friends, mostly prostitutes and drug addicts at various stages of recovery, would come and go constantly, day and night. There was basically no food, either. I was too depressed to go out to buy any, so I just copied Robban and survived on sweets and instant noodles. It was grim.

I was already living in a state of constant anxiety. My safety net was gone and I was alone. When I was with Eddie I knew that I could leave the firm; that I could shrug my shoulders and kiss them goodbye as I was beyond their control because I was his. Now, I was so afraid of going back.

The flat was often pretty busy at night so I started following Robban's sleeping pattern, staying up all night. I couldn't sleep in the daytime either so inevitably I got run down and eventually ill, with a sore throat and headache. Robban didn't seem to have much sympathy at first, but one day he came home with a shopping bag full of throat lozenges and canned soup.

'You'll have to look after yourself, brother,' he told me briskly, pushing a mug of the Swedish equivalent of Lemsip into my hand. 'I'm too busy.'

'I know,' I croaked. I was all curled up on the sofa wrapped in a plaid blanket. Robban looked at me as he pulled a red t-shirt over his head. He was putting on his hooker clothes, which always made me feel uneasy.

'Alright,' he said, perching on the arm of the sofa. 'I'm expecting a guy over tonight. He's a long-standing client, I see him once a month. So, you might want to make yourself scarce.'

I sighed. 'I'm too tired… can't you wake me up when he gets here? Then I'll go out? Please, please, I just want to sleep.'

'Colt,' groaned Robban, 'You're bad for my business, you know. Alright, stay there, if you want.'

I didn't remember falling asleep, but when I next opened my eyes, it was morning. I sat up and my blanket slid onto the floor. I still felt rubbish, really shivery and sick. I glanced over at the bed. Robban was lying on top of the sheets, fast asleep and naked. Someone was lying next to him, I didn't look too closely. The whole thing creeped me out. I felt so alone, and the more I thought about life, the more depressed I became. No friends, no family, no boyfriend. Well actually… I did have a boyfriend… even though I didn't love him and I had been cheating on him for the past two months. I badly needed affection.

I found my phone charger amongst my jumble of belongings, and when the mobile was a little bit charged I found that I had fourteen messages. Some were from Eddie from the night I left, demanding to know where I was and that I come home. The next ones from him were just flight info, no miraculous message of love or regret… his last message to me, an exasperating piece of advice, 'Be safe. Don't take any drugs,' was so irritatingly fatherly, that I deleted it crossly.

There were a few messages from my wee brothers. I hadn't called them in too long, I was a bad brother. Sorry guys, I thought sadly. I'd been pretty selfish, blind to everything except Edvard.

Then there were millions of texts from Manpyre. I read them, each message was patient, loving.

'Honey. I haven't heard from you in weeks. I know you said you don't have good reception. Hope you can call me soon. Hope you come back soon. I love you. I can't wait to just hold you in my arms.'

I read that last message ten times. To be held by someone who loved me that much. Suddenly, I knew I wanted nothing more. I needed someone who cared. I picked up Robban's phone and called the hotel.

'Hi… um, can I speak to David Manpyre?

'Dave's not here right now, can I take a message?'

'No… it's okay.' Despondent, I hung up and stared at the phone. I grabbed it again and called my brother Clarke, on his mobile but there was no answer. Frustrated, without thinking, I called his house phone, forgetting that he didn't live there anymore.

'Hello.' My heart started banging in my chest. My dad's voice, I hadn't heard it in over a year. I wasn't surprised that he sounded drunk.

'Hello… Hello…?'

It was strange to be speaking to him today, of all days. Maybe it was fate. Maybe he would remember that today was a special day? Maybe, just maybe… after everything, today could bring some kind of reconciliation?

'Daddy,' I choked, 'It's me.'

Impatiently, 'Who is this? Clarke?'

I was shaking. 'It's Bryce.' I said. There was a long pause, then, the line just went dead.

I put my head on the kitchen worktop. I was shaking badly. So, that was it, I was completely alone. I started to make myself an instant coffee, feeling sick and tired.

A deep voice speaking a bunch of Swedish made me jump. I turned around and this guy was standing there smiling at me. Robban's client. He was a middle-aged Swedish guy with a blondish beard and glasses combo.

'Sorry. I dunno,' I mumbled, turning away. He came up behind me and repeated in English,

'Is there any coffee for me?'

'Oh, um… yeah, sure.' I made him a cup and we sat together on the sticky sofa watching Swedish morning telly.

'So, you work with Robban?' He asked.

I shrugged, couldn't be bothered telling him my life story. He told me his name was Anders. As he talked, his hand crawled on my thigh, his fingers inching up into my shorts.

'You don't look like a junkie. How much would you cost me?'

I shrugged again, glancing over at Robban who was still sleeping.

'I… don't think I cost anything. Anyone can have me for nothing.'

I let Anders pull me over onto his lap, peel off my pyjamas and position me on the sofa. Things were happening fast and I just went with it.

'You're lovely,' he whispered, stroking my hair. 'Are you happy? Can I do this? Are you sure?'

I couldn't speak, so I nodded.

While he was having sex with me, I let myself think about Eddie. Look at what you did to me. A few tears dropped onto the carpet. Anders was taking his time doing me nice and slow, moaning quietly in my ear. It felt like my humiliation would never end but I didn't really care. This was my penance to myself, it was what I deserved, and it was all I was good for.

'Vad i helvete?' Robban was suddenly there, yelling at Anders in Swedish. He jumped up and I curled up into a ball while Robban really laid into this guy, I didn't realise that he was capable of shouting until that moment. The door slammed and there was silence.

'Colt?' Robban was kneeling beside the sofa. I lifted my head, I was all alone, my face sticky with tears. 'What did you do, little brother?' He said regretfully.

He sat me up and hugged me. 'You idiot. Look, it's okay... that guy is one of my regular clients, he's totally clean and everything but... oh, man.'

I felt utterly numb. Robban dragged me into the shower and stood just outside the curtain while I washed. 'Why did you do that, kid?' He asked, exasperated.

I rested my forehead against the tiled wall as the water rushed over me. 'I don't know.'

Robban yanked open the curtain. 'I'm not gonna let you self-destruct, bro.' He threw a towel at me, 'You're a nice kid. What would your family think if they knew what you just did?'

He got to me. The shame engulfed me and I just started crying. I pushed past him and grabbed my clothes.

'Hey hey,' said Robban, 'I'm sorry if I was harsh, I didn't mean to- it's what you need, believe it or not.'

I turned to him, 'Shut up! Shut up and leave me alone! You don't know anything about my family! You're just... a junkie.' I was breathing hard.

Robban just shrugged good-naturedly.

'Yeah, I've made mistakes. I know what I am, but I'm trying hard to get myself out of it. I'm trying to better myself but you, cutie, you're already better than this.'

I grabbed my boots and coat and ran outside. I fell against the wall and closed my eyes, my heartbeat refusing to slow down.

'Hej. Robban's friend.'

I opened my eyes. Anders was sitting in his car, the engine running. I dropped my head miserably. Anders wound the window down further. 'You look like a lost puppy. Come on, you're cold, get in. You must be cold.'

I shrugged, but he was right. I was freezing.

'You hungry? I'll buy you breakfast. Better; I'll make you breakfast, how does that sound?'

I was hungry, too. I looked at Anders, searching his face, but I didn't see anything that made me feel any better.

'Come on,' said Anders impatiently, 'Are you getting in or not?'

Dazed, I stumbled across the pavement and got into the car.

'You know,' said Anders, stroking my damp forehead, 'Normally when I have a young man in my bed... I expect him to take care of me. Not the other way round.'

I opened my eyes and saw that he was smiling.

'Thank you for looking after me,' I said faintly. I was feeling so sick, but the clean, quiet calmness of Anders' apartment felt nice after Robban's filthy apartment. I got the impression he didn't usually live alone, but the house was empty for the moment. He had made me some breakfast, just like he promised, in his clean and sunlit kitchen.

'Starving,' he observed grimly as I wolfed down my food.

'Oh... I'm sorry.' I wiped my mouth; I was behaving like a pig. I just hadn't eaten properly since I arrived at Robban's. I was hungry, but I was kind of falling asleep in my food, too. I still felt really ill. Anders came over and felt my forehead.

'You're burning up,' he murmured. 'Come on.' He took me upstairs to his bedroom. I felt so sleepy.

'I feel like I'm gonna faint,' I murmured.

'Just get into bed,' he said. 'Have a rest.'

I lay down and closed my eyes. He sat on the bed beside me and stroked my hair, which was a really kind gesture. The occasional tear ran down my hot, feverish cheeks, and he brushed them away carefully.

'What's the matter?' He asked kindly.

'Everything. Oh, everything. My boyfriend dumped me, but the thing is…' I opened my eyes and stared at the ceiling, 'the thing is I really, really loved him. And I miss my family. I miss my brothers.'

'Your brothers? In England, yes?'

'Yeah.' I snuggled deeper down into the bed, and closed my eyes. It was so comfortable.

'How old are you?'

I opened my eyes. 'Twenty-one. Today, actually.'

He had the grace to look embarrassed for me. 'Oh. Happy birthday,' he said awkwardly. I just looked at him. It was almost funny.

'Um, thanks?'

Anders was quiet for a moment and then, he sighed, 'Hell. You're just a very sad, mixed-up young kid, aren't you? I didn't realise how young… I'm old enough to be your dad.'

I shrugged. He was, probably older, if anything.

'How did you end up doing this? Are you using?'

'Drugs? No. I'm just… it's a long story. I'm not using drugs and I'm not a prostitute.'

'O-kay…'

'I'm not. I'm just staying with Robban.'

'Okay. So, I took advantage of you this morning,' Anders said quietly, 'I'm sorry. I thought you were working, like Robban. I thought that you were older, too… I misunderstood. Argh.' He rubbed his eyes.

'It's okay,' I said. 'I don't know what happened this morning.'

Thinking about him, my eyes filled up with tears again.

'I was so mean to Robban.'

'Oh, hey now. Robban's a tough cookie. He'll be fine.' He sighed and chuckled, 'I think I pissed him off, though. I'm probably off the books.'

Despite Anders' kindness, I still felt lost. 'Could you… please hold me for a while?' I asked, in a small voice.

With Anders spooning up to me, I felt a tiny bit better. He was a big, solid man and his arms would have gone around me twice. I didn't know him at all, but the simple gift of contact with another person was very healing. Before I knew what I was doing or why, I began kissing him.

We had sex a couple more times. Each time I felt a little more lost, even cheaper and more frightened, right in my gut, than before. I couldn't stop, because if I did then I would be alone, which was worse.

Later, I got up, fixed coffee in the clean white kitchen and tried to gather my thoughts. I couldn't imagine what I was going to do. I hadn't much money and I was in a strange country. Sure, I could go back to the hotel, but my old life terrified me now. I breathed out, shakily. Fear was shearing through me.

I looked out of the kitchen window; outside, the late afternoon sun was fading quickly and the street was growing frostily darker. I could do this, I thought. Do what Robban does. Fleetingly, I thought of my old medical school. My former classmates would be graduating as foundation doctors, by now.

I went back upstairs and Anders was awake, I passed him a coffee.

'Thanks.' He sat up to take it and I lay beside him, propped up on my arms. He tucked a bit of hair behind my ear. 'You know… you cannot stay here,' he said gently. 'I'd love it if you could, but you just can't.'

I shrugged, nodded. Crazily, I was disappointed. I don't know what I expected. He got up to get dressed and I just buried my face in the pillow. I took deep breaths through the cotton of the pillow, trying to control my anxiety, trying to alleviate this horrible tightness in my throat. My anxiety felt like a chunk of ice in my stomach. It felt like dread; deep and heavy.

Anders touched my shoulder softly; he was holding out a bunch of notes. 'For you.'

'I told you. I'm not a whore.'

He looked at me, one eyebrow arched. I didn't move so he said, impatiently, 'Not for this, then.' He gestured towards his bed, 'Just take it for your birthday or something. I can't pay you nothing, I'd hate myself.'

My jeans were folded on a chair beside the bed. He picked them up, put the money into the pocket and handed me the jeans.

'For you,' he repeated.

My fingers closed around them, tightened. I took them. I turned away and put them on, zipped them up and when I turned back Anders was standing watching me.

'You're fine,' he said, gently. 'Come on. I will take you back to Robban's.' He passed me my top and sweater. Finally, I spoke. I cleared my throat, blinking back a prickling feeling in my eyes.

'Actually if you don't mind, there's somewhere else I need to go first.'

The church was more or less empty. The first thing I did, was shove all of that money that Anders gave me, right into a big Perspex donation box. My hands felt all itchy and dirty from holding the money. As I crossed myself and sat down near the front, I felt calmer straight away. I closed my eyes, rested my forehead on the pew in front, crying silent tears of relief. It was crazy but, my eyes just kept welling up. A priest approached me and began speaking to me.

'I'm sorry Father, I don't speak Swedish,' I blushed, wiping my eyes.

'English?'

'Yes Father.'

The priest sat down with me and asked me if I was on holiday or if I was living in Stockholm. I tried to answer him but I was literally too choked up to speak.

'Sorry,' I wept, covering my face with my hands. How humiliating.

'Just pray,' he said kindly, 'and when you feel ready, make your reconciliation with God. 'Cast all your anxiety on Him, because He cares for you.'

'Thank you,' I managed to say. I calmed myself down then I went to the confessional. Kneeling in the darkness I whispered, 'Bless me Father for I have sinned. It has been… one year since my last confession.'

I went back to Robban's with a box of cakes from the 7- 11.

'I'm sorry,' I said, as he opened the door. 'I'm so sorry about the way I spoke to you.'

'Oh, don't apologise.' He brought me in from the cold and shut the door. 'Kid,' he said, taking a bite of one of the cakes, 'You have nothing to be sorry for. Forget it. Just forget it.'

I looked at him. On impulse, I hugged him tightly,

'Robban, you've been amazing, thank you.'

'No problem.' We stayed like that for a few minutes in silence, Robban munching on a cake while I hugged him, my head resting on his shoulder. I loved how calm he was all the time. I listened to his slow, steady heartbeat and closed my eyes contentedly.

'I'm not going to work tonight,' said Robban suddenly, through a mouthful of cake, 'I figured you might need some company.' He brushed the crumbs from his fingers.

'That's nice of you… Robban, you must think I'm so disgusting…' He laughed and squeezed me tight.

'Me? No. I don't think anything bad about you. I promise.'

'I just want you to know that… I'm not like that.'

'I know, brother. Don't worry anymore.'

I moved my head from his shoulder and kissed him gently. He responded a little, let me taste the icing sugar on his tongue and teeth, then he rested his chin on my head and said, 'Colt. I don't want to make you feel rejected honey, but let's not go there. There are all sorts of reasons why that's a bad idea.'

I hung my head in shame, 'Sorry.' I was craving affection. Maybe he could sense that. He pulled me into his arms and started kissing my neck. He was strong and confident.

'Mm. Your skin is so nice and soft,' he said. He nuzzled my neck, 'You're very desirable, brother. God knows you are. But I'm not that much of a… how do you say it in English? A prick. I don't want to take advantage of you.'

'No,' I shook my head, 'No you're not. I just need somebody to be nice to me.'

Robban wrapped his arms around my waist.

'I think I can do that, brother.' He smiled. 'But let's just keep things friendly, hey?'

So, we watched a movie, talked. Robban did some heroin and I just stuck with lemonade. That night, I fell asleep in the arms of a friend and for that, I was truly grateful.

As soon as it was dawn, while Robban was still asleep, I got up and phoned the hotel.

'He's not available right now, can I take a message?'

'He's asleep, right? I know, it's early but please, call his room. Wake him. He will want to talk to me. I promise. It's Colt.'

Seconds later a sleepy voice said, 'Honey, it's so early. Are you okay?'

'Yes.'

'Are you crying?'

I didn't answer.

'Colt?'

'Sorry. The line went weird. I… I want to come home, like, now. But I ran out of money.'

'Oh. No problem! I'll send you some, honey. Anything. But… Bodansky's got enough money, surely?'

'No. He can't give me any.'

'Okay. Well, are you sure everything's okay?'

I closed my eyes and held the phone with both hands.

'Yes.'

'Fine. Oh, bloody hell, I'm so excited. I have missed you to death. I was starting to think… but that was just me being paranoid.'

'What were you… starting to think?'

He chuckled, 'Well. I thought that you and Eddie might be… back together, or something. Stupid, I know. I'm sorry for even thinking it, it's so stupid!'

'It is stupid. Really stupid.'

After the call, I went out on to the balcony and smoked a cigarette, staring out at the street with the sun coming up and spilling all over the pavements, buildings and gutters. It was freezing, it made me feel clean and pure. I lifted my head, closed my eyes against the bright snow-reflected rays as the light washed over my face. The street was rousing to life. I took a deep breath of fresh snowy air and held it. Robban appeared behind me, blinking and yawning and stretching and scratching his arms.

'Morning brother. You alright?'

I nodded, my eyes roving all over the city. I picked out bursts of colour like sour explosions on the tongue; a red scooter, a bright yellow pushchair.

'I made a little decision,' I said. I took a long, slow draw on my cigarette.

'You decided something?' Yawned Robban.

'Yeah. I'm gonna go back to the firm. Don't argue, man. I don't have the nerve to leave without Eddie.'

Chapter 33

Eddie

As I followed the nurse through the corridors I recalled my last visit to Jason at the Harbour Centre. Back then, I had been in shock. I remembered feeling terrified and trying not to let Colt see just how afraid I was. I had been afraid of what kind of a mangled stranger I might find, but what I had found was my Jason, and that was harder to accept than anything else. My Jason, Eel Prescott, sitting in a hospital for sixteen years. That was intolerable; I almost wished that he had been damaged beyond recognition, that he was not Jason anymore. I think I could have handled that slightly better.

This time, as I walked through the Phillip Wren hospital, I was not afraid, I was stronger. I breathed in. I was stronger...

The hospital insisted that I be escorted by two male nurses, they were anticipating trouble. I was unsure what to expect. I knew, from a brief meeting I had with the lead nurse, that Jason was getting weaker from lack of food and sleep, every day. He was also becoming more disturbed, attacking nurses very regularly. I ached to think of how tormented he must be feeling.

The two nurses showed me into the day room, and they stood against the wall close to where he was sitting in a comfortable chair, his legs tucked underneath him. Unfortunately, no one had been exaggerating his shocking weight loss. He was resting his head on one curled fist, his face red and angry. Someone was clearing up the tray of food that he had just thrown across the room.

When he saw me his face drained of all colour. He looked even more terrified than the first time I visited. I felt huge and awkward, realising that my size could be intimidating to him, so I knelt down beside his chair. 'I am back now,' I whispered to him. 'I was away for a while but I am back now. Baby, I am not going anywhere.' He stared at me. I was so close to him and I could see that like me, he was shaking, his hands were shaking.

I was fascinated by his face, the familiarity of it. There were small white scars all over it where his piercings used to be. I became conscious of my own scars, my mutilated face and body. I was probably scaring him simply by looking the way I did. I felt bitter about it. I had never regretted my self harm quite as much as I did at that moment, because I wanted him to remember me properly, to love what he saw. I did not want to offer him something so damaged, nearly destroyed. I am sorry, I thought. This is all I have for you, my love.

He just stared at me. I was at his feet, offering myself to him completely. For sixteen years I had lived my life. Not happily, but I had lived it nonetheless, earning money, meeting people, experiencing. Everybody else had been living for the past sixteen years. Everybody except Jason. I had missed him daily, yet even I had come close to falling in love with someone else. He slid his hand towards mine and I touched his fingertips, my hand shaking almost out of control.

'Oh, God,' I said.

His lips parted slightly as though to speak. He said nothing, but grabbed hold of my hand, clenching my fingers tightly together. Though extremely thin, he was still strong. His arm was shaking from the effort of crushing my hand. It hurt, but I let him do it, of course. He leaned forward and grabbed me with his other arm in a sort of headlock. We were immediately surrounded by his nurses.

'It is alright,' I said softly from under his arm, 'Let him do what he wants. Let him hurt me if he needs to. God knows that I deserve it.'

Jason was holding me with his fragile arms. I could easily break out of his lock but I wanted to see what he would do. He was dragging me closer to him and I realised that he was trying to hug me. There was no malice in that awkward hug, no sense of where have you been, why did you leave me? He was just holding on.

One of the nurses said, warningly, 'Be careful. He sometimes bites people when he's angry.'

'Don't we all?' I murmured.

The nurse frowned and I said, 'Oh, relax; he's not going to fucking bite me.' I gently disengaged myself and looked at his face, which was wet with tears. 'I am with you, I promise.'

He nodded slightly.

I stayed with him all afternoon. He would not release his grip on my hand and he never stopped staring at me, though, I admit that this was mutual. I could hardly believe he was real.

At one point a nurse approached me and asked me, in hushed tones, if I would try to persuade Jason to drink some milk.

'It's got extra protein and some of his medication in it,' said the nurse.

He glanced at Jason, who was frowning slightly at him. I picked up the cup of milk, sipped a little of it then passed it to him, 'Finish it, Jason.'

He drank it, staring at me the whole time.

'Amazing,' said the nurse, 'None of us can get him to take anything today.'

'Obviously. No one else can help him,' I said. 'Only me.'

Jason's medication made him drowsy so I picked him up, took him to the bedroom and stayed with him while the nurses helped him into bed. I held his hand as he fell asleep, kissing his fingers. I wanted to stay but, the policy of the hospital was not that lenient. I had checked into a B&B, five minutes down the road. It was grimy and the bed was literally too short for me, but I collapsed into it anyway, exhausted.

I woke up in the middle of the night in a cold sweat. As my phone began to vibrate again in earnest I realised what had woken me.

'Jason is missing,' said the nurse nervously. 'The police are searching for him. He got out of the window in the ward, we- he doesn't usually get out of bed at night-'

I hung up on her. I knew he would be looking for me. The river ran about a mile from the hospital, and if he was anywhere, he would be by a river, I just knew.

The car crawled slowly along the path. It was pitch dark, the road ahead illuminated by fingering headlamps. I stared into the looming thickets of trees as they crept by. The radio played quietly beside me. It was a comfort. My skin was tingling.

Suddenly he was there. Of course he is there, I thought. He was leaning against a tree using one arm, and he lifted up his head as the light shone on him. He was a poor sight in pyjama bottoms and a thin long sleeved vest. His feet were bare. Even from a little distance I could see how hard he was shaking. I stopped the car and jumped out, the engine still running. I ran to him and grabbed his face in both hands.

'Look at us, Jay,' I whispered urgently. I was crying now, from sheer relief at having found him safe. 'Can you remember those two twenty-one-year-olds? I can't,' I sobbed. I stared down towards the river, seeing only darkness. I turned back to Jason, feeling suddenly fierce. 'It is not over, Jay,' I whispered tearfully, through gritted teeth. 'We are strong, we are still alive, and we won. It is not over, okay?'

Suddenly I felt a cold touch on my face. I opened my eyes as Eel deliberately traced my oldest scar from chin to forehead, and he looked at me with a calm understanding in his dark eyes. I took off my coat and spread it the ground, in the shelter of some trees by the road. I sat Jason down on the coat, and then I took off my cashmere sweater and arranged it around his thin shoulders. Sitting down beside him, I wrapped my arm around him while I phoned the hospital to say that he had been found.

An ambulance arrived quickly, blue lights flashing but no siren. As the paramedics hurried towards us bearing a stretcher, Jason seemed to panic and clutched tightly to me.

'Shh, it is okay,' I said, 'I am going to stay with you. He does not need a stretcher,' I added, to the two paramedics. 'I will walk him to the ambulance. He is okay, just cold.'

'Step away please,' said the first paramedic, dropping his case of equipment. 'This patient can be really aggressive.'

I paused. I had not had much sleep, and the night's events had unfolded fairly quickly, so I was struggling to understand what was happening.

'Aggressive?'

The paramedic put his hands on Jason and I swiped him away in confusion.

'No, he is not being aggressive. What do you mean? What are you doing?'

'Step back,' said the second paramedic firmly, taking hold of Jason's arm, and before I could stop him he drove a needle into his skin. Jason cried out, and then his eyes seemed to roll back into his head. I froze in shock and horror as his knees seemed to give way, and the two paramedics lowered him to the floor, onto the stretcher.

'What the fuck?' I cried. 'What did you just do?'

The paramedics were strapping him onto the stretcher; he was unconscious now. One of them ran a different needle into the back of his limp hand, fiddling with a temporary drip.

'We were told to sedate him,' explained the first man, 'as he can be violent and difficult to manage. Don't worry, he's fine and it's for his own good.' The paramedic threw me a relaxed grin.

A vein in my left temple began to throb deeply. I breathed out, clenching my back teeth, grinding them slowly. 'Is it really? Is it for his own good? That is very, very noble of you. Thank goodness you came along.'

I crouched down beside the two paramedics as they worked over Jason.

One of them was holding a third syringe. As he prepared to inject it into him, I snatched it from him and slammed the paramedic on his back on the cold ground. I jumped on top of him. Straddling him, I held the syringe up and let it glisten in the light, saying, 'Do not worry... this is for your own good.' I plunged it into his pulsating neck.

Leaving him on the floor, I jumped to my feet and tackled the second man as he tried to run back to the ambulance. I shoved him up against the ambulance, looking at his terrified expression in the pulsing blue lights.

'Turn around, and face the ambulance,' I ordered softly. I glanced over my shoulder at Jason lying motionless on the stretcher. The paramedic was visibly shaking.

Desperately he made a last appeal, 'This patient needs to be in a hospital. He's very underweight; he needs to be there-'

'Shh. Shh.' I brought my face up close to the young paramedic's, my mouth touching his cheek.

'Do not tell me what he needs, darling. I know what he needs. Face the wall.' I flipped him around and pushed him against the ambulance. 'Stay.'

I looked around, and then stooped elegantly to pick up a fist-sized rock. I tossed it in my hand, once, before slamming the rock against the side of the paramedic's head. The man crumpled to his knees then fell sideways on the grass.

Colt

Dreaming about being in Stockholm, I woke up suddenly, wondering where I was. I stirred in the crisp, clean sheets of my bed at Lake Martin. The room was cool and airy, scented sweetly with fresh flowers and suddenly, I fiercely missed the hot grimy smell of the Stockholm apartment. I stared at the ceiling, wondering if I would ever feel happy again. I was no longer living in a state of anxiety, just sadness. This was my life, now. I was a fully-fledged member of the firm now.

Earlier that night, the whole firm had gathered for a drinks party to welcome me back. I had stood there in the bar, drink in hand, suit on my back, looking around at the familiar faces and thinking, how did this happen? How can I be back here? I was a whole world away, I had a new life, and now this, again? How? I had felt dazed, like I was in a bad dream. And Manpyre was leaning against the bar, watching me hungrily.

'To my little accountant!' Ilya had joked, raising his glass. 'My books are a disaster, thank goodness you are back!' No one had any idea that Eddie was back in England too, though I thought of little else.

During the drinks party Manpyre had coaxed me outside, and without much preamble he sat me down on a low wall in the car park, stood between my legs and began kissing me, slobbering all over my face, like a dog marking its territory. I turned my head away in aversion as he licked my face. I had lost any self-respect and I felt entirely worthless.

'I missed you,' Manpyre panted, pushing his hands into my underwear, tearing the zip on my favourite suit. 'So much, honey.'

I was quite drunk. I kissed him back and told him I had missed him, too. I rested my arms on his shoulders while he fumbled with my trousers; I even raised my hips a little so he could get his hands down more easily.

His aftershave smelled weird and he felt too thin. He was all eager with no finesse, and he was an unbelievably bad kisser. He just wasn't Eddie. I did feel bizarrely at home with him, though, as if he was the gutter, and the gutter was very much where I belonged.

He pushed his face into my neck as he played with me. The night air was fresh and cool on my face and in my hair. I was lightheaded from the alcohol and I was tingling all over from his fumblings.

'Tell me honestly honey,' he murmured, his words buzzing against my neck, 'While you were away... did you let Bodansky fuck you?'

I looked up at the stars, feeling dreamy and tipsy. The way he phrased the question made me feel dirty.

'Yeah...' I answered him, without really thinking. Manpyre paused, his lips still against my throat.

'Wow. At least... I guess at least, you're honest. So, I bet that he taught you a few things?'

'Yeah, he did,' I droned, still without thinking. Like how much broken hearts hurt, I thought. Impulse made me tell him that I slept with that guy

Anders too. I didn't want to lie by omission. He slapped me across the face so hard, it made both of my eyes fill up with tears. I kept my head turned to the side, feeling numb. My eyes burned with shame. I sat there with my trousers undone, finding that I could not look at him. I actually didn't care. I felt like a twig being washed along a river, just waiting to see what would happen to me next.

'I didn't have you down as a little slut,' he spat. 'I really didn't.'

'Don't say that. I'm not.'

Manpyre stared at me for a moment, then said, 'Fuck.' He shoved his hands into his pockets, turned and walked away from me.

A wave of misery washed over me. He had just given me a damn good slap, but I couldn't handle another rejection.

'Dave,' I croaked.

He turned around, looking as wretched as I felt. 'Don't go.'

He stood where he was, looking at me. Then he took one hand out of his suit pocket, and held it out to me.

'C'mere,' he said softly. I just hung my head and he came to me instead. We didn't go back to the party, we went upstairs instead and sat on his bed, talking and kissing a little. I was so glad that he was there. He pushed back my hair with both hands and looked at me seriously.

'You look so bloody sad,' he murmured. 'What's he done to you, mate? What has he done to you?'

I felt choked up. What had he done to me, anyway? I wondered if I would ever feel happy again. Manpyre kissed me, deeply, and then began to take things further. I eagerly agreed to everything. I wanted him to fuck me. I felt that I owed it to him, but also, the way he was looking at me... he seemed almost grateful to be with me. I was feeling so low and unattractive after Eddie, and here was someone practically worshipping my body. Eddie took what he wanted as though it was his right to do so, but Manpyre was acting differently, as though he couldn't believe his luck.

He was extremely careful and gentle in bed, not at all the way Eddie warned me that he would be. He was actually more careful with me than Eddie himself had ever been.

'I love you,' he kept saying, '… honey, my baby, I love you so much.'

Afterwards, Manpyre hugged me from behind and laced his fingers through mine. I stared at our hands, his dark, hairy fingers stroking lovingly against my pale, girly ones.

'Where's the ring I gave you honey?' He asked me sleepily.

My face flushed. 'Eddie threw it away,' I whispered.

He didn't reply but, suddenly he tightened his hold on me, constricting my breathing. I tried to wriggle out of his arms subtly so as not to offend him. But his grip was strong.

'Ah, Dave? I'm getting kind of hot…'

'Why?' He said suddenly, fiercely, breathing hard on the back of my neck. 'Why did you have to let Bodansky fuck you? This is good but… it could have been perfect, you know? You let that mutilated, ugly, bastard shag you for weeks, not to mention half of Sweden by the sounds of it… I feel like you're second-hand, now.'

Stung, I said nothing. Manpyre loosened his grip on me and I could breathe again.

'Oh… I'm sorry, babe. I didn't mean that. You're not second-hand.'

'It's okay…' I guessed I deserved him to be a little upset with me.

Suddenly an unwelcome image popped into my head: Paul Russell's long, elegant writing fingers. All I could think about was Dave, pinning down Paul's wrist and slicing them off. I turned over and looked into his almond-shaped, dark eyes. It was difficult to imagine him carrying out such a cruel act. The thought was quite distressing, and it must have showed because he suddenly frowned in concern, 'Honey? Honey, you look all scared. I'm not angry with you, you know.'

I shook my head. 'No, I'm not scared,' I whispered.

He pulled me close to him and I snuggled against his chest. I repeated it, trying to convince myself. 'I'm not scared.'

It was still dark. Not having a clue what time it was, I groped for my glasses and mobile simultaneously and propped myself up on my arm, blinking at the greenish words of a text message glowing sinisterly. My glasses brought them into focus.

'Help me. Meet me. In Martin, at the West gate, bring key. Hurry up.'

There were also eleven missed calls because my phone was on silent. The message had been sent before midnight, it was now one am. I stared dumbly at my phone, starting to wake up properly. Eddie should be in Hallam, at Jason's hospital.

Quickly, I phoned him, but there was no answer. I slipped quietly out of bed and began to fling on my clothes. As I dressed, my phone buzzed in my hand.

'What took you so long?' Eddie exploded when I answered.

'Sorry.' I hopped into my trousers, balancing the phone. I took the rest of my clothes into the bathroom and shut the door. 'What's wrong?' I whispered. My heart was pounding; it was actually the first time we had spoken since we broke up.

'Why are you whispering?'

'Dave.'

'Ugh.'

I ignored him, though I tended to agree.

'Why are you here? I'm coming down to the gate now.'

'No, no, I managed to get in. I am in the stables now. Please come quickly.' I cradled the phone against my head. As far as I could recall, Eddie had never, ever pleaded with me before.

'I'm coming right now,' I whispered softly into the phone. I opened the bedroom door as quietly as I could and crept out into the corridor.

'What's wrong?'

'Please, just hurry,' said Eddie. His voice sounded like he was on the verge of tears. I stole down the corridor, to the fire escape and ran down the stairs. The night was sharp and cold. My feet crunched on the gravel as I ran away from the hotel, past the leisure complex and to the stables. I pushed the door nervously; the flimsy wood shuddered and creaked.

'Eddie?' I whispered, 'Eddie?' A torch beam clicked on and shone full in my face.

'Colt. Look at him. Is he going to be okay?' I stepped forward. My pulse accelerated as I realised that Jason was lying in the straw.

'God, what… what did you do?' I shook my head quickly, 'Give me that torch,' I ordered. Something was very, very wrong. Jason's eyes looked dull, unfocused. In the light of the torch he blinked several times, very slowly, a small noise coming from the back of his throat. His pupils didn't contract properly in the torchlight; it was clear he was heavily sedated. Eddie was supporting his head.

'The paramedics injected him with something, it practically knocked him out. And he was being hooked up to some sort of an I.V. drip, do you know what that was?'

I hadn't a clue. Kneeling in the straw in the weak beam of light, I had never felt less like a doctor.

'He needs a hospital.'

Eddie said nothing, so I flicked the torch beam at him. His dark eyes were serious as he shook his head. I was speechless. I had no idea what to do. It was the middle of the night in a dark, freezing stable, and Eddie was asking me to help someone I knew nothing about, who had been given a drug that could be anything. I had never felt less qualified.

'It's not a question of 'no'. This guy needs to go to hospital. I don't know what he was injected with. He's seriously underweight and, most importantly, he has epilepsy. Do you have any medication to prevent him from fitting, because I sure as hell don't!'

Eddie took the torch from me.

'He's not going back to hospital, Colt. Either you help me, or…' he dropped his head. 'I came here because I am desperate, I am begging for your help. Please, Colt.'

Eddie

We crept back up the fire escape, which was still open, soft yellow light seeping into the cold darkness of the night. Jason was able to walk in a painfully slow manner, leaning heavily on both myself and Colt. He stopped when his bare foot touched the metal step of the fire escape and I lifted him up. His head flopped back, eyes open but seeing nothing. We took him into my suite and sat him down on the bed, where he lay down immediately and closed his eyes. Colt sat beside him and checked him over more thoroughly than before. I did not ask Colt anything. I stood by, staring at the slight sheen on the green satin bedspread, trying to manage my emotions. After a while Colt stood up and I felt his warm hand on my arm.

'Honestly, I think it's just the medication. If you won't take him to hospital, then I'm going to have to make the decisions, and I say he just needs to sleep it off. But keep an eye on him. Any problems with breathing… any seizures, Eddie, and he has to go to hospital. I'm not kidding.'

I could not look at him. I just nodded once, staring at Jason, thinking that his hospital-issue pyjamas were awful.

Colt was still touching my arm. 'It will be okay, mate.'

I could not speak.

Colt squeezed my arm once. 'I'll make you some tea.'

I nodded again, dumbly. I had always hated the way Colt made tea, very weak and milky. I liked mine Russian; strong, and Colt would forget this, as always.

I stood next to my bed for a few minutes, gathering my thoughts. The enormity of the situation profoundly struck home for the first time. I had taken Jason from hospital, which meant that this very ill man was now completely dependent on me. I had not the faintest idea where to begin. Jason's trousers were wet, and he seemed to be shivering as he lay there with his eyes closed. This snapped me back into consciousness. I quickly turned up the heating to the maximum setting, and lit the fire. I then went into the mirror-free bathroom and ran the corner bath. 'Come on, Jay,' I murmured, ignoring the pain clutching at my chest as I gently lifted him, he weighed nothing. 'Let's get you out of these clothes.'

Helping him to get undressed and into the bath was very automatic. Peeling off Jason's top, I did not allow myself to feel, though the sight of his prominent ribs caused my breath to catch in my throat. My own full name screamed out at me, emblazoned across his sunken chest in huge letters.

The memories came flooding back. Eel lying on the leather chair in the tattoo parlour, looking at me in amused exasperation as the tattooist prepared. I had stood there coldly, overseeing everything. I had been blazing angry with him at the time.

'Come on, bloody hell,' he had said, as he studied a stencil of his soon-to-be tattoo. 'I don't want it to be that big. I'm gonna be more ink than skin.

'Shut up, unless you want the writing on your face,' I had snapped. At the time, I had been deadly serious. Eel had rolled his eyes to the tattooist and said, 'Mate, you had better make a bloody good job of this. Spell his crazy Russian name right, and all.' Then he switched his gaze to me. 'I'm doing this 'cause I love ya, you mad bastard. No other reason, right?'

'You are about to find out how much love hurts,' I had said emotionlessly.

Jason kept falling asleep, and it became difficult to hold him up, so I kicked off my shoes and, fully-clothed, got into the warm water. I kneeled behind Jason and held him as I carefully washed his ravaged, skinny body. All of his muscles were gone; the powerful arms that I used to love to lie in were wasted to nothing. I began talking to him and wondered aloud if Eel remembered me, if he remembered how much I had loved him.

I told him that he was safe, and that I would never leave him again. It physically hurt, as I told him that I was sorry, I was so, so sorry. I could not stop saying it, my mouth close to Jason's ear, and the soothing repetition of the words melding with the sound of the taps.

Colt coughed discreetly. I looked up at him as he stood, elegantly, by the door, holding a mug of tea. He shook his head at the sight of me, my silk shirt completely ruined and Jason in my arms, fast asleep. Turning off the taps, Colt shot me a look of pity and exasperation.

'Thought I said he needs to sleep,' he chided gently.

'He is asleep,' I could not help pointing out.

'Let me help… hey, are you okay?'

'Yes. Soap in my eye.'

With Colt's help; Jason was soon dried and dressed in some of my clothes. The clean black jeans and grey cashmere pullover were both several sizes too big.

Jay was fast asleep by the time we laid him back on the bed. I glanced at Colt, who was arranging some of the nine pillows under Jason's head. He was so pretty and beautiful and a good person. I had missed him terribly since Sweden.

'Thank you,' I said quietly.

'No bother,' smiled Colt. 'It's really no bother.'

His smile made me feel suddenly heartbroken. I was, however, getting used to that emotion, and I managed to bury it. Putting my sensitivity down to my inordinate tiredness, I pulled up a chair beside the bed and gently stroked Eel's hair, studying his face. 'Now, go and tell my brother I am here. I cannot hide, and I do not want you to get into trouble for me.'

'I don't care about getting into trouble for you.'

I kept looking at Jason as I stroked his hair.

'Okay… that is nice. But go and tell him anyway.'

Colt made to leave and, without taking my eyes from Jason, I said his name.

'Yes?'

I felt in my pocket and found what I wanted; Manpyre's ugly gold Egyptian ring. I held it up, 'Found this on the bedroom floor at Ava's… do you want it?'

To be fair to him, it was a loaded question. There was a long pause, then, 'Yeah, give it here.'

He sounded ashamed and I wondered how far he had let the grubby bastard go with him. Whether Manpyre had shown his true colours yet, I could not tell, but I knew that if I looked at him and saw his face then I would know.

I heard myself laughing quietly. 'Ouch. I must stop thinking of you as mine.'

Colt shifted uncomfortably. 'Eddie don't… Dave's, like, there for me.'

I said nothing to that. Manpyre would always be 'there' for Colt; he would never let him go. I had fed the boy to the lions; I knew, at that moment, that I had probably ruined Bryce Colt's life. But, as I sat there, holding Jason's hands and stroking his hair, I barely noticed Colt slipping out of the room.

Chapter 34

Eddie

'You have some nerve showing up here.' Ilya looked at me, then at Jason, his expression unreadable. Every muscle in my body went tight. I was more tired than I was sure Ilya could appreciate. My eyes itched from the effort of keeping them stretched open. All I wanted to do was curl up beside Jason and fall asleep. I was not in any fit state for fighting again, but certainly, I would if need be.

'Don't. Do not say anything about him, Illy. Don't make fun of him.' I stopped just short of saying 'please'. Ilya just shook his head. He came over to the bed and I bristled, holding myself protectively over Jason. Ilya, however, was looking down at his former love rival without hostility.

'I would never,' he said quietly. 'You will not believe me, but truly, I am so sorry about what has happened to him. Seeing him like this, it's real. I would not wish this on my worst enemy… so to speak.'

Kindness; I felt that I could take anything but kindness. My eyes boiled over with tears and I turned away, watching as they dripped and became dark grey spots on Jason's lighter grey pullover.

'Do you need anything?' Asked Ilya gently. I kept my face turned away from him and cursed myself; I could not stop crying.

'Yeah,' I managed to mutter darkly. 'Shoes. Nice ones. Mine are all too big, he's size ten like you.'

Thankfully, Ilya ignored my tears. 'I'll get some right now.'

'Black ones please, Illy,' I wiped my eyes and called after him, 'In fact- do you have any two-tone black and grey to match his outfit?'

Illy came back a few minutes later and tossed two pairs of shoes, both black and both ugly, onto the bed. He watched as I began to lace the more tolerable pair onto Jason's foot.

'When are you leaving? Do you know where you are going to go?' He asked.

'No.' I yanked the lace tight and Jason stirred. 'No, I don't. Tonight; any hotel. Thereafter, probably Paris, Stockholm, or…' I shook my head. 'I do not know. I have to call some friends.'

Ilya scratched his neck. 'Stay here for a few days. Make your arrangements from here. As long as you keep a low profile, it should not be a problem. The hotel is plenty big enough for you to stay hidden.'

I paused, looked down at Jay. He was sleeping peacefully, his chest rising and falling slowly, his curled fingers twitching sweetly like a child's. I could hardly keep my own eyes open, and the idea of staying where we were for even one night was very, very appealing. But, I wanted to get away. More importantly, I needed to get Eel away. I could not trust anyone in the firm. 'I don't want them to get what is left of us' I thought.

Ilya read my thoughts. 'Edik,' he said gently. 'No one wants to hurt you.'

'Good, because if anyone tries, I will kill them.'

'Of course, look, no one even knows you are here. You are safe. Rest.'

'You know. You know we are here.'

He looked at me. 'Even if I wanted to hurt you... how could I make things worse? Forgive me for saying it, but... you two are already living a personal hell, you especially.'

I shook my head. Ilya was wrong. He would never understand it, but I loved Eel, even this way. It was heart wrenching, but even on that first night, I knew that I never wanted to be without him. Ilya was also wrong in thinking that he could not make things worse. I knew only too well that if Ilya contacted the police, I would be arrested for the assault on Mischa, or for taking Jason from hospital. The thought of being separated from Jay again was more than I could bear. No, it could not be risked. Jason would be taken back to hospital, and I knew it would not be long before he died in there and he would die without me.

I slipped the other shoe onto Jason's foot and shook my hair out of my eyes. It was not going to happen. I supposed that Ilya would have phoned the police already, if he was going to. There was a silence, then Ilya gestured to Jason. 'Is this normal for him? To be just... lying there?'

'No. It's drugs. I hope it will wear off soon. Colt thinks it will.'

Ilya took a step closer. 'When he first went into hospital,' he said, his voice low, 'and he woke up from his coma after a month, he was on a lot of sedation. Normal doses wouldn't touch him.'

I did not really want to hear about this. It killed me that I had not been there for Eel. Yet, the larger part of me was compelled by a masochistic curiosity. I wanted to know everything about those early days when he was first injured. I needed all that information, needed to nervously pick and dig at that wound. So, fingering the lace on Jason's shoe for comfort, I listened.

'He kept screaming out... these long, drawn out screams.' Ilya took a deep breath. 'It... sounded... like an animal. His lips were all split. They were holding him down but he was kicking, screaming... he had the nurses black and blue. Biting and head butting. He was up all night, screaming, for you. I can hear him now, will never forget it. It was horrendous. I suppose he didn't know what was happening to him.'

The shoelace was wrapped around my finger so tightly I almost cut off the blood supply. 'What are you saying to me, Ilya?'

'I'm saying… you were only twenty-one. What kind of a burden is that for such a young person? I thought if he was… gone, you could move on.' He gestured to me, helplessly. 'You're handling it now, but you are closer to forty. Back then, you were just a child.'

I knew what Ilya was searching for; Forgiveness. My capacity for that was unknown to me. When I thought of what Ilya's lie had cost me; the agony of losing Eel. The blood I lost over him. The scars I sustained. More than that; Jason had suffered alone without me and I could never forgive that. I made my point simply, 'It was not your choice to make.'

Before Ilya left, I made a point of apologising to him. 'I just want to say, I am sorry about Mischa. I was unwell. I did not mean any harm.'

Ilya shrugged. 'It's fine. Now that you're back, I'm having him discreetly guarded around the clock. Which, incidentally, I loathe having to do.'

'Really, there's no need for a bodyguard. I pose no threat to him, I promise. I was having a breakdown, for God's sake. I am better now. He's safe.'

Ilya shrugged again, and repeated, 'He is being guarded around the clock.'

My throat was dry. I felt indignant at the lack of trust, but I knew I deserved it. My eyes narrowed. 'Yeah? Well, so is Jason. So be warned.'

Colt

Manpyre's bedroom was dark and quiet. I snuck back in and undressed silently, then I got into bed without touching him. I lay there in the dark, my heart hammering. Eddie was back. He was in the hotel. Anything could happen. The ring was still clutched in my hand. Lying on my back, I held it up and studied it in the moonlight. Manpyre's ring. My 'boyfriend' again… Oh God. What a bloody mess I was in.

Manpyre suddenly turned over in his sleep and I jumped, the ring fell on the carpet and rolled under the bed. I dived down to get it. Under there, Manpyre's shoes were all lined up in neat-freak rows. My eyes fell on a pair of black cowboy boots. Their steel toecaps winked dully at me. I sat back on my heels, on the carpet, just staring. Those boots, crunching into my ribs... oh my God. Oh, God, no...

'Honey? What you doing down there on the floor?' I squinted up at him, unable to speak.

'Babe, whatcha doing?'

I was out of options. I held up the ring. 'I dropped this,' I said faintly.

'Okay... Jesus, it's the middle of the night... I thought you said Bodansky threw that away?'

I climbed into bed and lay down, shivering as though I was cold.

'Yeah, I... turns out, he didn't. I found it in my jeans.'

Manpyre snuggled up to me and I tried not to tense up too much.

'You know something, honey?' He said, 'You're weird. I like your strange behaviour, though. You're eccentric and it's cute.' He kissed the side of my head. 'G'night.'

I stopped shaking after about an hour, and lying there in his arms I started to feel angry. Manpyre seemed so chillingly normal. Supposedly, he cared about me, yet he had beaten me, in a dark stable with steel toecaps and a belt. He must have been jealous at the time, about Eddie's drawings of me.

I felt too angry to sleep. I went to get a drink of water and then I stood by the window staring out on the floodlit driveway. Mostly, I was angry at my own stupidity in getting myself into such a tight corner. I had no choice but to get back into bed with that monster, and the tomorrow night it would be the same. I felt like such an idiot, like things were going from bad to worse. I slammed down my glass on the windowsill and got back into bed, feeling sick with anxiety and fear.

'Where have you been?' Manpyre sat up and switched on the light. 'Where have you been this time? Don't you ever stop messing around at night, for fuck's sake?' It was like a switch had flipped. My mouth was dry with shock, which delayed my reply for a few seconds.

'I went to get a drink,' I said. 'Sorry if I woke you up. There's no need to shout.'

He leaned over me. 'Yeah?' he said. 'I don't really like restless sleepers. I don't like waking up and finding you gone. And I don't want you to do that again, got it?' He wasn't smiling. I was baffled and a little scared. I didn't know what to say to that.

He reached under his pillow and drew out a thin, leather belt with a brass buckle on it. 'Do you see this?' He asked me, his voice flat. I saw it, I remembered it. I nodded, my eyes filling with tears, which he ignored. 'You see it? Okay, put your arms up, like this. Through here.' He pushed my arms through the metal railings on the headboard and threaded the belt through. He looped it around my wrists and yanked it painfully tight.

'There. There, that's better.' Manpyre stared down at me, expressionless. 'Now you're not going anywhere, are you?' He laughed, then he switched off the light and rolled over, leaving me. I stared into the darkness listening to my own rapid breathing. The tendons in my shoulders burned. 'Stop crying and go to sleep,' said Manpyre.

Eddie

I shifted on the couch, wincing at my stiff neck. I did not want to sleep, and in fact it was already getting light outside, but I felt exhausted. Despite this, it seemed that my troubled mind would never let my spent body sleep. I lay awake, thinking constantly about what to do. I doubted that Ilya would keep his word and let us stay in the hotel for a week or two, not even to give Jason time to recover properly. I knew how changeable Ilya could be, and that he had good reason to hate Jason. No, we needed to find somewhere to go.

There was a scuffing noise and I sat up stiffly and saw Jason sitting bolt upright in bed. He was looking around the room, sleepy and disorientated. I wondered if he remembered it, if he remembered the hotel at all. I could not help recalling that we had lost our virginity to each other in that room, in the same bed in which Jason now sat. I hurried over to him, but before I reached him, Jason looked up with large, apprehensive eyes and said, 'Eddie.' His voice sounded slightly muffled, as though he were deaf.

'What did you say?' I sat beside him and had to stop myself from grabbing hold of him. 'Baby, say it again.'

Jason looked at me steadily and again said, 'Eddie.' He paused and touched his lips. 'Drink. Water, Eddie.'

I was stunned. 'Water... I'll get you some now.' I was thinking, 'You can speak. This is not new to me, you could always speak, and it was new to me when you could not.' I gazed at Jason, bewildered.

Running some tap water into a glass, I heard voices passing by on the landing outside the room; loud voices, laughter. Pressing my eye to the spy hole in the door, my field of vision was obscured by one figure; Ilya, knocking lightly on the door.

'Sorry to bother you,' he apologised, when I opened the door a crack. 'Can I come in for a minute?'

'What's going on?' I switched on the light as Ilya stepped in to the room. My mind was still reeling from my exchange with Jason. Ilya stood stiffly by the door.

'Mischa has some friends over. I just wanted to remind you...' He glanced awkwardly at Jason and trailed off. Jay was staring at him with his deep, dark eyes, his face expressionless.

'He's awake,' said Ilya.

I needed them to stop staring at one another. I stepped between them, passing Jason the glass of water.

'Yes, he is. Illy, what is it that you want?'

Ilya spoke, still staring hard at Jason. 'It is vital that you stay out of sight.'

Jason began to drink from the glass, spilling most of the water on himself. I sat on the edge of the bed and steadied the glass for him while he drank. I answered Ilya distractedly, 'Not a problem. We will not leave this room. Colt can bring us what we need, food and things.'

'Yes, Bryce is good at doing that, isn't he?' Said Ilya sarcastically. His eyes swept over to Jason again and I watched his face tighten. His voice grew sharp, 'Keep away from the twins and keep him,' he jerked his head at Jay, 'Away from them, too. Fucking freak show.'

'Hey,' I said sharply. 'Mind how you talk to him.'

Ilya ignored that. His eyes glittered with naked hostility now. Jason shakily climbed out of bed and made his way unsteadily to the bathroom, using the wall to support himself as he walked. He closed the bathroom door after himself, and Ilya rounded on me. 'I actually can't believe that you brought him here, to this house. How dare you?'

'You've changed your tune.'

'Maybe I have. Maybe I just remembered how sick you both make me feel.'

I must have been feeling tender with tiredness; Ilya's comments usually failed to hurt me.

'Do not worry about it,' I said. 'As I said, I only came back to make some arrangements. We are leaving… as soon as we possibly can.' Distracted, I tapped my knuckles lightly on the bathroom door,

'Jason? Baby, you okay?' It felt strange and stressful, getting used to what Jason could do for himself, and what he needed help with.

Ilya lost patience, 'Surely he can piss by himself, Eddie,' he said scornfully.

Chapter 35

Eddie

It was agreed that I could stay in the hotel for one week. During this time, Colt helped me to make my plans, using the internet to find accommodation for rent in Paris, where I had decided to go. Colt seemed exhausted and subdued. I tried not to think about this too much. His sleeves crept up as he typed on his computer, and I saw how his wrists were red and bruised with friction burns. Manpyre had obviously started on him.

'Is everything alright, Colt?' I tried asking him.

He nodded quickly. 'Yeah! Everything's fine. Thanks.' Then he promptly changed the subject. 'I've found a great apartment in Rue de la Bucherie, look.' He turned the laptop around to show me. I looked at the pictures of the apartment. It was boring, and too small.

'Mm… Things going alright with Manpyre?' I asked quietly.

'Yeah.'

'Is he being nice to you?'

'Mm hm… Yeah, he is, always… anyway, look at the apartment, Ed. It's got two bedrooms and it's right in the area you wanted…'

'Because I get the impression that he is abusing you. He has a habit of doing that, you see.'

Colt turned scarlet. He stared straight at the screen, rigid. I had gone too far. 'I am sorry,' I said. 'It's none of my business. Show me the apartment. I am sorry, Colt.'

He was standing up, 'I'm just gonna get my glasses,' he murmured. 'Looking at the screen is making my eyes itchy. Want anything from the kitchen, the bar? Does Jason want anything?' He was talking fast, I had completely embarrassed him. I knew I was right about Manpyre, though.

'No thank you honey, we're fine…' I felt rather bad. 'Colt? If you want to talk about anything… I am always here.'

He hurried out of the room.

I looked over at Jason, sleeping so peacefully on the couch. I sighed. Manpyre; that dirty bastard. I wondered if I should talk to Ilya about it. After all, Colt and Manpyre were two of his employees, perhaps he could intervene somehow if Colt's work was being affected… but no. It was their private business and I very much doubted that Ilya would want to involve himself in any way. I was worried about Colt but I had other, more pressing concerns to attend to.

Jason was growing stronger every day. Caring for him was exhausting. I had never done anything like that before in my life but, I would not have it any other way. Colt warned me that the greatest danger to Jason's health was his epilepsy, and that Jay would be safest back in hospital… I knew, however, that I was doing a better job of looking after him than any hospital could.

Ilya had discreetly arranged with Dr Bell, to get the medication Jason needed for his epilepsy. No questions asked. Once I had the medication, I felt much calmer about Jason's health. Still, it was incredibly nerve-wracking. In some ways, I was waiting for that first seizure to happen.

When it did I rather panicked and called Colt. He came running, and found me watching helplessly. Colt immediately started timing the seizure on his phone while he moved a desk chair that was too close to Jason's head. Thankfully, the fit soon stopped and as Colt put him into the recovery position, he looked up at me, exasperated. I was holding my head in my hands, and I looked helplessly back at him. He was breathing heavily from running.

'What the hell was that?' He sighed. 'You know what to do, we talked about this. Remember the recovery position? Like this?'

His face softened. 'You okay? That looked scary, right?'

I could not speak. Colt pushed back his long hair. 'Okay. Listen. If you're going to live with him, you have to learn to do this yourself. It's really important.'

'I can't.'

'What?'

I shook my head. Colt did not realise what it was like for me, to see Jason fitting like that and know that I did that to him. Helping him to look after himself was one thing, but this felt like quite another.

'I said, I can't.'

'You have to.' Colt waited until I met his eyes and repeated, firmly, 'You have to.' He sighed again, 'Next time, you can do it while I watch. It's easy, really easy. Okay?'

I picked up Jay, laid him on my bed, where he ended up sleeping for the next fourteen hours. I watched him for a while, then I went into the bathroom and unwrapped my razor blade. I stared at it, breathing hard. This time it was different. My breathing slowed down and became regular. Ten minutes later I was still holding the blade but, it was clean. With one finger, I pushed it through the overflow drain in the sink. It fell and was gone.

Very sweetly, Colt got me some books and articles about epilepsy and they did help to demystify the whole thing for me. The next time Jason had a seizure, which was only, in fact, two days later, I dealt with it myself, as much as I wanted to run away. Afterwards, I fell asleep beside him in sorrow and most of all, relief.

While Colt sorted out accommodation and Ilya organised passports and other travel documents for us, I was simply building up my relationship with Jason. There was so much he needed help with. He was slowly beginning to eat, though he would not accept food unless it was given to him by me. I showered him, shaved him and dressed him. It was intensely difficult, and I often thought about the 'old' Jason, missing him acutely.

I adored the present Jason with all of my heart and I lived for amazing moments. As his confidence grew he began to talk more. He was different, but he still had his own sense of humour, still had his own expression of love. Looking out of the window one morning, he sat up a little straighter and said clearly, 'Eddie, Eddie. Horse.' And he was indeed looking at a horse being led across the driveway, a familiar sparkle in his eyes and his gorgeous half smile on his lips. Jason was always wild about horses, and I knew exactly what he would love… it was at around midnight, when all of the staff had gone home and the twins were both out at a party. Jay seemed afraid as I led him out of the hotel and into the dark. He gripped tightly to my arm with both hands. Yet, when he saw those horses, his hands fell to his sides and he gazed at them, eyes sparking. He gently touched the biggest animal, and made an excited noise, like a strangled scream.

'Hush, baby, do not scare them,' I shushed, but I was grinning, and trying not to let Jason see the tears of joy in my eyes. 'To think that you have not ridden a horse for so long… you! As soon as we are settled somewhere, babe, I promise I will take you riding. God, do you remember your old mare, Steph? You spent more time with her than you did with me.'

Eel smiled at me. Perhaps I was deluded, but I truly felt that he was remembering.

Thereafter, Jason emphatically asked for the horses every single day. I was almost sorry that I had taken him to the stables at all, since he asked to go so often.

Colt and I also took Jason to the hotel swimming pool, one memorable night. Jay was a surprisingly good swimmer, he was slow but he did not want me to help him. I paddled along beside him in the shallow end while

Colt swam lengths. Suddenly there were footsteps on the tiles.

'Who's in here?'

Colt whipped around. 'Manpyre?'

'Fuck.' I grabbed Jason and pulled him out of view behind a pillar. 'Babe,' I said urgently, 'You must be quiet. Shh.'

He looked at me, confused. I peered around the pillar. Manpyre was kneeling at the edge of the pool as Colt swam over to him.

'I just got back from Bristol and I saw lights down here. Honey, it's 2am. What the hell are you doing? Why are you always doing crazy things in the middle of the night?'

Colt cleared his throat. He leaned his arms on the side of the pool, his wet hair glistening. 'I just... fancied a swim.'

'At 2am?'

Colt shrugged. 'Yeah...'

Manpyre sighed and rubbed his face. 'I swear to God, you are mad.' He chuckled. 'It's a good thing you're so cute. You look hot in your little Speedos.'

I bit my lip. My feelings about Colt were buried very, very deeply, but still... I loathed the sound of Manpyre talking like that. Jason seemed to be getting impatient, he squirmed beside me and whimpered.

'Shh, babe. Wait,' I urged. My whisper sounded loud in the silent room but it was abruptly drowned out by the rushing sound of Colt getting out of the water.

'Hey,' said Manpyre. 'Where you going?'

'Let's go upstairs,' said Colt. 'Come on.' Colt stood at the poolside, dripping wet. He looked so vulnerable with his pale skin and goggles on his head, while Manpyre, dressed all in black, seemed cool and in control. He started kissing Colt, while unzipping his own trousers. Colt would hate that. He was prudish about sex in public, if he thought anyone else was watching or listening. Colt didn't like to be watched, he preferred to make love in private, preferably in the dark, or under a blanket if he could get away with it. His 'lights-off' penchant was something he and I had often disagreed on... Still. As long as he kept Manpyre distracted I could sneak

Jason out of there. I helped him to climb the ladder and he turned to me looking confused and a little irritated.

'Swim.' He said.

'Babe, shh. I'm sorry babe.' I put my hand gently over his mouth, glancing anxiously across the room.

'Stop,' I heard Colt pleading gently. I gritted my teeth.

'Not here.'

Manpyre sighed. 'What is it this time? Let me guess, what are the usual excuses… you're tired. You're late for work. You have too much work to do. What else, oh, you're stressed. You're late for someplace. You have to call your brother. You have to get to the gym. You-'

'Alright. You're right, sorry. It's just… not here. It's embarrassing.'

'There's nobody here.'

'There's all those big windows.'

Manpyre said nothing.

'Hey,' Colt tried, putting his arms around Manpyre's shoulders. He kissed him gently on his moody face. 'Let's go upstairs. C'mon.'

Manpyre started kissing him roughly again, whilst trying to push him down onto his knees.

'Just get on with it. What's the problem?'

Colt raised his voice slightly, 'Dave. Not here. I'm not going to-'

'Fine. Shut up with your fucking whining.' Manpyre turned away, then back to Colt. 'Christ, you know how to kill my mood, don't you?'

There was a short silence then a solid smack. Colt made a heart-breaking yelp.

'Oh, get up,' said Manpyre scathingly. 'I haven't hurt you.' He swore. 'I'm done with you for tonight, just sleep in your own room.' He stormed off.

As soon as he was gone I jumped out of the pool and hauled Jason out. Colt was scrambling to his feet. 'Don't!' He flinched, when I made to touch him. 'Just don't, Eddie!'

'Oh, Colt. That bastard… are you alright?' He grabbed a towel and started walking to the changing rooms.

'Why bother asking?' He said over his shoulder, 'You just sat there and watched.'

I tied a towel around Jason's waist and said nothing. Colt knew I could no longer fight his battles; I had Jay to think about now. I glanced over at the changing rooms. 'Babe,' I said to Jason, 'Sit here… can you dry your hair with the towel, like this? That's it… wait here for me, babe.' I left him towelling his hair and I followed Colt to the changing room. He was shaking, throwing on his clothes in a fit of uncharacteristic rage. I just watched, taking in all of the marks on that beautiful body under the fluorescent lights. This wasn't just classic Manpyre, this was worse. Bruises, old and new, and buckle marks, just like before. 'Oh, Colt.' I said. 'I did not realise… that things were so bad.'

'He does it all the time. He does this every day.' Colt was bright red with anger, humiliation. 'He hurts me in bed now too. We can't just be a normal couple, I have to be tied up and he makes me do things… say things.'

My mouth was dry. 'Colt-'

'It's your fault,' he added. 'He does it because of you. He says that he can't get you out of his head. He always brings you up and calls me things.'

'Things like what?'

'Like slut… or whore,' he said, colouring up. 'Used up. He says I am so used up, no one else would ever want me. He's really rough sometimes Eddie, and it hurts, it really hurts and I can't make it stop. I keep making excuses now and he- he's getting angrier.' He threw his shampoo into his bag so hard that it bounced out and clattered to the floor, then he sat down on the wooden bench with his face in his hands.

'Shit. Sweetheart, I am sorry.' I hugged him, his head on my chest. I wanted to kill Dave Manpyre. I breathed in the chlorine smell on Colt's hair and for a moment, dreamed back to those happy days in Stockholm, just Colt and I, far away from all of this.

Chapter 36

Colt

'Maybe you shouldn't come to the meeting,' said Manpyre doubtfully. 'Your bruises look worse today, babe.'

It was Friday. Manpyre and I were getting ready to head downstairs to the firm meeting but apparently, he didn't want me to go.

'It's fine,' I said, 'No one will notice.'

Everyone was getting used to seeing me with bruises nowadays, and no one seemed to care.

'I do love you, cutie,' Manpyre was watching me in the mirror as I knotted my new tie; an apology gift from him.

'Yeah, love you too,' I replied softly. I sighed and turned to face him. I wondered how cute I looked, really. I had two black eyes as a result of being punched in the nose. We'd had a big fight the night before. The usual rubbish, I was a little bit exhausted from work and helping Eddie so, when

Manpyre came to me looking for sex I just told him I was too tired. It was true, kind of. Anyway, that didn't go down too well; not at all, actually.

It wasn't just that I was tired. He knew that, and it made him livid. But I couldn't tell him the truth; that every time I even thought about sleeping with him I got so anxious that I got a really bad stomach ache. He could hit me all he wanted, it was all better than going to bed with him, doing the bloody weird stuff he was into. I wondered how long I could avoid it, really though. As we headed for the door my phone beeped; a message. As I reached for it, Manpyre scooped it up first. I felt a little tingle of dread as I watched him reading it. His face was completely blank and expressionless.

'Who's 'C'?'

My shoulders drooped in relief. 'Oh. That's just Clarke. He's my little brother,' I said. The next second, Manpyre had thrown the phone at my head. I ducked. It hit the wall.

'Liar. Your fucking brother wouldn't put two 'x's' on the end of a message, would he? And why would he write 'miss you'?'

'He would put 'x's'. And he always says he misses me, why not?'

When I picked the phone up I saw that the screen was cracked. I was about to complain about it, but I saw Manpyre's face and thought better of it.

'Sorry,' I said automatically. That sent him flying at me.

'Sorry?' He was screaming as he pummelled me on my arms and head. 'Sorry for what? Are you fucking cheating on me again?'

My forehead exploded in pain as he head-butted me savagely and threw me against the wall. I slid down onto the floor, head pounding in slow motion. Manpyre sat down heavily in his desk chair, one hand over his eyes. I sat there catching my breath, watching him. My head was banging. Minutes passed. Neither of us knew what to say. I couldn't tell if he was still angry, or just upset. I couldn't see his face. I was afraid to say anything so I just stayed where I was.

There was a knock on the door. Manpyre stood up to answer it, he wasn't crying but his face was grim. I got up too, but instantly a wave of nausea hit me. I scrambled to the bathroom and, on my knees, started throwing up half on the floor. When Manpyre appeared in the doorway, minutes later, he found me rinsing towels in the sink.

'That was Ilya, he's on his way down to the meeting. You,' he closed his eyes briefly, 'You can't come down now; you look awful. And you've got sick on your tie.'

I looked. 'Ah, shit. Sorry.'

He shook his head, 'It doesn't matter. Here,' he said, taking a step towards me. 'Let me.' He took off my tie, began washing it briskly. Without looking at me, he said, 'Shit, honey… look at us. This really isn't working out. I mean, even if that was your brother… which it probably was… I can't trust you. I think we have to finish this now, mate, otherwise I'm gonna end up hurting you bad.'

'No.' Was that really my voice, that desperate pleading voice? I felt the same sort of terror churning through me as when Eddie left me. It was that same feeling that made me sleep with Anders, the same feeling, in fact, that had gotten me together with Manpyre in the first place.

'Please don't break up with me,' I heard myself saying, in a wobbly voice. 'I can't be on my own. I need somebody.'

'You need somebody? Or me?' Manpyre was looking at me expectantly, so I nodded.

'You,' I whispered. 'I need you. Please.' He came down and sat beside me on the edge of the bath, wrapped me into his arms.

'Honey. C'mere. You know I love you so much.'

We kissed lingeringly. I felt empty inside, but that terrifying desperation had subsided, for now. Manpyre left me pressing a cold, wet flannel to my forehead.

'I'll tell Ilya you're sick,' he said, 'and I'll come up to check on you later, okay?' He stopped in the doorway and said, 'I won't do this again, Colt. Next time, I'll be better.' He seemed as though he believed himself. Then he left.

I lay on the bed, holding my battered head and staring up at the ceiling. I imagined Manpyre downstairs, telling everyone that I was too sick to work… when really, he had head butted me. I jumped up and scribbled a note to Manpyre;

'*Dave,*
I am still sick so just want to sleep in my own room tonight.
See you tomorrow,
Love Bryce xxx'

I tossed it onto his dresser, then I ran straight upstairs to Eddie's room.

'Hello!' He grinned, when he saw me. 'I am so glad you came up, I need someone to hide behind.'

I stepped into the room. 'We are watching horror movies,' explained Eddie, as he locked the door. He rolled his eyes as he passed me a bowl of popcorn and a beer. 'I hate gory movies,' he whispered with a smile.

'Me too.'

He winked at me, chewing some popcorn. 'Too bad. It is a very disgusting one too, they seem to be his favourites... right, my sick puppy?' He ruffled Jason's hair. (Jason watched at least three hard-core horrors every day. I was aghast about this the first time I saw Eddie put on the Japanese version of The Grudge.)

'You can't let him watch that!'

'Why not? He isn't a child. He's thirty-four years old.' Eddie had smiled. 'He laughs at all the jumpy parts. He used to fucking love horror films; still does, evidently. That is why I put it on for him.'

I lay on the bed while Eddie and Jason huddled together on the sofa, wrapped in a blanket. Eddie was making Jay laugh, by throwing popcorn and catching it in his mouth. I felt a twinge of envy as I watched them together. I missed Eddie, and I missed being the one who made him laugh like that. I ignored the film and watched instead as Eddie stuffed as much popcorn as he could into his mouth and was now making hideous faces to amuse Jason, his cheeks bulging.

Jason fell asleep halfway through the movie, so Eddie put him to bed. He dimmed the lights, turned the volume on the TV down really low and put subtitles on, and gestured to me to come and join him on the sofa. I scurried over gratefully. 'Mm. This is nice,' he grinned, putting his arm around my shoulders and pulling me in close. 'Just like old times.'

It was just like in Stockholm. Snuggled against his big, warm body I felt my troubles evaporating. I smiled happily to myself, and subtly I breathed in his smell, which was dusty vintage velvet and cologne. Eddie stroked my bruised forehead, showing me that he had noticed and that he cared. He tucked the blanket around me and settled back to watch the movie. I closed my eyes and listened to his slow heartbeat. He was killing me. I wanted him so much. There was a hot scene between two of the characters in the movie. It was torture, sitting pressed up against Eddie watching a sex scene. I stole a glance at up him, he was watching the movie impassively. If anything, he looked bored. Eddie's arm was around me, his fingers dangling teasingly close to my face. I couldn't resist anymore. I took the tip of his finger in my mouth and gently, I sucked it. Eddie snatched his hand away.

'Stop it,' he whispered, 'Calm down.'

I stared at the movie, my face burning.

Eddie glanced down at me. 'What is wrong? Do not tell me that this stupid film is making you horny. It is the silliest film ever.'

'So what if it is?' I snapped.

'Wow… okay, grumpy. What is wrong?'

On the screen, the monster advanced on the couple.

'I just…' I shrugged. I lowered my eyes, lowered my voice and said, 'It's you.' I looked up at him, seductively I hoped. 'Man, I want you so bad.'

The movie monster raised his arm, knife gleaming.

Eddie looked at me carefully. 'Are you joking?'

I shook my head. 'Feel my heart, it's totally racing.' I unbuttoned my shirt and placed his hand on my chest. 'There, feel it? That's just from being close to you.'

He rolled his eyes and said, 'Enough.' And with the decisiveness that I loved, he held my face with both hands and kissed me. The blanket slid onto the floor. The movie kept murmuring, flickering and screaming. I felt light-headed. I just wanted more and more and more.

Eddie disengaged his mouth and said, 'Alright, alright. You deserved a few kisses for that performance, but that really is enough now.'

'It isn't.' I straddled him and kissed him on his neck. 'Just… come to bed with me,' I begged, between kisses. 'Nothing more, just… just fuck me, please.' I blushed, shocked at speaking that way, but it's how I felt.

He looked at me incredulously, 'Have you heard yourself?'

I noticed he was perspiring lightly. Despite himself, he was stroking my thighs, letting his hands move up my thighs.

'You are being very bad tonight, baby. You are making me think bad thoughts.' His thumb brushed against the tip of my penis and I shuddered and gently bit his neck, dizzy for him.

'Please,' I begged.

'Baby,' he groaned softly, 'I want to but I can't. I simply cannot.'

I was aching from wanting him so badly.

'But you're not a couple,' I said, 'It's not like you'd be cheating on him.'

'Ah… no, I know that. But it is complicated.' He swallowed and cast a tortured glance at Jason, who was fast asleep.

'Why is it complicated?' I couldn't help it, I was touching his chest now. 'How complicated is it?'

He looked at me then, and something flickered in his eyes. He stood up, brushed me off and said, 'Complicated enough.'

I followed him into the bathroom and found him splashing his face with cold water.

'Oh Colt, stop it, now.' He looked quite pissed off, but I ignored that. I dropped to my knees in front of him, grabbed his flies and gently eased his trousers open.

'Leave me alone,' he said in a ragged voice, but he didn't move. As I gently pleasured him, planning my next move, I looked up and saw him biting his fist, his eyes clenched tightly shut.

'Enough.' He hauled me to my feet and flipped me to face the wall. Bent over the sink, I yelped loudly as he entered me and he clamped his hand firmly over my mouth. I was light-headed and I came hard, moaning helplessly into his hand. Eddie came into me with a repressed groan. He held me as our heartbeats slowed together.

I rested my forehead on the cool enamel of the sink, catching my breath. I laughed quietly, 'Hey. I win.'

He punched me lightly on the arm. 'Yes. You win… do not… ever do this to me again,' he panted. 'I'm too old for this.'

We went to my room and he gave me what I wanted. We made love to each other for hours. I couldn't get enough of him, I just wanted him constantly.

'You are not tired yet?' He laughed, as I begged to have sex with him again.

'No,' I said, 'I won't ever get tired of being with you.'

Eddie's face turned serious. 'This,' he said, touching one of my many, many bruises, '… is very bad.' He got hold of my wrist and examined the chafed stripy rope burns. 'Sick bastard… how dare he do this to you? Do you know what I would do to David Manpyre if I could? I would give him one of these around his neck.'

Sometimes, I had a fantasy like that, about Eddie beating up Manpyre, but I didn't want to talk about Dave right now. I shrugged and kissed Eddie again. He pulled away and looked at my face.

'You do not suit blackened eyes. Next time he does it, hit him back. Punch him in the throat.'

'Yeah, right.'

He shook his head, 'Heh. Obviously, do not do that, he would kill you… baby, I wish I could help. I thought that maybe, if you- or I- talk to Ilya…'

'Don't you dare! How embarrassing would that be? He wouldn't care anyway. He knows. Look at the state of me, everyone can see what's happening and no one cares. It's alright, anyway.' I kissed him again, slowly, lovingly; so perfect, until he stopped it again.

'If you talk to Ilya…' he began.

'Don't,' I said. 'Don't let's talk about it. Let's do… this… instead.'

'Alright,' he said, laughing, 'Go gently this time… I do not have your energy.'

He was lying on his front, and the tattoo with Jason's name was right there, glistening with sweat; mine and his. I closed my eyes and rested my cheek against his shoulder blades. I made love to him nice and slow, like he wanted. 'I really love you,' I groaned.

'Oh, Colt. Do not say that,' he whispered roughly.

After, he snuggled up to me for sleep. I was wide-awake, though. I traced my fingers across his back and shoulder, again and again. This was my paradise. It was heaven, exactly where I wanted and needed to be.

'Hey,' I whispered, 'what are you thinking?' Such questions usually annoyed him.

'I'm not thinking, I'm relaxing. Shh.'

I smiled. 'You did need a break,' I thought, out loud.

Eddie stiffened slightly. 'A break from what? From Jay?'

Shit. 'Um, no... more like, a break from all your responsibilities? You know, a little escape. From life. Know what I mean?'

Eddie was quiet. Then he sat up, rubbing his face. He looked so sexy with his hair all undone.

'I had better go, baby.'

'Wait, no. Was it something I... said?'

He laughed quietly and kissed me lightly on the lips. 'Yes. But do not feel bad.' He kissed me again, quickly and began to get up, holding a sheet around his waist. 'Baby... perhaps you would like to escape from your life. But my life is Jason, and I do not want to escape, or break, from him. Thank you for tonight, it was special. I have to go now.'

'He's fine,' I groaned. 'He's probably still asleep. Don't go yet. Please, please don't go...'

He was already going. My bed felt freezing afterwards. I gathered the sheets that smelled of him, and breathed deep.

A couple of hours later there was a knocking on my door. Unfortunately it wasn't Eddie, it was Manpyre. 'Hey, honey bun. How are feeling? Aw, you look so beautiful in the morning... your cheeks are all flushed, how cute is that?'

I blushed really, really hard at that. If he knew why I looked flushed…

'Hang on a minute,' I mumbled. I shut the door, ripped all the sheets off my bed and flung them into the bathroom. Then I smoothed the duvet over the bare mattress, composed myself and opened the door properly.

'Don't ever keep me waiting, Colt.'

'Sorry. Come on in.'

He sat on my bed and told me all about last night's meeting, and by the time that story had ended, I had calmed down, though my stomach still ached with guilt. Manpyre didn't seem to notice anything amiss, at all. How could he not notice? I could still feel Eddie's hands all over me and I could taste him in my mouth. His smell was on my skin, on the bed and in my hair, everywhere. I noticed a glittery pink stain on my inner thigh; lip-gloss. Maybe I was imagining it. I rubbed it surreptitiously.

'Aren't you gonna give me a kiss, honey?' Said Manpyre, and his hand on my face almost made me flinch.

'What is it?'

'Nothing…' I was panicking that there might be scratches, or hickies from Eddie on my body, or that Dave would go into the bathroom and find the stained bed sheets. And thinking these things, I just felt disgusting. I realised I was becoming exactly what Manpyre was always accusing me of being.

I tried to just get on with life. I didn't try to sleep with Eddie again, there was never a good opportunity and besides, I decided I didn't want to behave in that slutty way again. Like it or loathe it, I was with Dave. I was busy with work but I tried to help Eddie out as much as I could in my free time. Eddie tried to make me go shopping for Jason, handing me an extensive list… Underwear, razors, toothbrush, socks, a coat, an iPod, all available Patti Smith and Dickies albums and DVDs, a netbook computer, horror movies (certain ones, there was an A-Z), a selection of tops in various specific colours (memorably, he had written 'Long-sleeved fitted top in white; not cream, but not white white. A nice white.').

'Oh Eddie… what the hell is 'nice white'? Come on…' I put my foot down, offering instead to stay with Jason while Eddie went shopping. It surprised me when he agreed, in fact, I was flattered that he trusted me. Maybe he needed to take a break from caring for Jason, to get out of the house.

As Jason ate his breakfast, Eddie explained to him. 'Babe,' he said, holding a piece of buttered toast as Jason took a small bite, 'I am going shopping this morning. I am going to buy things for you. You need to stay here with Colt, and I will be back soon… okay? Understand, babe?'

Jason glanced at me, looked back at Eddie and said, 'Coat,' which is how he generally pronounced my name. Eddie kissed him on top of his head, and left, looking tense.

'Take care of him, Colt… sorry, sorry- I had to say it. You know I trust you. '

It was a beautiful, bright day. I felt bad for Eel being stuck indoors, confined to Eddie's suite. There wasn't much for him to do, but on the other hand, he seemed content… he had just spent sixteen years in hospital, I mused, it could not have been enormously exciting. The suite must have been a luxurious step up for him. Even having a double bed to himself must have felt like a bit of an extravagant treat.

Jason watched carefully as I built a few Lego models for him. He liked dismantling them afterwards. I read aloud a few articles from a magazine about horses. I let him brush and play with my hair, which he always seemed to love doing to both myself and Eddie. He was really very gentle. While Jason was messing around with my long hair, bunching it all together and wrapping it around his fingers, he found my silver crucifix and he held it, examining it closely.

'Do you like that, buddy? Yeah, it's God. I'm sure you know that…'

He was kind of trying to pull it off of me. Suddenly, I wanted him to have it. 'Do you want it? Yeah? Hang on.' I unfastened it and clasped it around his neck. He stroked it gently between his fingers with an almost-smile. Then he reached for my other necklace which was a thin, leather string threaded through Manpyre's gold ring. 'Aw, no buddy, you can't have this one. I'm stuck with this one, I'm afraid.'

I fetched him some tea and some crisps, stuck on one of his horror flicks. He was soon absorbed in the film, some teenage torture movie, and I was soon bored watching that gore. I needed a book, so I decided it would be safe to leave him alone for twenty minutes while I went to the library. I came out of Eddie's suite, locked the door behind me then I turned around and gasped. Manpyre was standing in the corridor with a curious expression.

'Dave... jeez, you scared the shit out of me,' I laughed. I walked quickly down the corridor, away from Eddie's suite, hoping he would follow. He did not.

'Hey.' He jerked his head towards the door, 'What were you doing in Bodansky's old room?'

I was panicking a little, and I knew that Manpyre could read me like a book. I tried to create some excuse. 'I thought there might be... I'm looking for an invoice, can't find it anywhere, I was checking Eddie's old desk.'

'Oh, right.' Manpyre walked really close to me as I hurried on down the corridor. 'Was it in there?'

I shook my head, 'No. It'll turn up.'

'Did you check inside the desk? Sure you looked right inside in all the drawers?'

'Oh... yeah, I think so.'

Manpyre suddenly pushed me against the wall.

'Except, that little story is fucking bullshit, isn't it?' He grabbed my arms and slammed me back against the wall again. 'Isn't it? '

'No!'

'A few weeks ago, I personally carried that desk into one of the new suites. So I know it isn't in there. I carried it myself, Colt. I'm sick of your fucking lying. You've been in there for ages and I can hear a TV. Is Bodansky back here?'

'No.'

He slapped me hard. 'Is he back here? Have you been in there getting fucked by Bodansky?' He slapped me again, again. A slap for every question. 'Is he here? Is he?'

'No, no, he isn't. I made a mistake, I didn't mean his desk... Dave, don't, please.'

Manpyre dug in my pocket and pulled out the key I had just used to lock Eddie's room. I threw myself at him, trying to wrench it out of his hand.

'Dave,' I was gasping, slightly hysterical, 'Please, don't.'

He swept me aside, looking incredulous.

'You're pathetic,' he said coldly, his eyes full of anger and pain, 'And once I'm finished with Bodansky, you had better run boy, because I don't like people fucking me around.'

He went to Eddie's room and began unlocking the door. I grabbed onto his hand and tried everything to stop him.

'You stupid... little... slut,' grunted Manpyre as he struggled with me. He bent my fingers back and pushed me over.

'No.' I scrambled to my feet as Manpyre burst into the room. He stood staring for a moment, and then he gave a single bark of laughter.

'What... the fuck. Eel Prescott?'

Jason was lying on the couch watching his movie. He hugged a pillow to his chest and stared thoughtfully at Manpyre. It was difficult to tell whether or not he recognised his former colleague.

'Where's Bodansky?' Said Manpyre without taking his eyes from Jason.

'Out,' I whispered, 'He'll be home soon.'

Manpyre smiled and shook his head. 'You lying little fuck. So he is back.'

I didn't say anything. Manpyre looked around the room, looked at Jason surrounded by all of his Lego toys and colouring books. He shook his head again, 'What a fucked up situation... I always liked Eel. He was one hell of a nice bloke.'

'He still is,' I blurted out. 'Just because he has brain damage doesn't mean-'

'Shut up.' He jerked his head at me, 'Come on. You come with me.'

'I... I have to stay here to look after Eel-'

'No. You come with me.'

I followed him, cringing, apologising and talking fast the whole time. I was in a right panic but Manpyre just walked ahead of me, he didn't seem to be listening. He led me into the lift.

'Dave,' I said nervously, 'I'm sorry I didn't tell you.'

'Hm.' He looked hard at me, his pupils were really small. He pressed some buttons on the panel. I shifted uncomfortably.

'Okay… I'm sorry, Dave! Please don't be so angry!'

'I'm not angry, it's just…' Manpyre looked at me fully, 'Are you sleeping with him? Eddie?'

I looked down. 'Yeah.'

He made a little noise like a small, wounded animal.

'Colt… seriously? Again?'

I sighed. 'Oh, Dave… yeah- but we only just started, I've only done it once-'

'Only once? Colt, why the fuck didn't you just tell me he was back? Why didn't you trust me with the truth? I could have handled that, I know you love him…' He looked down. 'Fuck. Fuck, I can't handle that you've been cheating on me again. You little dickhead. You dirty little slut.'

I shook my head, speechless.

'Where's the respect? What have I done to deserve the way you've treated me, Colt?'

I didn't know what to say. He was scaring me now.

'Well, now I know. And with one phone call to the hospital, I could blow their lives apart.'

'Oh, please don't.'

He shook his head, 'I wouldn't do that, Colt. Fuck, you don't trust me one inch, do you? I'm not a bad person, I love you. You may have treated me like shit, but I've done nothing but love you.'

By now he was gripping my neck, squeezing it so I couldn't breathe.

'Don't be scared of me. Colt, did you ever love me even a bit? Look at my eyes.' They were filled with tears. He released my throat a bit and I took a rough gasp of air. The doors of the lift opened. Manpyre pushed me out and shoved me towards some stairs.

'Where… are we going?'

He started up the stairs behind me.

'The roof,' he said quietly. 'You're not afraid of heights, are you?'

I turned on the stairs and looked at him, clutching my sore throat.

'Are you crazy?' I croaked.

'Come on.' He looked edgy now. 'Come on. Don't make me out to be some kind of… just keep going.'

I pushed open the door at the top. It was cold, the wind was whipping loudly. He was going to throw me off the roof. He came behind me and closed the door. As he turned to face me I grabbed him and kissed him desperately.

'I'm sorry,' I mumbled, half crying. 'This is my fault. I'll make it up to you. I'm sorry.'

He didn't move. Suddenly he clamped my lip between his teeth and bit down hard. I froze as he ground his teeth together, sawing into my flesh. I squealed. His teeth tore into my flesh, harder, it was agony. He seemed to decide against it, pushing me away. I held my mouth with both hands, it was throbbing and bleeding. 'I don't know what to do with you!' He shouted, raising his fist. I cowered, but he didn't hit me. He slapped his palm against the wall in frustration. 'I could honestly kill you!' He reached towards me again but changed his mind and aimed his punch into the brick wall, slamming it again, again. My mouth was dry with fear. His knuckles were grazed and bloodied. He turned and looked at me in absolute anguish. 'Can't we just be happy?'

It was freezing and I wanted, more than anything, to get down from the roof.

'Oh, please, please can we just go inside and talk?' I begged, holding onto the door handle with one hand, my face with the other. Maybe if I was quick, I could just open it, run like hell down the stairs. But then what? Then where?

'Colt. Can you just be my guy? No more cheating? Just be mine. Let's get fucking married, or something.'

'Sure, Dave. Let's get married,' I said incredulously. I took my hand away from my mouth and he winced visibly at the sight of all the blood on me.

'See? You think I'm joking. Let's leave this place, start again somewhere. No more stress, then I'll start treating you better. That's why I lose my temper sometimes, because I'm stressed in this place.' He smoothed his greasy ponytail, staring out over the grounds of the hotel. 'If I wasn't so stressed, we would have more fun together. You would be happy and you wouldn't want to cheat on me.'

I decided to play along. 'Your... your job is totally stressful.'

Manpyre sat down slowly, beside the door, his back against the wall.

'Colt, it is. It really is honey, you have no idea. And you're causing me a ton of extra stress. I just want a happy home life.'

I thought about all the bad stuff he had done to me. The horrible things he had done, and said. My head was throbbing. I looked out across the fields stretching in each direction, and from up here I could see a nearby farm with a drift of smoke above one of the chimneys. There were a couple of horses grazing in a paddock, and these made me think about Jason. I knelt down beside Manpyre and put my hand on his knee, and although my fingers curled involuntarily, I kept my hand there and touched my fingers against his trembling lips, still stained with my blood.

'Babe,' I said, 'this is my fault. But we can fix this.'

He looked at me. Our faces were inches apart. I prayed that he believed me. 'We can fix this,' I repeated.

He studied my face for the longest time.

'I never felt like this about anyone,' he said thoughtfully, his eyes wet. 'My whole life. And then I get to my age, and I go and fall in love with a little slut. Because that's what you are,' he added. 'Don't bother looking pissed off. You know what you are, and I know you.'

I really hated him calling me that word. My self-preservation momentarily vanished. 'You don't know me that well,' I muttered.

'No? I think I do. For example, I know... what 82 Yale Road, Edinburgh is.'

I froze. I tried not to react, but how could I keep my composure when he had just mentioned my little brothers address? Manpyre was watching me.

'Clarke Colt and James Colt. Nice names. Two lovely brothers, you're lucky, I never had any- '

'Is this a threat?' I burst out.

'Wha-hat? Of course not. I'm just showing you how well I know you! Hey? Don't look so scared! Okay?'

I nodded dumbly.

'As if I would threaten your brothers, honey. I'm merely showing you that I know exactly where they live, where they go to school and where they play football on Sundays. Nothing sinister, hon.' Manpyre stood up. 'Come on, honey. Let's get off this goddammed roof. And you're right... we can fix this.'

He opened the door for me. I hesitated so he didn't wait, he brushed past me, walking back down the stairs. I watched him go, and I followed, gratefully slamming the door behind me.

'Where you going?' He snapped, at the bottom of the stairs. He sucked the blood from his knuckles. I said, with a nervous shrug, 'To check on Jason. He's still alone.'

Manpyre shook his head. 'No you ain't. Leave him. I don't want you involved in Bodansky's shit anymore.'

'Um, no, I know, but... it's not about Eddie. It's not safe. Jason has fits. Epilepsy. And he's due to take some medication in...' I checked my watch, 'Oh great, fifteen minutes ago. Shit.'

Manpyre smiled, 'I love it when you play Doctor.' He laughed, then snapped his fingers. 'The answer's still no. Bodansky can look after his own baby. C'mon.'

I wanted to scream. Instead, I followed Manpyre.

We went to the bar. Mischa and Ilya were there, arguing about something. Ilya gave us an impatient, hand-flapping wave of greeting before turning back to Mischa.

I stood at the bar, biting my nails and fretting while Manpyre ordered us a couple of teas. I glanced over at Ilya. My boss wouldn't be able to help, he didn't care. No one in this Hotel cared about Jason. Eddie, please come back, I thought feverently.

I reached into my pocket and, glancing at Manpyre who was still talking to the waitress, I took out my mobile. My fingers shook as I tried to tap out a message.

Manpyre grabbed my wrist. 'Give,' he said shortly. He placed my phone on the bar, humming softly as he dismantled it, piece by piece. He passed the pieces back to me: the phone, the back cover and the battery. He kept the SIM card, casually snapping it in two against the bar. Then wordlessly, he passed me that, too.

The waitress had just finished making our teas. Manpyre brought them over to a table by the window, and setting them down he said, 'I was serious upstairs, you know. I do want to marry you. I would marry you twice.'

I looked out of the window, wondering if he even knew what marriage was, what love was, at all.

Manpyre sipped his tea, 'I know what you're thinking,' he added. 'You can't be with me, because you still love Bodansky?'

I put down my tea. Here in the bar, surrounded by other people, I felt safe enough to be honest. 'Yeah,' I said gently. 'That's not the only reason, but… yeah, you know, I do.'

Manpyre shrugged. 'He'll be in prison soon anyway. Kidnap, assault, GBH on some poor paramedics… he's good at caving in people's heads, isn't he? Yeah, he'll be in prison soon enough.'

My fingers felt numb. Flexing them, I said, 'Well. Hopefully not. You said you wouldn't tell the police that Eddie's here, and I trust you because you're not a liar.'

'You're right. I'm not a liar, and I won't tell the police.' He took hold of my hand and studied my fingers. I watched his face. Then he let go of my hand, leaned back in his chair and called over his shoulder, 'Mischa?' Mischa and Ilya looked across to our table, Mitch scowling as usual.

'What?'

I stood up, 'David, no.'

'Shut up. I have to.' He turned back to Mischa, 'C'mere, for a second, kid. Want to know a secret?'

Eddie

I knew something did not feel quite right as soon as I opened the door to my suite. I had returned from shopping for Eel. It had taken slightly longer than expected, because I stumbled across a vintage jewellery store and got carried away buying opal rings and cameo brooches. However, I knew that Jason was safe being looked after by Colt, so I did not hurry back. Getting into the hotel unnoticed was very easy; I simply walked across the rear car park and in through the gym entrance.

'Baby, look what I bought for you!' I opened the door and dropped my thousand bags. 'Colt…? Hello?'

Eel was alone in the suite. His DVD had finished and he was sitting quietly by the window, his trousers all undone. He needed help with buttons and belts after using the toilet, but obviously no one had bothered to help him.

I dropped my bags. 'Hello babes… look at you, come here, darling.' I fixed his trousers and looked around, the room was freezing cold and there were crisps and tea spilled all over the carpet.

'Colt?' I called again, irritably. I checked the bathroom, it was empty, also. Worst of all, Jason's two o'clock medication, which I had laid out and taken great care to explain to Colt, was still sitting there by the sink. It was now almost time for his next pills. I glared around the room, seeing hazards everywhere. There were thousands of pills in the cabinet, the window was unlocked, and my gun was under the bed… not to mention Jason's fits. With no one to help him into the recovery position, he could have just fitted and died there in my room. I was breathless with anger. Yet at the same time, I was worried. It was so very unlike Colt to be irresponsible.

'Where the hell is he?' I asked Jason. I hardly expected Jay to answer me, but in fact, he did. Giving me a languid hug of greeting, he said, 'Day.'

I smoothed his hair back. 'Say that again, sweetheart.'

Arms around my neck, he looked at me seriously and tried again, with effort. This time it sounded more like, 'Dabe.'

'Oh, sorry babe, I do not understand-' Suddenly someone was hammering on the door... hammering and kicking.

Outside my bedroom door, Ilya was trying to calm Mischa down, to no avail.

'I'm calling the cops,' Mischa said, his voice hoarse from crying. 'Why are you letting him stay here, Dad?' He broke into rough sobs.

'You're not calling anyone,' said Ilya. 'Mikhail, try to calm down, no one is going to hurt you.'

I stared in shock.

'Eddie,' said Ilya tightly. He gave up trying to comfort the hysterical boy. 'Get out. You have twenty minutes to just get out of our lives. Twenty minutes,' he repeated, 'then, we really will call the police.'

I accepted this, grateful at being given the chance to leave. Wordlessly, I turned to go back into my room but Mischa barged into the doorway.

'Is he in there?' He demanded, squaring up to me aggressively.

I shook my head and said quietly. 'Not the time, kid. Now is not the time.'

'Mischa, come on' said Ilya quickly, 'go and wash your face, go to your room, and stay there, please.'

Mischa ignored him. 'Let me see him,' he snarled at me. He barged into me, trying to shove his way into the room. I just sighed.

'Mischa...' I felt suddenly sad. 'Jason and I are just two middle aged men, living our lives. For God's sake, he is brain damaged. What harm could we possibly do to you? Leave us be. Ilya is still your father, he loves you. You will still inherit all of his money; Christ, you will even eventually have all of mine. I don't have anyone else to give it to, and you are, after all, my partner's son.' I looked at Mischa, searching his young face. 'So, please, leave me alone. What can you possibly want?'

'I want to see him. I want him to see me.'

I regarded him. 'You're such an angry young man... Listen, I'm not about to let you see Jason. End of story. I understand that you are curious about seeing your father...'

'He isn't my father, you fucking prick.'

I shrugged. I looked helplessly at Ilya, lost for words. Ilya spoke for me, his voice weary.

'Just go. Get your things, get Jason. What do you need? How can I make you leave more quickly?'

I opened my mouth to answer and Mischa gave me a sudden shove in the stomach. I staggered and he pushed past me into the room. The teenager stopped dead. Jay was curled up elegantly on the couch, legs tucked under his body. His dark eyes regarded Mischa for a moment, then he looked uncertainly at me.

'It's alright, baby,' I said softly. 'Kid, get away from him, before you scare him.'

Mischa stood right in front of Jay, his chest and shoulders heaving, fists clenched. Jason gave him another cool glance, up and down.

'Mee-sa,' he whispered timidly, looking at me to check if he was correct.

'Yes, it is Mischa, darling. From the photographs.' I swallowed. I was leaning slightly forward, I wanted to grab Mischa and haul him away.

'So… this is him.' Mischa's mouth was jerked into a sneer, angry tears still running down his cheeks.

'Yes,' I said quietly. 'This is him. And whatever you think, whatever you say, will not change the fact that he is wonderful.'

Mischa had his hands in his hair, staring in disbelief. 'Wonderful? In what way? He's a retard. He should have been put down like a dog a long time ago. Freak, why don't you say something?'

As he spoke, Mischa suddenly slapped the remote control from Jason's hands. Without hesitation I knocked Mischa sprawling on his knees.

'Eddie stop!' Ilya yelled, panicking, 'You'll kill him!'

I was not listening. The familiar darkness was entering my brain as I stared down at Mischa. I grabbed the boy by his collar, picked him up like a rag doll and with my free hand I seized the bronze horse head statue. I knew that I was quite capable of it.

'Daddy,' whispered Mischa. His eyes were like liquid close-up, like Jason's, 'Please help me.'

Ilya was on me, grabbing at the statue while trying to wrench Mischa free.

'Eddie!' He yelled. 'Stop. Look at Jason. Look at him.' I glanced towards Jay. He was crouched on the floor, hyperventilating with his hands over his ears. The statue fell from my hand and splintered the wooden floor. Mischa collapsed into Ilya's arms, sobbing.

'Fuck... Eel, I'm sorry babe,' I murmured, dropping to my knees beside him. He tightly gripped the lapels of my jacket, twisting the velvet into his hand and laid his forehead against my chest, breathing quickly in fear. I wrapped my arm comfortingly around him.

'It's alright,' I murmured, and looked up at my family. Mischa sobbing against Ilya, who was leaning against the door, eyes closed in sheer relief.

'Now, I think would be a good time to leave,' I whispered to Jason.

Colt

I was alone in the meeting room. It was late and I was so drunk, I was slipping in and out of dreams and wakefulness. Slumped on the table, Dave had finally come to unlock the door to release me and tried to hug me, telling me everything would be okay now... I had pushed him away, disgusted. Then I limped away to find a drink and be alone with it.

Eddie left, and I didn't get to say goodbye to him. I was actually kind of glad about that. I didn't have any tears left to cry, I felt the same sort of desperate depression as I had in Stockholm.

I stepped out onto the terrace, it was a cold night but the electric heaters kept me warm with their steady humming. Someone followed me out; Dave. He sat down on a chair, I stayed standing.

'I know you love Eddie mate, but he doesn't feel the same, and it's over, he's gone,' he began. His words made a little rip right in my heart, I actually felt it rip. I closed my eyes.

'I love you,' Dave said, his voice shaking with emotion, 'Me. And I am here. I know I'm gonna have to be patient. But I want you to know, I'll do whatever it takes to put a smile back on your face, mate. Even if it's just being your friend for now.'

I turned to face him. 'Friend? You just...' I croaked and swallowed, my throat still hurting. 'You just ruined everything.'

'No, nothing's ruined. Everything's fixed! I had to get rid of Bodansky because he was between us. I wasn't trying to hurt you, I was just protecting what's mine.'

'But I'm not yours.' Finally, from somewhere I had found a little core of self-defence. 'This doesn't make me yours, neither does this.' I pointed out a couple of marks that he'd recently added to my flesh.

He kept shaking his head, looking horribly regretful. 'Honey I'll stop doing that. Now that he's out of our life, I know I can. I swear, I love you, I love you. You are mine, you're my whole life.'

I put my head down on my arms. How could he ignore the things that had passed between us? The hurtful, embarrassing things that he had subjected me to, things I could never talk about, had effectively broken us. Respect, trust, feeling safe, he had taken those things out of our relationship. It couldn't be rebuilt. And I could hardly bear to talk about it. I tried. 'You make me-'

'Don't say it, honey. I don't make you. I would never do that. You always had a choice.'

I looked away. He was right, I did have choices. Not many, but there were some.

Chapter 37

Eddie

Jason was in the arbour. A magazine lay on his lap, its pages fluttering gently in the warm breeze as he gazed down the garden, to the small wooded area with a thin river at the end. I kneeled down beside him. 'Jay, someone is here to see us. Okay? Say hi.'

Jason looked up at me, then, glanced at Colt who was standing shyly beside me with his hands in his pockets. 'Hey, Jason,' he smiled. 'How you doing, buddy?'

Jason nodded, with the smallest hint of his trademark half-smile. 'Coat,' he said.

I felt a flicker of delight. 'That's right, sweetheart. Colt. Will you say hi to him? Just say, 'hello.''

Jason looked down. 'Hello,' he said quietly.

I stood up. 'I love it when he responds like that. It's beautiful,' I laughed.

Colt nodded, his hands still in his pockets. 'You're looking really well, Jason,' he said. To me, he added quietly, 'I can't believe you painted his bloody nails, Eddie…'

'I had to. It is punk stuff, he wanted it.'

'Sure, sure.'

We went inside and I showed Colt all around the house. It was a very pretty building, with classic Victorian features. We climbed the stairs, stepping carefully over discarded Italian shoes and a collection of miniature oil paintings drying on the top six steps. A large framed painting of a horse hung at the top of the stairs. I showed him Jason's bedroom, which was the master suite. It was an expansive luxurious room overlooking the garden and beyond that, the forest. There were no less than three double wardrobes in the room.

'I keep a lot of my clothes in here,' I explained, 'My room is quite small.' My bedroom, next door to Jason's was indeed very compact, once having served as a dressing room. Everything was rather untidy, for I was not the best housekeeper. 'I should hire someone to do it,' I apologised, lifting up a two-thirds full wine bottle from the bathroom windowsill, then absently setting it down in the same place. 'But I rather like it being just the two of us, for now.'

I ended the tour in the kitchen, which was bathed in light and overlooking a neglected yet charming walled garden. I inexpertly prepared tea for everyone, feeling that this was the correct thing to do, and we sat down at the table. Jason sat huddled up in the window seat, a cushion hugged close to his chest, watching us contentedly.

'So, how are you doing, mate? How are you managing all this on your own?' Colt asked me. He sipped his tea, keeping his other hand in his pocket. I tried not to think about that.

'We are alright. He is no trouble,' I added, tipping my head towards Eel. 'He's very… chilled out, as you would say. He sits around reading comics, or watching the birds in the garden. I make little comic strips on bits of paper for him; little stories, memories, anything, and he sits and reads them. When I paint, he likes to sit somewhere near me and watch.

311

It's very, very sweet.' I looked down at my tea, embarrassed. I gave a small, sad smile, and looked over at Eel, who was gazing back at me with his lovely dark eyes.

'Jay, come and sit with us,' I said softly. Eel leaned back against the glass pane of the window, and continued to look at me. After a pause, he shook his head once, with a tiny half smile playing at the corner of his lips.

'You are beautiful,' I told him, laughing a little. 'Fine, be antisocial. Drink your tea, at least.'

Colt smiled, I could see he was glad that I was happy. Colt knew how much love there was between us, despite that our relationship had been so drastically altered.

After a while Jason drifted out into the garden, leaving his tea behind. I took it out to him and checked that he was alright, then I returned to my guest. 'Would you like something stronger than tea?'

'Sure,' smiled Colt.

I could hardly believe that he was here, sitting on my couch. I poured us both some wine and passed him a glass; he took hold of it awkwardly with his left hand and almost dropped it. 'Sorry,' he said.

'It is alright.' I bit my lip. I promised myself I would not say anything, he had asked me not to.

'So,' said Colt, his eyes sparkling with excitement, 'I'm going back to uni.'

I sank into the couch beside him. 'Baby, that is great.' I reached out to stroke his pretty hair but I stopped myself, awkwardly dusting the back of the couch instead. 'That is great,' I repeated.

'Yeah. Gonna try to get back into medicine, specifically-,' he dropped his head and glanced shyly sideways at me, '-Psychiatry. If they'll take me. If I don't get accepted, then I thought I could try Psychiatric nursing.'

I moved to hug him, then stopped myself. 'Oh, baby,' I said, 'that is wonderful. You are so clever, and you will make a great psychiatrist, or nurse, I know you will.'

Colt sipped his wine and smiled. 'Aye. I thought you'd be pleased.'

He told me about his brothers. He was living close to them now, and they had moved to a foster home which Colt felt was a far better environment than the communal home.

'They let me visit, and I do, like all the time,' he said. He leaned his head on the back of the couch, smiling, shaking his head, 'And it's awesome, because I've missed them for so long and nothing's changed.' He laughed, 'The other day, Clarky said-' Suddenly, he fumbled his glass and dropped it completely. 'Oh no... I'm sorry... your couch.' He began scrubbing the blossoming red stain with his sleeve.

'Have you got any soda water? It might stop this from staining...' He looked up. 'Eddie?'

I never cried. I never cried in front of anyone.

'I am so sorry,' I said. 'I am so sorry, babe. You did not deserve this. It just is not fucking fair.'

Colt hesitated, then he placed his right hand on his lap, where we could both see it.

'Don't blame yourself,' he said, looking down at it. 'I wanted to leave. I'm... I'm really okay with this. It's a small price to pay, isn't it?' I hoped that he meant that.

'Manpyre did it?'

'Yeah.'

'Did he hurt you?'

Colt sighed, 'Eddie, I don't want to talk about it, man. Yeah, course he hurt me. What do you think?' He looked at his hand again, gave a short, grudging laugh, 'I almost bled to death. I wasn't... conscious, for most of it; because of the pain. The last thing I remember is Ilya saying like, okay Dave, that's enough, okay Dave, stop, you're going too far... but obviously he didn't stop, so Ilya's yelling at him and like dragging him off...' Colt winced and shook his head, 'But I guess, I broke his heart, so... anyway, I passed out. Somebody dropped me off at the hospital and... that was it.'

'Christ. Stupid of Illy to get Manpyre to do it... fuck, I am sorry.'

'For goodness sake. It's not your fault. And I don't want to talk about it anymore. It's in the past.'

This punishment was brutal, but I understood why my brother had done it. This maiming would serve as a daily reminder to Colt to keep his secrets. I did not doubt that Ilya had threatened his life, maybe even the safety of Colt's brothers, if he ever betrayed the firm.

I picked up his hand and looked at it, rubbing my finger gently over the healed tissue. Just his little finger was left. The rest had been sheared off, leaving twisted knots of scar above the knuckles. I used to love his little hands. There were deep scars at the wrist where Manpyre had tried to hack his entire hand off. 'Oh, baby. Look at this… are you sure you are happy?'

Staring at his mutilated hand, he answered firmly and without hesitation. 'Yes.' There was peace in Colt's expression, his eyes were relaxed and I realised he was no longer afraid.

'Ed,' he said, 'I'm free now. Besides, I can write almost perfectly with my left. I can still do most things easily. I'm okay, I promise.'

I looked at him adoringly.

'I did not realise how strong you are. I have not fucked you up completely- not at all, in fact. You really are, truly going to be alright, aren't you?'

Colt nodded, and said.

'Aye. I will be.'

I watch him smiling as he drives away from me. I wonder if I will ever see him again. I close the door slowly. I go back to the kitchen where Jason sits at the table, flipping through the book that Colt brought him. It is the perfect book for Jason; a huge, heavy volume of horses in art throughout history. I sit across from him and watch as he examines every picture, skimming his black-painted fingernails over the glossy pages. 'Do you like that book, Jay?'

'Yes. Yes, I like this.' He speaks a lot more to me when we are alone, like this. He seems to become rather shy in front of other people.

'Who brought you the book? Can you remember who came to visit us today?'

He thinks about it, sucking his bottom lip. 'Coat.' Then he turns his attention back to the book, touching at a dramatic painting of a true black stallion. Peacefully, he turns the page and studies the next one.

'Oh, Jay,' I say, feeling a rush of affection for him. 'I love you darling, do you know that?'

He glances up at me and smiles; not the shy smile that he showed Colt, but his big, lopsided smile; the one that he reserves just for me; the warmest and friendliest smile in the world. My heart thuds in my chest, as it always does when I am caught unawares by it. That smile is my reward at the end of each long day. It is what motivates me to get out of bed each morning. My heart beats irregularly now and again, a little thud just to remind me that it is there. More than anything I fear dying, leaving him on his own. He simply would not be alright. I place my hand on my chest, feel it thumping away; still going, keeping us both going for as long as I can.

He goes back to his book and I look at him and I just think this,

'I adore you. My love, I adore you.'

ABOUT THE AUTHOR

S F Lindsay was born in Dumfries, Scotland. She has a background in social care as well as a stint in the retail and hospitality industry. She is a member of a multi-national English-speaking writers and poets circle and enjoys writing about socially awkward characters. Having lived in Glasgow, Liverpool and Stockholm, she has now made her home in Dusseldorf, Germany. Scratches is her first novel.